Jenny Holmes lives in Ilkley, the gateway to the beautiful Yorkshire Dales, and sets her sagas in her beloved home county and in neighbouring Lancashire. She enjoys playing tennis, being around horses and walking her dog by the river. She also writes children's books as Jenny Oldfield.

Find her on Facebook at
www.facebook.com/JennyHolmesAuthor

www.penguin.co.uk

Also by Jenny Holmes

The Mill Girls of Albion Lane
The Shop Girls of Chapel Street
The Midwives of Raglan Road
The Telephone Girls

The Land Girls
The Land Girls at Christmas
Wedding Bells for Land Girls
A Christmas Wish for the Land Girls

The Spitfire Girls
The Spitfire Girls
The Spitfire Girls Fly for Victory
Christmas with the Spitfire Girls

The Air Raid Girls
The Air Raid Girls
The Air Raid Girls at Christmas
The Air Raid Girls: Wartime Brides

The Ballroom Girls
The Ballroom Girls
The Ballroom Girls: Christmas Dreams

THE *Ballroom* GIRLS HIT THE BIG TIME

JENNY HOLMES

PENGUIN BOOKS

TRANSWORLD PUBLISHERS
Penguin Random House, One Embassy Gardens,
8 Viaduct Gardens, London SW11 7BW
www.penguin.co.uk

Transworld is part of the Penguin Random House group of companies
whose addresses can be found at global.penguinrandomhouse.com

First published in Great Britain in 2024 by Bantam
an imprint of Transworld Publishers
Penguin paperback edition published 2024

A CIP catalogue record for this book
is available from the British Library.

ISBN 9781804994061

Typeset in Baskerville by Falcon Oast Graphic Art Ltd.
Printed and bound in Great Britain by Clays Ltd, Elcograf S.p.A.

The authorized representative in the EEA is Penguin Random House Ireland,
Morrison Chambers, 32 Nassau Street, Dublin D02 YH68.

Penguin Random House is committed to a sustainable
future for our business, our readers and our planet. This book is
made from Forest Stewardship Council® certified paper.

For all ballroom dancers everywhere

CHAPTER ONE

May 1943

The band at Blackpool Tower Ballroom played on as two burly doormen ordered a badly behaved couple off the crowded dance floor. Overhead, chandeliers glittered and gilded plasterwork glowed.

'Quite right,' Pearl Greene murmured to her friend Joy Rossi as they observed the incident from the sidelines. 'There was too much funny business and not enough fox-trotting for my liking.'

'His hands were all over her,' Joy agreed with evident distaste.

Sylvia Ellis joined Pearl and Joy at their table. 'Did you recognize the culprits?' she asked above the swell of saxophones and clarinets.

Pearl was all ears. 'No; who was it?'

'Only Fred Salter and an ARP ambulance driver from the White Swan first-aid post.' Careful not to crease her royal blue satin skirt, Sylvia perched prettily on the chair next to Joy's. 'She ought to know better.'

Over by the exit Salter continued to kick up a fuss, while on the stage a singer in a purple dress came to the microphone to croon the words of 'Paper Doll': a lachrymose song about a boy who has lost his sweetheart.

‘I don’t know this one.’ Preferring to ignore the fracas, Joy tapped out the rhythm with her fingertips and concentrated on the colourful swirl of dresses and the graceful moves of the dancers closest to her.

‘It’s a new Mills Brothers number.’ Pearl’s attention was still fixed on the entertaining antics at the exit. ‘The silly idiot will get himself banned if he’s not careful. Yep; the doorman isn’t standing any nonsense – he’s got Fred by the scruff of the neck. A hefty shove and down the stairs he goes.’

‘And good riddance.’ Sylvia was all for having fun on the dance floor but there was a limit. Besides, Salter, who worked on the assembly line at the Vickers-Armstrong aircraft factory, was notorious for regularly pawing his way through the waltz and quickstep. As for his conduct during energetic swing dances, the less said the better. ‘Ugh!’ She shook her head in disgust.

‘“I just quarrelled with Sue, that’s why I’m blue.”’ The singer’s sweet voice was loaded with regret as she delivered the chorus line and the couples on the floor continued to sway and turn.

‘Let’s hope the next one is more cheerful.’ Once the excitement had passed, Pearl’s gaze wandered to the five members of the band, dressed to impress in white dinner jackets, black trousers, red cummerbunds and bow ties, and the svelte singer in the strapless, amethyst dress. Sure enough, the musicians segued into a lively jive number and before Pearl knew it, she was swept on to the floor by none other than Errol Jackson.

‘Howdy, Miss Pearl, how you doin’?’ The GI sergeant seized her right hand then swung her into a space close to the stage.

‘Errol, where did you spring from?’ Pearl was pleased

to see her regular dance partner. This man knew how to jitterbug and jive like there was no tomorrow. Here he was, swinging her out and pulling her back in again, leading her into an underarm turn, smooth as you like.

'I been here a while,' he informed her in his attractive Southern drawl. 'I was drinkin' with the guys over by the bar.'

The room was chock-full of American soldiers in their smart uniforms, pockets full of chocolate treats and pairs of nylon stockings if a girl was lucky, and all bussed in from their Warton base. 'I never spotted you,' Pearl confessed mid-twirl.

'Yeah, but I spotted you.'

'Did you now?' She threw in a few low kicks and a shoulder shimmy. 'Phew, it's warm tonight.'

'Sure is,' he agreed, with moves to mirror hers.

'They should open the roof.' Pearl's voice was lost in the wah-wah-wah of trumpets and trombones.

'Come again?'

'Nothing. It doesn't matter.' Time to shake her hips and swivel her feet.

Errol cottoned on. 'You mean, this roof opens – for real?'

He looked up at the frescoes high above their heads, depicting medieval maidens playing lutes and floating on clouds. 'The whole thing?'

'Yep.' She grinned at his look of disbelief. 'Later in the summer they'll slide the roof back. It's magic – you can look up as you dance and see the stars.'

'Gee whiz.' Here he was, jiving like crazy with the girl of his dreams. But she only happened to be married, goddammit, with a soldier husband last heard of scrapping it out in North Africa. Pearl Greene – small, petite and cute as hell, with cropped dark hair and big green eyes – yeah, those eyes! Off limits, though; that's what they'd agreed.

'How's business in Blackpool's premier penny arcade?' Errol enquired as the tempo quickened.

'I'm rushed off my feet now that the weather's warmer.' Pearl told him how much she relished the sound of coins dropping into the Little Mickeys and Lucky Stars, less so the ker-ching of the occasional payout. Still, summer was just around the corner and business at her North Pier amusement arcade was booming. She bounced to the syncopated rhythm of 'Jingle Jangle Jingle', glad that she'd opted for a sleeveless white blouse and her floral-patterned cotton skirt for coolness. 'Aren't you boiling in that uniform?' she asked as Errol drew her in for a lightning-quick turn.

'Sure am,' he confessed with a grin and casual clicks of his fingers in time to the beat. Six foot tall, broad shouldered, slim-waisted; a fine figure of a man.

'Good evening, Errol.' Sylvia swung by with Terry Liddle, who provided stiff competition for Pearl's Yank in the looks department – though Terry was fair, not dark. She and Terry had dazzled on the dance floor ever since their success in the Latin section of the North of England Allied Championship in January. There was no romance, however – their relationship was strictly professional. 'You're in your element, I see,' she remarked to Errol.

'Yes, ma'am. Jive, lindy hop, jitterbug – you name it, I'm your guy.'

Terry slid his arm around Sylvia's waist then sidestepped her into a gap between the jiving couples.

'Don't have too much fun!' Sylvia called to Pearl with a meaningful look.

'Really?' Terry frowned as he snaked his hips, toe to toe with Sylvia.

'Yes, really. If Pearl's not careful, tongues will wag.'

'Ah, wagging tongues.' Terry knew all about those due to his 'friendship' with dance teacher Cliff Seymour. He and Cliff had weathered the gossip storm, but only just.

Sylvia's blonde ponytail bobbed and swung as she jived, and her blue skirt flared to reveal long, slim legs. 'Pearl's one of my closest friends,' she insisted. 'I'm keeping a weather eye out for her, that's all.'

On Terry and Sylvia went, swinging out, drawing together, spinning faster and faster until the music ended and the MC announced an intermission: a signal for Pearl and Sylvia to separate from their respective partners and rejoin Joy at their table.

'Phew, it's sweltering!' Pearl sighed as she flopped on to her chair.

Sylvia ignored her. 'Wedding pictures!' she demanded of Joy. 'You promised to show us.'

So Joy dipped into her handbag and proudly produced a yellow Kodak envelope containing photos from the event that had taken place a few weeks earlier. 'Here's me and Tommy outside the church. And here's one of all of us – me, Tommy and you two as my maids of honour. And one of Tommy and me with his mother.' Colouring up self-consciously, she spread the prints across the table.

'My, Mrs Rossi, you look a million dollars in that dress and with your hair up. And look at that teeny-weeny waist of yours!' Sylvia's praise only deepened Joy's blushes.

Mrs Rossi – the words still sounded strange to her, and the wedding itself was a blur of white silk, spring blossom and confetti. The one image that stayed fixed in Joy's memory was of her beloved Tommy at the altar, turning with a bemused expression to watch her walk down the aisle; was it really happening or was it a dream?

'Tommy looks like the cat that got the cream,' Pearl added. 'And who can blame him? Anyway, how does it feel to be a married woman at last?'

Joy's cheeks burned at the clear innuendo behind these words.

'Pearl!' Sylvia remonstrated primly.

'What? I'm only asking.' Pearl had never been slow to express her views on the wait-until-you're-married issue. During the three girls' cosy heart-to-hearts in Sylvia's flat, she'd been astonished that Joy and Tommy had managed to keep their hands off each other even though Joy had lived under the same roof as Tommy and his mother, Lucia. 'Well?' She pressed for an answer.

'It feels marvellous,' Joy answered in the softest of voices. 'Better than I ever could have hoped.'

'Satisfied?' Sylvia gave Pearl a small jab with her elbow.

'No, but I can see that's all I'm going to get.' Noticing that the band had returned to the stage, Pearl scanned the room for likely partners. She didn't have far to look: Errol was already on his way over from the bar so she just had time to slip in one last quick question for Joy. 'How's Tommy's ankle, by the way? Is he still laid up?'

'Yes, worse luck.' An accident in the circus ring, when a routine involving Tommy, two other clowns and a see-saw had ended in disaster, had kept her new husband off work for a week or more. *Husband!* There was another word that Joy would have to get used to. 'It's a bad sprain. The doctor says he has to rest it for another few days.'

'Then you two will be back on the dance floor, showing the rest of us how it's done.' Sylvia commiserated while noting Pearl's eagerness to accept Errol's invitation to join him in the waltz. 'I only hope she knows what she's doing,' she muttered.

Joy frowned. 'She does – Pearl's made it plain that it's a dancing partnership and nothing more. Besides, Errol is a perfect gentleman.'

'If you say so.' Seeing that Terry was deep in conversation with Cliff by the bar, Sylvia made a snap decision. 'You and me?' She surprised Joy by springing to her feet and extending her hand.

The familiar introductory notes to 'We'll Meet Again' filled the ballroom, inviting hundreds of couples on to the highly polished, parquet floor. The tempo was slow and sedate, the mood decorous. 'Why not?' Joy decided. She'd spruced herself up and chosen her favourite lilac dress with broad shoulder pads and ruched, nipped-in bodice, ready to dance the night away in Tommy's absence. 'After all, you only live once.'

'I'm in a rush,' Joy told Tommy on what promised to be a drab, grey Monday in mid May. 'Honestly, I have a train to catch.'

'I know you do.' He sat in bed with his right ankle bandaged, unshaven and bleary eyed. 'Surely you have time for one little kiss?'

'Just one.' Joy checked her reflection in the dressing-table mirror – shoulder-length dark hair brushed until it shone, pale cheeks powdered, pearly-pink lipstick neatly applied – before she skipped across the room to give Tommy a peck on the cheek.

'Sorry, I must look a sight.' He made a vain attempt to smooth his tousled hair.

'You do,' she declared as she reached for her jacket. 'An absolute sight!'

'*Assolutamente*,' he echoed in his mother's native Italian. *Giù di morale* – that's how he felt. Down in the dumps, out of sorts, fed up.

Handbag, hat and gloves; Joy gathered her belongings then paused at the door to take one last look at the disgruntled invalid. 'Cheer up; it's not the end of the world.'

'If you say so,' he grunted, followed by a gruff, 'Go on; off you go.'

The notion that men made poor patients had turned out to be true in Tommy's case – he'd been like a bear with a sore head since his accident in the circus ring, so unlike the happy-go-lucky joker who'd made the first moves when she'd worked as a cleaner at the Tower. Joy blew him a final kiss then flew down the stairs, calling a quick goodbye to Lucia as she ran through the café to exit by the front door, past the 'Rossi's Genuine Italian Ices' sign and out on to the promenade.

'*Ciao!*' Tommy's mother's faint voice issued from the small kitchen at the back of the house.

Luckily a tram approached as Joy reached the stop. Yes; it was a chilly day with choppy waves breaking on the shore and hardly anyone on the beach as yet. The town's three Victorian piers strode far out to sea, each with a cluster of cafés and amusement arcades at the far end; on the grey horizon a flotilla of Royal Navy frigates rested at anchor.

Joy flagged down the tram and exchanged hellos with the cheerful clippie. She took her ticket then sat down, hardly noticing the temporary water tank that had recently been installed next to the lifeboat station by Central Pier or the piles of sandbags stacked outside entrances to the hotels that lined the seafront. Blackpool North was Joy's stop. As she alighted, she happened to spot Pearl in the distance. The two girls waved to each other then hurried on – long gone were the high spirits of Saturday night at the Tower, now replaced by the grey monotony of weekly routine. With a sigh, Joy entered the train station then threaded between porters, piles of mail bags and hordes of glum passengers to step from the grimy platform on to the Manchester express.

Clickety-click, clickety-click; the soothing rhythm of wheels on steel tracks helped her to get her thoughts in order for the day ahead. Firstly, there was a backlog of orders on women's lambswool jumpers to sort out then a difficult telephone call about overdue invoices to be made. Her cousin George had indicated that he would travel down from Glasgow either today or tomorrow to discuss future plans. Joy must be ready to pitch in with ideas on where next to take the knitwear company that they now jointly owned thanks to George's determination to right the wrongs committed by his dishonest father.

It was hard for her to get to grips with the dizzying changes that had taken place in such a short space of time. A mere twelve months ago she, Joy Hebden as she then was, had been a single girl living in a shabby boarding house on Silver Street, with no family and a lowly job as a cleaner to make ends meet. Then she'd fallen in love with ballroom dancing, which was how she'd met rising circus star Tommy and fallen in love with him as well. Now they were married and she was a bona fide businesswoman running the distribution branch of an up-market knitwear company.

The squeal of brakes pulled Joy back into the present and she stepped from the carriage – a trim figure emerging from billowing clouds of steam in her crisp cream jacket, royal blue dress and straw hat, white handbag hitched into the crook of her arm – onwards and upwards along the platform at Manchester Piccadilly with a fiercely determined air.

Dearest Pearl, Do you want to hear the good news first or the bad?

Pearl sat behind the till in Great Scott's North Shore Amusement Arcade reading the latest missive from her husband Bernie for the fourth time that day. The letter had landed on the mat at the family home on Empire Street and had been scooped up by Pearl's little sister, nine-year-old Elsie, who had recognized the handwriting and announced its arrival in a high-pitched screech while holding it aloft and prancing around the breakfast table.

'Pearl has got a letter! Pearl has got a letter!' she'd crowed.

'Give it here!' Pearl had snatched the envelope then run upstairs to scan its contents in private.

Dearest Pearl . . . the good news first or the bad? All right, I'll start with the bad . . . am writing this in the middle of a sandstorm that's lasted all through the night . . . a bloody awful wind is howling so loud it gets inside your head . . . sand everywhere – in your eyes and ears, up your nose, between your toes, up your jacksie; you name it . . .

With a faint smile she turned over the letter to see again how Bernie had signed off – how much love, how many kisses – before clutching the letter to her chest, closing her eyes and taking a deep breath.

Her soldier husband was alive and kicking in North

Africa, thank God, mithering on about the blasted sand, the scorching desert heat and the sheer boredom of sitting on his backside, awaiting the next set of orders from the bigwigs. Pearl supposed that he meant Churchill and Roosevelt, who had got their heads together at the start of the year to work out how to drive Rommel out of Tripoli. For many months the German troops had hung on by their fingertips until just last week, when they'd finally surrendered. The Allied victory had been trumpeted on Pathé News and in every British newspaper; Hitler could rage and rant all he liked but his army of *Übermenschen* had been given a severe drubbing.

Now Pearl could heave a sigh of relief that Bernie had survived the worst the Nazis and the Sahara could throw at him, despite being blown up by a booby trap and being reported missing presumed killed. Oh, the agony of thinking she'd lost him so soon after they'd married; the days of disbelief and denial that she'd suffered, holed up in her bedroom, not sleeping, not eating. A widow at the age of twenty-one; how was that possible?

Then the Christmas miracle had happened: Bernie had been reported missing after the landmine had exploded but he had not been killed after all. Alone in the sand dunes, hallucinating and severely dehydrated, he'd been close to death when an American reconnaissance party had rescued him and returned him to the land of the living and afterwards to his grieving widow. Pearl had been presented with the greatest gift of all: Christmas with her husband at home in Blackpool, back in the arms of family and friends.

Then, come January, the lousy war had claimed Bernie once more. Now there were only increasingly rare letters written on flimsy airmail paper, his spidery handwriting that strayed from the lines and rarely followed a train of thought to its conclusion.

'How's he doing?' Pearl's mother Maria had poked her head around the bedroom door after Pearl had taken in all of the letter's contents.

'Good news,' Pearl had reported. 'He's getting out of the desert at last. His regiment is being moved on; he's not allowed to say where.'

'Most likely to the Med, to deal with Mussolini,' Maria had predicted and Pearl had agreed.

'You're right – they're going at it hammer and tongs in Sicily. Anyway, Bernie's glad to be on the move. I'll write back and warn him not even to think about eyeing up any of those Italian *signorinas*!'

And now, in the calm of the empty arcade, before Pearl opened the doors to the day's paying customers, she revelled in every word of Bernie's rambling, chatty letter. Sitting by the doorway, surrounded by shiny Playballs, Wizards and Fill 'Em Ups, she read that he had holes in all his socks, worse luck, and that he was doing his best to give up smoking as she'd suggested but it was well-nigh impossible when you were bored out of your skull and the only way of killing time rather than Jerry was by playing endless games of dominoes and gin rummy.

He'd signed off with twelve kisses (more than his usual number) and all his love. His name was smudged where he'd folded the paper before the ink was dry.

Pearl counted the crosses again and was happy. *My Bernie, my darling, my love.*

Faces peered through the arcade window and she heard a crotchety cry of, 'Open up!' – a coach load of wrinkly pensioners with money to burn were champing at the bit. Slipping Bernie's precious letter back into its envelope and placing it carefully in her skirt pocket, Pearl unlocked the door to welcome them in.

Sylvia was all too well aware that there was nothing glamorous about teaching the tango to a bunch of beginners with two left feet. Her afternoon session with a group of office workers and RAF recruits had proved it yet again.

'What's up?' Cliff asked as her students gathered their belongings before heading for an evening on the beach, where they would roll up their trousers or hitch up their skirts to paddle, flirt and eat chips. He'd come into the studio at the end of the lesson to find a disgruntled Sylvia sporting a deep frown. 'Your face will stick like that if you're not careful and then you and Terry won't win any more Viennese waltz competitions.'

'Ha ha – very funny,' she retorted. Waltz demanded grace and serene smiles whereas tango was all about the drama of clipped, staccato moves building to exciting crescendos. It involved stealth on the male dancer's part and a series of sinuous, inviting hip swivels from the female. 'Think of the way a cat moves,' Sylvia had instructed as she'd lowered the needle on to a recording of Edmundo Ros's '*Los Hijos de Buda*' then demonstrated a series of progressive side steps as she faced the floor-to-ceiling mirror that lined one wall of the North View Parade studio.

'Feet together, weight on the right foot. Step forward with the left foot to finish forward and across the body.'

For the most part it had been like talking to a brick wall, except for a couple of earnest typists from the Inland Revenue office who had mastered the basics but were a million miles away from achieving the predatory stealth required.

'Anyway, how come you're looking so cheerful?' she asked Cliff with a huffy edge to her voice.

He informed her that he was fresh from a meeting with his bank manager, a Mr Cecil Perkins, who had perused the dance school's latest figures and promised to give serious consideration to Cliff's request for a loan of two hundred pounds.

'Most satisfactory.' Perkins had finished studying income versus expenditure columns over a six-month period. 'And what would the two hundred pounds be spent on, Mr Seymour, should the bank choose to advance you the money?'

'Mostly on advertising our classes, Mr Perkins. My partner, Miss Sylvia Ellis, and I wish to print more posters and leaflets to spread around town, together with improving our sign above the entrance to the studio.'

'Improving in what way?'

'In an ideal world we'd like to replace the current board with a striking neon-pink version: "Live Your Dream!" with "Learn to Dance with Cliff and Sylvia" in smaller script underneath.'

'But?' Perkins had peered inquisitively above the rim of his spectacles.

'But that's not possible during the present blackout,' Cliff had conceded. 'So instead Sylvia and I propose to design a new painted version, only twice the size of the present one and in brighter colours.'

The two men had shaken hands and Perkins had promised an answer within the week, so Cliff was eager to bring Sylvia up to date. 'I talked nicely to the bank manager and the loan is practically in the bag,' he informed her as he set her Edmundo Ros record playing again. 'Aren't you pleased?'

'Yes, of course I am.' Backing from the bank meant a lot. 'It seems our hard work is paying off.' Spreading her arms wide, Sylvia took in the sleek, modern styling of the refurbished studio. It had a touch of the ocean liner about it, with jade-green walls and streamlined, pearlescent wall lights. The sprung floor was highly polished and the gramophone in the alcove behind her was new and top of the range. 'If only,' she sighed.

'If only what?'

'If only we could attract a higher calibre of students.' There; dyed-in-the-wool dancing snob that she was, Sylvia had come out with what she really thought. 'Honestly, Cliff – sometimes I'm ready to give up.'

'Oh no you don't.' Cliff scooped her into a close hold then swept her across the floor. 'Hip to hip, progressive link into closed promenade,' he instructed. 'On the count of four: one, two, three and . . . prowl!'

Together they tangoed around the empty room; Sylvia in white capri pants and a short-sleeved pink blouse, Cliff in his best pinstriped suit and collar and tie for the bank manager's benefit, his hair slicked back and immaculately parted. Suddenly the door was flung open and Terry breezed in wearing an open-necked shirt, fawn slacks and sandals.

'Not interrupting, am I?' He set down a bag of shopping then stood with hands on hips.

'There you are, love of my life!' With a delighted laugh Cliff abandoned Sylvia mid-turn and dragged Terry on to the floor, assuming the same close hold and resuming where he'd left off. 'Quick, quick, slow, quick,' he reminded him. 'I've just been telling Sylvia the good news: our bank loan is likely to come through later this week, in time for the summer rush.'

Despite the clumsy crêpe soles of his open-toed sandals, Terry prowled like a professional: feet parallel, slow and smooth. 'Then the world is your oyster. Sylvia, why aren't you over the moon?' he called across the room.

'I am – look.' Repressing a shudder at the thought of yet more clodhoppers queuing up for an hour's tuition, she forced a grin. 'I'm ecstatic; can't you see?'

'The problem is, I'm bored with my little life,' Sylvia confessed to Joy and Pearl as they strolled along the beach to enjoy the setting sun. The grey clouds of earlier in the day had lifted and the smooth sands of the Golden Mile stretched endlessly before them while gentle waves lapped the shore and gulls wheeled overhead. 'It's all right for you two – Joy, you have Tommy; and Pearl, you have letters from Bernie to keep you going. I have nothing and no one except teaching dance.'

'And whose fault is that?' As usual Pearl rushed in where angels feared to tread. 'One snap of your fingers and you could've had Eddie Winter down on bended knee; but no, he wasn't good enough apparently. And now he's firmly paired up with Mavis Thorne – and not just as a dance partner either.'

Not good enough. Sylvia mulled over Pearl's verdict. It was true that she'd been the one to end the on-off relationship with Eddie. He was kind and endlessly considerate, but he no longer made her heart go pitter-patter in the way that girls dreamed of.

'Steady on, Pearl – no need to rub it in.' Feeling the breeze lift the hem of her pleated skirt, Joy lowered it with both hands. 'Eddie wasn't right for her so there's an end to it. And anyway, Sylvia, you still have a lot going for you.'

'Such as?'

'Think about it – you're not just a common-or-garden dance teacher – why, you and Terry have won prizes in competitions across the North of England, which makes you shining stars of the amateur dance world.'

'Ah.' Sylvia stopped short, lowered her gaze and dug her toes into the soft, dry sand. 'Not for much longer, sadly.'

'Why ever not?' Pearl demanded. 'Cliff and Terry haven't had another bust-up, have they?' The volatile pair rowed on a regular basis; Terry would threaten to pack his bags and leave town before agreeing to kiss and make up, then they would carry on living together in rooms above the studio as before.

Sylvia pulled her cardigan across her chest for warmth. 'No – I just left them dancing the tango to Edmundo Ros; very sweet. But the fact is, Terry's past has caught up with him.'

'Uh-oh.' Joy shot her a look of serious concern. Terry's previous existence, before arriving in Blackpool, had involved going by a different name and had included an ex-wife who had divorced him when his true nature had come to light.

'No, I mean that the ISTD are on to him for earning money as a professional dancer,' Sylvia explained. The Imperial Society of Teachers of Dancing had a rule that entrants into their competitions must be strictly amateur. 'Once they learned that Terry was part of the chorus line for *Sleeping Beauty* at the Grand last Christmas they banned him for good.'

'Who snitched?' an outraged Pearl demanded.

'I have no idea.' Sylvia shook her head disconsolately. 'Most likely one of our rivals, but we'll never know for sure.'

'But the *Sleeping Beauty* stint was theatre dance,' Joy pointed out. 'It's a world away from ballroom.'

'It makes no difference – he was still earning money from dancing.' Sylvia knew that there was no chance the ISTD would change their decision. 'And all this leaves me high and dry – no Eddie to enter competitions with and now no Terry either.'

'Boohoo; you poor thing.' Pearl resolved to count her blessings and also to remind Bernie how much she loved him when she wrote her next letter. 'But someone will soon step into Terry's shoes, surely?'

'Yes, men will queue up to take his place.' Joy too was convinced that the setback was temporary. She pointed to the horizon, where a setting sun had turned the sea to liquid gold. 'Don't let it get you down,' she advised. 'Take it on the chin and remember: you'll succeed in whatever plan you make – you always do.'

CHAPTER TWO

Joy waited for Tommy beneath a colourful poster advertising twice-daily shows at the Tower Circus. Tommy's clown act, the Trio Rossi, didn't appear high on the bill – they came below the Devils of the Forest and Twenty Wonder Horses – but she was proud that his name appeared at all and relieved that his ankle had healed and he was back at work. Waiting for him in the elaborately tiled, curved corridor that overlooked the circus ring, she watched the high-wire act with bated breath: one slip and Polish acrobats Irena and Alina would plunge . . .

'Hello, Joy – did you catch our new act?' Ted Mackie emerged from the clowns' dressing room with streaks of greasepaint still on his face. Small and thin as a whippet, he was the fall guy of the comic trio, dressed in baggy trousers, false moustache and bowler hat à la Charlie Chaplin. Now in civvies, comprising checked sports shirt and dark blue flannels, he looked surprisingly dapper.

'I did,' she confirmed with a bright smile.

'It's good to have your hubby back in action.' Ted returned the smile then went on his jaunty way, hands in pockets and whistling under his breath.

Tommy had returned with a bang – cavorting around the ring, clowning away in his fabulously sequinned pantaloons, white make-up and dunce's hat, playing his trumpet and orchestrating a sequence of pratfalls performed by Ted and Leo Court, the third member of their group. Tommy the whited-face clown was a jack of all trades – musician, juggler and acrobat combined – popular with the crowds and rapidly working his way up the billing.

Joy breathed in the smell of sawdust, relieved when the high-wire act concluded without incident. My, but those two girls were brave! They swung fearlessly between trapezes in scarlet leotards and fishnet tights, twisting in mid-air, catching hold of the hands of their male counterparts to loud gasps from the audience. Such perfect timing, such athleticism! Joy was so absorbed in their performance that she wasn't aware of the dressing-room door opening once more.

'Boo!' Tommy whispered in her ear.

'Oh!' She started then quickly recovered to kiss him on both cheeks, demonstrating how glad she was to have her old cheerful Tommy back.

'Sorry to keep you waiting.' He gave her a hug and a longer kiss on the lips. Meanwhile, the audience broke into loud applause as the acrobats dropped one by one into the safety net at the end of their act. 'I don't know about you, but I'm peckish.'

'Likewise.' Slipping her hand into his, they headed for the exit.

'What do you say to a bag of chips and a stroll along the beach before we head home and get ready for a night on the town?'

'Perfect,' she replied.

They bought their chips from Maria Scott's stall close to Central Pier. Pearl's mother, glamorous and vivacious as ever with a red bandanna tied around her curly dark hair, topped up their portions with a comment about Tommy being in need of building up after his accident. 'You too, Joy,' she added with a knowing stare. 'Our Pearl tells me that you're running yourself ragged.'

'Pearl's right,' Tommy agreed as he tucked into his chips. 'Joy catches the early train to Manchester every weekday. Sometimes she doesn't get back until eight in the evening.'

'But I enjoy my job,' Joy countered. 'Most of the time.'

There'd been one day last week when this hadn't been the case – Wednesday, to be precise, when her cousin had caught the overnight sleeper from Glasgow and they'd spent the entire day with their manager, Alan Henderson, examining stock lists and working out how to cut down on expenses. Money was tight due to wartime shortages and increased transport costs, so George Hebden had suggested staff cuts in the warehouse as a necessary next step. Joy had resisted. 'I haven't considered getting rid of anyone,' she'd protested. 'I don't mind if people leave of their own accord, but sacking them is a different matter. They have families to support.'

Luckily Alan had agreed and they'd decided to hang fire to see if sales of gentlemen's lambswool jumpers and ladies' cardigans picked up in the autumn – a reprieve at least. George had caught the late train home, leaving Alan to give Joy the benefit of his thirty years' experience. 'It's the tough side of business,' he'd explained in his kindly manner. 'Unless we make a profit, the whole company goes under, not just two or three employees.'

'I'll come up with other ways to balance the books.' Joy had been unable to countenance sacking Dora in the canteen (a war widow with three young children) or Walter the caretaker (over sixty years old, with poor eyesight and no prospect of other work).

'You're too soft hearted,' Tommy had pointed out when they were in bed that night. 'That's why I love you so much.'

Snuggled under the covers in the warm darkness of their room, Joy had let go of her worries. The blackout blind cut out light from the moon and stars and they lay entwined, surrendering to soft touches and kisses – still new and exciting for them both.

'I love you too,' Joy had whispered.

'For better or worse?' He'd pulled her closer.

'For richer or poorer,' she'd added, entranced by the feel of his skin against hers and the way their bodies folded into each other so tenderly and perfectly.

Even on their wedding night, there'd been none of the awkwardness that she'd feared. Making love with Tommy for the first time had been pure delight – nothing rushed, no shyness in their coming together, only surprise afterwards that it had felt so natural, that she'd given way to passion and been able to lose herself in the moment after months of nerve-tingling wondering and longing.

'Happy?' Tommy had developed the habit of murmuring this single word in the moments that followed, lying on their backs, his arm around her shoulders, her hand resting on his chest.

'*Assoluto*,' she would whisper back.

It was obvious to everyone who knew them that Joy and Tommy's was a match made in heaven; even to battle-hardened Maria as she served them their extra-large helpings of chips. After more than twenty years wedded to wheeler-dealer Henry Scott, and four children later, she still recognized true love when she saw it. 'Eat up,' she encouraged, leaning over the counter and sending the happy couple on their way. 'And keep an eye on Pearl for me if you end up at the Tower later on. Make sure she behaves.'

'We will,' Joy promised as she and Tommy descended the wide concrete steps on to the beach, past hundreds of striped deckchairs stacked against the sea wall for the night, between the rusted, seaweed-clogged legs of the pier. They walked south towards the ice-cream parlour with its bright green and white awning, and found Lucia waiting at the door to welcome her *due piccioncini* – her two lovebirds – with hearty hugs and smiles.

'Do you come here often?' The evening was well underway when Joe Taylor crossed the ballroom to approach Sylvia with a wink and a cheeky smile.

'Very funny,' she remonstrated as she accepted the invitation to dance the quickstep with the market trader whom she'd known all her life. The snappy rhythm and energetic hops, runs and skips would allow her to show off her skills to their best advantage.

'Nice dress,' Joe commented mid-turn. Sylvia was a vision in pale blue, with flounces and frills to bodice and skirt.

'Thanks. You don't look too shabby yourself.' Joe had obviously made an effort in his crisp white shirt, open at the neck, and cuffs rolled back to show off his outdoor tan. He'd smoothed down his dark hair, which he wore longer than most men, and he danced with loose-limbed confidence, shoulders back and head held high.

'I heard the latest about Terry,' he commiserated, steering her into a space in the middle of the floor, where they paused then twirled to lively music from Reginald Dixon – Mr Blackpool himself – whose fingers skipped lightly across the Wurlitzer keys.

'That's right, he's been banned from competing, worse luck.' They attempted a lock step followed by three chassés, smooth as you like.

'That leaves you in the lurch?' Since hearing the news earlier in the week, Joe had pictured stepping into the breach, learning the moves and performing with Sylvia at the Blackpool Mecca or the Winter Gardens, or here at the Tower Ballroom itself. After all, he was a decent dancer with plenty of potential to improve, given the right instruction. Mind you, Sylvia was very picky about who she competed with.

'It does.' Sensing what was going through Joe's mind, she briefly considered the possibility then dismissed it. True, Joe was the right height and build, with a fair amount of natural talent, but he had no formal training so it would be necessary to start from scratch. She quickly shook her head. 'No, Joe – it wouldn't work.'

There was a thud of disappointment in his chest which he concealed with a chirpy retort. 'Blimey, Sylvia – are you a mind reader all of a sudden? You don't even know what I was going to say.'

'Yes, I do. You were about to offer to step into Terry's shoes.'

'Maybe.' A quick smile and a fib glossed over the awkwardness. 'On second thoughts, count me out. I'm far too busy with the market stall, ta very much.'

The quickstep ended and a languid, lilting waltz began. Sylvia and Joe danced on. 'No offence?' she checked with him as he swung her on the first beat of each bar then swayed her towards the centre of the turn.

'None taken,' Joe assured her. He saw now that it was ridiculous ever to have imagined that Sylvia would say yes. This was as much as he could hope for: casually partnering her on a Saturday night, having a joke and a laugh, worshipping her from afar.

'I feel sorry for Joe.' Dancing the quickstep with Tommy, Joy had glimpsed him and Sylvia in between the runs and whirling turns. 'He keeps on hoping against hope, poor bloke.'

Tommy agreed. 'Joe's a nice chap – salt of the earth. Can't you ask Sylvia to give him a chance?'

Joy shook her head. 'It's not that she keeps him dangling. She makes it perfectly clear that she's happy to be friends but that's as far as it goes.'

'Friends – huh.' They danced on, exchanging greetings with other couples. Sylvia's old flame, Eddie, was dancing with Mavis Thorne, who looked spectacular as usual in a slinky emerald-green dress. Then there was Doris Morris (whatever had her parents been thinking when they gave her that moniker!) dancing with circus ringmaster Gerry Martin, and young Len Fraser from Ibbotson's tobacconists with an old school friend, Valerie Ward. They were a sweet, shy pair, new to the courtship game and obviously enjoying every minute.

'I thought young Len was head over heels in love with Sylvia,' Tommy commented as the quickstep segued into a waltz. 'He was last time I heard.'

'Oh, everyone's head over heels in love with Sylvia.' The modern waltz was one of Joy's favourite dances; second only to the more complicated Viennese version with which she and Tommy had won the North of England championship. 'Now stop yakking and let's just enjoy the music.' Head tilted sideways, with Tommy's arm resting across her shoulder blades, smoothly into a reverse turn – one, two, three, and on across the floor.

For once, Pearl had decided to sit out the quickstep and

had selected a quiet corner under the balcony from which to watch others dance. She soaked up the atmosphere, tapping her feet and admiring her pals, Joy and Sylvia, as they effortlessly put other dancers to shame.

I must ask Joy where she bought the material for that dress. Pearl made a mental note, expecting the answer to be the name of a big department store in Manchester. Joy's style had grown more sophisticated lately; the sweetheart necklines of last summer had been replaced by strappy numbers with more flesh on show and a tighter fit over the hips. Tonight she was wearing silk flowers in her hair – a paler shade of purple than her dress – and she'd definitely lost a bit of weight. She was now almost as slim as Sylvia, which was saying something. *Must warn them both not to overdo the dieting*, Pearl resolved.

'Don't be mad at me, Miss Pearl – I bought you a drink.' Appearing out of nowhere, Errol put two glasses on the table then sat uninvited beside her.

She smiled and thanked him. 'Why would I be mad?'

'I didn't ask what you'd like.'

'Nothing to make me squiffy, I take it?'

'No, ma'am – it's orange squash, pure and simple.' Neither mentioned the horrid time just before Christmas when Pearl had drunk too much and had staggered alone out of the ballroom into the fresh air, only to be set upon by three GIs from the Warton base. If Errol hadn't stepped in the night would have ended in disaster for Pearl. Since then she'd stuck to a strictly no-alcohol rule.

'How come you're not out there showin' 'em how it's done? Are you feelin' OK?'

'I'm grand, thanks – just catching my breath. How about you?'

'Same,' he replied. Stifled by his uniform, he leaned

back in his chair and loosened his khaki tie. Then he delved into the top pocket of his belted jacket to draw out a pack of cigarettes and offer one to her.

'No thanks – I've given up.' She took a sip of squash. 'Bernie's regiment is on the move at last,' she informed him.

'Yeah?' Errol lit a cigarette then slid his lighter back into his pocket.

'I don't know where to. Mum thinks he'll be shipped off to Italy.'

'Italy, huh? Anythin' is better than the desert, I guess. Is he due home leave any time soon?'

'Not as far as I know – unless he gets one at the last minute.' Pearl sipped again then relaxed into the conversation. 'Have you ever been to North Africa?'

'No, ma'am. The only desert I've visited is in Arizona. To my way of thinkin', you seen one giant cactus you seen 'em all.'

She smiled. 'Anyway, I'm glad Bernie's regiment is moving on.'

'If you're glad I'm glad. Say, I got a letter from my sister Maisie this week.' Errol took a swig of beer. 'She's expectin' a kid in the fall.'

'Why, that's grand news! Tell her congratulations from me.'

'I sure will.' The trick with Pearl was to play it cool, talk family stuff, keep the conversation flowing. If Errol gave even a hint of how he really felt about her, he was damned sure she would run a mile. Well, that's the way it was – for now, at least. When the music underwent a change of tempo he seized the moment, stubbing out his cigarette and standing up. 'You wanna dance this one with me?'

'Why not?' She'd had her breather and this would most likely be the last dance before the interval.

So Errol led her on to the floor. She stood out from other girls in her short dress, designed for jive and swing – all the so-called freak dances that the oldies complained about. 'Waltz ain't exactly my thing,' he mentioned as they took up position close to Tommy and Joy, while Sylvia and Joe, also near by, looked to be deep in conversation.

'Just follow me,' Pearl said brightly as she placed his hand in the small of her back. 'It's easy as pie – and one, two, three, here we go.'

Early the next day Sylvia and Cliff set off for the Winter Gardens to meet Sylvia's mother, Lorna. It was a glorious, sunny morning with a fresh breeze, and soon hordes of day trippers would pour from coaches to sample the town's delights. For now, though, fortune tellers lit incense sticks inside their darkened booths and sorted through their packs of cards in preparation for the day ahead, while souvenir sellers took their time to set up stalls along the seafront, chatting as they worked.

'Well, Mr Perkins approved the loan as I thought he would.' Cliff was in a good humour as they stopped to allow Clive Rowse to lead his string of donkeys across the promenade. Just lately he'd taken to stabling his beasts of burden in Mason's Yard along Empire Street, much to the neighbours' annoyance – 'Terrible racket; ee-aw, ee-awing all night long!' – but now, bedecked with jingling reins and colourful pompoms, they plodded unenthusiastically towards the beach. 'That means we're well and truly on the up,' Cliff added.

Sylvia, too, was in a better mood than when she'd spoken with Pearl and Joy earlier in the week. It was hard not to be cheerful on a day such as today; just one look at the sea sparkling in the sunlight like a million diamonds was bound to raise the spirits. 'Thanks to you,' she told Cliff. 'Mind you, I'm not surprised – I've always said you could charm the birds out of the trees.'

'Pot – kettle – black.' Cliff raised an ironic eyebrow.

They went on discussing business as they walked; Sylvia knew of a printer in Lytham who would agree a decent price for their new posters and leaflets if she spoke nicely to him. She insisted that it would be up to Cliff to sweet talk her mother when they met for coffee in the glass-roofed promenade that connected the two grand entrances to the magnificent Winter Gardens. 'I'll leave it to you to convince her that our latest plan is worthwhile.'

'I'll do my best.' Beset by an uncharacteristic attack of nerves as they reached Coronation Street, Cliff slowed his pace. 'Your mother's not keen on me,' he pointed out. 'She's dyed-in-the-wool Imperial Society – waltz, foxtrot and quickstep. I'm a samba and swing merchant; not her cup of tea at all.'

Sylvia did her best to soothe his jitters. 'Don't be silly – Mother might turn up her nose at jive, and so on, but deep down she does respect you. And even she recognizes that the world of dance is changing; in the long run she has to change with it in order to survive.'

'If you say so.' Taking a deep breath, Cliff approached the impressive arched entrance that led to a vast entertainments complex containing a theatre, dance halls, exhibition spaces, function rooms and cafés. 'Where exactly did you arrange for us to meet?'

'Follow me.' Sylvia led the way past an exhibition hall redesigned more than a decade earlier in the style of a Moorish village, presently used for training RAF recruits. Further on, they crossed the foyer of the spectacular new Opera House until they reached a wide arcade lined with tables set beneath palm trees. 'There she is.' Pointing at an elegant figure, dressed in palest lilac and sitting, ramrod straight, by one of the palm trees, Sylvia rushed ahead.

'Ah, Sylvia dear.' Lorna tilted her head to receive a kiss on the cheek.

Her mother's smooth skin smelt of face powder. There wasn't a fair hair out of place beneath her small, brimless hat. Her white kid gloves were neatly folded across her lap. 'Mother,' Sylvia began, a touch breathless after the rush to arrive on time. She felt underdressed in white blouse, blue slacks and white canvas sling-back shoes as she sat down opposite, leaving space for Cliff next to Lorna. 'Have you ordered?'

'No, dear.' Lorna turned to Cliff. 'I'd like tea, please. Nothing else.'

'The same for me,' Sylvia added.

An attentive waitress in a lace-trimmed apron and cap arrived on cue.

'A pot of tea for three, please.' Cliff's voice was strained. He was beginning to think that this whole thing was a bad idea.

Lorna's face gave nothing away. If she was intrigued by the invitation to meet she was determined not to show it. 'Such a pity that the Royal Air Force has been permitted to take over parts of this building,' she remarked. 'The war is spoiling everything. Everywhere you look there are troops doing physical jerks – on the beach, on Central Pier and now here. Nowhere is safe.'

Sylvia gave a loud tut. 'It's a small price to pay if we want to beat Hitler, Mother.'

'You're right, of course.' Lorna acknowledged the arrival of the tea tray with a gracious nod. Teaspoons rattled in their saucers as the waitress transferred them from tray to table. 'Eddie has explained to me that many thousands of RAF personnel are housed here in Blackpool at any one time, not to mention the WAAFs and the Americans out at Warton—'

'You've seen Eddie?' Sylvia interrupted a touch sharply.

'Of course, dear. He and Mavis come to me twice a week for private lessons; you know that perfectly well.'

'Ah, yes.' The mild reprimand put Sylvia in her place.

'Shall I pour?' Cliff ended an awkward silence. It was time to turn on the charm. 'I take it you're keeping busy, Mrs Ellis?'

'Yes, thank you, Cliff – too busy, as a matter of fact. Eddie relieves the burden by teaching waltz and quickstep in the evenings when he's not on duty at his ARP post. Otherwise I'd be run off my feet.'

Eddie again! Sylvia was sure her mother was doing it on purpose. Eddie remained in Lorna's good books, so she lost no opportunity to reproach Sylvia for what she regarded as her heartless rejection of him. 'Yes, yes – we're aware that he's a Civil Defence volunteer,' she muttered.

'And doing a grand job as a first-aider.' Once again Cliff saved the day. 'You must be chuffed by his and Mavis's recent successes. They've reached the very top of the tree in the amateur world, thanks to you.'

'Why, thank you, Cliff.' He was a flatterer and no mistake; extremely well turned out and with lovely manners to boot. 'Now, please enlighten me: what's behind this invitation to take tea?'

Feeling a light kick on his ankle from Sylvia beneath the table, Cliff cleared his throat. 'It's to do with the town council's decision to cancel this year's Easter Dance Festival.'

'Yes; I'm not alone in thinking that was a poor show. Do tell me more.'

'A very poor show, considering the ongoing popularity of ballroom dancing.' As Cliff eased into his pre-prepared pitch, he kicked Sylvia back – *Come on; back me up*.

Emerging from her sulk, Sylvia cut to the chase. 'And this set Cliff and me thinking: since the official dance festival didn't happen, why don't we three set up one of our own?'

'Goodness gracious!' Lorna's eyes widened. 'And how do you suggest we do that?'

'First we choose a date,' Cliff explained. 'Possibly in late July or early August.'

'And a venue,' Sylvia added. 'That's most important.'

'Of course, we'd have to apply for a licence.'

'But that shouldn't be a problem; most licences are granted without any difficulty. Then we would advertise in the *Gazette* and print posters, and so on.'

'We would hire a band – live music is essential, don't you think?'

'It wouldn't be as grand as the official event, which had been running for years until this rotten war put a stop to it,' Sylvia conceded. 'But think about it, Mother – with your involvement, our competition will cover all styles of Latin and ballroom dance and attract people as far afield as Manchester and Liverpool.'

'The name of the Lorna Ellis School would appear in big letters on all the advertising material, alongside ours,' Cliff promised. 'A reporter from the *Gazette* will no doubt wish to interview you.'

Lorna raised both hands to halt the enthusiastic flow of ideas. 'Consider the costs,' she cautioned. 'How can we be certain that we would make a profit?'

'We can't.' Sylvia sensed by the attentive tilt of her mother's elegant head that she was ready to take the bait. 'But don't you see; this is a wonderful chance to enhance our reputations. Surely it's worth the risk.'

'As for a venue . . .' Lorna mused.

'We already have one in mind.' With a glad smile Sylvia jumped up and reached out her hand.

'Follow us,' Cliff invited.

Sylvia led the way out of the glass arcade, up some broad stairs to the first floor of the Winter Gardens, past the Renaissance Room and various small meeting rooms, until they reached the entrance to the exotic Spanish Hall.

'You mean we can hire this space?' Lorna asked in mounting astonishment as she gazed at the grand, vaulted room, styled like a village in Andalusia. The walls and arched ceiling were covered in painted, sun-drenched scenes, with battlemented balconies overlooking a central hall and on the ground floor there were colonnades to either side.

'Of course we can!' Sylvia cried. 'We'll invite all the well-connected figures in the dance world; they might even take the train up from London if we play our cards right.'

'And you mentioned a band?' Lorna was warming to the idea, well aware that the Spanish Hall would be a significant draw.

'With a singer,' Cliff confirmed.

Sylvia drew in her mother for a closer look. 'Why do things by halves?' she enthused, her eyes alight with a new dream that would lift her out of the rut she was in. 'We don't want our dance festival to be a small affair. No, Mother, Cliff and I are aiming for the big time. Please say you'll come along for the ride.'

CHAPTER THREE

Joy and Pearl suspected that something was in the air. For days Sylvia had been going around with a secretive smile, humming tunes and batting away queries with a spirited waft of her hand.

'What's got into you?' Pearl had demanded on more than one occasion. Or, more forcefully: 'For goodness' sake, wipe that smile off your face and spill the darned beans.'

'All in good time,' Sylvia had teased. She and Cliff were waiting for the venue for their dance weekend to be confirmed and a licence to be granted, but once this was done she would happily share the good news.

'Pearl hates being kept in the dark,' Joy had reported to Tommy and Lucia after a few days of Sylvia's secretive behaviour.

'*Pazienza*,' Lucia had murmured as she'd tied her apron around her ample waist and made her way into the ice-cream parlour, ready to begin the day.

'Patience isn't Pearl's strong point,' Joy had reminded Tommy as they set off from the house together – Tommy for an early-morning rehearsal of a new Trio Rossi routine, Joy to catch her Manchester train. 'She has many good qualities but patience definitely isn't one of them.'

They'd parted ways with a fond kiss and Joy had reached the warehouse at her usual time of nine o'clock. She'd gone straight up to her cramped office overlooking an asphalt courtyard, and watched as Dora Simmons and her fellow canteen worker, young Mildred Kershaw, clocked in at the machine situated by the entrance to the main building. Two vans bearing the name Hebden Knitwear in large red letters against a green background were parked in the yard and Joy could see their drivers in conversation with Alan, her warehouse manager, who appeared to be dishing out instructions for the day. Shifting her gaze back to the clocking-in machine, she saw that three warehouse workers were stamping their cards, hard on the heels of Dora and Mildred.

So far, so ordinary. Joy was sorting invoices at her cluttered desk, surrounded by piles of buff-coloured files, a typewriter and a telephone, when Alan knocked on her door.

'Only me,' he said with a smile as he entered the room. He was a tall, ruddy-faced man in his fifties, still with a full head of fair hair and with a strong Scottish burr to his voice – the type of figure featured wearing a kilt and putting the shot on the side of a packet of Scott's Porage Oats. 'I took a telephone call from Mr George first thing.'

Joy stopped what she was doing. 'Oh?'

'Yes, he would like you to call him back when you have a minute.' Alan wandered over to the window and looked out at the clear blue sky. 'Too nice to be inside,' he remarked, hands deep in his pockets. 'Train journey all right?'

'Yes, fine, thanks.' Alan's relaxed, friendly manner had been a godsend when Joy had first joined the company. He'd been sent down from Glasgow to assist with the everyday running of the new warehouse and often harked back to the days when Joy's late father had been at the helm of the business. 'I hope you don't mind me mentioning your dad,' he'd checked with her before telling her what an excellent boss he'd been and how upset he, Alan, had been when Joy's father had been unfairly kicked out of the family firm. 'Your dad didn't deserve it; he was honest as the day is long. Still, Mr George put right the wrongs of the previous generation when he brought you in.'

Grateful for the manager's openness and his solid reliability, Joy had taken to Alan at once and now that she was settled in she trusted him to run the practical side of distribution while she concentrated on the paperwork.

'By the way, this is from Mildred.' Alan took a scrappy piece of paper from his pocket and slapped it down on Joy's desk. 'She passed it to me right after she clocked in.'

Joy read the note. 'Oh goodness, she's handed in her notice with immediate effect,' she told Alan with a touch of alarm. 'Is it because she's not happy working here?'

He shook his head. 'No – I pressed her for a reason and it turns out she's up the duff.'

'Having a baby!' Joy's alarm turned to surprise. 'I didn't even know she was married.'

'She isn't – she's not old enough. Apparently her mother plans to pack her off to an aunt's house until after she's had the kid.'

'Poor girl.' Mildred, no more than fifteen years old, was a shy, innocent type with long, light brown hair that she wore in plaits pinned across the top of her head, Austrian style.

'Aye, but look at it this way: it'll be one less wage packet to pay out at the end of each week.' Alan pointed out the silver lining as he sauntered out of the office.

The news about Mildred bothered Joy for the rest of the morning. How would the young canteen worker cope with being hidden away for the duration of her pregnancy? And what would happen to the baby after it was born? Determined to find out more and to offer help if it was needed, Joy went down to the canteen, where she found Mildred setting out knives and forks in preparation for the lunchtime rush. One glance at her red-rimmed eyes told Joy that she'd spent the morning in tears.

'May we have a word?' Joy asked before inviting her up to the first-floor office. 'Dora, can you manage by yourself for a while?' she called into the kitchen.

'Yes, Mrs Rossi,' came the reply, accompanied by a resentful rattle of plates and cutlery.

So Joy led the way upstairs then sat Mildred down and offered her a clean handkerchief as the tears started to flow once more. 'There, there,' she murmured, patting the girl's shoulder and waiting for her to stop crying.

'Sorry, miss—' Mildred managed two words between a series of loud sobs. Her head was bowed and her slight frame shook beneath her green overall.

'Take your time,' Joy told her. 'Mr Henderson showed me your note and he explained the background – about the pregnancy, I mean.'

Mildred gasped. 'Please, miss . . . I'm sorry you found out . . . Oh, what a mess!'

Joy crouched beside her and spoke softly. 'Look at me. There's no need to apologize. You're in a fix and I'm keen to know if there's anything I can do to help.'

Mildred drew a long, jagged breath then blew her nose. 'No thanks, Mrs Rossi. Mum is sending me to stay with my Aunty Myra in Kendal until it's all over.'

'Is your mother angry with you?'

Mildred nodded. 'She proper blew her top; said I was a disgrace and swore she'd throw me out for good unless I kept my mouth shut. Then what do I do? I only go and blab to Mr Henderson . . .' Her voice trailed off and she started to sob once more.

'Don't worry; it goes no further than this room,' Joy promised. 'The baby – will it be adopted?'

'I don't know. I can't think that far ahead.' Mildred buried her face in Joy's handkerchief and cried as if her heart would break.

Joy refrained from asking any further questions. 'I want to be clear about one thing,' she went on in a more determined voice. 'Your job here is safe – you can come back to work whenever you're ready, or not at all if you choose not to. You don't need to decide until after the baby is born.'

Mildred raised her head in bewilderment. 'No, miss, really . . .?'

'Yes, really,' Joy insisted. 'It'll be up to you. And in the meantime, do you have enough money to be going on with? There may be extra things that you need to buy – a bus ticket to Kendal, new clothes and such like.' Prepared to dip into her own pocket, she made the offer with no strings attached.

'No. Thank you, miss – but no.' With a sharp intake of breath, Mildred gathered what remained of her dignity. 'I'll find the cash for the bus fare. I don't need handouts.'

Joy was forced to backtrack. 'Good – very good. I didn't mean to cause offence.'

'It's half twelve. I'd better get back to work.' Mildred got shakily to her feet.

'My offer to keep your job open still stands.' Joy knew

she would have to square this decision with Alan and her cousin George, but her heartfelt sympathy for the girl drove her forward.

'Thank you, miss – I appreciate it.'

'And if . . . Well, don't hesitate to ask for whatever you need.'

'There's nothing,' Mildred said firmly. 'I'll manage somehow.'

Joy showed her to the door and held it open. The girl was halfway down the stairs when an urgent voice called from the canteen.

'Mrs Rossi, come quick!' Dora had pushed her way through a group of men in overalls and was calling for help. 'Walter's had a bad turn – we need to telephone for an ambulance!'

'It was one thing after another today.' Joy took a cup of tea from Lucia and put her feet up on the leather pouffe that Tommy brought her. 'First a resignation out of the blue – I won't go into the reason – then poor Walter Coulter collapsed in the queue for the canteen. No warning – the poor man just keeled over.'

'*Santo cielo!*' Lucia fanned her warm face with a folded copy of the *Gazette*. 'He is dead?'

'No, luckily he came round after a few minutes. I called for an ambulance and they carted him off to hospital. He has no family so I went with him.'

'What was up with him?' Tommy took off Joy's shoes and gently massaged her feet, aware that he had less than half an hour before he must set off for the circus.

'It's his heart. They're keeping him in overnight to do tests.' Resting back in her chair, she closed her eyes wearily. 'Walter tells everyone he's sixty-three but his medical record has him down as seventy-two with a weak heart and kidney stones.'

'So you'll have to find a new caretaker?'

'It looks like it.' Life seemed to present problem after problem, and with too little time in the day to solve them, Joy felt thoroughly worn out.

'You must rest.' Lucia fussed and fretted, as was her wont. Having come to terms with the sudden arrest of her husband, Tommy senior, as an enemy alien, followed by his incarceration in a prison camp on the Isle of Man, her instinct to shower love and affection on other family members had come to the fore. She brought a cushion for Joy's head and stroked her hair back from her face. 'I cook, you eat. I do everything – *tutto*.'

Joy sighed. 'I arranged to meet Pearl. We're planning to go to Mrs Ellis's Wednesday-night quickstep class.'

'*Sicuramente non!*' Lucia wouldn't hear of it. 'Tommy goes to work, you stay here.'

'Save the quickstep for the weekend.' Tommy backed his mother up. 'I've got a matinee on Saturday but then I have the night off. You can take it easy during the day then we'll dance our socks off in the evening.'

'Right you are.' Joy smiled weakly. 'Will you tell Pearl not to wait for me?'

'Yes, I'll knock on her door on my way to the Tower.' Glancing at the clock on the kitchen dresser, he saw that it was nearly time to leave. 'Early to bed,' he recommended. 'Don't wait up.'

So little time in the day. Too worn out even to go dancing with my friends. Joy drifted off in the chair to the sounds of Tommy getting ready for work upstairs and Lucia moving quietly around the kitchen. *There must be more to life than this.*

*

Lorna Ellis kept her pupils on their toes; there was no relaxed 'classes for the masses' approach for her. Pearl was aware of this after an exhausting hour spent perfecting the quickstep at the King Alfred Street academy. Sylvia's mother was hot on what she called 'correct' dancing – no wriggling, twisting or flouncing was permitted, only precise walks, runs and chassés in rapid 4/4 time and the occasional lock step followed by a jump and a skip.

'Very good on the promenade chassé, Mavis.' Lorna had lavished praise on her two star pupils. 'Eddie, please demonstrate the heel lead followed by two forward steps on the balls of the feet. Excellent, thank you.' For others in the class there had only been beady-eyed criticism. 'No, Pearl; you must allow your partner to left-shoulder lead without losing body contact. And don't swivel your feet. Please try again.'

'I might as well stick with Latin,' Pearl said with a sigh as she and Mavis changed their shoes at the end of the class. 'I'm never going to be able to dance the way Mrs Ellis wants.'

Mavis let her fair, shoulder-length hair fall forward as she tied her laces. Since she'd begun her partnership with Eddie her own confidence had come on in leaps and bounds. 'Don't take it to heart. She wouldn't bother with you at all if she didn't think you'd get there in the end.'

'I know, but . . .' But dancing was meant to be fun, not a version of the Spanish Inquisition. 'I don't suppose you and Eddie have time for a quick drink?' she suggested.

'Count me out,' Eddie cut in with an apologetic shrug. 'Duty calls – I go from here to start a shift at the first-aid post.'

'It's just us two then.' Mavis was quick to take Pearl up on her offer. No sooner said than the girls were out of the studio and heading for the Queen's Arms at the end of the street; Mavis chirpy and bright in a kingfisher-blue blouse, outshining even Pearl in a yellow cotton dress with an appliquéd border of big white daisies around the hem. 'Where's Joy tonight?' Mavis asked as they entered the busy pub.

'Tommy called at my house to say she's having an early night. But I spy Sylvia, over by the bar with a bunch of GIs. Let's see if we can cadge a drink.'

Mavis hesitated. She and Sylvia weren't exactly best buddies; not since Mavis had got together with Eddie – and not prior to that either, for that matter. The two girls were chalk and cheese and Mavis always felt that Sylvia looked down her nose at her, knowing that she lived in a poorer part of town and that she'd left school at fourteen to take a job as a cleaner at the Tower.

'Come on,' Pearl urged. 'Sylvia won't bite. In any case, it looks as if she's leaving.'

She was right – Sylvia hurried over to them, clutching a pile of leaflets with the words 'Live Your Dream' emblazoned across the front. 'Learn to Dance with Cliff and Sylvia' appeared in smaller letters beneath. 'Sorry I can't stay,' she told Pearl. 'I'm in a rush to deliver these to the Tower before the ticket office closes for the night.'

So Mavis was off the hook and she and Pearl were hailed by the group of American soldiers at the bar. Calls of, 'Hey, honey, come join us,' and, 'Say, you two sure look swell,' rose above the general hubbub, and the girls were soon inundated with offers to buy them sweet martinis and lemonade, sherry or whatever their hearts desired. 'Orange juice for me, please,' Pearl said, quick as a flash.

The evening was going swimmingly when one of the

crewcut GIs who had made a point of cosying up to Pearl spotted her wedding ring. He demanded the lowdown – which branch of the forces did her husband serve in, what rank, where was his latest posting, et cetera.

'Take it easy,' his pal warned. 'Maybe the little lady don't like to be reminded—'

'I don't mind talking about Bernie,' Pearl cut in. 'I'm proud of him.'

'Victory will be ours, huh?' the over-friendly GI prompted.

'You bet.' A long, steady stare from Pearl warned him not to step out of line.

'But I guess you miss him?' The second soldier gave her arm a sympathetic pat.

Despite insisting that she'd been happy to discuss Bernie, the conversation sent Pearl on a downward spiral. Yes, she missed her handsome, brave husband. Though she kept herself busy and carried on dancing to lift her spirits, still her heart was sore and each day demanded every ounce of willpower to overcome the constant gnawing fears over his safety. 'I get up in the morning and the worry is at this level,' she'd confessed to Joy only the day before, placing her hand at waist height. 'By the end of the day it's right up here.' Up to her chin and still rising.

'Are you all right?' Glass of martini in hand, Mavis checked with Pearl.

'Yes, but I'm dead on my feet. I think I'll head on home.' With this rapid excuse she said her goodbyes and was gone. She'd reached the promenade when she felt a light touch on her shoulder and turned to see Errol.

'Howdy, Miss Pearl,' he said quietly. 'You OK? I didn't get a chance to say hi back there.'

'You were in the pub?' she queried.

He nodded. 'It'll be dark soon. You want me to walk you home?'

'Yes, if you like.' He'd caught her at a weak moment, still thinking about Bernie. 'Just as far as the Tower.'

They set off together towards the town's most famous landmark. 'We both know it's not good for a girl to walk alone at night.' To prove his point he gestured towards a gang of raucous youths hanging around in a tram shelter twenty yards ahead.

'I can look after myself.' Pearl glanced up at his face and saw from his sceptical expression that he was recalling the night of the attack and her narrow escape. 'Most of the time,' she conceded.

No more was said as both recalled the shocking attack by three GIs, when one had grossly assaulted her while the others had encouraged him. If Errol hadn't stepped in to prevent it, the worst would have happened and for this Pearl would be forever grateful.

'I'll always look out for you,' Errol promised, shortening his stride to keep in step and offering her his arm. 'I guess you know that?'

They strolled along in the dusk, past the rowdy youngsters then on past a group of ARP men in wardens' battledress and helmets, who were busy offloading sandbags from a stationary lorry. The wardens grunted as they shifted the heavy bags and stopped for a breather as a tram rattled to a stop, sparks flying from its overhead cables. Walking on, Pearl and Errol inhaled the smell of the men's cigarette smoke mingled with a strong odour of rotting seaweed blowing in off the shore. Errol remarked how he'd grown up in Georgia, many miles from the sea. He talked of cotton groves and peanut farms, baseball matches and American football, and explained how the army had offered him an escape from an unhappy home life.

Pearl listened quietly, occasionally nodding her head. America seemed so big, so different and so far away. 'We two would never have met if there wasn't a war on,' she pointed out.

'I'm sure glad we did,' Errol said in his slow drawl, deliberately letting a silence develop as he waited for her response.

Not far ahead Sylvia emerged from the Tower building after successfully delivering her leaflets. Spotting Pearl walking arm in arm with Errol, she instinctively stepped back into the shadows.

'I'm glad we did too,' Pearl replied as she came to a halt. 'Here is where I turn off into Empire Street.'

'It's pretty dark down the alley – I'll walk you all the way,' Errol offered.

'No – here is fine,' she insisted with a grateful smile.

Squeezing her arm then leaning in towards her, he only just managed to resist the urge to kiss her. Not even a peck on the cheek. 'Miss Pearl,' he said with a soldierly click of his heels. 'See you soon, I guess.'

'Bye for now.' She smiled and broke free, watching him turn back the way they'd come, admiring his long stride and upright bearing. *I'll always look out for you* – she recalled his assurance with mixed feelings then turned for home down the alley.

'Pearl!' Sylvia emerged from under an awning, her face aghast.

Startled, Pearl stepped backwards off the pavement, narrowly avoiding a collision with a man on a bike who yelled a warning as he swerved wide.

'How could you?' Sylvia accused.

'How could I what?'

'You and Sergeant Jackson – I saw you!'

'Saw me what?'

'Kiss him.'

'I did no such thing,' Pearl protested with a sudden rush of blood to her head. 'I wouldn't – I didn't!'

Sylvia was having none of it. 'I witnessed it with my own eyes – you gazing up at him, him grabbing your arm and leaning in for a kiss.'

'He didn't have his arm around me and we never kissed.' Pearl was furious. How dare Sylvia . . . how *dare* she? 'You're supposed to be my friend!'

'I am your friend.' Sylvia spread her hands helplessly. 'I warned you to be careful but you took no notice. And now look.'

'You need to get your eyes tested,' Pearl said bitterly. 'Nothing happened. Errol walked me home, that's all.'

'Oh, Errol this and Errol that!' Convinced that she was in the right, Sylvia's voice was full of scorn. 'I can hardly move without seeing you two together – dancing cheek to cheek at the Tower, having cosy heart-to-hearts at the arcade during the week and now this.'

'"This" – whatever you think it is – was his idea. He happened to be in the Queen's Arms. I never asked him to walk with me.'

'But you didn't say no. It looks as if you're leading him on – and I'm not the only one to think so, by the way.' Sylvia called to mind the many sideways glances and disparaging remarks directed at Pearl and her GI that she'd noticed in recent weeks. 'As for letting him kiss you just now—'

'How many times do I have to tell you – I didn't!' Pushing Sylvia out of the way, Pearl stormed off down the alley, emerging on to Empire Street still furious, leaving Sylvia high and dry.

'What's got into Pearl lately?' Henry Scott asked his wife at the sound of their front door opening then being slammed shut, followed by footsteps stomping straight upstairs. 'Banging about the place, going around with a sour-lemon face.'

Maria shifted his feet so she could sweep under the kitchen table. 'Take no notice,' she advised. 'I'll ask her in the morning when she's calmed down. It'll be something or nothing, I expect.'

'It won't be a festival, exactly.' Sylvia had arrived at the Rossis' spotless ice-cream parlour to bring Joy up to date. It was Friday evening and the café was already closed, although it was still daylight and they were able to sit at a window table looking out across the prom at the silver horizon beyond. The sun was low in the sky, partially obscured by a thin veil of clouds. 'Cliff and I don't claim that our event will be on the same scale as the official Easter shindig, so we've decided to advertise it as a Blackpool Ballroom Dance Weekend instead of a festival.'

'Good for you.' Joy found Sylvia's enthusiasm infectious. 'Whose idea was it – yours or Cliff's?'

'Both,' Sylvia said proudly. 'We agreed that it would be a big step up for us if we were to rent a really good venue and advertise it properly.'

'The Spanish Hall is definitely top notch,' Joy agreed. 'I love that place; it always makes me want to visit Spain and see the real thing. But surely it's expensive to hire for a whole weekend – aren't you taking a bit of a risk?'

'It's a *lot* of a risk!' Sylvia's eyes continued to sparkle with excitement. 'That's part of the reason why Cliff and

I persuaded Mother to come in with us. She'll share the expense. The plan is to hold both Latin and Standard ballroom competitions, including all the dances across the board. You and Tommy will be able to enter for waltz, quickstep, foxtrot – whatever you fancy.'

'And when will this be?'

'We've plumped for the seventh and eighth of August. Meanwhile, Cliff's job is to find the best band available on those dates and mine is to advertise the event as widely as possible – through posters and adverts in the *Gazette*. We're hoping to attract the top amateur couples in the whole of the North of England.'

Joy's eyes widened in surprise. 'Goodness, you're aiming high.'

Sylvia nodded vigorously. 'We are. You and Tommy will enter, won't you?'

'Yes, if we can.'

'What do you mean, *if* you can?' It was Sylvia's turn to express astonishment. 'Of course you can. There's heaps of time for Tommy to arrange time off from the circus.'

'But life is so busy for me just now.' Joy tried to be realistic. 'I hate to throw cold water over things, but when would Tommy and I find the time to practise?'

'Nonsense! You know the saying about all work and no play. Besides, there's *always* time for dancing.' The girls' shared passion was what had brought Sylvia and Joy into contact in the first place, when Joy had started taking lessons at the Lorna Ellis Dance Academy and Sylvia had assisted her mother in teaching the basics of quickstep. From there the friendship had blossomed and had included Pearl as well. Every Saturday night during the summer and autumn of 1942, Sylvia Ellis, Joy Hebden and Pearl Scott – three dance-mad girls before any of them were married – had whirled around the Tower Ballroom together, waltzing and jiving their cares away.

'What about Pearl?' Joy asked now. 'Have you told her?'

Excitement drained from Sylvia's face, replaced by an uneasy frown. 'Pearl and I have had a disagreement,' she confessed.

'But we three never argue – we stick together through thick and thin.'

Their talk was interrupted by Lucia bustling into the café to pull down the blinds and offer them a free ice cream apiece.

Sylvia stood up from the small table. She smiled apologetically. 'Not for me thanks, Mrs Rossi. I have to dash.'

'No, *per favore* – you sit.'

'I really can't. Thanks all the same.' Sylvia had no wish to stay and be cross-examined by Joy, but as she stepped out on to the prom she found that she'd been followed.

'What did you and Pearl row about?' Joy demanded.

Sylvia sighed heavily. 'If you must know, I took her to task for going behind Bernie's back with Errol Jackson.'

'You did what?'

'I couldn't help myself. I saw them together the other night – outside the Tower.'

'Doing what exactly?'

'What do you think?' The more Sylvia had stewed over the matter the more convinced she'd become about what had taken place. The sickening idea that Pearl was betraying Bernie had taken root and kept her awake at night. *Poor Bernie – if only he knew!* 'They had no idea I was watching them and of course Pearl denied it when I confronted her afterwards.'

'Hang on a moment.' Joy asked Sylvia to backtrack. 'Tell me what you actually saw.'

Sylvia pulled her friend close to prevent being overheard by passers-by. 'They were hugging and kissing,' she whispered. 'Well, Errol had his back to me but I saw him with his arm around her. He leaned forward and they kissed.'

Joy swallowed hard. 'Pearl would never . . . Are you sure?'

'Certain. Didn't I say she was playing a dangerous game? It's one thing to keep cheerful by going to the Tower on a Saturday night like Ruby Donovan and some of the other married women we know. But take Ruby as an example – she makes sure she dances with a lot of different partners so no one can get the wrong idea. Pearl, on the other hand, makes no bones about jiving the whole night away with her sergeant.'

'Stop!' Joy put up her hand like a policeman directing traffic. A falling-out between the three of them didn't bear thinking about. 'What was Pearl's reaction when you challenged her?'

'Like I said, she denied it. Well, she would, wouldn't she? Then she stormed off. And don't groan at me like that.' Exasperated, Sylvia took a few steps towards the approaching tram that would take her the length of the Golden Mile as far as North View Parade.

Joy raised her voice to be heard above the sound of the tram. 'It doesn't feel right for you and Pearl to be at loggerheads. Maybe I should talk to her?'

'Go ahead – for all the good it'll do.' Sylvia shrugged. 'Don't mention the dance competition, though – not yet anyway.'

'Why ever not?' Sylvia's tram had almost reached the stop so Joy had only seconds in which to negotiate the choppy waters that lay ahead.

'It wouldn't do for Pearl to enter with Sergeant Jackson – that's why not. Let's wait for her to come to her senses before we tell her.'

So now there was a secret to keep as well. Joy watched in confusion as Sylvia hopped on to the open platform at the back of the tram. The sun had sunk below the horizon, leaving Joy standing in a colourless landscape, in a world that seemed a two-dimensional cut-out in shades of grey. *I can't let this happen. Pearl would never . . . Sylvia must be mistaken.* She shook herself to bring some order back into her thoughts. Tomorrow was Saturday. She would seek out Pearl at her North Pier arcade and get her version of events. Tempers would cool. All would be well.

'I'm on a mission to make peace between Pearl and Sylvia,' Joy explained to Tommy as they lay in bed that night, her head resting on his chest. 'I'm sure it's a misunderstanding that's been blown out of proportion. By tomorrow night we'll all be bosom pals again.'

CHAPTER FOUR

'You and Sylvia have no idea what it's like.' Pearl turned her head to hide her tears from Joy as they stood outside the entrance to her arcade, buffeted by a fresh sea breeze. Her voice rose above the sound of waves lapping against the legs of the pier and the screech of gulls overhead. 'Every moment of every day I think of Bernie. He's always, always on my mind!'

Joy reached out a hand. 'I understand – I do.'

'How can you? Your Tommy is still here in Blackpool, helping to boost morale, but my Bernie is God knows where – in some hellhole on the front line. They've moved him out of Africa but his new posting is probably just as bad. I haven't had a letter from him for two whole weeks. I can hardly sleep for worrying.'

This time Joy didn't offer words of comfort; she only clasped Pearl's hand and let her speak. Why oh why had she opened these floodgates by tackling the thorny topic of Errol Jackson?

'Why hasn't Bernie written?' Pearl's green eyes were dark with desperation. 'Every morning I wait for a letter to drop on the mat and every morning without fail my heart breaks into tiny pieces. I've written to him twice in this last week, reminding him how much I love him. I draw little hearts with our initials down the margin and rows of kisses at the end . . .'

'Stop,' Joy begged. 'Please don't do this to yourself. I know how much you miss him. Believe me, I do.'

Pearl withdrew her hand then leaned on the railing to stare at the dark water below. In five short minutes she must open the arcade. 'What will I do if . . .?'

'Please don't!' Joy begged again.

'If it happens a second time?' Pearl continued as if she hadn't heard. 'If I get another telegram?' *That heart-stopping moment, the thud of dread as the door opens to a boy clutching a flimsy official envelope, the disbelief, the agony . . .*

'Let's pray that you won't,' Joy murmured.

Pearl's imagination charged on. 'I'll cope if the telegram says he's injured again – of course I will. They'll send Bernie home and I'll look after him, no matter what. In sickness and in health; I'd never break that promise. But "killed in action" – no!' Leaning heavily on the railing, she hung her head and her voice was almost inaudible.

'I'm so sorry. Please don't be angry – I should never have broached the subject.'

'I'm angry with Sylvia, not you.' Pearl rallied, stepping back from the railing and casting her gaze along the length of the pier, towards the turnstiles at the entrance. 'You were only trying to help.'

'Not very tactfully, I'm afraid,' Joy said with a sigh. She'd arrived at the arcade without warning and had handled things badly – simply relaying the conversation she'd had with Sylvia, followed by, 'I'm sure we can sort this out between us.' Pearl had hit the roof, said she'd already had it out with Sylvia and wasn't prepared to discuss the matter any further.

'Did Sylvia tell you that she was spying on me?' she'd

demanded. 'And that she got the wrong end of the stick as usual? Well, it tells you more about her way of going on than mine. When it comes to flirting and leading men on, she's the expert – not me.'

The force of Pearl's anger had knocked Joy off balance and she'd mumbled a feeble excuse on their friend's behalf. 'I'm sure Sylvia was only saying how it might look from the outside.'

'Wrong! She accused me outright of betraying Bernie.' Pearl had flared up again. 'Anyway, I don't give a fig how it looks. Errol and I are friends, that's all. We both know the truth of it and that's all that matters. Other people, including Sylvia, can go to hell!' Then, without warning, she'd dissolved into tears. Between sobs she'd confessed to Joy how it felt to have a husband serving on the front line – like thousands, nay millions, of other women who had men in the army, the navy and the RAF – youngsters, scarcely more than boys, willing to make the ultimate sacrifice, while their wives, sweethearts and mothers put on brave faces and soldiered on at home. 'You and Sylvia have no idea what it's like,' she cried.

So Joy's visit had solved nothing and now several families were coming through the turnstiles, braving the wind and a damp sea mist, intent on buying trinkets at souvenir stalls before losing money on Pearl's slot machines – dads in shirtsleeves and braces, mums in flowered cotton skirts that billowed in the wind, kids carrying buckets and spades as they cantered ahead.

'I'd better get ready for the onslaught.' Pearl pulled herself together. 'And I mean it, Joy – I'm not angry with you. I'll see you at the Tower later on.'

'I'll be there with the rest of the gang.' Joy had to stop herself from mentioning Sylvia by name. 'I hear that

Mr Blackpool himself will be playing the organ tonight. Ruby and the girls will be thrilled – Reggie Dixon's their favourite.'

'Mine too,' Pearl assured her as she opened the doors wide and set down a sandwich board sporting the words 'Great Scott's North Shore Amusement Arcade' in bold red and gold letters. 'Why not give it a go, sir and madam?' she called to her first customers of the day. 'You too could hit the jackpot. We have Spitfires, we have Little Mickeys and Wizards. Come inside and try your luck!'

Blackpool Ballroom Dance Weekend. Sylvia slid a recently printed leaflet with this bold headline across the desk in the front office of the *Gazette* situated on the corner of Temple Street and Sefton Street. The walls of the stuffy room were painted a sickly shade of green and it was sparsely furnished with a single desk and chair, with bundles of newspapers stacked by the door from which a strong smell of printers' ink emanated. 'Excuse me; I'd like to know how much it will cost to place an advert for this event.'

A bored, bespectacled receptionist scanned the contents of the leaflet and informed her that it would depend on the size of the advertisement, number of words, and so on, before pointing to a typed list of prices pasted to the wall behind her head.

Sylvia suppressed a gasp of surprise. 'Might there be a special rate?' she enquired.

The woman behind the desk – obviously a bit of a battleaxe with her tight perm and prim twin-set and pearls – raised an eyebrow. 'Special in what way?'

'If we were to place the advert on consecutive Saturdays in June and July, for instance?'

The receptionist took her time to study the leaflet more closely. 'If you can afford the Spanish Hall and a live band, I don't see why you shouldn't pay the full price here.'

'It's our first venture.' Sylvia conjured up her most persuasive smile. 'If it's a success we hope to make it an annual event, which would mean repeat business for you.'

'And who's "we" when we're at home?'

The smile had obviously not had the desired effect so Sylvia tapped the front of the leaflet with her tapered forefinger. 'You see there – it tells you that it's a joint enterprise involving the Lorna Ellis Dance Academy and Cliff Seymour's Latin Dance Studio on North View Parade.'

'Cliff Seymour.' The receptionist repeated the name, again with the raised eyebrow and a knowing expression that spoke volumes. 'He's sent you to do his dirty work, has he?'

'I'm his business partner,' Sylvia replied stiffly.

'Are you now? Well, I knew Cliff before he set sail from Blackpool for distant shores – for Berlin and then London, wasn't it?'

'That's right. What of it?'

'Nothing – only, I was as surprised as everyone else when he had the cheek to come back here and set up a dance studio, all things considered.' The receptionist spoke with slow deliberation as she shifted papers on her desk without looking Sylvia in the eye.

Stung by the innuendo, Sylvia hit back. 'He – *we* – are doing good business,' she insisted. 'Our Ballroom Dance Weekend will be another step up.'

'Then, as I pointed out, you'll have no difficulty in paying the full price for your ads. When would you like to start?'

Sylvia was juggling figures in her head when the door behind her was flung open with a loud warning jangle and a burst of fresh air. In breezed a man in a tweed jacket, open-necked sports shirt and trilby hat set at an angle.

'Anything new for me, Angela?' he asked the receptionist before pausing to take in Sylvia's back view.

'No, Vernon – nothing,' was the terse reply.

The newcomer approached the desk. Now he could see Sylvia in profile and he wasn't disappointed – besides the blonde hair tied up in a ponytail, the extremely pretty face and perfect complexion, there were just enough curves to satisfy. 'What's this?' He picked up her leaflet and examined it. 'I say, this looks right up my street.'

'A small ad; that's all.' Angela did her best to downplay its significance.

'It says here there's going to be a dance weekend. Why haven't I heard about it?' Taking off his hat, he offered to shake hands with Sylvia. 'I'm Vernon King, by the way – the new entertainments reporter, covering theatre, cinema, music, and so on.'

The handshake was firm, the gaze steady. Sylvia immediately felt she was on firmer ground with her smile. 'Sylvia Ellis; pleased to meet you.'

'Likewise, I'm sure.' The young journalist tapped the leaflet. 'And where do you fit in?'

'I help Cliff Seymour to run the Latin Dance Studio,' she explained.

Vernon narrowed his eyes and nodded. 'Mind if I keep this?' he asked as he pocketed the leaflet. 'I take it you have plenty?'

'Yes, please do.' Without doubt her winning smile was working wonders now. 'Might you be prepared to run a feature covering our event nearer the time? You could include photographs of the venue and contestants rehearsing in our studios to whet readers' appetites – a dramatic tango or a rumba. It could make quite a splash.'

Angela slid a sheet of paper into her machine and began to type rapidly – clickety-clack-clack-zing! – the carriage slid back to its starting point.

'It's possible.' Rather than commit himself, Vernon reached for the spiral notepad on the receptionist's desk then handed it to Sylvia. 'Here – write down your name and number and I'll be in touch.'

Joy was acting like a dog with a bone over the matter of Sylvia versus Pearl, not content to let it rest.

'Maybe it would be better to stand back for a bit?' Tommy suggested as they walked hand in hand along the prom. 'Allow time for tempers to cool.' They were heading towards the Tower, where he was due to perform in the Saturday matinee – always a busy point in the week for hard-working circus performers. Though pressed for time, he offered Joy a word of advice after she told him that her next step was to waylay Eddie outside Lorna Ellis's academy.

'But I feel that I put my foot in it and it's up to me to make amends.'

'What makes you think Eddie will be any use?' Tommy asked. 'He and Sylvia haven't been together as a couple for I don't know how long.'

'But he still knows what makes her tick better than anyone,' she explained. 'I'm hoping that he'll be able to suggest a way to get her to say sorry to Pearl.'

Swinging her arm gently as they walked in step, weaving between groups of holidaymakers and making the most of the warm spring sunshine, Tommy came up with another objection. 'You don't think that Sylvia has a point?'

Joy came to a sudden halt by Maria Scott's fish and chip stall close to Central Pier. Music drifted from the nearby Pleasure Beach, mixed with strangled screams from the famous Big Dipper ride. 'What do you mean?'

'This business with Pearl and her Yank – maybe they *ought* to be more careful?'

Joy shook her head. 'You weren't there when Pearl poured her heart out to me,' she pointed out. 'She misses Bernie more than she lets on. In fact, she's struggling to keep her head above water, not knowing where he is or what danger he might be in. Dancing is her one way of easing her worries on that score.'

'Yes, but does it always have to be with him – the Yank?'

'It's not *always* with him. Sometimes she dances with me or Sylvia, or with Joe or whoever happens to ask her.'

'If you say so.' Tommy tugged at her hand and they crossed the road. 'Anyhow, let's not argue over it.'

'We're not arguing.' But they were and she knew it, which was why when Tommy suggested that it might be better to stand back for a bit she'd dug in her heels. 'It won't harm to have a word with Eddie,' she insisted, accepting a kiss on the cheek without returning it. 'I know for a fact that he's helping Mrs Ellis teach a waltz class this afternoon. If I time it right, I'll catch him on his way out.'

It happened just as Joy had planned. After parting from Tommy she soon reached the Majestic Hotel then turned up King Alfred Street, where she killed time by looking at Brown's window display – one of the best dress shops in town. There were styles she could copy if she bought the right sewing pattern; a dress in cream-coloured brocade caught her eye.

'You can't afford it,' a voice whispered over her shoulder and Joy turned to see Mavis winking at her. Her face was flushed and she had a pair of dance shoes tucked under her arm – a sign that she'd left Lorna's studio in a rush. 'On second thoughts, what are you waiting for? I hear you're rolling in lovely lolly these days.'

Joy blushed then smiled. 'Is Eddie still around?'

Mavis tilted her head towards the studio. 'He's getting changed into his ARP uniform. He'll be out in a couple of ticks. Why?'

'I just need a word, that's all.'

Scrunching her features into a quizzical expression, Mavis waited for more.

'I have to go – Eddie will tell you about it later.' Seeing him emerge from the studio then head off in the opposite direction, Joy ran after him, calling his name.

He turned and waited; smart and upright in his forage cap and dark blue battledress and giving off an air of quiet confidence.

Joy arrived slightly out of breath. 'I've never seen you in uniform before,' she commented. 'I almost didn't recognize you.'

'Hello, Joy. We missed you and Tommy at today's class.'

'Tommy had to work. But you'll see him tonight, all being well.'

'Good – I look forward to that.'

'I'm glad I caught you.' Gathering her breath, she walked with him up the street towards a Yates's wine lodge. 'Do you mind if I ask your advice?'

'Fire away.' If he was curious he didn't show it.

'About Sylvia,' she added.

Eddie's expression changed. He glanced sideways with narrowed eyes and a slight frown. 'Why – what's she done now?'

'She and Pearl have had a row.' Joy outlined the situation, making it clear that she'd taken Pearl's side. 'I can see that she does run the risk of being gossiped about – Tommy thinks so, anyway – but I'm sure it would all be settled if Sylvia could be persuaded to say sorry.'

'And that's my job, is it?' Eddie turned the corner on to a street of smart terraced houses, all with 'No Vacancies' signs in the window, and walked steadily towards his first-aid post on the northern edge of town. 'You do realize that Sylvia doesn't listen to a word I say? I'm sorry if that sounds flippant, but honestly, Joy, I fail to see what I can do.'

'Perhaps have a quiet word with her?'

'Telling her to mind her own business and apologize? I don't think that would go down very well.'

'No, but you could remind her that it's not worth us three girls falling out over, considering all that we've been through together. You'd be more tactful than me, and Sylvia does respect your opinion.'

Eddie stopped at the kerb before crossing the street, acknowledging a toot of the horn from a passing ARP ambulance. It was Eileen Shaw, on her way to the White Swan first-aid post. 'I like to think she did at one time.'

'She still does; believe me.'

Eileen squealed to a halt a few yards ahead then leaned out of the window to offer Eddie a lift.

'Well?' Joy prompted.

Eddie teetered on the edge of the pavement. 'All right, I'll give it a go,' he promised as he jogged towards the ambulance. 'Tonight at the Tower if Sylvia's there.'

*

'What did Joy want to talk to you about earlier?' Mavis asked Eddie. The Tower's huge, brightly lit entrance hall was abuzz with excited chatter, as dancers queued on the wide oak staircase leading to two ticket booths on the first floor. Ornate tiled panels displayed fish swimming through coral reefs and the fan-shaped window at the top of the stairs cast shafts of coloured light on to the expectant crowd.

Eddie had almost forgotten about his conversation with Joy. His afternoon shift had been action packed – a trainee flight engineer with the RAF had collapsed from over-exertion during a PT session on the beach and had been rushed to hospital in Eileen and Eddie's ambulance. Then they'd been called out to the scene of a sea mine stranded on the beach out at Fleetwood, standing by as a bomb disposal crew got to work. This had meant a nerve-racking wait of over an hour before the mine had been rendered safe, thank heavens. After that, some blithering idiot at Warton Aerodrome had fallen from a ladder while making minor repairs to the brick control tower. He'd ended up with a broken leg and as Eddie and Eileen had loaded him into their ambulance swearing his head off they'd picked up the distinct whiff of alcohol on the man's breath.

'Eddie?' Mavis nudged him with her elbow. 'What about Joy?'

The queue inched forward and Mavis and Eddie shuffled up two steps towards the ticket booths at the top of the stairs. 'Oh, she asked me to have a word with Sylvia. She and Pearl have fallen out – probably a storm in a teacup.'

Mavis adjusted the delicate silver bracelet on her wrist – a recent gift from Eddie. As usual she'd made a big effort in the glamour department, sweeping her hair back from her forehead and fixing it in place with a mother-of-pearl clasp. She'd attached a corsage of silk peonies to the strap of her long emerald-green dress, which had a slit in the skirt to just above the knee to allow for freedom of movement; all in all it was a winning outfit. 'Why drag you in?' she asked with a definite pout.

Eddie shrugged. 'I suppose because Joy thinks I can help heal the rift.'

Mavis said nothing as they edged forward once more. She looked over her shoulder to see, among others, her work supervisor, Ruby Donovan, rounding up fellow cleaners Ida, Doris and Thora by the main entrance, all dressed up to the nines and ready to fling themselves into a night of carefree pleasure. She noticed Joe Taylor join Tommy and Joy then Pearl arrived by herself, standing out from the crowd in a daringly short, flared skirt and gypsy-style white blouse trimmed with red ribbon. Pearl immediately attached herself to Joe. As yet there was no sign of Sylvia.

'Are you all right?' Eddie sensed that something was up.

'Yes – why shouldn't I be?'

'You're not bothered by me talking to Sylvia?'

'It's a free country,' Mavis replied with an ungracious shrug.

Eddie dealt with the rising tension by resorting to generalities: the weather was warming up nicely, which meant that day trippers were flooding in; and had Mavis heard, the word on the grapevine was that Allied forces were preparing for a full-out assault on Sicily?

'I need to visit the Ladies,' she interrupted mid sentence. 'Won't be long.'

As Eddie waited alone, he became aware of Sylvia's breezy, lilting voice calling out excuse-me and thank-you.

He turned to see that she was jumping the queue by brandishing a batch of brightly coloured leaflets. On spotting Eddie, she pushed on towards him. 'Hello there. Sorry to push in but I promised Cliff that I'd drop more of these off at the ticket office before the start of tonight's event. Typical of me: I've left it to the last minute.'

He stood to one side, noting the elegant tilt of her head and the familiar little flutter of her eyelashes that she used to win people over.

'Why not come on up with me?' she suggested.

'I can't – I'm waiting for Mavis.'

'Ah yes, of course.'

She hesitated just long enough for him to ask if she was here to dance as well as to deliver leaflets.

'What do you think?' She gestured towards her gown: a strappy, three-quarter-length, peach-coloured confection of graceful pleats and ostrich-feather trim. Then she floated on up the stairs just as Mavis returned.

'Well? Did you sort her out?' Mavis asked abruptly before doing her best to smooth out her expression. 'I'm sorry – ignore me; I'm being an idiot.'

'Yes, you are,' Eddie agreed, putting an arm around her waist then guiding her up on to the next step.

From inside the ballroom the first strains of the Wurlitzer sounded to the accompaniment of impatient grumbles from those still waiting in the queue.

'We're missing the first dance,' the woman behind Eddie and Mavis muttered, while down in the entrance hall, stragglers debated whether or not to give the whole thing a miss and try the Empress instead.

Up on the stage the famous Reggie Dixon worked his keyboard magic and couples were soon transported into an enchanted world of gilding and gold braid, of crimson swags, sparkling cut-glass chandeliers and painted garlands held aloft by medieval maidens in swirling garments. Down on the dance floor there was a hot crush of bodies and trampled feet as the workaday world was left behind.

Once inside the ballroom, Pearl took care to avoid Sylvia, who had bagged a table beneath the balcony and sat there now with Tommy, Joy and Joe. She gravitated instead towards Ruby and her gang by the bar, where they didn't have long to wait before a bunch of Royal Navy men descended. Their smooth blue uniforms were a cut above the khaki serge battledress worn by British Tommies and their invitations to dance were eagerly accepted. Ruby glided on to the dance floor in the arms of a chief petty officer, leaving the lesser ranks to Ida and co., while Pearl snagged an actual warrant officer and spent an enjoyable ten minutes being expertly led into pivot turns and chassés to Benny Goodman's 'Sing, Sing, Sing', while the usual banter filled the air: 'You're a smashing dancer' . . . 'You're not so bad yourself' . . . 'the bee's knees', and so on. A polite thank-you after an energetic quickstep left Pearl free to make her way back to the bar, where she was acknowledged by Errol who kept his distance and merely raised his glass in her direction.

Across the floor, Joe returned Sylvia to her seat while Tommy and Joy chose to stay and dance their speciality, the Viennese waltz. Ever eager to please, Joe went off to the crowded bar to buy Sylvia a drink and while she sat by herself, Eddie seized his chance.

'Mind if I sit?' he said.

Sylvia nodded her assent. In the old days, when they'd gone everywhere together and been the star couple on the dance floor, he wouldn't have needed to ask. 'So long as you promise not to mention Pearl.'

Eddie blinked in surprise. 'How did you know?'

'Easy – I can read you like a book, Eddie Winter. Let me guess: Joy's been whispering in your shell-like ear. She's fretted for days about the row between me and Pearl so she's hit on the idea of getting you to build bridges. Am I right?'

'Spot on,' he admitted with an embarrassed grin. 'Well?'

Sylvia shrugged. True, she hated the ill feeling that had developed between her and Pearl, but her conviction that she was in the right was as firm as ever. 'You want me to say sorry to Pearl but I have nothing to apologize for. I saw what I saw, which was Pearl getting far too friendly with Sergeant Jackson.'

'But she denied it?'

'Yes. You know what they say about the lady protesting too much.'

'I take your point. But try seeing it from Pearl's angle – perhaps Jackson was the one coming on strong and she's the innocent party. Look over there right now – he's obviously got the message that she's not keen to dance with him.'

Sylvia wasn't convinced. 'Can we please change the subject? Where's Mavis got to?'

'She won't be long – she went to powder her nose.'

'And how are you two getting along?'

'You mean dance-wise?' Eddie hid his discomfort behind a dry cough.

'Of course dance-wise. What else?'

Out of the corner of his eye he saw Mavis return to the ballroom. 'We're making good progress,' he assured Sylvia.

Taking a leaflet from her handbag, she handed it to him. 'So you'll be sure to enter our dance weekend at the Spanish Hall – quickstep, foxtrot, anything you like? This tells you all about it.'

It was the first Eddie had heard of Sylvia's latest plan. He scanned the front page as Reggie Dixon transitioned from waltz to jitterbug, to the delight of the younger couples on the floor.

'I'm surprised Mother hasn't mentioned it to you,' Sylvia commented. 'We're hoping to attract some big names, including you and Mavis, of course.'

'What's that?' Hearing mention of her name, Mavis approached with an apprehensive expression.

There was no time for an explanation. A partner for Sylvia appeared out of nowhere, approaching from behind and tapping her bare shoulder.

'Good evening, Miss Ellis – care to show me how it's done?' Vernon King from the *Blackpool Gazette* offered her his hand with a confident smile.

'Why not?' she replied. Then, with a whisk of her pleated organza skirt and a light brush of ostrich feathers, she was gone.

CHAPTER FIVE

'The Yanks have all the best dances.' Vernon delivered his verdict as he swung Sylvia out then drew her in again, easing into the jitterbug with a few gentle bounces and low kicks. 'Charleston, East Coast swing, lindy hop, jive – you name it, they invented it.'

'That's one reason why my mother dislikes them.' She gave a wry smile. 'They're so un-English – all this kicking and gyrating.'

'So unladylike?' Vernon added.

She nodded. 'Unregulated, undignified, un-everything.'

'Remind me – your mother is Lorna Ellis, right?'

'Yes and she's ISTD through and through.' Sylvia felt herself spun round, blonde ponytail swinging, then pulled back in – straight into another underarm turn. 'The Imperial Society of Teachers of—'

'Dance. I know what it means,' he assured her, co-ordinating his rapid, across-the-body kicks with hers. He was an expert with the finger clicks, too. 'So she's old school?'

'Extremely.' Sylvia drew Vernon into an upright ballroom hold to demonstrate. 'Everything standardized – one, two, three; one, two, three – no side stepping, very Victor Silvester. Lean to the left, no rise-and-fall; like so.'

'And no fun at all,' Vernon said with a laugh as they broke out of formal hold. 'Who wants to dance like a robot?'

As if to prove his point, a nearby couple went the whole hog with one of the more extreme jitterbug moves. The girl bent forward, head down, hands on her knees and arms braced, waiting for her partner to leapfrog over her. He performed the trick with inches to spare and then they reversed their roles. The girl's skirt flared up to show her petticoat and stocking tops as she leaped. Then they were off into an empty space at the edge of the dance floor, bouncing, shimmying and finger clicking as they went.

Vernon's smile broadened. 'You're only young once. Do you fancy a go?'

Sylvia shook her head. 'I draw the line at leapfrogging, especially in this dress.'

'Yes, I don't see you as a natural leapfrogger,' he admitted.

She wondered whether or not to take offence. Vernon King was a smooth-talker, no doubt about it. And there was a definite twinkle in his blue-grey eyes. He had a strong jawline with an attractive cleft, she noticed, and his hair was dark and wavy, without a parting.

Standing at the crowded bar, Pearl gave Joe a dig with her elbow. 'Psst – who's Sylvia dancing with?'

'No idea.' Whoever it was, he was no slouch in the jitterbug department. Tall, good-looking in an open-necked shirt with cuffs rolled back – and with the gift of the gab, to judge by the way he was making Sylvia laugh as they swivelled and swung. Joe turned his back on the spectacle. 'Forget that glass of lemonade,' he told the barman with a frown. 'Just the usual pint of bitter for me, please.'

'Who's that, dancing with Sylvia?' Pearl asked Joy and Tommy the same question as they jitterbugged by.

'Not got a clue,' they answered in unison.

'His name's Vernon King,' the obliging barman informed Pearl before pulling Joe's pint. 'He works for the *Gazette*.'

'Since when?'

The barman pushed Joe's full glass across the bar. 'Since a couple of weeks back. Didn't you read his review on the latest Greer Garson flick?'

Joe shrugged. 'I don't bother much with film reviews.'

But Pearl's eyes sparked with curiosity. 'So that's the *Gazette*'s new entertainments critic. Blimey, he looks like one of the Hollywood stars he writes about. And he has some nifty moves, too.'

'No need to harp on,' Joe said with a glum sigh as he got stuck into his pint, for how could he compete with a chap like that?

Pearl motioned for him to wipe the beer foam from his top lip. 'Never mind, Joe – there are plenty more fish in the sea.'

Jitterbug segued into quickstep, but not before Vernon and Sylvia had executed several cross swivels and whisks, which were, however, no match for the leapfrogging couple's wildest move of all. Taking hold of the girl's ankle and wrist, the boy had flexed his muscles, leaned back then swung her round in a circle, lifting her off the floor as he'd gathered speed. He'd raised her to chest height then lowered her until her nose practically skimmed the floor, causing cries of ooh and ah, followed by a smattering of applause. Stocking tops had been on display again and this time suspenders and lacy knickers.

'Has she no shame?' Vernon murmured with a wink and a smile.

Sylvia laughed out loud. 'Lord knows where they get the stamina.'

The quickstep proved tame by comparison, and pretty soon Sylvia had had enough of being jostled and barged by beginners. Vernon picked up on her mood. 'Follow me,' he urged, leading her from the floor back to her empty table. He sat down beside her, leaning back in his seat, legs splayed. 'Did anyone ever tell you that you're an open book?' he ventured as he offered her a cigarette.

'No thank you; I don't smoke. What do you mean?'

'Easy to read,' he explained. He lit his cigarette with an expert flick of his lighter then inhaled deeply. 'I could tell you weren't enjoying that – your expression gave you away. And when I first came across you in the *Gazette* office I could see at a glance you were fizzing with excitement over your pet project.'

'Our Dance Weekend is not a pet project,' she objected. 'Mother, Cliff and I have our hearts set on entering the big time.'

'The big time,' Vernon echoed from behind a thin plume of blue smoke. 'Well, the Spanish Hall is definitely a step in the right direction.'

'Did you read our leaflet?'

'Not all of it – I've filed it away until nearer the time.'

'Make sure you don't lose it.'

'I won't. And may I say, Miss Ellis, I spotted you across a crowded room the moment you came in tonight?'

'Really? I didn't see you.'

'No, because I was up on the stage, rounding off an interview with Reggie Dixon, who by the way is a very nice chap. He does excellent work, travelling around to boost the morale of our troops both at home and abroad.

I was standing in the wings, just out of sight, when all of a sudden I saw this vision in pink.'

'Peach, actually.' Once more Sylvia couldn't quite put her finger on the intention behind Vernon's compliments.

'I dashed down from the stage intending to claim you for a dance but at the same time pretty sure there'd be a sweetheart somewhere around and damn it; there you were dancing the foxtrot with the lucky fellow.'

Sylvia quickly put him straight. 'Joe Taylor isn't my sweetheart.'

'No, I worked that out by the way you were in hold – very formal and proper. But what about the matinee-idol type you were talking to afterwards?'

'Do you mean Eddie?' She blushed then shook her head. 'Once upon a time, but not any more.'

'That ship has sailed?' Vernon was satisfied that he'd got the lie of the land. 'Not that it's any of my business.'

'You're right – it's not.' Eager to discover more about her new acquaintance, Sylvia turned the tables. 'How about you? Any sweetheart or fiancée I should know about?'

'Not guilty, your honour.'

'And where did you learn to dance?'

'Here and there.' Vernon shrugged off the question. 'Before I landed this Blackpool post I was based in Manchester. It was my job to report on professional ballroom competitions across the North West. I thought it best to learn the basics so I knew what I was talking about.'

'You must have had a good teacher – I was impressed.'

'Eight out of ten?' he prompted with the same disconcerting upwards twitch of his mouth.

'More like a seven.'

'Still room for improvement, then?' He stubbed out his

cigarette. This was going rather well, he thought. 'Maybe you could give me lessons?'

'Certainly – you'd be welcome at the studio on North View Parade any time you like.' Sylvia decided that Vernon's half-smile was an attractive attribute. It suggested playfulness, in marked contrast to her old flame Eddie's guarded politeness. So she launched into a series of enthusiastic questions. 'Tell me, what's it like being an entertainments critic? Which do you prefer: theatre or cinema? I like cinema best. Who is your favourite Hollywood actor? I love Cary Grant – you look rather like him, by the way.'

'Whoa!' Vernon rocked back in his chair. 'I'm off-duty, remember. I'll definitely take you up on the lessons, though.' Deciding that it was time for more action, he swept Sylvia back on to her feet. 'Come on; this must be the last dance before the interval.'

It was a tango and the close hold and drama of the dance seemed to suit Vernon. He led with his right shoulder into progressive side steps, their hips touching and his left arm pressing against Sylvia's shoulder blade. By the end of the dance, after much swaying and prowling, she was convinced that he had the makings of an excellent ballroom dancer.

The organ notes faded and the MC, a rotund man in a crimson dinner jacket and bow tie, came to the mike to announce tonight's competition – the rumba. 'For all you Latin dancers,' he enthused over the sound system as the floor emptied. 'So by all means take a breather but don't go away. The rumba will be your chance to shine.'

Train journeys provided Joy with much-needed thinking time.

'A penny for them.' The passenger in the next seat

struck up a conversation at the start of a new week. She was a stout woman in her fifties whose cheerful expression and hand-knitted cardigan over a flowery cotton dress lent her a reassuring air.

'Oh, they're not worth it,' Joy replied with a smile. She'd been reflecting on how Saturday night's session at the ballroom had ended unsatisfactorily, with Sylvia making a surprise early exit with the new critic from the *Gazette*, followed by a defiant Pearl accepting Errol Jackson's invitation to enter the rumba competition with him. Pearl and Errol had reached the final six couples before being eliminated – giving plenty of opportunity for those tongues to wag.

'Who are you trying to kid?' the kindly woman next to Joy persisted. 'You look as if you're carrying the weight of the world on those young shoulders.'

'No, really – nothing's the matter.'

'If you say so. My name's Edna, by the way. What's yours?'

'Joy.'

'That's a nice name – just make sure you live up to it. I named my girl Clara, after the film star, Clara Bow. How time flies – she's married now, with two little kiddies.'

The conversation lapsed and Joy stared out of the window as green fields gave way to rows of terraced houses then to factories with tall chimneys that belched out grey smoke into the blue sky. What a pity that Eddie's attempt at bridge-building had fallen on deaf ears and Sylvia and Pearl were still at daggers drawn; if anything the situation was worse than before.

'Here we are – the end of the line,' Joy's neighbour announced to the squeal of brakes and the grinding of steel wheels on metal tracks. 'Take the advice of someone who's seen more of life than you have,' she added as she lowered her shopping basket from the luggage rack. 'Whatever is worrying you right now will soon be over and done with.'

'Thank you.' Joy stood aside to let her exit the carriage. 'I hope you're right.'

'I am,' the woman assured her. 'Trust me – the problem is never as bad as you think.'

Joy took heart from the friendly woman's advice, only to find when she arrived at work that the opposite was true – sometimes existing difficulties could balloon out of control. She'd scarcely had time to hang up her jacket and take off her hat when Alan tapped at her door.

'Bad news,' he informed her. 'Poor old Walter didn't make it.'

Joy gripped the edge of the desk to steady herself. 'I see. What happened exactly?'

'I visited him in hospital on Saturday afternoon and he seemed cheerful enough. But apparently his ticker packed up without warning in the middle of the night – there was nothing that the doctors could do.'

Joy sat for a few moments, collecting her thoughts. 'Walter doesn't have any relatives, does he?'

'None that I know of.'

'Then we must make arrangements for his funeral,' she decided. 'He deserves a decent send-off.'

Alan dipped his head in acknowledgement. His wide stance and steady gaze were welcome at a time like this. 'Leave it to me. And in the meantime, I'll set about finding a new caretaker. I know of a few chaps who are looking for work, so it shouldn't be too hard.'

'Thank you; I don't know what I'd do without you.'

'I'm just doing my job. But that's not all . . .'

'Spit it out,' Joy urged as her manager, seemingly now lost for words, shifted from one foot to the other.

'I'm afraid this needs a woman's touch,' he mumbled. 'Dora Simmons caught me on my way up here and informed me that young Mildred has locked herself in one of the women's lavatories. She's crying her eyes out and refusing to open the door.'

'I'll go and see.' Joy followed him down the stairs then headed to the ladies' cloakroom, where she found Dora still trying to persuade Mildred to come out of the cubicle furthest from the door. The cloakroom was a small, green-tiled area with a row of wash basins along one wall, mirrors above and a linen roller-towel to one side. It was harshly lit with up-to-date fluorescent tubes and had a smell of disinfectant that combined with the lighting to give off a soulless, clinical air.

'I've done my best.' Dora squeezed her stout frame past Joy before beating a hasty retreat.

Mildred's sobs filled the room. Joy tapped on the door and called her name. 'It's Mrs Rossi here. Why not come out and tell me what's wrong?'

There was a gasp from inside the cubicle, followed by more muffled sobs.

'Mildred, you'll make yourself ill if you go on like this,' Joy pleaded. She tapped on the door for a second time. 'What will help to make it better? Can I fetch you a drink of water or a cup of tea?'

The sobbing faded to silence. Still Mildred refused to emerge.

Joy waited on tenterhooks, wondering what on earth had reduced the girl to this desperate state.

'Shall I stay outside while you pull yourself together? Then you can come out and we can have a chat.'

'No need.' At last there was the sound of a bolt being slid back and the cubicle door swung open.

Joy was shocked by what she saw. Mildred stood with her overall unbuttoned and her long plaits hanging loose. Her face was red and swollen and there was a large purple bruise under her left eye. 'Who did that to you?' she demanded.

'No one – I fell over. No one, honestly!'

'Come here.' Joy took the girl's hand and led her gently from the cloakroom, straight upstairs to her office where she sat her down. Closer inspection revealed more bruises on Mildred's hands and arms. 'Tell me the truth; what really happened?'

'I had a row with Mum after she found out that I'd blabbed about the baby.'

'Your mother did this?' Joy could scarcely believe her ears.

'Yesterday. Then first thing this morning she dragged me out of bed, told me to pack my bag and never come back.' Mildred turned her head away in shame and misery.

'She's thrown you out of the house? Are you sure she won't change her mind?'

'Certain. You should've heard her, Mrs Rossi – calling me all the names under the sun then clouting me again for good measure.'

'That's not right.' Joy's face was hot with anger; the mother's behaviour was downright wicked, placing Mildred in grave danger.

'I'm a proper fool, I am. I can't even keep my mouth shut. Mum will never forgive me.'

Joy sprang to the girl's defence. 'Your mother ought not to hit you and shove you around when you're pregnant;

in fact, not under any circumstances. And you're not a fool – you hear me?'

'I told her I didn't want to be sent away to Aunty Myra's.' Mildred continued her tale of woe. 'That really set her off.'

Joy pushed stray strands of damp hair from the girl's forehead. 'Why don't you want to go there?'

'I just don't.'

'There must be a reason. Come on; tell me.'

Mildred took a deep breath before deciding to confide in Joy. 'Aunty Myra has taken against me; that's why. She told Mum she'd get Uncle Keith to knock some sense into me while I'm there.'

'Oh, Mildred – that's awful. You definitely can't risk going back home, but do you have somewhere else you could stay?'

'Who would want me while I'm in this pickle?' she wailed.

'The baby's father – won't he help?'

The question led to a fresh outburst of crying. 'I don't even know where he lives. I'd only just met him at a dance when it happened – in an alleyway behind the Mecca dance hall. I didn't want him to do it but he wouldn't take no for an answer, even with someone else standing at the end of the alley watching what went on.'

Worse and worse! Joy took out her hankie to wipe the tears from Mildred's cheeks. 'This man's name?' she prompted in a soft voice.

'He said everyone calls him Frank because he looks like Frank Sinatra, but I don't think that's his real name.'

'And did he look like the singer?'

'Yes – he was skinny, with a thin face and he had the

same smile; that's what struck me when he first asked me to dance.'

Joy decided she'd heard enough. 'We can't have this,' she declared. 'Did you manage to pack a bag?'

'Yes; I left it in the cloakroom.'

'Good. Now, can you fetch it and bring it back here while I make a quick telephone call? You can? That's a good girl.'

As Mildred did her bidding, Joy dialled the number of Nixon's newspaper shop next door to the ice-cream parlour. Once she was connected, she asked the proprietor if he would pop next door to ask Lucia if she, Joy, could bring someone home with her? After a few minutes Lucia herself came to the phone. Joy told her that the girl in question was in a spot of bother – would it be all right for her to use the spare room?

'*Si, si, si,*' good-hearted Lucia assured Joy without hesitating. '*Ma certo, senza dubbio. Si!*'

'Now listen to me and no arguments,' Joy told Mildred when she returned with her bag. 'Everything is arranged – at the end of the day you're to come home to Blackpool with me.'

'Mrs Rossi, no! You don't have to do that.' Dumbfounded, Mildred let her canvas duffel bag drop to the floor.

'I don't have to but I want to,' Joy said firmly. 'It doesn't need to be for long – just until we find you something more permanent. And I want you to carry on working here so you can save money for when the baby is due. Your secret is safe with me and Mr Henderson, you hear me?'

'You're sure you don't mind?' Her employer's kindness fell like manna from heaven; it was almost impossible for the poor, downtrodden girl to believe.

'Quite the opposite,' Joy declared. 'Keep on working

for as long as you like. Stay with me and my husband and my mother-in-law, Lucia. She's a lovely Italian lady who runs an ice-cream parlour. You'll like her, I'm sure.'

'Our new sign is in place above the studio door.' Sylvia was brimming with excitement when she visited her mother to share some good news. It was midday on Monday and Sylvia had skipped lunch in order to travel over to King Alfred Street. 'It's bright as anything and twice the size of the old one. People can't help but notice it.'

Lorna had just finished giving a private lesson to a well-heeled, retired couple from Lytham. Guessing that her daughter had had nothing to eat, she led her from the studio to her first-floor flat and insisted on making her a fish paste sandwich and a cup of tea. 'You're looking awfully thin,' she commented with a worried frown. 'I assume that you don't always cook yourself a proper meal in the evening?'

'Of course I do, Mother – don't fuss.' Sylvia nibbled at the sandwich. It was true she was losing weight again; Cliff had commented on it and he and Terry had recently insisted on taking her out for a slap-up meal of roast beef and Yorkshire pudding. She'd forced it down but the sensation of being too full had left her feeling nauseous. The following day she'd eaten hardly anything. 'Anyway, when will you come to the studio to see our new sign?'

'On my next day off.' Lorna's promise was deliberately vague. 'Tell me, have you come all the way across town just to inform me about a sign?'

'Of course not.' Once, just once in her life, couldn't her mother show more enthusiasm? But no; there she perched on the edge of the sofa, ankles neatly crossed, hands resting in her lap, the picture of refined elegance. 'My big news is that Vernon King has agreed to conduct an interview about the dance weekend with you, me and Cliff.'

'And who is Vernon King?'

'The new entertainments critic at the *Gazette*. I've met him twice now: once at the newspaper office when I went to place a small ad and then again at the Tower on Saturday night. It turns out he's a keen ballroom dancer himself – mostly Latin, so he won't necessarily be your cup of tea.'

'Slow down.' Lorna held up her hand imperiously. 'This man's offer to conduct an interview – it will lead to an article in the newspaper?'

'Yes, which is so much better than placing a number of small ads, don't you see? There will be a proper feature with photographs and information about the classes we run as well as publicity about our weekend.'

Sylvia thought back to her conversation with Vernon after they'd left the ballroom and he'd escorted her along the prom, walking arm in arm all the way to North View Parade. It had been a fine night with a clear moon and hardly any wind. The compliments had continued to flow: didn't Sylvia realize that she danced well enough to turn professional, how come a girl as good-looking as her didn't have a sweetheart and hadn't she ever thought of broadening her horizons by moving to London where the real action was? She'd made it crystal clear that she wasn't taken in by the flattery, had told him in no uncertain terms to cut the flannel and focus on the interview that he'd offered to do.

'It's a definite,' Vernon had confirmed outside her studio, with its brand-new sign over the doorway gleaming in the moonlight. Cars with hooded headlights crawled along the unlit thoroughfare, briefly illuminating the two figures standing deep in conversation. It was time to say goodnight. 'Let's meet again to arrange a time and a place.'

Wednesday at 7 p.m. Winter Gardens. All was agreed. A brief kiss was exchanged, followed by a self-conscious smile and a soft goodnight from Sylvia.

Now, sitting in Lorna's beautifully tidy living room, surrounded by her dance mementoes – a display of silver trophies in the glass cabinet, won in the twenties when Lorna had been a rising ballroom star, next to signed photographs of her heroes, Victor Silvester and Josephine Bradley – Sylvia fought to communicate the thrill she'd felt when she'd secured the interview. 'Don't you see, this is an extremely valuable contact for us – one that we must follow up, come what may?'

'I do see,' Lorna conceded. 'But ideally I'd like to meet Mr King in person before I consent to his writing the article.'

'Whatever for?' Sylvia was irritated by her mother's caution. 'Can't you just be glad that he's taking an interest?'

'Not until I get a measure of the man first. Listen to me, darling – you wouldn't be the first girl to be swept off her feet by a man in his position. And journalists are notorious for their unscrupulous behaviour. Are you quite sure of Vernon King's intentions?'

Sylvia sprang to her feet. 'Why do you always have to doubt me?' she protested. 'I'm not a girl any more – I'm a grown woman and perfectly capable of taking care of myself.'

'Calm down, Sylvia dear. All I'm saying is that you need to tread carefully. For instance, can Mr King guarantee that his editor will find space for this article, and if so when? Are we quite sure that his message will be positive?

Will he show us in a good light or seek to undermine our efforts with negative comments? Have you thought of that?'

'Vernon is one hundred per cent on our side,' Sylvia insisted. 'Like I said before, he's a decent dancer with a good deal of knowledge about the world we inhabit. All we have to do is show him around our studios, answer his questions then let him take a few photographs. Where's the harm in that?'

'You may be right.' Lorna nodded slowly.

'So you agree?' Sylvia plonked herself down beside her mother and squeezed her arm.

Lorna's face softened into a fond smile. 'Yes, but promise me that you'll be careful,' she pleaded.

'I will,' Sylvia vowed. She stood up again with a fresh burst of breezy energy. 'And now I must be on my way. I've decided it's high time to enter the lion's den and I only have an hour in which to do it.'

Lorna followed her out of the living room on to the landing. 'What do you mean?'

The quarrel with Pearl had started to weigh heavily on Sylvia's conscience – besides leading to an unbearable awkwardness whenever their paths crossed, small doubts had eventually wormed their way in; had she actually seen the fateful kiss take place or just imagined it? Finally she'd come to the fretful conclusion that the only way forward was for her, Sylvia, to back down.

'Pearl and I have had a disagreement. She's been avoiding me for days because of something I said about her precious Sergeant Jackson, which by the way happens to be true. Oh Mother, the details don't matter – I've just reached the conclusion that the only way to repair the friendship is for me to eat humble pie.'

'You?' Lorna made no attempt to hide her surprise. After all, humility didn't come high in her headstrong daughter's list of attributes.

'Yes, me,' Sylvia said firmly as she skipped downstairs. 'I'll track Pearl down at the arcade. She won't be expecting me so I'll ambush her and shower her with so many apologies that she won't be able to resist.'

And with this she was gone – on to a tram to take her north along the prom, past the Tower and the lifeboat station, past the imposing seafront hotels with their sandbagged entrances, with serried ranks of RAF trainees doing physical jerks on the beach, as far as North Pier, where she hopped off then paid her penny at the turnstile. Sylvia ran lightly over the worn wooden planks, taking care not to look down at the gaps and the swirling sea below, until she reached a row of gaudy souvenir shops and a café with a domed white roof beyond. Here she heard big band music blaring from loudspeakers over the doorway to Great Scott's Amusement Arcade. Humming along to the tune of 'I've Got a Gal in Kalamazoo' to hide her nerves, she stepped inside.

'Blimey, Sylvia, cut out the squawkin',' Pearl's fourteen-year-old brother Ernie grumbled from his seat behind the cash desk. He wore a grubby green jumper with holes in the elbows and his upper lip showed the downy beginnings of a dark moustache. 'You'll scare away the customers.'

'Ha ha, Ernie; very funny.' Peering between the rows of fruit machines, Sylvia waited for her eyes to adjust. Three lads in short trousers and well-worn plimsolls inserted pennies into a Little Mickey while a couple of uniformed GIs claimed a jackpot payout from a shiny Playball, complete with flashing lights. 'Where's Pearl?' Sylvia demanded.

'Not here,' was Ernie's churlish reply.

'I can see that. Where did she go?'

'How should I know? She's only gone and left me stuck 'ere without tellin' me when she'll be back.'

'Did she leave alone or with someone?' Sylvia watched the GIs pocket their winnings then eye her up, no doubt exchanging off-colour remarks as they did so. An uneasy feeling created a small knot in her stomach.

'With that Yank,' Ernie informed her huffily. 'The one she goes dancin' with – Errol what's-'is-name. He asked her to go for a walk with 'im and, blow me, off she bloomin' well trots.'

CHAPTER SIX

'*Povera bambina!*' Lucia fussed mightily over Mildred. A fire was lit even though it was almost June and Lucia invited her to sit by it while she brewed a pot of tea. She asked no questions; she simply made the girl welcome in her effusive, Italian way. 'Your room; it is clean – *fresca.* I have put flowers by bed for nice smell. My Tommy, he take your bag. Joy, she explain everything to him.'

Mildred sank into the chair. Her boss had been as good as her word. They'd left the warehouse ten minutes early, before the hooter signalled the end of the working day, and they'd caught the train to Blackpool together – a town that Mildred had visited only once during a Sunday school trip when she was nine years old. Today she'd scarcely taken in the famous sights during the tram journey from North Station to South Shore, only dimly aware of the Tower and the Pleasure Beach as she sat next to Joy, head down and doing her best not to draw attention to her blotchy skin and swollen features.

Upstairs in the spare room, Joy described to Tommy what had taken place while keeping her promise not to give away Mildred's secret. 'I couldn't abandon her. Who in the world thrashes a fifteen-year-old girl so badly that she ends up covered in bruises then turns her out on to the street with scarcely a penny to her name?'

'You did the right thing.' Tommy drew her close. 'You always do,' he murmured as he kissed her gently on the lips.

'You're sure you don't mind me bringing her here?'

Without answering her question, he stroked her long, glossy hair back from her face. Joy was lovelier than ever; so sincere and brave, with dark brown eyes that would melt the hardest of hearts. 'I understand why you've done this – it's because you know what it's like to be alone in the world at Mildred's age.'

'True,' she whispered. Alone in Blackpool after her mother, father and sister had been killed during an air raid; left to fend for herself as best she could. 'But my situation wasn't as dire as Mildred's.'

Tommy took a step back so he could make out her features more clearly. 'What do you mean?'

'Oh dear!' Too late Joy realized she'd given too much away. 'Never mind – forget I said that.'

'No.' He kept hold of her hands and made her look him in the eye. 'What's so dire about Mildred's situation?'

'I promised not to tell.'

'We're married,' he reminded her gently. 'We're not supposed to keep secrets.'

What to do now? For a few seconds Joy was torn between the promise that she'd given in the heat of the moment and her husband's tender reminder of her loyalty to him. The latter won the day. 'Mildred is pregnant,' she confided at last, 'by a stranger who took advantage of her. I don't know much more than that. Will you please keep it to yourself?'

Tommy nodded then kissed her again. 'Thank you for trusting me.'

She hugged him for a few moments. 'Shall we go down and help to settle her in?'

Down to Lucia's cosy, cluttered kitchen where copper pans hung from a rack above the cooking range and a bright fire burned in the grate, to the smell of roast potatoes in the oven and a display of blue and white plates on the dresser and the rattle of cutlery as the table was set for dinner.

Huddled close to the fire, Mildred's cheeks had gained a healthier colour, except for the bruise under her eye that was turning dark blue. She gazed around in wonderment at the gleaming pans and crockery, at onions hanging from a string and chopped liver frying in the pan and most of all at the short, plump figure of Lucia in her green and white striped apron, with her greying hair pinned back into a bun, smiling as she chattered in a mixture of English and Italian.

'Sit,' Lucia instructed as Tommy and Joy entered the room. '*Avete fame?* You are hungry? Food is ready – *sedetevi*; sit!'

Queen of her domain, Lucia piled food on to their plates. Her smile was bright as she watched them eat, then she wouldn't hear of Mildred lifting a finger to clear away the plates afterwards. 'You sleep now,' she told her. 'Tomorrow you make a new day.'

Tommy and Joy agreed that an early night would do Mildred the world of good. Joy took her upstairs, pointing out the bathroom door at the head of the stairs. She gave her a clean towel from the airing cupboard then showed her the wash-stand in the corner of her new bedroom, complete with porcelain basin and ewer filled with water – 'In case the bathroom is occupied when you wake up,' she explained. The sheets on the bed were pristine, the eiderdown a pretty shade of cornflower blue, matching the jug of flowers that Lucia had placed on her bedside cabinet. 'Will you be all right?' she checked before she left.

Mildred felt tears of gratitude well up. 'You're too good to me, Mrs Rossi – I don't deserve it.'

'Nonsense and please don't cry.' Joy took care to stick to practical matters, recalling how she'd damaged the girl's fragile self-respect by offering to pay for a bus ticket to her aunt's house in the Lakes. 'We have to be out of the house early tomorrow morning to catch the Manchester train. I'll knock on your door at seven o'clock sharp, to give you time for breakfast.'

'Yes, Mrs Rossi.' Mildred clasped her hands in front of her, slowly taking in more of her new surroundings – soft pillows, crisp net curtains, a small fireplace framed by blue and white tiles.

'Call me Joy – please. We can be informal when we're at home.'

Mildred gasped. 'Oh, I couldn't.'

'I insist. You can carry on calling me Mrs Rossi at work, but here we're friends on an equal footing.' Joy left the room before Mildred could object, closing the door quietly and going downstairs to help Tommy with the washing-up. She too felt tired after the day's events and was soon shooed upstairs to bed by Lucia, followed soon after by Tommy.

Leaving the blackout blind up and the lights off, they undressed by moonlight then slipped between the sheets. Joy's breathing soon slowed to keep pace with Tommy's as they lay side by side, gazing out at the stars.

'So peaceful,' she murmured. 'Have I ever said how the sky at night reminds me that we're tiny specks in a massive universe – how much I love that feeling?'

'It doesn't scare you?' he asked. 'Don't you feel helpless in the face of everything that goes on around us?'

'No, I don't look at it like that. It lifts me out of myself when I see how beautiful the moon is, sailing clear of the clouds and shining down on us.'

Tommy said nothing to spoil the mood. These quiet moments with Joy were precious. 'What would you wish for if I could wave a magic wand?'

She turned her head towards him to study his profile in the half-light, remembering how they'd begun as friends – Joy, a cleaner at the Tower, occasionally crossing paths with Tommy when he came away from a matinee performance at the circus, always bright and cheery, fond of practical jokes, cheeky and funny – until the magical point when she'd realized there might be more to it than friendship. A first kiss had done it – out there on the beach, under the same starry sky. 'I'd wish that nothing will ever part us,' she whispered. 'That this war will end tomorrow and the world will breathe a sigh of relief. That you and I will carry on dancing together for ever and ever.'

'Blimey, you don't want much.' Tommy laughed as he turned on to his side and drew her close. What more could he hope to hear?

Sylvia wasn't sure what to wear. The meeting with Vernon was important as far as the big dance weekend went but was there more to it than that? Had he too felt the frisson when their lips had briefly touched at the weekend? The question was this: ought she to dress in a businesslike way to firm up details for the interview or wear something more fetching, like the summer dress that she held up to the mirror to study its effect. The dress was in her favourite pale blue, exposing her long neck and slim arms but not too much cleavage. It was made of smooth brushed cotton, with a floral pattern; altogether fresh and feminine.

Yes, the blue dress would do. But now she must hurry to reach the Galleon Bar inside the Winter Gardens at the time they'd arranged. Quickly on with the dress and her white wedge-heeled sandals, a flick through her blonde tresses with her silver hairbrush, a rapid dab of coral-pink lipstick then out of the door and downstairs on to North View Parade. She prayed that she wouldn't have to wait long for a tram, with butterflies causing havoc in her stomach. Finally, just in time, she approached the entrance on Coronation Street.

A sudden thought stopped Sylvia in her tracks as she entered the splendid vestibule that was crowded with theatre-goers queuing for a performance at the Opera House and with dancers waiting for the doors of the Empress Ballroom to open – *What if Vernon doesn't come?* How foolish she would look. Taking a deep breath, she walked on towards the Galleon, prepared for all eventualities.

As its name suggested, their meeting place was done out as a replica of a Spanish warship, complete with oak beams supported by carved pillars and old-fashioned oil lamps that cast a subdued light over the captain's bridge and ship's wheel. None of it was real; every inch was fashioned in clever, *trompe l'oeil* plasterwork – the beams and scrolls, the pillars and arched ceiling – all fake. Sylvia hesitated in the doorway. It wasn't customary for a woman to come here alone, unless she was a certain type. Her jitters increased and she was on the point of turning back when Vernon came up behind her.

'Francis Drake at your service, milady,' he announced with a flourish. 'Here to rescue you from devilish Spanish pirates!'

'There you are.' She let out a sigh of relief.

'Don't sound so surprised.' Escorting her towards the bar, he found two empty stools and ordered drinks: beer for him and sweet martini for Sylvia. 'Will it go to your head if I tell you how pretty you look tonight?' he asked in the teasing manner that seemed second nature. He looked relaxed and summery in a white sports shirt with a soft collar and dark blue trousers, teamed with brown suede shoes.

'I'll take the compliment and ignore the big-headed dig,' she retorted.

He drew his stool closer. 'Well seriously, you do look exceptionally pretty. How has your day been?'

'Rushed off my feet, as usual.'

'Business is booming, I take it?'

'Yes; our new advertising campaign seems to have paid off. Cliff and I have put on extra classes as a result.'

'Good for you,' Vernon said.

'How about you? Have you seen any good films lately?'

'No previews, but I took in *Casablanca* again – it's showing at the Odeon. Warner Brothers have a giant hit on their hands so it's probably worth reviewing a second time.'

'Their love story makes me cry.' Sylvia had seen the film three times in as many months and never tired of Bogart's and Bergman's performances. 'I'm jealous that you get paid to see everything before the rest of us.'

'Yes and we hold a good deal of power,' he said with a wink. 'A bad review from us can kill a show or an event stone dead.'

She raised an eyebrow. 'Then I'd better watch out.'

Vernon leaned in closer still. 'Oh, I wouldn't do that to you. I'll be very kind about your dance weekend.'

He was near enough for her to notice the fine hairs on his forearms and feel the warmth of his breath, but it was his eyes that held her attention – a cool blue-grey in colour and set deep, emphasizing his well-defined cheekbones. 'You promise?'

'Promise,' he agreed before breaking the spell by reaching for his cigarettes. 'Just state a time and a place for this interview.'

'I think you should call in at King Alfred Street first,' Sylvia suggested. 'I persuaded Mother to come on board, but I have to warn you that she's rather grand and a touch prickly about journalists.'

'Forewarned is forearmed, eh?' Vernon mentioned that since their last meeting he'd done his research; he'd looked up the name Lorna Ellis in the ISTD records and read about her impressive achievements back in the day. 'You're telling me to watch my Ps and Qs?'

'Yes; best to stick to facts with my mother: the ins and outs of our competition, how many entrants are allowed, the types of dance, and so on.'

'So flattery is out.' He made a mental note before they fixed on Friday at noon for his visit to the Ellis Academy. 'And what time shall I visit you?'

'Why not come straight from there? The chances are Cliff and I will be busy, but one of us will be able to break off from what we're doing to answer your questions.'

'I'd rather it was you.' Bold and direct, teasing, willing her to react.

'We'll see, shall we?' She made an effort not to make the attraction too obvious, to keep him at arm's length and play the game.

'Right – that's all arranged. Now it's time to let our hair down. How about taking a spin around the floor?'

Vernon nodded towards the Empress Ballroom next door, stubbing out his cigarette and whisking her from her stool without giving her time to say no. Before she knew it he'd wangled their way in for nothing and joined hundreds of other couples for a spritely quickstep with renowned organist Horace Finch at the Wurlitzer, running, hopping, skipping and turning under dazzling chandeliers and a barrel-vaulted ceiling that vied in gilded splendour with the Tower Ballroom itself. Once again, Sylvia revelled in the speed and agility with which Vernon led her around the floor, and when he slipped in some extra, tricky syncopations, she laughed out loud.

'Keep up!' he urged with a grin.

'Less of the cheek!' Sylvia showed him that he'd met his match by seizing the lead and throwing in several nifty chassés until the quickstep ended and an American smooth began.

Vernon kept firm hold of Sylvia's hand. 'Come on, Ginger Rogers – we can do this.'

'Of course we can, Fred.' A combination of waltz, tango, foxtrot and Viennese waltz, the dance required a good deal of skill. There were frequent breaks of hold and experiments with open, side-by-side footwork that demanded quick thinking. Not to be outdone by her partner's free-flowing natural turns and travelling chassés, Sylvia executed a perfect individual spin before coming back into hold.

After the American smooth had melted into classic Viennese waltz they danced on, followed in quick succession by foxtrot, followed by samba. 'Thirsty?' Vernon asked as an interval was announced.

Sylvia nodded but instead of heading for the crowded bar, Vernon led her out of the ballroom, across the vestibule and into the street.

'There's a pub I know just off Church Street,' he explained. 'It'll be quieter there.'

Glad to catch her breath, Sylvia soon found herself ensconced in a corner of a dingy lounge bar with only a few customers and a run-down, old-fashioned air. It was partitioned into private booths, each dimly lit by flickering gaslight, an increasingly rare hangover from pre-electricity days.

'This is more like it,' Vernon said when he brought over drinks from the bar. 'Now we can hear ourselves think.'

Sylvia's heart was still racing. It wasn't only the high-energy dancing that had caused this fluttery, breathless feeling; it was also the excitement of being with Vernon. The sensation was new to her and stripped away her air of aloofness. 'That was smashing – I really enjoy dancing with you,' she confessed.

'Likewise.' About to offer her a cigarette, he thought better of it. 'You don't, do you?'

'Not usually, but go on then; where's the harm in the occasional one?' She took a cigarette from the packet and let him light it. The smoke burned slightly as it hit the back of her throat.

'I enjoy talking to you too,' he said before adding, 'and not just about work. I hope we can get to know each other better.'

'Yes, that would be nice.' Her heart gave a skip and a jump.

'How about tomorrow night? I'll pick you up in my car at six.'

'You have a car?' she asked eagerly.

'Yes – my pride and joy. We can drive along the coast road.'

Sylvia gave a quick shake of her head. 'I teach a samba class on a Thursday evening.'

'Say you're poorly. Ask Cliff Seymour to stand in for you.'

His flippant suggestion made her smile. 'I live next door to the studio. He might see me sneaking off.'

'All right, then – I'll pick you up after you've finished teaching. The pubs will still be open, won't they? Say yes!'

'Yes.' She didn't pause to think it through. Floating on air was an expression Sylvia had often read but never experienced until now. It felt most peculiar; as if she was separate from her own body. 'The Sun Lounge at the Norbreck Hydro is open to non-residents. We could go there for a drink.'

'This place isn't good enough for you?' Vernon jerked his thumb in the direction of a group of scruffy market traders playing dominoes in the booth opposite. 'Only kidding; the Norbreck it is.'

A decision was made and Vernon insisted on walking Sylvia home to North View Parade. Her head was spinning, her heart pounding all the way along the prom. Vernon chatted easily – about his fuddy-duddy colleagues at the *Gazette* and Angela, the fiery dragon on Reception, then his ambition to make it to the top in the world of journalism. 'A big London paper is what I'd like,' he told her. 'Theatre critic for the *Evening Standard* – that's my ambition. Does that sound big-headed?'

'Yes – very.' She too could tease. 'But there's nothing wrong with aiming for the top.'

'Does the same go for you too?' They'd reached the turn-off onto Sylvia's street so it was almost time for them to part.

'Why not?' She jutted out her chin. 'I work hard at what I do.'

'And you've won almost every competition there is. I've looked you up as well,' he added. 'Like I said, I do my homework.'

'But those competitions were in ISTD standard categories, when Eddie Winter was my partner,' she reminded him. 'I hoped until recently that I was part of another winning combination with Terry Liddle, but the Society has banned him.'

'Poor you.' Vernon tilted her head back with his thumb. 'I'd step in like a shot if it weren't for work commitments.'

Their faces were so close that the kiss was inevitable. Their lips met then they each pulled back to judge how the other had reacted. Then Vernon reached for her and held her close, kissing her cheek and then her mouth so that Sylvia melted into him and lost herself in the feel of his lips pressing against hers, his arms around her waist, hers around his shoulders, her head back, thrilling to his touch.

Dark thoughts crowded in on Pearl. She failed to keep them at bay during idle moments when there were few customers in the arcade or at night-time as she lay awake, unable to sleep. Why hadn't Bernie written to tell her where he'd been posted? Or perhaps he had but the letters had never got beyond the censor's desk? Yes; the need for secrecy on military matters was very likely the reason, but knowing this didn't ease Pearl's heartache or the constant worrying that wore her down and made all of life seem bleak.

It didn't help, either, that she and Sylvia were still not on speaking terms or that Joy was preoccupied with other matters. Pearl had run into Tommy when she'd been heading for the arcade and he'd been crossing the market square en route to an early rehearsal at the circus. He'd hailed her and told her the latest news – Joy had offered their spare room to a girl who worked in the Hebden canteen. Pearl had tried to squeeze more information out of him – the whys and the wherefores – but Tommy had clammed up. 'All I'm allowed to say is that Mildred's mother chucked her out and she had nowhere else to go. Joy's taken her under her wing, bless her.'

They'd both been in a rush so Pearl's many questions had remained unanswered. 'Tell Joy that I'm here if she needs someone to talk to,' she'd told Tommy as they'd parted.

That had been at the start of a long, uneventful day spent sitting at the entrance to the arcade, staring out at grey, gusty weather. Few holidaymakers braved a persistent drizzle to venture this far along the pier to play the slot machines; fewer still frequented the Seaview Café selling lukewarm tea, tired sausage rolls and limp sandwiches. By mid afternoon boredom had set in and with it Pearl's deep-seated worry about her beloved Bernie had reared its ugly head. To distract herself she wandered across to the café and collared one of the waitresses. 'I'll pay you a tanner to run along to my house and tell Ernie that I need him to step in for me here,' she explained. 'He'll be home from school by the time you get there.'

'I'll do it for a shilling,' the girl shot back.

The deal was done and a damp Pearl returned to the arcade, where she waited impatiently for her brother to show up. Once relieved, her plan was to go home and begin yet another letter to Bernie. She waited and waited and still no Ernie. A few customers trickled in. A Chip and Bust machine paid out to a sou'wester-clad angler who had left his station at the end of the pier and taken refuge from the dreary weather. An off-duty Yank – a thin, sad-looking private with none of the typical GI bravado – entered with a low-key 'Hi.' He took up position in front of the latest Spitfire game and played doggedly without a win.

'Time for me to shut up shop,' Pearl informed him at last. She felt weary and frustrated, willing the working day to come to an end.

The GI sighed and tapped his empty pockets. 'Just as well, I guess.' He'd stepped out on to the pier when he added as an afterthought, 'Sergeant Jackson said to say hi.'

'Say hello to him from me,' Pearl said automatically. Thinking no more about it, she closed the shutters and raised the canvas awning. Boy, would she give Ernie a piece of her mind when she got home!

'What happened to you?' she demanded the moment she stepped into the kitchen at Empire Street.

Her brother looked up from a football magazine to find a damp and scowling Pearl gunning for him. 'What are you on about?'

'You know perfectly well what I'm on about – I sent a message for you to come to the arcade.'

Maria was standing at the sink, keeping a watchful eye on her offspring.

'That's the first I heard,' Ernie said with a careless shrug.

Pearl turned to her mother with a questioning look.

'There was no message so far as I know,' Maria informed her.

Pearl was fuming. 'What? I paid the little swine from Seaview Café a whole shilling! Ernie, I needed you there, damn it. Now I won't have time to write to Bernie before I go out to my dance class.'

'Boohoo!' he muttered scornfully. 'Poor diddums.'

'Ernie!' Maria raised a warning finger.

'How often do I ask you to stand in for me?' Pearl demanded. 'Hardly ever.'

'Fibber,' Ernie mumbled under his breath then jumped to his feet as Pearl launched herself at him. He backed towards his mother. 'She made me do it earlier this week. I missed a game of footie cos of 'er.'

'When exactly?' Pearl was too exasperated to remember clearly.

'Monday. Yes, Monday. Sylvia came looking for you and you weren't there.'

'Sylvia came to North Pier?' For a moment Pearl was taken aback. 'What for? What did she want?'

'How should I know?' Ernie came out from behind his mother and sidled towards the door. 'I told her you'd gone for a walk with the Yank and she stormed off again.'

Pearl gasped. 'You told Sylvia where I'd gone?'

Slowly Maria dried her hands on her apron then motioned for Ernie to leave the room. She told Pearl to sit down then sat opposite her, leaning forward, with her elbows on the table and her hands clasped. 'Well?'

'Well what?' Pearl's attempt to meet her mother's gaze ended in failure. Instead, she squirmed and covered her face. 'All right, it's true – I did go for a walk on the beach with Errol and it's just rotten luck that Sylvia found out. I've no idea why she came to the arcade – we're not even on speaking terms.'

'That's beside the point and you know it.' Maria waited for Pearl to calm down before she spoke again. 'You're an adult and what you do is your business, unless . . .'

'Unless what?'

'Unless you carrying on with a Yank reflects badly on us as a family. And you'll see that it does if you stop to think about it.'

'I'm not carrying on with Errol!' Pearl cried. 'You sound like Sylvia, for heaven's sake.'

'Yes and imagine how it looks to other people besides her,' Maria pointed out. 'And what a disaster it would be if Bernie got to hear about it.'

The thought hit Pearl like a punch to the stomach. 'How would he?' she whimpered.

'Gossip gets carried on the wind. Soon it's everywhere – blown to four corners of the earth in mothers writing letters to sons, wives to husbands, sweethearts to sweethearts. And those brave men serving abroad pick up the rumours, true or false, and can do nothing except sweat it out and try not to be eaten up by jealousy.'

'Stop,' Pearl pleaded, hands over her ears. 'Bernie knows how much I love him. He trusts me.'

Maria scraped back her chair and stood up, her expression grim. 'I've said my piece.'

She went out into the backyard to bring in a line of washing that had failed to dry. Silence descended. Pearl closed her eyes and took several deep breaths. Was it time for a rethink? Perhaps a note to Errol explaining the situation and her reasons for stepping back, or better still she would tell him face to face the next time they met. Meanwhile, she needed pen and paper to write a long, loving letter to Bernie.

CHAPTER SEVEN

The bruise under Mildred's eye was still clearly visible when she next clocked in at work. Nevertheless, the girl had had time to rest and get used to her cosy new surroundings. She and Lucia had spent their evenings chatting while they darned holes in Tommy's socks and mended rips in Mildred's threadbare dresses, so that she appeared at the warehouse looking less neglected than before.

Dora, her supervisor, noticed it straight away. 'You look nice.' She diplomatically ignored Mildred's black eye as the girl entered the women's cloakroom. 'Shorter hair suits you.'

'Do you think so?' Mildred glanced anxiously in the mirror before slipping her overall over her head. 'It was Mrs Rossi's idea for me to get it cut – not young Mrs Rossi; the older Italian lady. She took me to a proper hairdresser on King Street.'

'That was kind of her.' Dora was here to do an eight-to-five job and it wasn't her place to pry. In a way, the less she knew about the circumstances surrounding Mildred's misadventures the better. 'Anyway, it's a relief to have you back. I've been run off my feet trying to cope single handed.'

'Good morning, Mildred.' Alan greeted her cheerfully as she emerged from the cloakroom and made her way towards the canteen. 'What's on the menu for dinner today?'

'Fish and chips.' She kept her face turned away but she needn't have worried; Mr Henderson, who was with a man she didn't recognize, acted as though nothing bad had happened.

'Of course; it's Friday.' The manager was about to take the stairs up to the office two at a time when he paused. 'Nice hairdo,' he commented with a quick smile. 'Follow me,' he told the stranger. 'Mrs Rossi has read your application letter for the caretaker's job. She'll see you now.'

Mildred watched the man follow the warehouse manager at a slower pace, obviously hampered by a bad limp.

Hearing a familiar tap on the door, Joy called for Alan to enter.

'Good morning, Mrs Rossi. This is Robert Finchley, the young chap I mentioned to you earlier in the week. You have all his details written down so I'll leave you to it.'

'No; please stay.' Joy motioned for them both to take a seat. 'Alan knows more about the day-to-day operation of the warehouse than I do,' she explained to the candidate – an underfed, earnest and evidently nervous man in his twenties who, according to his application, had been badly wounded during the evacuations from Dunkirk and afterwards been declared unfit for service. Today he seemed to have taken trouble with his appearance, sporting a close shave, slicked-back hair, a white shirt and a dark blue tie. 'He's described your military background to me and vouched for your character.'

'Yes, miss – my dad knew Mr Henderson when he worked for Hebdens over twenty years back. The families kept in touch. And if you're wondering if this limp of mine will stop me from doing a good job, I can assure you it won't.'

Joy glanced at Alan, who nodded in confirmation. 'You're otherwise in good health?'

'Yes, miss. I'm stronger than I look and I stick at a job until it's done.'

'Very well. I want you to be quite sure about what you'd be taking on so I've asked Alan – Mr Henderson – to show you where everything is, in particular the cellar, where we keep the bags of coke to fire up the boiler, and the store-room for mops and buckets, and so on. Then he and I will have a chat and make a decision.'

As the two men left for the grand tour, Joy scanned Finchley's application – written in a cramped script with the odd spelling mistake here and there. She noted that he was married with one child and another on the way.

Of course Joy would give him the job. He had Alan's backing and that was good enough for her.

Another knock on the door interrupted her train of thought and before she could react, a red-faced, hatless woman in a light green jacket over a fawn jumper and dark brown skirt barged in.

'Where is she?' The intruder strode into the office, slamming the door behind her. Her eyes raked angrily across the room then outside to the yard and brick-built warehouse below. 'Where's my girl?'

Joy stood up from her desk. 'Who do you mean?' Although there was no obvious physical resemblance, she realized immediately that this was Mildred's mother.

'You know damned well who I mean. She works in the canteen. My name's Winifred Kershaw. I demand to see my daughter and you can't stop me.'

'Mrs Kershaw, please don't shout.' Joy positioned herself between the woman and the door. 'I really don't think that Mildred wants to see you.'

'What would *you* know?' The woman, who was several inches shorter than Joy but much heavier and fuelled by a savage, sneering anger, seemed to be about to square up for a fight.

'I'm aware that you sent her packing and warned her not to darken your door again,' Joy replied calmly. 'What made you change your mind?'

'Ah, she's come snivelling to you, has she? Just like her, that is. What sob story did she tell you? Well, never mind – all you need to know is that I've had second thoughts. It's better for Mildred to come home so I can stop her washing her dirty linen in public.' Spitting hot fury within inches of Joy's face, Winifred Kershaw was blind to reason.

'And if she refuses?' Joy continued in the same measured tone, playing for time in the hope that Alan would soon return. 'She has a black eye, Mrs Kershaw, and bruises all over her arms. How do you account for that?'

'What's it got to do with you?' The unwelcome visitor shoved Joy to one side then seized the door knob and wrenched hard. 'I want her back with me and there's an end to it. Open this door, damn you!'

Knowing that she was no physical match, Joy kept her distance. 'It's not locked – feel free to turn the knob.'

'If you do you'll find me on the other side of it.' Alan thrust the door open. The sudden movement sent Mildred's mother flying backwards. She crashed into Joy's desk, upending the telephone and scattering papers across the floor. 'What the devil are you playing at, woman?' he demanded, rushing across the room to haul her to her feet. 'No, don't tell me – you're the one that gave our wee lassie her shiner.'

Winifred shook herself free, switching in a split second from hot anger to cold cunning as she rolled back her sleeve to reveal a red mark on her bare arm. 'Two against one now, is it? Wait till I go to the coppers and show them what you did to me, you bloody brute!'

Alan didn't flinch. 'Go ahead; huff and puff all you like, but it won't be me who ends up in a police cell; not once we tell them how you mistreated your own flesh and blood – you understand me?'

'Says you – pah!' A feeble show of defiance was followed by the silent acknowledgement that Mildred's mother had met her match. Fists clenched and breathing noisily through her nose, she allowed herself to be escorted from the room, down the stairs and across the yard. 'You haven't seen the last of me,' she warned Alan as a low, parting shot. 'Or my brother-in-law, for that matter.'

She marched off towards a small black Ford parked some fifty yards down the road while Alan returned to the office, where he found Joy picking up her scattered papers.

'I wouldn't wish her on my worst enemy,' he observed with heavy understatement, noting that Joy's hand was shaking as she retrieved the dangling telephone and placed it in its cradle.

'Dreadful woman,' she agreed. 'What a good job that Mildred stayed out of the way.'

'Mrs Rossi, do you want my opinion?' Alan offered in his unruffled manner.

She thought for a moment then nodded. 'Yes please.'

'That nasty piece of work out there is threatening to

come back and bring a sidekick with her next time. It's not safe for the wee lass to work here any more.'

Joy sighed in reluctant agreement. 'Then what do you suggest?'

There was another pause before her manager delivered his verdict. 'If it was me, I'd stop young Mildred from coming into work for the time being and I'd keep her tucked away in Blackpool, out of harm's way. Yes; that's what I would do.'

First impressions were everything. Vernon reminded himself of this fact as he approached the Lorna Ellis Dance Academy, checking his watch to confirm that he was punctual and then his reflection in the plate-glass window of the Gift Emporium next door to the academy. He was aware that he looked the business in his lightweight linen jacket and Panama hat, yellow silk cravat, with a Kodak camera slung nonchalantly over his shoulder.

As a rule there would have been no trace of nerves; he would breeze in with his notepad and pencil, churn out a few standard questions, scribble quick notes, snap some pictures then leave. But today was different; for once it mattered what his interviewee made of him.

Waiting at the studio window, Lorna beckoned him in. *Presentable*, was her immediate thought. *Smart and spritely, with a spring in his step. Handsome, even.*

'Mrs Ellis?' He extended his hand politely. 'I'm Vernon King.'

'How do you do, Mr King? Please, do come in.'

Vernon saw immediately where Sylvia got her looks. From a distance he would have put Lorna in her early to mid thirties; head held high, perched on a long, swan-like neck, permanent smile, expertly made-up eyes and lips plus a touch of rouge – not overdone, though. It was only when he looked more closely that he noticed the fine lines at the sides of Lorna's eyes and mouth. 'I hope I didn't keep you waiting,' he said, nerves jangling in an uncharacteristic fashion.

'Not at all. But I must warn you that we only have thirty minutes before the start of my next class. I suppose that will be enough?'

'Plenty of time,' Vernon assured her, taking out his notepad. He'd visited many dance studios and rehearsal rooms in his time and this one was a cut above the average – large, with a ballet bar down one side, lined with floor-to-ceiling mirrors and with a proper sprung floor. There was an upright piano in one corner against which he could pose his subject when it came to taking photographs. 'First off, Mrs Ellis, could you confirm a few basic facts for me? Your ballroom dance weekend is scheduled for the seventh and eighth of August; is that correct?'

'Yes. The venue is the Spanish Hall in the Winter Gardens; perhaps you might include that in your headline? It will be a major draw. And please stress that the competition is restricted to amateur dancers; no professionals are permitted to enter. Tickets for entry will be sold in advance.'

Vernon steadied his hand to make quick notes. 'How much?'

'Five shillings per couple, paid in cash or by postal order.' Lorna met his quizzical gaze. 'To cover our costs,' she added defensively before he could comment on what was admittedly a fairly steep charge. 'There will be a live band.'

'Name of the band?' he asked, pencil poised.

'Ah – I have no information as to that, I'm afraid. Perhaps Mr Seymour will provide an answer when you visit North View Parade.'

He jotted down a reminder – *Seymour; name of band?* 'And now a couple of questions on your background, Mrs Ellis. I'm aware that you're a prominent member of the Imperial Society and have been for a long time. Is there anything else I should add?'

'Yes, I also keep up to date with the National Association of Teachers of Dancing. I attend lectures and conferences. In fact, I recently played a part in redesigning their tests for amateurs.'

'So you're right at the heart of things?'

Encouraged, Lorna continued. 'You might say in your article that I, like many of my National Association colleagues, was strongly opposed to the government-enforced closure of dance schools at the outbreak of war.'

Vernon scribbled again. 'But now it's business as usual, right?' In fact, he'd persuaded his editor to accept his article by emphasizing this angle. 'Your dance weekend is only possible because ballroom dancing has defied the lot: Blitz, enlistment, rationing and blackout. In fact, people across the country are clamouring for more dance halls, more competitions.'

'Quite right, Mr King. Now we have the Star Championships, the Lonsdale Cup and Gaumont British Trophy,' Lorna enthused. 'But they're all based in London. Here we have the Allied North of England Championship, with the final in Liverpool.'

Vernon nodded as he wrote. 'Sylvia won a prize there in January, I believe?'

'Yes, be sure to include that in your article, Mr King.'

Noticing her glance at her watch, Vernon moved things

on by putting away his notebook and taking his camera from its case. He suggested using the piano as a backdrop. 'I'm sure you've done this a hundred times before so there's no need for me to set a pose,' he told Lorna. 'Just a sec while I attach the flash . . . Yes, now I'm all set. In your own time, Mrs Ellis.'

Lorna leaned lightly on the piano, feet elegantly turned out in ballet first position, head tilted ever so slightly backwards, lips stretched to show her even, white teeth.

The flashbulb went off. She changed position to offer a sideways angle, then again for a close-up.

'Smashing,' Vernon said after each shot. 'I've got what I need – now I'll get out of your hair.'

The camera went back into its case, they shook hands again and he was gone.

'I'm calling to tell you that my interview went well,' Lorna hastily assured Sylvia on the telephone during the five minutes before the start of her next class. 'Your young man, Mr King, was most professional.'

'Your mother scared the life out of me,' Vernon confessed to Sylvia the moment he crossed the threshold at North View Parade after a short drive along the prom. 'I need a stiff drink.'

Was he serious or exaggerating for comic effect? 'Come in,' she said with a light laugh. 'Cliff, this is Vernon King. Vernon, meet my business partner, Cliff Seymour.'

Cliff's snap judgement on the young journalist was remarkably similar to Lorna's – *Lively and confident; the type that breezes through life by relying on his looks*. He couldn't blame him for that; Cliff had done much the same thing himself. 'We've arranged for two of our most talented couples to come to the studio for you to photograph,' he informed Vernon. 'They have full-time jobs but this interview coincides with their dinner breaks.'

'Good thinking.' As Vernon took out his notebook he gave Sylvia a quick smile. Their drive out to the Norbreck Hydro the previous evening had gone pretty well, all things considered. He'd had to wait for her at the end of her samba class and had teased her for being a few minutes late – 'I wouldn't normally sit twiddling my thumbs but I decided you were worth it.' He'd had the top down on his racing-green MG sports car (Sylvia's first view of the nippy little number) and had suggested that she pop up to her flat for a headscarf to protect her hair – 'We can't have you turning up at the Sun Lounge looking a total fright.' Sylvia had laughed at everything he'd said. She'd turned heads as they'd entered the bar – one of the classiest in town, frequented by minor royals and film stars such as Gracie Fields. Vernon and Sylvia had stayed for a couple of drinks then he'd driven her home. The only let-down had been that he'd hoped to be invited up to the flat but the evening had ended on the pavement with a warm thank-you and another chaste kiss. Well, better luck next time.

Vernon's smile brought colour to Sylvia's cheeks. She must force herself to forget about last night's romantic rendezvous and concentrate on the reason for his visit to the studio.

'We've managed to hire the Art Richardson Swing Band,' Cliff answered Vernon's question about the live music. 'They're one of the best around; a couple of trumpets, two saxophones, a piano, double bass and drums.'

'Any singer?' Vernon asked without looking up from his notepad.

'Rosie Johnson is on vocals.' Cliff provided the information with practised ease.

'Ah yes; Rosie Johnson.' Vernon scribbled another note. 'She and I go a long way back – we worked together in cabaret before the war; that's how I was able to book them at short notice.'

Vernon took everything down. When he queried the entry fee, Cliff justified it by saying there was time for couples to save up the money. 'Besides, it means we'll only attract contestants who are serious about their dancing.'

'Yes, I see that.' More shorthand jottings, another sideways smile at Sylvia. 'Mrs Ellis was keen to stress the more traditional component of the competition. Will it be all white tie and tails?'

'Half and half,' Sylvia answered. 'The Standard section will take place on the Saturday, with Latin on Sunday.'

'And you have ambitions to make this an annual event?'

'Definitely.' Cliff noticed that the first of their invited couples had arrived, soon followed by the second pair. He directed them to get ready quickly while Sylvia chose the record for their demonstration and Vernon took out his camera.

'Bill and Shirley, Andrew and Margaret.' Cliff made brief introductions as soon as the couples had changed out of their drab daytime clothes into colourful, close-fitting dance wear. They had emerged like butterflies from a chrysalis – the men in silk shirts and high-waisted Oxford bags, the girls in sleeveless, sequinned tops with plunging necklines and skirts above the knee.

'Let's try a jive.' Sylvia suggested the liveliest of the swing dances as she lowered the needle on to the record. Jazz music blared through the loudspeakers and the couples sprang into action: bouncing and swivelling their feet as an American voice rang out over the trumpets and saxophones – 'Come on you hep cats and 'gators – jive!'

As Bill and Andrew swung their partners to arm's length, the girls' skirts flared out. The flash on Vernon's camera went off; he captured the dancers in mid-swing, jiving away to their hearts' content. On they went, with Vernon's flashbulbs popping and Sylvia and Cliff standing by.

'It's a pity the *Gazette* can't print them in colour.' The dance ended and Vernon was happy with the images he'd taken. 'Still, a caption underneath the photographs will help capture the mood.'

While Sylvia thanked the dancers and sent them on their way, Cliff asked about the number of words Vernon would write.

'Don't worry; I'll talk it up and squeeze as much space out of my editor as I can,' Vernon promised as the two men shook hands. 'I'll convince him that a big new dance competition is just what Blackpool needs to see us through the war.'

They parted on the best of terms before Vernon hurried on to another appointment. Sylvia saw him out of the studio to his car parked close by.

'Thank you.' She felt exhilarated. Her heart soared as Vernon leaned in for a kiss.

'See you tomorrow at the Tower?' he asked softly. Not really a question; he already knew she would say yes. 'Dress up in your jazziest number – something tight and sparkly. I'll meet you outside the entrance at half past seven.'

Sylvia watched him vault into his car without opening the door then returned to the studio.

'Someone's fallen head over heels,' Cliff remarked with a knowing wink. 'And I can't say I blame you – you've got yourself quite a catch.'

'And vice versa,' she reminded him with her tinkling laugh.

'Touché!' Cliff laughed back. 'No doubt about it – it's a match made in heaven.'

'Your mother is a wonderful woman,' Joy enthused as she and Tommy got ready for a night out at the Tower. 'She said yes to keeping an eye on Mildred during the day before the words were even out of my mouth.'

Tommy knotted his tie at the dressing-table mirror then attempted to flatten his thick, unruly curls without success.

'That's my momma: kind and generous to a fault,' he agreed. 'It's the Italian way. Now that she's cottoned on to the fact that the girl is expecting, she'll most likely ask her to do odd jobs in the café to keep her mind off what she has to face in a few months' time.'

Tommy backed away from the mirror, almost bumping into Joy, who needed him to zip up her dress. Their bedroom was small and most of the space was taken up by a double bed that had been installed the week before they were married. Tommy's musical instruments had been tidied away to create more space and some feminine touches had been introduced – a dressing-table frill to match the counterpane, china ornaments on the mantelpiece and new net curtains – with vestiges of Tommy's bachelor life still remaining in the shape of his pipe and tobacco pouch on the window sill and a pile of car magazines on the bedside table.

'Oops, sorry,' she apologized, turning around for him to zip her up. She'd chosen her pale lilac dress; the one with shoulder pads and a floaty skirt. 'And you're wonderful, too.' She turned to kiss him then sat at the dressing table to do her hair. 'Up or down?' she asked.

Time for another kiss; this time on the back of Joy's neck. 'You decide. You look grand either way.'

'Up then.'

Tommy stood back to watch her insert hairgrips, her bare arms raised, fingers deftly achieving the desired effect. God, he was a lucky man to have her as his wife. And boy, was it difficult to resist her.

She caught sight of his reflection in the mirror and blushed. 'Don't stare.'

'Why not?'

'It puts me off.' Finishing what she was doing, she stood up and slipped her feet into her white, peep-toe shoes. 'It's a fine night; shall we walk?'

'You decide,' he said again.

Walk it was. They went downstairs to say a quick good-night to Lucia and Mildred, both busy in the kitchen.

'*Buona serata.*' Lucia's smile lit up the room. '*Bellissima!*' she cooed at Joy. 'This dress, your hair – *come sei bella*!'

Mildred went on stacking plates into the cupboard next to the sink. 'You do look lovely, Mrs Rossi.'

'Call me Joy, remember?'

'Joy,' the girl whispered self-consciously. 'Have a nice time.'

'It's a shame that Mildred can't come dancing with us.' Joy sighed as she and Tommy walked along the wide promenade in the warm evening sun. Blackpool was at its best; the cluster of buildings at the end of South Pier stood pristine white against a clear blue sky, its deep azure colour reflected in the sea. The smooth, wave-washed sand was golden, and ahead of them the Tower rose magnificently, dwarfing even the Big Dipper fairground ride and the row of impressive seafront hotels. 'She's young; by rights she should be out enjoying herself instead of stuck at home.'

Tommy swung Joy's arm as they walked along. 'Has she definitely decided to go ahead and have this baby?'

Joy gasped at the unexpected question; of course, there was a choice that she hadn't previously considered. 'I don't know – I haven't asked her and I don't think the alternative has even occurred to her.'

'It's just when you remember how Mildred fell pregnant,' he went on. 'According to what she told you, the man forced himself on her then left her high and dry. Besides, she's under-age.'

'But still.' Joy wasn't sure how she felt about an abortion. 'Lucia wouldn't approve, would she?'

'Definitely not.' Tommy shook his head. 'You're saying it's best not to interfere?'

'I don't know.' But the dilemma would remain in Joy's head in the days and weeks to come.

'On a more cheerful note,' he continued as they joined a steady trickle of couples all walking hand in hand towards the Tower, 'do we want to sign up for Sylvia's big dance weekend?'

'Oh, Lord – do we? Don't we already have more than enough on our plates?' She glanced at Tommy's face to judge his response.

'It would give us something to look forward to. I'd have to book some time off from the circus well in advance – Ted and Leo could cover for me.'

'It might be fun.' Joy imagined the pair of them whirling around the floor in the Spanish Hall to a live band, casting care to the wind.

'At least let's think about it.' Tommy spotted Sylvia in the entrance to the Tower building, greeting the chap who'd been taken on as entertainments critic by the *Gazette*. 'It's up to you, love. Best to decide sooner rather than later, though; that's all I'm saying.'

*

'Talk about making a grand entrance,' Pearl grumbled to Joe. They'd been chatting at the bar when heads turned towards the entrance to the ballroom, to see Sylvia on the arm of the man from the *Gazette*.

'Miaow!' Joe knew Pearl well enough to tease her. 'They look spiffing together and you know it.'

Sylvia wore a silver satin dress with a split down one side of the tight-fitting skirt. She carried off the halter-neck style with aplomb, basking in the attention she drew. Spying Mavis and Eddie close to the doorway, she put on her brightest smile to say hello. Then hello to ambulance driver Eileen and her friend Sandra, followed by a quick hug for Joy and Tommy and the rapid introduction of her new beau. 'This is Vernon. He's writing a feature for the *Gazette* about our dance weekend. Vernon – meet my friends Joy and Tommy Rossi.'

At the far end of the ballroom, the crimson curtains parted and the Wurlitzer rose into view with Reggie Dixon at the keyboard. Anticipation grew as the evening kicked off with his jaunty signature tune.

'How do you do?' Vernon shook hands with Tommy. 'You're not part of the Trio Rossi, by any chance?'

'Guilty,' Tommy replied.

And the two men were off – talking circus business while Sylvia drew Joy to one side. 'What do you think of him?' she whispered excitedly. 'Isn't he the bee's knees?'

'He seems very nice,' Joy replied with a hint of caution.

'He's asked me out twice this week,' Sylvia confided. 'Well, once properly; the first time was for me to tell him about our dance weekend. But on Thursday he took me to the Hydro Sun Lounge and it turns out he really likes me.'

'How could he not?' Joy grasped her friend's cold hand and noticed the goose pimples on her arms. 'Brrr, you're freezing, and on a warm night too.'

'I'm always cold; you know that.' Sylvia dismissed her concern. Catching sight of Pearl and Joe at the bar, a small frown appeared. 'I didn't have a chance to mention my visit to the arcade earlier this week, did I? No? Well, I was all for letting bygones be bygones and saying I was sorry for upsetting Pearl, blah-di-blah, and what did I find when I got there? No sign of her, that's what.'

'Oh dear.' Joy's heart sank. 'Why, where was she?'

'Only off with Errol, leaving Ernie to hold the fort!' Sylvia exclaimed. 'Now tell me, was I imagining things that night outside the Tower?'

Their conversation ended abruptly when Vernon slid his arm around Sylvia's waist then whooshed her on to the dance floor to the exuberant carnival sound of a samba being played on the Wurlitzer – all tilting pelvises, whisks to left and right and plenty of bounce.

'Vernon's a pretty good dancer,' Tommy remarked. 'And he seems a decent enough chap. Sylvia's having a whale of a time out there.'

The couple easily outshone all the rest. For a start, they were taller than most and their confident hip tilts and accentuated bounces on the second beat of each bar were perfectly coordinated. They were so self-assured that other couples naturally conceded the centre of the vast floor to what turned into an exhibition by Sylvia and Vernon of how samba should be done.

Afterwards Vernon proudly led Sylvia towards the bar, accepting compliments as they went.

'Well?' Hoping that he'd caught Joy at her most relaxed, Tommy reached for one of the colourful Blackpool

Ballroom Dance Weekend leaflets strategically placed by the entrance. 'Have you had that think?'

She opened the leaflet and studied it. 'Saturday would be the day for us. Sunday is Latin and you know I'm not so keen on that.'

'One little day,' he cajoled, stuffing the leaflet into his pocket and guiding her on to the floor. 'Say yes.'

Reggie Dixon was off again, this time with a quickstep: a crowd favourite. Joy's spirits soared as her body responded to the bright, happy rhythm. Her lightning-quick feet skipped and ran smoothly over the polished surface. Oh, this was pure heaven! 'Yes, why not?' she agreed mid-turn. 'Best foot forward and all that.'

'I love you.' Dancing cheek to cheek in close hold, promenade chassé into lock step into quarter turn. 'Light of my life, my best girl.'

Entering by the main door, Errol paused to take in the scene. He'd arrived in time to witness the end of Sylvia's samba in the arms of a guy he didn't recognize then saw her going into a huddle with Joy. Pearl wasn't on the dance floor. Ah, there she was: talking with her market trader friend near the far end of the bar.

Languidly, as if with no particular purpose, he took a leaflet and scanned its contents. Yep; this was the competition that Pearl had learned about on the grapevine. She'd dropped a hint about it during their walk along the beach. Apparently, helping to run the show was Sylvia's next step up the ladder. Pearl had confessed that the old gang of three (Pearl, Joy and Sylvia) had had a difference of opinion due to her friendship with him. He'd offered to take a step back until things cooled down but Pearl had said no; why should Sylvia rule the roost? She, Pearl, would be friends with whomever she pleased. Errol had been mulling over his next move ever since. *Seize the day*, he decided.

So he made his way through the crowd. Beads of sweat had appeared on his brow by the time he reached Joe and Pearl. 'Gee, it's hot – even for a Georgia boy like me,' were his first words as he arrived.

Pearl turned at the familiar voice. 'Errol, it's good to see you. You look as if you could do with a beer.'

Joe stepped in with a casual, 'Let me,' before shouldering his way to the bar.

Aware that people close by were listening in on their conversation, Errol showed Pearl the leaflet. 'Is this the contest you talked about?'

'That's the one.' Since the heated talk with her mother, doubts had taken root. Pearl had written her long, loving letter to Bernie and now she partly regretted having mentioned the blasted dance weekend to Errol in the first place.

'It might be fun, huh?' Overcoming his nerves, he spoke as one pal to another. 'We jive pretty good together. Maybe we should give it a go?'

All the reasons why not flashed in front of Pearl: Maria's advice, the row with Sylvia, the fear of Bernie finding out and the risk of general tittle-tattle, but they were drowned out by the memory of Sylvia's angry voice accusing her of something she hadn't done. Pearl's stubborn resentment pushed her onwards. 'Maybe,' she echoed softly.

Joe returned with just two drinks: a beer for Errol and an orange juice for Pearl. 'I ran into an RAF mate of mine at the bar,' he explained hurriedly before turning back the way he'd come.

'Is it a deal?' Errol asked in the same casual way. 'You and me entering the jive on the Sunday – who knows, we might even win the darned thing?'

To hell with the consequences. A defiant Pearl made her decision. 'Sunday the eighth of August – that gives us two months to work out a routine.' She shook her GI's hand with exaggerated vigour and said, 'You're on!'

'Gee whiz, that's swell,' he said with a broad grin. 'Watch out, you guys; Spanish Hall, here we come!'

CHAPTER EIGHT

For Sylvia the evening went by in a whirl. After dancing the samba with Vernon, they eased into a simple modern waltz, followed by a tango then a foxtrot. During the interval he suggested that they call it a day – as before, there were too many clodhoppers barging into them, treading on their feet, snagging Sylvia's stockings and throwing them off balance. So they left early and Sylvia knew nothing about Pearl taking up Errol's invitation to enter her competition. Just as well; she'd have blown her top.

'I'd far rather take a moonlight spin with you than put up with any more of that.' Vernon's voice was low as he drove his MG along the prom, one hand around Sylvia's waist, one on the steering wheel.

'Don't be mean – it's only people letting off steam,' she protested. 'The Polish Air Force brings in trainees by the coach load and so does the RAF, not to mention the Yanks.'

'That's all very well, but most of them have two left feet.' Vernon delivered his verdict. 'I don't mind the civil servant contingent so much – they generally know the basic moves and besides, some of the girls are not bad looking.'

Sylvia tried not to flinch as Vernon swerved to avoid a

bunch of Merchant Navy lads who had spilled out of a nearby pub.

'Don't worry – none of those typists and shop girls are a patch on you.' Vernon patted her thigh. 'Did I mention how marvellous you look tonight?'

'Yes – more than once.'

'Well, that's because you do.' He'd revelled in the way that she'd drawn admiring glances; it proved that he had good taste. When they reached the corner of North View Parade he signalled right and waited for an oncoming tram to trundle by, using the moment to lean sideways and kiss her on the cheek.

Sylvia closed her eyes. Vernon's lips had scarcely brushed her skin but a thrill ran through her whole body. She felt the car turn off the prom and swayed towards him, resting her head on his shoulder as they ended their journey.

'Are you going to invite me in this time?' he asked when he pulled up outside Ibbotson's.

'Why not?' Where was the harm in a nightcap and a chance to get to know each other better?

Vernon was out of the car like a shot, racing round to the passenger side to open Sylvia's door. Heart pounding, she searched in her handbag for her door key then stepped out on to the pavement. She fumbled the key in the lock before leading him upstairs and into her flat. Luckily she'd had the foresight to move the clothes horse from the living room into the bedroom before she'd left for the Tower, otherwise her freshly washed underwear would have been on full display.

'Nice place you have here.' Vernon lit a cigarette as they stepped into the room, noting that Sylvia shared her mother's unfussy, up-to-the-minute taste. There was a pair of the ubiquitous sleek and slender dancing-girl statuettes on the mantelpiece, a fashionable art deco shade on the standard lamp in one corner, a low coffee table in the middle of the room, set in front of a green sofa. A framed print of Degas' ballet dancers adorned the chimney breast.

'Here; take the weight off your feet.' Sylvia offered him an ashtray as he sat down then asked if she could get him something to drink.

'No, come and sit here with me.' He patted the cushion next to him. 'This is cosy,' he murmured. 'You smell as good as you look, by the way.'

'So, why not tell me more about yourself?' A nervous Sylvia launched into a breathless series of questions. 'Where were you born and where did you go to school? Any brothers and sisters? What's your taste in music? What made you decide to become a journalist?'

Vernon leaned forward to stub out his cigarette then rested back against the sofa with his feet up on the coffee table. 'Blimey, what is this – the third degree?'

'Stop teasing; I'm serious. But I don't mind going first if you prefer. I was born here in Blackpool. I never knew my father. From the start it was just me and my mother. Does that shock you?'

Vernon shook his head. 'I'm not easily shocked.'

'Before she had me she was a dancer at the top of her profession, mixing with the likes of Josephine Bradley, George Fontana and a famous American called Arthur Murray. My father was a judge on the ISTD panel in a competition that Mother had entered. He was already married; it was a fling and he went back to London. He never knew about my existence.'

'Your mother didn't tell him?'

'No; she was too ashamed. Two years after I was born he was killed in a car crash. Then there was nothing for it but for her to make her own way in the world, bringing me up as well as working to set up her dance academy.'

'Good for Lorna.' For once Vernon was in earnest. 'I mean it; it must have been hard for you as well as for her.'

Sylvia shrugged. 'It was normal, as far as I was concerned – sitting in on dance classes from an early age, perched on the piano stool and itching to be allowed to join in and wear what looked to me like dresses out of a fairy tale. I wanted to be just like my mother: graceful, elegant, beautiful.'

'And you are,' he whispered. 'Tall, blonde, slim – the loveliest princess imaginable.'

She gave a self-conscious laugh. 'That's me – now it's your turn.'

'Very unglamorous, I'm afraid.' Vernon skimmed through the basic facts. 'I was born and brought up in a small fishing port on the Yorkshire coast; father in the Merchant Navy, no brothers and sisters – that I know of,' he added with a sly wink. 'You know what they say about sailors.'

Sylvia gave him a dig in the ribs.

'Seriously, it was a regular family life – holidays at Butlins, Saturday matinees at the local Odeon. I did a paper round to earn pocket money – yawn, yawn. Oh, one thing that we do have in common: my father was away at sea a lot so my mother had to cope on her own. She used to take me to local hops at the village institute. That's where I learned the Lambeth walk, the polka, the veleta; you name it, Mum and I joined in. When I was twelve she entered me into a competition at the Bridlington Spa and, blow me down, I only went and won it to become junior ballroom champion for the whole of the East Riding.'

'Well done, you.' Sylvia was intrigued. 'And did you keep up with your dancing?'

'No; football took over. I didn't play the game; I stood on the sidelines and wrote reports on inter-school matches for the school magazine. Then Mr Newton, my English teacher, asked me to write an article about the end-of-year school play – George Bernard Shaw's *The Devil's Disciple*. That was it; I was hooked on writing theatre reviews. And all these years later, here I am.'

'Here you are,' Sylvia took a deep breath as she snuggled closer. She had many more questions but before she could ask them Vernon tilted her head back and kissed her on her lips.

He drew back to gaze into her eyes – wide and astonishingly blue, with dark lashes. 'You have no idea what you do to me,' he murmured before kissing her again.

She lost all sense of where she was. All she knew was that she wanted to be held in Vernon's strong embrace and for the kisses to go on and on. His lips touched her cheeks, her forehead, her neck. Only when his hand slid up her thigh to find bare flesh above her stocking did she pull away.

'Not yet?' Such a pity – the feel of her smooth, warm skin was driving him mad.

Sylvia shook her head.

'Are you sure?'

No, she wasn't sure. The urge was there, so why not let him go on? If they went the whole way, what was so wrong in that?

'Is it too soon?' he breathed. 'I take it you haven't done this before?'

'I haven't,' she confessed. Never with Eddie, who

hadn't pushed her further than was considered proper. And never with any other sweetheart either.

'Then we'll take our time,' Vernon promised. 'You know that I like you a lot – that's what matters.'

Sylvia shuddered as she drew breath. 'I like you too.'

'You're very special.' He stroked her cheek with his thumb. 'And hard to resist.'

Sylvia pulled him towards her until his features were blurred. She placed a finger on the curious cleft in his chin then ran it along his jawline. He was smiling, waiting to see what she would do next, disappointed when she kissed his cheek then broke from his embrace.

'Is that it? Are you giving me my marching orders?' The half-joking tone was back, the smile firmly in place.

'I am.' Her reply was low and full of regret.

Vernon stood up then pulled her up after him. 'Until next time?'

'Yes. I'll see you out.'

'No need. I can find my own way.' But not without another long, lingering kiss that left them both wanting more. 'I'm going now,' he whispered.

'Yes, goodnight.'

And then he was gone – footsteps on the stairs, sounds of the door opening and closing. There were more faint footsteps crossing the pavement, his car engine coughing into life then purring and fading into the distance. Gone.

Sylvia sank on to the sofa and closed her eyes. Was this the real thing? After all this time and so many disappointments, was she in love with the man of her dreams at last?

'In love' – what did it mean? Sylvia asked herself this question on her way to meet Joy first thing next morning. She'd hardly slept, had eaten no breakfast and was responding to a message delivered by young Len, elderly Jack Ibbotson's live-in assistant. He'd run up the stairs with news of a phone call from her friend, the young Mrs Rossi. 'She says can you meet her at nine o'clock outside the Tower? It's to do with Pearl Greene and it's urgent.' No more information than that before the lad had scarpered back downstairs.

If Joy, who seldom exaggerated, had said it was urgent then it must be. Sylvia could only suppose that something bad had happened at the Tower the previous night after she and Vernon had left.

So here she was, hurrying along the practically deserted prom before any stalls or shops were open, with only the sight of a team of ARP men and women shoring up the sandbag barricades outside the entrance to the Majestic Hotel. 'Love' – should it involve this whirlwind of unanswered questions, this torrent of contrasting emotions ranging from nerve-tingling longing to stomach-churning apprehension and everything in between? Was this normal? Sylvia was twenty-two years old, for heaven's sake, and yet she was acting like a green girl, lurching along on an emotional roller coaster more frightening and disorienting than the Big Dipper itself.

'There you are.' Joy broke into Sylvia's tumultuous train of thought by stepping out from under the glass canopy over the main entrance to the town's most famous landmark. 'Thank you for meeting me. I didn't fancy tackling this by myself.'

Sylvia came back into the present with a jolt. 'What's wrong? Is Pearl all right?'

'Yes and no.' Joy had been stewing over the problem all night. She'd talked it through with Tommy and they'd both agreed that some sort of action was necessary.

'Pearl won't like it,' he'd warned as Joy set out from the ice-cream parlour. 'You know how stubborn she is.'

'Why; what has she done?' Sylvia urged.

'She plans to enter your competition with Errol Jackson.' There; Joy had put it as succinctly as possible and now she waited with bated breath for Sylvia to react.

'Does she indeed?' In spite of everything Sylvia had said, the warnings she'd given, hot-headed Pearl had gone ahead and done exactly what she ought not to. 'Has she lost her senses?'

'It happened in front of everyone,' Joy continued. 'Errol came up to her at the bar and asked her to enter the jive with him. You should've heard the gasp that ran round the ballroom when she agreed.'

Sylvia frowned. 'Here's an idea: I could solve the problem by rejecting their entry.'

'On what grounds?'

'I could invent one; perhaps that they don't meet the required standard.'

'That won't wash,' Joy decided. 'Pearl and Errol can out-jive everyone in sight. No; we must have it out with Pearl face to face. There's no other alternative.'

'You mean right this minute?' Sylvia grimaced.

'Yes. She doesn't open the arcade until ten o'clock on a Sunday. We can catch her at home if we hurry.' Joy set off towards Empire Street as she spoke. 'We'll remind her again what damage this will do to her reputation and say she should think of Bernie, stuck out there in Italy or wherever – really rub it in this time. Surely she'll come to her senses.'

Unconvinced, Sylvia trailed after Joy across the empty market square then followed her along Empire Street. They passed the derelict stable yard that currently housed

Clive Rowse's donkeys then a grocer's and the Black Horse pub. The girls soon reached number six – the Scott family home – and Joy knocked loudly on the door.

A twitch of the net curtains told them that their presence had been noted. They waited for what felt like an age – presumably a discussion was going on inside the house. Finally Pearl herself answered the door, barefoot and dressed in a white blouse and dark blue slacks.

She kept the door half-closed and eyed them suspiciously. 'What do you want?'

Joy saw no point in beating about the bush. 'We need to talk about you and Errol.'

'Oh, not that again.' Pearl gave an exaggerated sigh then made as if to close the door in their faces. She was prevented by her mother, who came up quickly from behind.

'Let them in,' Maria ordered in a voice that brooked no argument.

'I don't have time for this,' Pearl protested weakly.

'Let them in,' her mother insisted. 'You three need to sort out your differences.'

Pearl reached for the first excuse that came to mind. 'But what about the arcade?'

'Ernie can open up for you. Show Joy and Sylvia into the front room and talk, you hear me?'

Maria disappeared into the kitchen, leaving Pearl to do as she was told.

'We're not here to have a go at you,' Joy assured her. The Scotts' little-used front room was in semi-darkness, with the blackout blind still down.

'Then how come that's what it feels like?' Pearl opened the blind, letting light flood into the room, which still had its original Victorian fireplace with an ornate mirror hanging on the chimney breast and with bare floor-boards only partially covered by a patterned rug. A sewing machine stood in an alcove and easy chairs were placed to either side of the fire.

'We're worried about you,' Joy insisted, while Sylvia hovered uneasily by the door.

'No need,' Pearl said airily. 'I'm tip-top, ta very much.'

Sylvia stepped forward. 'Come off it, Pearl. Joy's being her usual diplomatic self but let me spell it out for you. I'll say it one last time: no one's happy with the way you and Errol are carrying on – it's not just us, believe me.'

'Change the record, why don't you?' Really – did she have to go through this again?

'But your plan to enter Sylvia's dance competition with him is your biggest mistake to date,' Joy pointed out. 'It'll entail weeks of practice. You'll be spending more and more time together. Even if it is all perfectly above board, as you say, imagine how it will look from the outside.'

'I don't give a fig how it looks!' Pearl's exasperation boiled over in the shape of hot, angry tears. 'This is my business and no one else's. Why won't you two just leave me alone?'

'Because we've been through a lot together and we care about you.' Joy moved towards her but was fiercely rebuffed. 'Please don't cry.'

'You'd cry too.' In a sudden, unexpected shift Pearl slipped from fury to dark despair. 'You two have to remember what I owe Errol.' Sobbing helplessly, she sank into one of the chairs, shielding her face with both hands.

Sylvia glanced at Joy in alarm.

'Surely I don't have to rake it all up?' Pearl demanded.

'No; we remember,' Joy said softly.

'Then you know it was Errol who rescued me,' Pearl

reminded them. 'He ordered his soldiers back to base then made sure the main one, Chuck Sanderson, was sent back to America so I never had to set eyes on him again.'

Sylvia's irritation melted away. 'We do understand how hard it's been for you.'

For the first time Joy made a comparison between Mildred and Pearl's experiences and the realisation shocked her to the core. 'Honestly; these rotten men who force themselves on girls – they deserve to be locked away for good.' She glanced up at Sylvia.

'We never meant to make you relive all that. That's not the reason we came.' Sylvia approached Pearl and put an arm around her shoulder.

'Errol looked after me, took me all the way home, made sure I was safe. And afterwards I felt rotten, thinking it had been partly my fault.'

'It was not.' Joy's voice was quiet and firm. 'Three strong men against one woman, walking alone. How is that your fault?'

'But I was tipsy.' This arrow of guilt had stayed lodged in Pearl's conscience for months.

'So what?' Sylvia was equally firm. 'Joy's right – tipsy or not, you were in no way to blame.'

'Do you really believe that?' Pearl's sobs eased and she was able to raise her head.

'No question,' Joy confirmed.

'And I'm truly sorry I misjudged you,' a penitent Sylvia added. 'I ought not to have been so hasty.'

Feeling that she'd got through to them at last, Pearl managed a faint smile.

Relieved, Joy pulled her to her feet. 'Say we're forgiven.'

'Please,' Sylvia implored.

'Yes, I forgive you.' Pearl drew a deep breath then

hugged them both. 'We'll go on as before: three girls lighting up the dance floor with our foxtrots and our jives.'

'Sylvia and Vernon, me and Tommy, Pearl and Errol.' Joy's smile was broad. 'And who cares what people say?'

Whit Monday fell on June the fourteenth, meaning a bank holiday for all. Joy had the day off work and invited Mildred to watch the grand procession with her. She promised that there would be a brass band marching ahead of a float carrying the Whitsuntide queen attended by several flower girls, followed on foot by a fancy-dress parade.

'*Si, si* – go!' Lucia urged. '*Godetevi il sole.*'

'Enjoy the sunshine,' Joy translated her mother-in-law's parting remark as she shooed them out of the house. 'Come on; we'll find a good spot by Central Pier.'

The town buzzed with anticipation. Crowds of holidaymakers in sunhats and summer dresses, khaki shorts, socks and sandals gathered all along the prom, everyone eager for a glimpse of this year's queen. Even locals seized the opportunity to relax and join the fun. The Pleasure Beach was doing a roaring trade as Mildred and Joy passed its gates. For a moment they were tempted by the thrills of the Big Dipper, the dodgems, ghost train and waltzers – but no; today's parade was a once-a-year spectacle not to be missed.

So they found their spot by the pier and stepped on to a concrete ledge to give themselves a better view. 'Here they come!' At the sound of trumpets and trombones, Joy pointed towards King Alfred Street in time to see the procession emerge on to the prom. *Oompah – oompah*; brass instruments flashed in the sunlight and the gold-trimmed, scarlet coats of marching musicians stood out against the dull grey sandbags and emergency water tanks that lined the wide street. A cheer went up from the crowd as the band paraded ahead of the queen's float, which was decorated with patriotic Union Jacks, rosettes and ribbons.

'Each spring there's a competition to choose the queen and her attendants,' Joy explained. 'See; she wears a sash and a crown.'

'Her dress is beautiful.' Mildred gave an inarticulate gasp. 'And oh; the little girls too!' She had rarely seen a sight so wonderful.

This year's winner sat on her throne under an archway of artificial blossom, waving regally to right and left, acknowledging the cheering crowds. Her gown was primrose yellow, she wore long white gloves and her dark hair curled prettily over her shoulders. Her six attendants, dressed in white frocks with a red rosebud pattern and red satin sashes, sat on stools, clutching their posies and smiling bashfully.

The band played on, drowning out the cheers. The queen's float went by all too quickly, followed by a parade of townspeople in fancy dress. There were Brownies in tights and tabards, brandishing feather dusters, dressed as the mischievous children of the old woman who lived in a shoe. There were Wee Willie Winkies, Little Miss Muffets and Cinderellas galore, then a milkmaid wearing a yoke from which two pails dangled, then a pirate with a cutlass and eyepatch and a pantomime dame in a shocking pink dress, his orange wig askew. Joy and Mildred laughed as they picked out their favourites, clapping and cheering until the last of the parade had passed.

As the crowd began to disperse, they too made their way home, choosing to stroll barefoot along the beach.

When they came within sight of the ice-cream parlour, Mildred slowed to a halt.

'Is something wrong?' Joy asked. 'You're not feeling poorly?'

'No, I'm fine.' Mildred tilted her head to feel the warmth of the sun on her face. She never mentioned her early-morning bouts of sickness, accepting that this was normal for someone in her condition. In fact, she'd mostly succeeded in ignoring what was happening to her body, carrying out the light chores that Lucia gave her without complaint. Her main fear was that her mother would somehow discover her whereabouts, but so far there'd been no sign of this happening.

Joy watched her dig her toes into the wet sand. The girl cut a lonely figure against a backdrop of blue sea and sky, wavelets circling her thin ankles in small, foaming eddies. The sun had brought a touch of colour to her round face and given it a sprinkling of freckles. Her short brown hair was tucked behind her ears, making her seem achingly young. 'You're sure you're quite well?'

Mildred nodded. 'But how long do you reckon I can stay here without Mum finding out?' she queried in a querulous voice.

Joy reassured her. 'How would she? It's our well-kept secret. Besides, if your mother comes back to the warehouse Mr Henderson will soon see her off again.'

'Fingers crossed,' Mildred whispered.

'Yes, fingers crossed.' Joy linked arms with the girl and walked her slowly towards South Pier. The gentle sound of waves washing against the shore soothed them both. 'Tommy, Lucia and I are glad you've come to live with us – we like having you and we care a great deal about you. Only this morning Tommy asked whether we should make a doctor's appointment to check that all's well with the pregnancy.'

Mildred broke free and strayed deeper into the waves, turning away from Joy to stare out to sea.

'Don't be alarmed. All mothers-to-be should register with a doctor, to be on the safe side.'

Pregnancy, mothers-to-be – the very sound of the words made Mildred's stomach churn.

Joy waded through the swirling water to join her. How wide the horizon, how huge the sky – and how small and helpless Mildred looked against them. She stood beside her in silence.

Mildred spoke at last. 'Do I have to have this baby?'

'Don't you want to?'

'I don't know. I'm scared.'

'You're bound to be. It's only natural.'

'Do I really have to?'

Joy paused for a long time before she spoke. 'No – there's a way to stop it if that's what you choose. For a girl in your situation it's worth considering.'

Mildred's gaze didn't alter. The sea went on for ever. 'What kind of a way?'

'I'm not sure about the details. Would you like me to find out?' When there was no answer, Joy took Mildred's hand and waited.

It was too much to take in; she was too young, too terrified, too lost. Silent tears rolled down the girl's cheeks.

'Don't cry,' Joy murmured. 'You don't have to decide here and now. Just bear it in mind.'

Wiping away the tears with the back of her hand, Mildred turned to face Joy. 'Can we go home now?' she pleaded.

*

Late in the evening Tommy listened attentively to Joy's account of the conversation that she'd had with Mildred. They sat together at the kitchen table after the others had gone to bed, talking in whispers and wondering what to do for the best.

'I still reckon the first port of call is Dr Evans' clinic,' Tommy said. 'The nurses would check that all is well and give us advice on how to look after Mildred in the weeks to come.'

'But they wouldn't be allowed to tell us about her other option.' Reluctant to say the word abortion, Joy skirted around the issue. 'Who would we go to for that?'

Tommy thought long and hard. 'There's no point asking Momma – we already know she'd be dead set against it. But don't some of these women calling themselves midwives advertise in the *Gazette*?'

'How can they if it's illegal?'

'They don't come out and say so in black and white – but those in the know pick up certain clues. I'm not sure how safe it is to go for one of these so-called back-street jobs, though.'

Joy couldn't repress a shudder. 'Are you certain Dr Evans couldn't help?'

'I'm not certain about anything,' Tommy admitted with a sigh. 'All we can do is ask around and find someone with more experience of this sort of thing.'

Disheartened, they realized that they'd reached a dead end for the time being. 'Do you know what?' Tommy went on in a rush. 'I reckon we should go after the rotten so-and-so who did this to Mildred. Why should he be allowed to get away with it?'

'He shouldn't,' Joy agreed. 'But where do we start? It happened in Manchester and all Mildred knows about the man is that his nickname was Frank because he looked like Frank Sinatra.'

'It's not much to go on,' Tommy admitted. 'But you could get a better description out of her – his height and build, and so on; that would be a start.'

'I could try.' Joy was unsure what good this would do. 'Then what?'

'Then we'd go to the police.' It seemed logical to Tommy but he left out of account the extra pressure this would put on Mildred. 'They could go through their mug-shots with her. If he's attacked girls before they might have him on their files.'

'Let me think about it.' Joy was tired and confused but she was sure of one thing: they mustn't act without talking it through with Mildred first. 'I'm off to bed. Are you coming?'

'Soon.' He sat a while after Joy had gone upstairs. There had been something he wanted to share with her before they'd tied themselves in knots over Mildred's situation but now it must wait for another day.

Tommy took a folded page of Saturday's *Gazette* from his pocket and laid it flat on the table. He'd used a pencil to underline the 'Houses for Sale' section then circled one of the ads: *24 King Street – two-bedroom terraced house in need of modernization.*

He'd done the arithmetic and decided that the asking price was within his and Joy's reach. The town centre location was ideal. It would be a place of their own. But what would Joy say? And could they leave Lucia to cope alone while his enemy alien dad was cooped up in a prisoner of war camp on the Isle of Man? Maybe it would be better to wait until the war was over and life was back to normal.

But a house, a home with their own front door and a yard at the back, with rooms to do up: kitchen, living room, a bedroom where he and Joy could do as they pleased without worrying about being overheard and another bedroom with flowered wallpaper and a baby's cot. Tommy knew he was getting way ahead of himself but the seed was planted in his brain and in his heart. Folding the paper and putting it back in his pocket, he followed his wifc upstairs to bed.

CHAPTER NINE

Sylvia went through the motions of teaching the jive to the usual ragtag assortment of over-eager shop girls, timid civil servants and callow servicemen.

At least the girls made an effort with their appearance, showing up for class in all-the-rage pleated skirts and gymslip tops in decent imitation of the current American high school trend. But the boys shunned the latest fashions, sticking instead to workaday slacks held up by braces over their un-ironed white shirts.

'Jive is all about letting go and expressing yourself,' Sylvia would cajole from the front of the studio. 'There's no set formula; you don't have to do the same as everyone else.'

Her advice was often met with blank expressions. *Just show us how it's done*, was the sullen, unspoken demand.

What would it take to make her pupils abandon themselves to the swing music that she played? 'Try not to think too hard,' she urged. 'Just do what comes naturally.'

The problem was that, left to their own devices, the self-conscious boys shuffled around without direction and the girls proved too shy to experiment, though they would eagerly copy Sylvia's bounces, side steps, kicks and finger clicks and they went away happy with what they'd learned.

'Not to worry,' Cliff told her after one especially dispiriting session. 'As long as the punters pay their money and keep on coming back, we're happy.'

So thank heavens for the dance weekend and something more exciting to look forward to: namely a meeting here in the studio with band leader Art Richardson to discuss musical numbers for each of the two days.

'Sylvia – Art. Art – Sylvia.' Cliff made the introductions one Thursday evening in late June. 'Art happens to be passing through town, on his way to tonight's venue.'

'Nice to meet you.' Sylvia shook the band leader's hand. Not especially handsome with his thinning hair and lanky frame, still he had a certain presence – a confidence and charm that came from a lifetime of performing in front of large audiences.

'Likewise, I'm sure. Rosie agreed to join us, but don't count on it.' Art explained that his singer, Rosie Johnson, was easily sidetracked. 'She's not the most reliable girl in the world. In fact, she's probably still in the Pleasure Beach where I left her, screaming blue murder on the ghost train.'

'Same old Rosie,' Cliff said with an indulgent smile. 'A kid at heart.'

They got down to business, agreeing that the Saturday dance programme – standard waltz, foxtrot, et cetera – demanded big band ballads in the Glenn Miller style. 'A String of Pearls', 'Happy in Love' and 'White Cliffs of Dover' came top of the list, followed by Bing Crosby's 'Be Careful, It's My Heart'. On Sunday the band would pick up the pace for the Latin section with numbers such as 'Cow Cow Boogie' and 'Jersey Bounce'.

Sylvia smiled all the way through the discussion; the dance weekend was becoming ever more real, and when

Rosie did put in an appearance, straight from the famous funfair, she brought with her an extra dose of glamour and excitement.

'Rosie – Sylvia, Sylvia – Rosie.' Once more Cliff did the brief honours.

Sylvia rarely found herself overshadowed by another woman but boy, was Rosie Johnson a stunner! All of five foot two inches tall, she was a bundle of blonde, curvaceous energy, lipstick smiles, high heels and wiggling hips, of sugar-sweet greetings and fluttering lashes.

'Don't be fooled,' Cliff confided after the visitors had left. 'Rosie is twenty-eight years old and already on marriage number three. Plus, she can drink anyone you care to name under the table. But her saving grace is that she has the voice of an angel.'

Buoyed up by the day's events, Sylvia rushed to the town centre later that night to meet Vernon at the Galleon Bar as arranged.

'I'm sorry I'm late,' she apologized. 'I waited ages for a tram. In the end it would have been quicker to walk.'

Vernon gave a nonchalant shrug then ordered her a sweet martini. 'How was the famous Art Richardson?'

'Very pleasant and down to earth, as a matter of fact. And Rosie Johnson . . . Well, she was . . .' Sylvia was lost for words.

'Your typical blonde bombshell?'

'Yes; have you met her?'

'Once or twice. In my line of work you bump into the Rosies of this world on a daily basis. Not my cup of tea, if I'm honest.'

'Oh?'

'No – a bit too brassy for my liking. Down the hatch.' Vernon pushed Sylvia's glass towards her. For some reason his manner was cool, verging on the distracted. 'How are the competition entries coming along?'

'They're picking up, thanks to our new leaflets. Three couples signed up at the end of today's salsa class and Mother has four more names for the Saturday event.'

'How about further afield? I've got a list of contacts in Liverpool and Manchester – pals who run dance halls there. I can give you their names.'

'Yes please.' Sylvia sipped her drink.

'Did you eat before you came out?'

'No, I didn't have time.'

He clicked his tongue against his teeth. 'I guessed as much. Just as well I've booked us a table in a cosy little restaurant a short drive up the coast. Come on – drink up.'

And so it went on in a whirl from one week to the next: a round of car rides in the moonlight and candlelit dinners, of glittering Saturday nights at the Tower and visits to the cinema to see the latest releases, all culminating in close embraces on Sylvia's sofa; nearer and nearer to the point that played out endlessly in her imagination and made her heart race in anticipation.

'We hardly ever see you these days,' Joy complained on one of the rare evenings when Vernon's work commitments had taken him elsewhere. She and Pearl had arranged to visit Sylvia at home and had found her catching up with her laundry. Wet garments were hung over a clothes horse in front of the fire, steaming gently, and the rest of the room was in disarray, with cut flowers withering in vases and used glasses and cups left on the coffee table. 'What have you been up to, as if we didn't know?'

'Excuse the mess.' Sylvia moved the clothes horse out of the way. 'And I'm sorry I haven't been in touch.'

'No need to apologize; we know you're busy with the build-up to the competition.' Joy flopped down beside Pearl on the sofa.

Pearl made a burring sound with her lips. 'Come off it, Joy – it's his nibs who's taking up Sylvia's time.' His nibs being a certain entertainments critic at the *Gazette*.

Joy and Pearl made space for Sylvia on the sofa and they sat side by side in companionable silence, with their feet resting on the coffee table. The low fire crackled in the grate.

'This is nice,' Joy murmured. 'Just like the old days.'

Pearl nudged Sylvia with her elbow. 'So, what's the low-down on you and Vernon? Have you or haven't you?'

Joy gave a small yelp of protest. 'Take care, Sylvia; whatever you say may be written down and used in evidence.'

'Don't worry – I'm not about to spill the beans.' Sylvia passed her fingers across her mouth to imitate the closing of a zip.

'You haven't?' Pearl tried to guess from Sylvia's expression. Then, 'You have!'

Sylvia blushed furiously. If only they knew how close she'd been. But no; so far she'd managed to resist temptation. 'Vernon really is the best thing that's ever happened to me,' she confessed. 'I've never felt this way about anyone – you both know what it's like when you can't stop thinking about a man, how his face pops into your head when you're busy doing something else or how you spend ages deciding what to wear before you go out to meet him; how to do your hair, which lipstick to wear.'

'"Romeo, Romeo,"' Pearl teased. '"Wherefore art thou?"'

'Yes, we do know,' Joy admitted. 'Take no notice of Pearl.'

'I know it sounds corny but it feels as if my feet hardly touch the ground,' Sylvia continued. 'My heart does a somersault every time I see him.'

'Poor you!' Pearl couldn't resist making fun of their lovesick friend. 'Whatever happened to Sylvia the Snow Queen?'

Joy listened with a serious expression. 'Are you remembering to eat?' she queried.

'I might skip the odd meal,' Sylvia admitted, 'but most of the time I'm not hungry.'

'Not good enough,' Joy said sternly. 'We need three square meals a day to keep our energy up.'

'Says you, who eats like a little bird,' Pearl challenged.

'Not now that I've got Lucia to keep me on the right track.' Tommy's mother's cooking was impossible to resist. 'Really, Sylvia; you can't afford to lose weight.'

'Vernon has no complaints,' Sylvia insisted. 'He says he likes me the way I am. He's not fond of girls with too many curves.'

'Talking of Vernon . . .' Pearl dragged them back to the subject that fascinated her.

'If we must.' Sylvia heaved an exaggerated sigh.

'When's that article of his going to appear in the paper?'

'Soon. Mother's been on at me to find out but Vernon won't be pinned down to a date. He reckons it will have more impact if it's printed nearer to the actual weekend.'

Her friends debated the pros and cons of this argument: sooner was better if Cliff, Sylvia and Lorna wished to attract advance entries but later might make a bigger, last-minute splash. Meanwhile, Sylvia drifted off. What to wear tomorrow night? Vernon had arranged to pick her up in his MG to drive her to Stanley Park for a stroll around the Italian Gardens. She considered slacks and a white broderie anglaise blouse before remembering that he preferred her in dresses – to show off her figure, he said. So she decided on a pink sleeveless one with a flared skirt that she would team with white accessories.

'Sylvia, are you listening?' Pearl demanded. 'Joy and I agree with your mother – it would be good to have a firm date for the article to appear.'

'Stop fussing.' Brought back to the present with a jolt, she went through to the kitchen to put on the kettle and make tea, carrying on her conversation with Pearl and Joy through the open door. 'Vernon's the expert – he knows what works best. I leave it to him to decide. By the way, I've run out of sugar so you'll have to have your tea without.'

Stanley Park on a fine midsummer evening was hard to beat. Vernon and Sylvia sat in the bandstand overlooking the lake while ducks and swans paddled expectantly at the water's edge. Brightly coloured rowing boats were safely moored for the night and families were dispersing after a leisurely day of strolling, splashing about on the water, playing bowls and taking tea in the art deco café, far away from the garish thrills and spills of Blackpool's Golden Mile. The low sun cast long shadows. There was no wind.

'We should come here more often,' Vernon observed simply.

Sylvia felt a secret thrill at his use of the word 'we' and the casual assumption that there would be many more such outings. 'It's lovely and peaceful,' she agreed.

'I have more spare time during the day than in the evening. Perhaps I could take you out in one of those boats one afternoon.'

'That would be nice but I'm busy teaching most days.'

'Can't you palm off some of your classes on to Cliff or his sidekick; what's his name – Terry?' Vernon slid a cigarette from the packet he kept in his shirt pocket and smoothly lit it with one click of his lighter. He leaned forward to rest his elbows on his knees.

'It's tempting, but no – not really. Terry doesn't have a teaching diploma and Cliff and I are working our socks off in the build-up to the competition.'

'Couldn't you at least try to find the time for one little row across the lake with me?'

Smoke drifted across her face and she felt the sharp sting at the back of her throat when she inhaled it. 'Perhaps one Sunday morning,' she suggested.

But no, Sunday wouldn't do – it was Vernon's one day of the week for a lie-in and besides, weekends at Stanley Park were always rammed with day trippers. A romantic row on the lake would have to wait.

The sun sank slowly behind a stand of beech trees. The surface of the water was shiny and smooth as a mirror. Sylvia snuggled closer to Vernon as the air grew chilly.

'Time to move on?' he suggested.

They'd parked the car by the park entrance. Its roof was down and as Vernon pulled away from the kerb, Sylvia wished she'd brought a cardigan with her. Seeming not to notice that she was cold, he drove towards the coast before turning into the car park of the Norbreck, choosing a quiet spot overlooking the sand dunes and the wide open sea beyond.

'Isn't it a bit late for a drink?' Sylvia asked. By now she was visibly shivering.

'Who said anything about a drink?' Vernon got out of the car and invited her to follow suit. 'I fancied a moonlit walk with my sweetheart.' Taking her by the hand, he led her between grassy mounds towards the deserted beach. He slowed down as dunes gave way to soft, open sand then put his arm around her to shelter her from the wind. 'Would you like my jacket?'

Sylvia nodded. This was better; with Vernon's jacket around her shoulders she was happy to stroll on and listen to him chat about his show business contacts and then address one of his favourite topics: how he saw the *Gazette* as a stepping stone to greater things. 'Picture it; once I've made my move to the Big Smoke I'll be at the heart of things, living the high life. You'll come down for visits while I set myself up with decent lodgings. I'll be able to show you around and introduce you to the right people in the dance world. Then eventually you'll be able to find work and move to London too.'

'Slow down!' The very idea took Sylvia's breath away. 'You seem to be overlooking the fact that I have a dance studio to run here in Blackpool.'

Vernon smiled as he took hold of the jacket lapels to draw her closer. 'A man can dream, can't he?'

She put her arms around his waist and felt the warmth of his body through his shirt. 'I was on the verge of moving to London once,' she confessed. 'Cliff put me in touch with a man called Mitch Burns, a sort of talent scout.'

'"Sort of"? That sounds dodgy to me.' Vernon drew her closer still and murmured the words into her ear.

'Luckily Cliff put me straight and the arrangement fell through, so I'm still here in Blackpool.'

'And here we are, under the moon and stars. It must be kismet that has brought us together.' Sliding the jacket from her shoulders, he laid it on the sand. They sat facing a sea that sparkled and danced in the moonlight, his arm around her shoulders, hers around his waist. They exchanged soft, leisurely kisses, sinking back until they lay on the sand, staring up at the dark sky.

He turned on his side and ran his hand down her bare arm.

Her skin tingled at his touch. When he kissed her on the lips, she felt the tip of his tongue press against her teeth. She opened her mouth. His body was against hers, his hand moving from her hip, down her leg to lift up her skirt. He stroked her thigh and she didn't resist.

'Is now the time?' he whispered.

'Yes.' The touch of his hand, his lips, here on the seashore and a million miles away from civilization made her certain. She loved, adored, worshipped this man and wanted him and he wanted her.

'Blimey, it's fast!' The music that Pearl and Errol had chosen for their jive routine had left her seriously out of breath.

'You'll get used to it,' he assured her with a smile as he lifted the needle from the record then rested it in its cradle. 'Fast and furious is the name of the game.'

It had been decent of Cliff to offer them use of the studio once the day's classes had ended. 'Sylvia won't need it – she's off gallivanting with her latest beau,' he'd informed them. 'Just lock the door after you then pop the key through the letter box once you're done.'

So Pearl and Errol had sketched out a series of preliminary moves that involved much bouncing, clicking of fingers and shoulder shimmies, mostly out of hold to display their individual talents. Errol was loose limbed, almost casual with his kicks and retractions, while Pearl, who kept perfect time despite the tempo, was daintier and more precise. After fifteen minutes they'd taken a breather before trying out a more complicated sequence.

'I thought I was in decent shape,' she complained between deep intakes of breath. 'Now I'm not so sure.'

'Honey, your shape is just fine,' Errol said with a teasing wink.

She jabbed him with her elbow. 'You know what I mean. Anyway, how come you make it look so easy?'

He shrugged. 'I had plenty of practice back home in Fayetteville – I been jivin' since I was a kid. The secret is to loosen up and let yourself have fun.'

Pearl dabbed at the nape of her neck with her handkerchief, glad that she'd worn her lightest blouse and the yellow cotton skirt that gave her plenty of room to pivot and kick. 'But it's all those syncopations and foot swivels – they tie me up in knots if I'm not careful.'

Errol turned to the gramophone and carefully lowered the needle once more. 'Let's begin again with a swing-out move.' He offered Pearl his hand. 'Step to the side, bounce, step again and bounce. Now spin in towards me, sway together to the left then to the right. OK, now we strut.'

Pearl let out a peal of laughter. The strength of his arm as he'd swung her out was impressive.

'Try that again,' he cried as the music raced on. 'And again.'

Once they'd perfected the sequence they went straight on to the most ambitious move of the night so far: two low kicks with linked hands, followed by one high kick from Pearl and an anticlockwise pivot on her left foot, swinging her right leg over Errol's head as he ducked and kicked his legs forward from the knee like a Cossack dancer. It was their first attempt and Pearl's foot grazed his ear, knocking him off balance so that he landed flat on his back, limbs splayed.

'Jeez!' he groaned. 'What just happened?'

She darted forward to pull him to his feet. 'My fault,' she gasped. 'I didn't time it right.'

So they repeated the sequence and this time it worked – Pearl kicked even higher and cleared Errol's crouching Cossack form then he sprang up and they came together and went into the basic swing-out move, smooth as you like.

'That was more like it.' She was exhilarated as the music ended and the needle hissed with static. She followed Errol into the alcove that housed the gramophone then sat on a bench to regain her breath. 'This is going to be super,' she predicted. 'We'll work in some lifts and maybe a cartwheel or two.'

'Good thinkin'.' He sat beside her. 'There will be stiff competition come the actual night.'

'Bill and Shirley Jones and Andrew and Margaret Pearson, for a start.' She pointed to photographs of Cliff's star pupils that were pinned to a noticeboard above their heads. 'Not to mention contacts that Sylvia's Vernon says he has if they ever materialize.'

'Rehearse, rehearse, rehearse.' Errol tapped her knee for emphasis as he repeated the word.

Pearl closed her eyes and leaned back against the wall. 'I don't mind how much we have to practise – learning this jive helps keep my mind off things I'd rather not think about.'

'Yeah; I get it – Bernie.' Errol tackled the elephant in the room.

'There's still no word about where he's been posted. I

haven't had a letter for I don't know how long, which is a good thing in a way.'

'No news is good news,' he agreed.

'But I'm still longing to hear from him, even if it's just to read about the holes in his socks that need mending or some daft, schoolboy joke that he wants to pass on, or how lousy the bully beef and spuds are – I don't care.'

Errol studied her face; eyes still closed, beads of sweat on her forehead, dark hair slightly damp. It was all he could do not to reach out and pull her towards him.

'It'll happen,' he promised. 'You'll go down one mornin' and the letter will be there on the mat – maybe two together, if you're lucky. That oughtta keep you goin' for a week or two.'

Pearl opened her eyes and turned her head towards him.

Green eyes with flecks of brown. Errol's heart skipped a beat.

'Thank you,' she murmured.

'For what?'

'Just thank you.' Standing up suddenly, she set the record playing once more. 'Come along, Sergeant Jackson, we have work to do. Step and kick, step and kick, shimmy, shimmy, shimmy and again!'

'She's back.' Alan rushed into Joy's office without knocking.

Startled, Joy looked up from the balance sheet she was working on. 'Who do you mean?'

'The wee lassie's mother; ranting and raving, demanding to know where Mildred is. She's cornered Dora in the canteen and is kicking up a stink.'

Joy swallowed hard. This had to be dealt with

immediately, so she followed her manager down the stairs to find that what he'd said was true – Dora was pinned against the wall and Mildred's mother was wagging a finger in her face, threatening to administer a good slap unless Dora divulged her daughter's whereabouts.

'Mrs Kershaw, that's enough.' Joy dragged the angry woman away from Dora. 'I won't have you upsetting my staff. You must leave the premises now, this minute.'

Winifred Kershaw gave a scornful laugh before squaring up to Joy. As before, the match was unequal: Joy's slight frame against the stockier middle-aged matriarch whose permed grey hair sat like a steel helmet on top of her jowly face. 'Who'll make me?'

Just then the canteen door swung open and Robert Finchley, the new caretaker, joined them.

'Leave,' Joy repeated. 'You have no right to be here. And understand this: even if we did know where your daughter was, we're not obliged to pass on the information to you, given what you did to her.'

'Ha!' Winifred sneered. 'The whining ninny has got you twisted round her little finger. I only gave her what she deserved.'

'Mrs Kershaw – please!' The brutal comment had brought a gasp from Dora and an uneasy shuffling of feet from Robert. What now? 'Robert, Alan – stand guard by the door while I call 999.'

'Yes; and be sure to say she shoved me against the wall and threatened me with a black eye,' Dora added.

Still Mildred's mother defied them. 'I dragged that girl up to know better but did she listen? Did she heck! She egged the men on – dancing these new-fangled jitterbugs and jives – and look where that landed her: up the duff, that's where.'

Joy shook her head in despair. 'Yes, we'll have to fetch the police,' she decided. 'Alan and Robert, please make sure she doesn't leave the building while I go to my office and make the call.'

Seeing the lie of the land, Mildred's mother bellowed a protest then charged for the door ahead of Joy. As she attempted to shoulder Robert out of the way, he tackled her to the floor and pinned her down, sending a trolley stacked with plates flying in the process.

Calamity! This time the woman might have sufficient grounds to charge them with manhandling her when all she'd been trying to do was to discover the whereabouts of her errant daughter.

'All right, everybody.' Alan stepped in to cool tempers. 'Get up, both of you. We'll forget about the police, Mrs Rossi, and sort this out between us.' Helping Mildred's mother to her feet, he suggested a way forward. 'We're prepared to overlook the fact that you're trespassing on Hebden property and making threats against our employees if and only if you're willing to leave the premises and promise never to return.'

'Why should I?'

'Because you're in the wrong and we have witnesses.' Alan's gaze bore into her. 'If you break this agreement by coming back a third time, we'll have no choice but to prosecute.'

The woman narrowed her eyes and directed her bile towards Joy. 'Bloody stuck-up bitch – "I won't have you upsetting my staff", mim-mim-mim! A jumped-up little nobody, that's you! And you keep your hands off me,' she warned Alan. 'You can see I'm leaving.' Backing through the door into the yard, she let off a final volley of insults. 'It's over to you, Mrs Holier-than thou Rossi – that girl of mine is your problem now. And tell her not to come begging at my door with her brat after it's born. Say I'm done with her once and for all.'

That same afternoon, Joy left work early in order to take Mildred to Dr Evans' maternity clinic. She watched as the dejected girl was weighed and her blood pressure taken by a kind, efficient nurse who showed no reaction as she wrote down the patient's age, took her behind some portable screens to examine her then wrote down her stage of pregnancy – thirteen weeks, give or take.

All through the visit Mildred barely spoke a word. Her face was pale and drawn. Nurse Myers said she must eat and get as much sleep as possible before making a date for her to return to the clinic. 'See that she looks after herself,' she advised Joy while Mildred got dressed behind the screens. 'She's underweight and her blood pressure is on the high side.'

With Mildred's mother's parting words still ringing in her ears, Joy felt the responsibility weigh heavily on her shoulders. After they reached home and had been fussed over by Lucia, she broached the two subjects that were at the forefront of her mind.

First, she wanted to share with Mildred what she had found out about the so-called midwives who advertised in the back pages of the *Gazette*. 'I'm not saying that this is what you ought to do,' she cautioned as Lucia returned to the ice-cream parlour and she and the girl sat in the quiet kitchen. 'But I've followed up two of the names I found in the paper and these women are known to provide a reliable service for girls in your situation.' Joy spoke quietly and framed her words carefully, noting the flash of panic in Mildred's eyes.

'Oh, Mrs Rossi, I'm not sure . . .'

Joy patted her hand. 'Neither am I, Mildred. I'm only telling you that it's possible.'

'But I don't have much money. And would it hurt? How would they do it?'

'The money isn't important – I can take care of that. We'd go to one of these women and they would explain it to us if you decide that's what you want. Going ahead and having this baby will change your life for ever – you have to consider that.'

'I know it will.' Mildred's lips trembled. 'I'm ruined; everyone will look down their noses at me.'

'Not necessarily,' Joy argued. 'I'm sure Sylvia wouldn't mind me mentioning that her mother found herself in a similar situation to you twenty-three years ago and managed to make the very best of it. Look at how well mother and daughter are doing now.'

'I never knew that.'

'It's no secret. Mrs Ellis set up her dancing academy when Sylvia was a baby and she's never looked back.'

'I'm not sure I could do that,' Mildred murmured. Her eyes were wide in her pale, freckled face and she had the air of a rabbit caught in car headlights.

'You don't have to make up your mind right now.' Joy decided to move on to the second topic that troubled her. 'Listen, I've been talking to Tommy about the man who attacked you. We both believe that he should be brought to account.'

Mildred shook her head wildly. 'No, no; please.'

'But why not? What he did was a crime.'

'But how would we find him? And even if we did, it would be his word against mine.'

'Except there was a witness,' Joy reminded her. 'You

mentioned a man at the end of the alley who saw what was happening.'

Mildred carried on shaking her head. 'Yes, but he didn't do anything to stop it. I can't remember the first thing about him, except he was taller than the other. Yes, the second man was tall.'

'And the attacker was skinny and he said his name was Frank?'

'That's right,' Mildred confirmed.

'And we know the date and if you thought hard you could remember what he was wearing and a few other things about him – the sound of his voice, and so on.'

'He had a blue blazer that he kept unbuttoned all of the time he danced with me and afterwards.' Unwelcome memories flooded back. 'At first I thought he was nice – he told jokes and made me laugh. It was only later when we went outside . . .' Her voice trailed off and she hid her face in her hands.

'Mildred, I'm so sorry.' For a while Joy let her cry. 'If this upsets you too much we needn't talk about it any more.'

'He tricked me,' she sobbed. 'He promised to walk me home, only he led me down an alley with big dustbins and cardboard boxes where nobody could see . . . I know he wasn't very tall but he was still stronger than me. He put his hand over my mouth.'

'It's all right. Take some deep breaths.' The tearful account strengthened Joy's belief that such men were monsters. 'You're safe now.'

Mildred clutched Joy's hand. 'I tried to explain to Mum – she wouldn't listen.'

Joy pictured the scene: the daughter in floods of tears, the hard-bitten mother boiling over with fury. 'Hush. Me and Tommy, *we* believe you.' She promised to support Mildred every step of the way. 'Whatever you decide, you can count on us,' she vowed as the sobs subsided. 'That's better,' she soothed. 'That's it; take a deep breath and again – breathe.'

CHAPTER TEN

'I've filled in our entry form and given it to Mrs Ellis,' Tommy informed Joy as they came away from the King Alfred Street studio exhausted but jubilant after a rare rehearsal of their Viennese waltz with Lorna's praises ringing in their ears.

'Lovely, smooth undulations, excellent fleckerls, a nice reverse turn – very well done, Joy and Tommy.' Their dance teacher had picked them out from five other couples, all intending to take part in the fast-approaching dance weekend.

Joy kicked off her shoes as they reached the beach and felt the warm sand beneath her bare feet. Rays from the setting sun fell on their faces. 'I'm glad you talked me into it,' she confided. 'I've been snowed under lately, what with work and Mildred's problems, but spending an evening dancing with you is just what the doctor ordered.'

'That's my girl.' Tommy squeezed her arm. 'Talking of doctors . . .?'

'Mildred saw the nurse again today. Lucia took her to the clinic this time. She's like a mother hen clucking after her chick.'

'And no more mention of . . . you know what?'

Joy shook her head. 'I've offered, but so far Mildred

hasn't taken me up on the midwife idea. I've a feeling she's decided to go ahead and have this baby.'

Tommy thought through the implications. 'At least Momma will be pleased.'

They walked along in silence, under Central Pier and on towards the ice-cream parlour. They watched a woman throw an orange ball for her frisky black dog and the dog gallop into the sea after it. The tide was coming in, washing away the day's sandcastles.

'As I've mentioned before, she's still not keen on tracking down the man who did this to her,' Joy went on.

Tommy seemed distracted. 'Who isn't – Momma or Mildred?'

'Mildred. Perhaps it's too much for her to cope with.'

The dog ran into the sea for a second time. 'Toby, fetch!' the owner cried. But the dog shook itself dry while the ball was carried out to sea.

'Here; what do you think of this?' Tommy held his breath as he suddenly handed Joy a neatly folded sheet of paper. He'd been carrying it around in his pocket for weeks, but now seemed like the right time.

She opened it up and read the bold print at the top of the type-written sheet. *Harrison and Boyd, Estate Agents.*

'I've had it for ages.' He thrust his hands deep into his pockets, keeping his fingers tightly crossed.

'"Houses for Sale . . . 24 King Street."' Joy scanned the page with mounting interest. Living room, kitchen and two bedrooms. Backyard and outside toilet. In need of modernization.

'It's going for a song.' Tommy studied her face to judge her reaction.

'For us to move into?' she asked shakily.

'Yes. We'd have Joe as a neighbour and the market

square is a stone's throw away; and anyhow isn't it high time we had a place of our own?' he gabbled.

'But your mother?'

'I haven't mentioned it to her yet. I wanted to test the water with you first.' The idea had filled Tommy's thoughts since the moment he'd seen the advert in the paper. In his mind, without even stepping over the threshold he'd decorated the house from top to bottom and worked out a way to divide one of the bedrooms into two and install plumbing for an indoor toilet, sink and bath.

'Butterfingers!' During today's matinee performance Ted had barked at him for dropping two of the brightly coloured balls he was meant to catch as part of their juggling act.

'Bloody hell, Tommy lad; keep your mind on the job!' Leo had also been furious with him for missing his cue for a trumpet solo. Leo had covered for him but afterwards the two other members of the trio had torn Tommy off a strip. 'If this is what being married does to you, I'd recommend getting divorced pronto.'

'And never mind your mother; what about Mildred?' Joy asked, her fingers shaking as she handed the sheet back to Tommy.

'What about *us*?' he countered quickly. 'Don't we matter?'

'Of course we do.' Her forehead creased into a deep frown. 'Aren't you happy where we are?'

Tommy caught Joy by the hand then swung her round to face him. 'Be honest, love; it's a bit cramped. If we had our own place we could spread out and relax without having to tiptoe around.'

Joy slowly absorbed what he was saying. 'That would be nice.'

'Nothing against Momma and Mildred, but . . .'

'Our own place,' she echoed in a tone of wonder.

'And Dad will be home from the POW camp before we know it. Mildred can stay with them and carry on serving in the café and looking after the baby at the same time if she wants to; I'm sure that would work out.' Tommy saved his trump card until last. 'I think we should put in an offer before someone else snaps it up. There's already plenty of interest.'

Our own place. Shut out the noise and bustle of the seafront café, be a couple. Even start a family. Joy held her breath as their future blossomed in her imagination. *But, but . . .* Her feet dragged through the soft sand. The waves crept up the shore and washed away another child's sandcastle dreams. 'Let me think about it,' she pleaded as the last sliver of fiery red sun sank below the horizon.

The first time that Vernon spent the night at Sylvia's flat was a Friday in early July. To her it was another huge step; as significant in her mind as their lovemaking in the sand dunes close to the Norbreck Hydro had been.

Back then Sylvia had ridden a wave of desire so strong that she'd been unable to resist. The moon and stars, the waves, Vernon's sure touch as he took her through the stages had carried her along. He'd led and she'd followed, astonished by how it felt, a swooning combination of apprehension, longing, shyness and desire.

'Relax,' he'd murmured in her ear. 'Don't be scared.'

Sylvia had closed her eyes and clung to him. Though she'd pictured this moment in her mind's eye, with images drawn mostly from Hollywood films, the real thing had been nothing like what she'd expected – the pressure of his lips, the weight of his body, the loosening of her inhibitions and again the sound of waves breaking on the shore, driving them on. Afterwards there was confusion. Is this how it was for everyone? Had she done it right? Oughtn't she to feel more fulfilled?

But Vernon had covered her face with light, tender kisses and told her he loved her. Another first. The three little words had meant so much – far more than the deed itself.

Vernon loves me, she'd reminded herself as she'd lain awake in her own bed for nights afterwards, sleeping fitfully, running through their conversations and reliving their kisses.

'Aha!' Pearl had cried on their first encounter after the event. It had been in the North View Parade studio, where Pearl and Errol had got together for a rehearsal of their jive routine. 'I know that look.'

'What look?' Sylvia had blushed and been unable to meet her gaze.

'Come off it; who are you trying to kid?' Pearl had a sixth sense that had correctly identified the significant shift in Sylvia and Vernon's romance. 'I'm happy for you both. Well done, you.'

Joy's reaction had been more circumspect.

'Pearl guessed the truth so I might as well let you in on the secret,' Sylvia had confided over cups of tea in the ice-cream parlour. 'I went all the way with Vernon the other night.' The banal phrase sat awkwardly on her lips.

'You did?' A wide-eyed Joy had rattled her cup down into its saucer. 'That was a big step.'

'He said he loves me.'

'Have you said it back?'

'Not yet,' Sylvia had confessed as she put a hand on her heart. 'But I do.'

'Good; that's the main thing. But don't rush things and definitely don't do anything that you'll come to regret.'

'Of course not.' Sylvia had resented Joy's cautious note. 'Pearl was happy for me. Aren't you?'

'I'm happy if you're happy,' Joy had assured her.

Now Sylvia and Vernon woke together in her narrow bed as dawn filtered into her bedroom around the edges of the blackout blind. He lay on his back with his hands behind his head, eyes open, while Sylvia was curled on her side, one arm across his chest that rose and fell gently as he breathed.

'Let's never move an inch ever again,' he suggested, turning his head towards her.

'I won't if you don't,' she murmured back.

Vernon began humming their favourite Fred Astaire song, and Sylvia picked up the tune, gazing gently up at him.

They went on in harmony then he smiled and turned towards her. 'If there's anything better than being here with you, I've yet to discover it. You're the best girl in the world – you know that?'

A warm glow of contentment spread through her body.

'It's amazing how well we fit together. We love doing the same things, share the same tastes – Fred Astaire films and letting our hair down when we're dancing at the Tower. There's a kind of magic in it.'

All this was true; still, Sylvia was astonished to hear Vernon say it out loud. Her eyes filled with tears as she ran her fingers over his cheeks and gave him a lingering kiss on the lips.

'Not crying, are we?' he whispered.

'Only because I'm so happy,' she confessed.

'Honestly, I can't imagine a future without you. I want you by my side, always and for ever.'

'Hush,' she breathed, afraid that her full heart would burst.

But he went on. 'I knew the moment I saw you, standing there in the *Gazette* office with that determined glint in your eye. I thought, *This is a girl in a million.*'

'But why?'

He moved his head back so he could run his gaze over her body. 'Look at you,' he whispered. 'Smooth skin, long limbs, soft hair, blue eyes – you're every man's dream. As for what goes on inside that lovely head; I discover new things every day.'

'Such as?'

'I'm learning that you're less confident on the inside than you appear on the outside and that you've no idea how gorgeous you are and that you definitely worry too much about what people think. It makes me want to look after you. Will you let me do that?'

'Yes,' Sylvia agreed. 'But please don't treat me like a china doll. I can stick up for myself.'

Vernon gave her a quick hug. 'I've been thinking.'

'Oh dear.' She kissed him. 'No thinking allowed.'

'I'm serious. We agree that we're made for each other, you and I.' He pulled her closer and planted kisses on her forehead, cheeks and neck. 'Tell me that you love me – say it.'

His lips caressed her and he was so close that his features were blurred. 'I love you,' she whispered for the first time.

'There, that wasn't so hard. Listen, I've thought of a way we could spend more time together.' Pausing, he gazed intently into her eyes.

What was coming next? Did it perhaps involve a ring and a walk down the aisle? Sylvia held her breath.

'Why don't I stay here more often?' Vernon stroked her hair back from her face. 'Instead of me racing around, arranging to meet you at the Galleon or the Tower, wouldn't it make more sense if I moved in with you?'

'Oh.' Taken aback, she echoed his words. 'Move in? Here, with me?'

'Not all at once. Perhaps at weekends to start with, to see how it goes. Like today, for instance – it's Saturday so we'll doubtless be dancing at the Tower later on, which, as things stand, means me having to drive all the way over to Manchester for a change of clothes then back here again, when we could have been spending the whole day together.'

This came as another surprise. 'You've never mentioned that you lived so far away.'

'You've never asked. When I landed this job I was renting a room from a pal in the city centre. I haven't had time to look for anything else.'

'I see. I'd have to check with Mr Ibbotson first – he'd probably want to charge more rent.' A practical obstacle came to mind, followed by a nervous fluttering in her stomach. 'My mother might not approve.'

Vernon propped himself upright with a pillow then reached for a cigarette. 'But you're a big girl now – your mother has no right to interfere if it's what you want. And anyway, you can tell her that I've promised to make an honest woman of you.'

Sylvia gasped in disbelief. 'What are you saying?'

'Eventually,' Vernon mumbled the afterthought as he lit up then inhaled deeply. 'We wouldn't rush into anything, but we do love each other and we want to be together for the long haul, don't we?'

'I suppose we do.' Still she had no clear picture of what lay ahead.

'And we're living in different times,' he reasoned. 'Lots of people our age are breaking the old rules by moving in together without needing a wedding ring on their finger. The sandbags in the street and ARP wardens yelling for us to turn our lights out are proof enough that life's too short for the till-death-do-us-part rigmarole.'

When Sylvia thought about it later, after Vernon had sped off in his sports car for his change of clothes and she was getting ready for their night out, she convinced herself that what he'd said made perfect sense. Real life during wartime wasn't a 'princess meets and marries her prince' dream. For a start, there was the hardship of rationing to contend with – Vernon had driven this point home by mentioning that his journeys to and from Manchester gobbled up most of his petrol coupons. And he was right about rules being broken when the threat of being blasted to kingdom come was at the forefront of everyone's minds. Sylvia had read about the looting that went on in the aftermath of such attacks and there were endless, more trifling examples of people breaking the law – housewives who fiddled their ration cards to wangle extra butter and sugar and farmers who slaughtered pigs on the sly to sell ham and bacon on the black market.

We're living on the edge, Sylvia thought as she chose her peach-coloured dress with the floaty organza skirt. Most of her dance dresses were hand-me-downs from Lorna, painstakingly remodelled and brought up to date – something which proved the point about everyone doing whatever it took to make ends meet. *So we have to find happiness where and when we can.*

She'd finished getting ready and was on her way downstairs when Jack Ibbotson emerged from his shop.

'A visitor?' the old man quizzed abruptly, waving his walking stick in the direction of her first-floor flat. 'Don't deny it; I saw his sports car parked outside all night.'

Sylvia's heart thudded. 'What of it?'

'I don't blame a good-looking girl like you for having a fancy man.' He spoke the words with narrowed eyes. Under the bare light bulb his pink scalp gleamed through his thinning white hair while his scrawny neck and knobbly hands served to emphasize his frailty.

Sylvia pressed her lips together and waited.

'I take it he's the one who works for the *Gazette* that my lad Len has told me about?' Jack continued in the same suspicious tone.

'You mean Mr King. What about him, Mr Ibbotson?' She looked down from the third step of the staircase.

'He seemed decent enough when he dropped by earlier in the week.'

The sudden change of tack caught her off guard. 'He is.'

'If you like that kind of thing. Not from around here, I gather?'

'He's from Yorkshire originally.'

'Ah.' Enough said. Jack allowed the ancient Wars of the Roses rivalry to resurface.

'As a matter of fact, Mr Ibbotson, Vernon and I have been wondering . . .' As she descended the final stairs, her feather-trimmed skirt brushed against the old man's legs.

'Spit it out. No, let me guess – you want your young man to shack up with you.'

'That's one way of putting it.' A fiery blush coloured Sylvia's cheeks and neck. 'I guarantee Vernon wouldn't be any trouble. He might only be here at weekends to start with.'

'Spare me the details,' the old man growled. 'One overnight stay is enough for the meters to tell me that he'll be gobbling up my electricity and gas. I'll have to put the rent up by two and six a week if he's here part time, five bob for full time. How does that sound?'

'Fair enough,' Sylvia said softly. Events were unfolding before she'd even had time to announce to the world that she and Vernon would live together.

'He can't use my telephone, mind. He'd have to pay extra for that.'

'I'll tell him.' As the elderly tobacconist hammered home his demands, Sylvia caught a glimpse of Len Fraser standing behind the counter, backed by shelves of black and gold canisters next to racks of briar and meerschaum pipes. The boy had obviously overheard every word but was not letting on. Now she was sure that the news would spread like wildfire, from Len to his sweetheart Valerie and on to the Idas, Thoras and Eileens of the ballroom circuit. She groaned inwardly before agreeing to the last of Jack's conditions. 'I must go,' she told the shopkeeper hurriedly. 'I promised to meet my friends at the Tower and it wouldn't do to be late.'

Ruby Donovan left her place in the long queue and made a beeline towards Pearl, who stood in the entrance to the Tower building. 'All on your own-some?' she asked, bright and chirpy as a parakeet in her shiny scarlet and emerald dress.

'I'm waiting for someone,' Pearl explained.

A group of Royal Navy trainees made their rowdy, rollicking entrance, eyeing up Ruby and Pearl before checking the foyer for other potential partners for their fun night out.

'You two are a bit of all right.' One of the lads who sported a wayward blond forelock and a cheeky grin hung back behind the rest.

'Get away with you – I'm old enough to be your mother.' The cleaning supervisor's rich laugh rose above the general hum.

'What about you, love?' The sailor turned enthusiastically to Pearl, dressed for Latin in a tight dress and high-heeled shoes.

'She's waiting for someone.' Ruby gave him a shove in the direction of his pals. 'Are you sure you're all right?' she asked Pearl with a concerned expression. 'I thought you looked a bit peaky.'

Pearl forced a smile. 'I'm grand, thanks. Or I will be once I'm let loose on that dance floor.'

'Have you heard from hubby lately?' Ruby didn't wait for a reply. 'No, me neither. My Douglas has been posted to Italy – that's as much as I know.'

'Bernie, too.' More days had dragged by without a letter. 'At least, I think so.'

Hard on the heels of the sailors, a gaggle of ARP girls entered the building, chattering, waving and calling out to people they recognized – among them Sandra and Eileen from Eddie's first-aid post, dressed up to the nines in vivid flounces and frills.

'Yoo-hoo, Eddie! Yoo-hoo, Mavis! Have you saved us a place?' Sandra trod on Pearl's foot in her haste to jump the queue.

'Ouch! Watch where you're going,' Pearl grumbled.

'Sourpuss,' Sandra muttered as she barged ahead.

Eileen, too, got in a quick dig at Pearl's expense. 'What's the matter, has your handsome hunk stood you up?'

Pearl was ready with a spirited reply but Ruby got in

first with a cat-like miaow. 'Take no notice,' she advised Pearl before rejoining Ida and Thora in the queue. 'Eileen would scratch your eyes out for the chance to jive with Sergeant Jackson.'

'I expect you're right.' Nevertheless Pearl's spirits had sunk to an all-time low before Tommy and Joy eventually showed up. What was the point of coming out on a Saturday night and carrying on as normal? Why put on a brave face when her heart ached for Bernie every minute of every day?

'Sorry we're late,' Joy apologized. 'Tommy insisted on making a detour along King Street. There's a house there that he's interested in buying.'

'You don't say!'

'I was as taken aback as you are,' Joy confessed before quickly changing the subject. 'No sign of Sylvia?'

'Not yet.' Pearl drew her back to the original topic. 'Don't you two have enough to deal with without contemplating a house move?'

'Don't remind me.' Joy's first view of the exterior of 24 King Street hadn't filled her with delight. The front of the house was north facing, its paintwork was peeling and some window panes were cracked.

There was no time to voice her doubts because an anxious-looking Sylvia put in an appearance. 'Oh dear,' she sighed. 'I've had such a rush to get here – the usual long wait for a tram, and so on. I was worried I'd be late. Is Vernon here yet?'

'I haven't seen him.' Pearl noticed red patches on her friend's neck and put it down to her eagerness to arrive on time. 'Calm down – you're here before him,' she advised.

Sylvia continued to scan the crowded foyer, acknowledging people she knew and exchanging small waves with Eddie and Mavis, who were halfway up the stairs. 'Mother tells me they've handed in their entry form for the Viennese waltz at last,' she reported. 'Naturally, she couldn't resist reminding me that Eddie and I would have beaten the opposition into a cocked hat if we'd still been together.'

'But you couldn't have entered your own competition,' a literal-minded Joy pointed out. The queue for the ballroom had begun to move more quickly, leaving the spacious foyer relatively empty.

'Try telling my mother that.' Sylvia wafted away the comment. '*En garde*, Pearl – here comes the American contingent.'

A bus had pulled up at the kerbside and was disgorging soldiers from the Warton base. Errol was the last to alight before issuing instructions to the driver about when to return. His sergeant's stripes and authoritative manner set him apart and he seemed in no hurry to make his way across the wide pavement towards the Tower entrance.

Spotting Pearl's group, he greeted them with a relaxed salute and a low 'howdy' but without picking out Pearl in particular.

She returned his smile then watched him join the end of the queue where his group of GIs was pounced on by Sandra and Eileen, each flirting shamelessly in order to bag themselves a good-looking partner – and why not?

Joy raised her eyebrows then laughed. 'Some people!'

Pearl managed another smile, guessing that Errol would follow his usual pattern of waiting for the first jive number to begin before inviting her on to the floor. 'They know he's a free agent.'

No more was said. Now it was Vernon's turn to make an entrance, and to Sylvia's surprise he wasn't alone.

'Evening all!' He breezed through the glass doors with two companions in tow: a slightly built man in his twenties and bandleader Art Richardson, who Sylvia recognized from his drop-in visit to the studio. 'Look who I ran into on the way here,' Vernon proclaimed.

'Is that who I think it is?' Pearl whispered to Sylvia, who nodded. 'I once saw Art Richardson's band in a concert at the Opera House – it was before the war. They played the latest songs – Bing Crosby, Benny Goodman, and so on – and got everyone tapping their feet in no time.'

'We've hired them for our dance weekend,' Sylvia said quietly.

Vernon brought the newcomers across to Sylvia, one arm slung carelessly round the younger man's shoulder. 'This is Alfie Matthews – the pal I spoke about,' he told her. 'The one who's been letting me kip in his spare room, who, as it happens, plays the drums in Art's band. I caught up with them while they were playing at the Hydro.'

'A tea dance,' the drummer informed her. He spoke in a soft voice and had a modest air in contrast to his band leader's more confident manner. He wore his hair in a quiff and he was clean shaven. 'Foxtrots and quicksteps – all very genteel.'

'I hung around until they'd finished then persuaded Art and Alfie to come along to the Tower and have some fun,' Vernon explained.

'It might look like a bit of a busman's holiday,' Art chipped in, 'but I'm hoping there's a chance for us to put out some feelers, business-wise.'

'I'll introduce you to the right people,' Vernon assured

him. 'I know the chap who books the acts both here and at the Winter Gardens.'

'Vernon knows everyone who's anyone.' Art winked at Sylvia.

'Come on – no time to natter.' Pearl pulled at Sylvia's arm. 'I can hear Reggie Dixon's theme tune. We'll miss the start if we're not careful.'

Tommy and Joy led the way up the grand staircase, with Pearl and Sylvia tagging along and Vernon and his friends bringing up the rear. As they reached the ticket booth, they bunched together to sort out payment.

'"I do like to be beside the seaside."' Tommy whistled the tune as he drew silver coins from his pocket. 'Two tickets; one for me and one for Joy, please.'

'"Oh I do like to stroll along the prom, prom, prom."' A chivalrous Art stepped forward. 'Allow me, girls!' he said to Sylvia and Pearl before paying for their tickets and his own, leaving Alfie and Vernon to squabble over who should stump up.

'My turn,' Vernon offered.

'No, mine.'

'Right you are.' Vernon clapped his pal on the back. 'It's my shout next time. Oh and by the way, everyone – Sylvia and I have an important announcement.' He spoke above the sound of the organ so that they all paused before entering the ballroom.

There was a glimpse through the doorway of glittering crystal chandeliers and of the arched ceiling with its ornate, gilded plasterwork, a sense of the vast dance floor beginning to fill with couples in anticipation of the first dance of the evening.

'Please, Vernon; now isn't the time.' Sylvia's cheeks were aflame.

Pearl's vivid imagination anticipated a diamond ring at the very least; perhaps even a date for an actual wedding. 'Flippin' heck, he doesn't hang about,' she muttered to Joy out of the side of her mouth.

'I'm planning a move to Blackpool to be closer to my place of work.'

'To live where exactly?' Tommy voiced what everyone was wondering.

'"So just let me be beside the seaside,"' Art crooned along to Reginald Dixon's signature tune, inviting Alfie to join in. '"I'll be beside myself with glee!"'

'Why, on North View Parade with Sylvia, of course.' *Fait accompli.* Vernon enjoyed the impact – shocked faces all round, except for Alfie, who had got wind of it a few days earlier.

'Are you sure you're not jumping the gun?' Alfie had ventured over two bottles of beer in his chaotic kitchen – unwashed dishes in the sink, broken blackout blind, no bulb in the overhead light, the room dimly lit by a foul-smelling paraffin lamp on the shelf above the sink – after Vernon had outlined his latest plan. 'Do you think Sylvia will fall for it?'

'I don't just think it; I *know* she will,' Vernon had assured him. 'That girl is like putty in my hands. This time next week I'll be out of your hair for good.'

CHAPTER ELEVEN

'Never lean back – you must shift the whole of your weight forward for the jive,' Sylvia reminded Joy during an impromptu Latin lesson. 'And when you kick forward, the retraction is equally important – sharp and snappy, like this.'

She demonstrated the move in the comfort of her living room after inviting Joy and Pearl round for tea. All were casually dressed in slacks, blouses and flat shoes as befitted a Sunday-afternoon get-together. The sofa and coffee table were pushed back to create more space.

'It feels unnatural,' Joy complained as she attempted to copy Sylvia. 'I'm so used to ballroom hold – leaning back, head turned to the side, shoulders down.'

'You old fuddy-duddy,' Pearl teased. 'It's time to get with it.'

Joy tried again.

'That's it – shake those hips and shimmy those shoulders,' Sylvia instructed. 'Click your fingers as you kick.'

After practising hard, Joy collapsed back on to the sofa. 'I'll stick to ballroom, thanks very much.'

'Mother will be relieved to hear that.' Sylvia refilled their teacups. 'So far the number of entries for the ballroom section of our dance weekend is lower than expected.'

'Why might that be?' From the window Pearl glanced down at the busy street, cheered by the sight of holiday-makers in shirtsleeves and sunhats making their way towards the prom. She'd left Ernie in charge of the arcade, confident that he'd be able to cope with the expected influx of customers this fresh but sunny Sunday afternoon.

'We're not sure,' Sylvia confessed. 'Perhaps because Art Richardson is known for his modern swing numbers and that's what attracts the youngsters to the Latin section.'

'That's good news for you and Cliff.' Pearl stood with her back to Sylvia and Joy, hands in pockets. 'Maybe Vernon could give ballroom more of a push when the *Gazette* finally prints his article.'

'How would he do that?' Joy wondered.

'Perhaps by giving Mrs Ellis star billing. You know: "Waltz Away Your Cares Says Blackpool's Premier Dance Teacher".'

Joy turned to Sylvia for her response.

'I can hardly tell Vernon how to do his job,' she pointed out. 'He and Cliff reckon that Art could be the main attraction; you saw the two of them with their heads together at the Tower last night.'

'Thick as thieves.' Pearl recalled how the evening had ended, with the two men at the bar talking business, leaving Sylvia without a dance partner until Alfie Matthews had gallantly stepped up for the last waltz. 'Why didn't they include you in their discussion?'

'Yes, the dance weekend wouldn't be happening without the hard work you and Cliff have put in.' Joy realized that it would soon be time for them to leave – Pearl was due back at the arcade at five and Joy had promised Mildred an evening trip to the circus. 'Never mind; I'm sure Vernon will bring you up to date when you next see him.'

The elephant in the room trumpeted loudly. 'Where is Vernon, by the way?' Pearl made a point of asking.

Where indeed? 'He drove Alfie back to Manchester last night.' It had made sense to Sylvia at the time – Vernon had explained that he would spend the night in his old digs then pack the rest of his belongings before driving back today. 'Then we can celebrate my moving in properly,' he'd said with a tender kiss in the shadow of the Tower before heading off with his pal. There'd been no mention of a part-time arrangement and she hadn't pressed him on the matter. 'I'll be back before you know it.'

Sylvia had felt deflated for a reason she couldn't explain. She'd slept badly and spent the entire morning expecting to hear Vernon's car pull up outside the tobacconists then the sound of his rapid footsteps taking the stairs two at a time, the sight of him in the doorway, suitcase in hand and her flying across the room to greet him.

'I take it Mr Ibbotson's happy with your new arrangement?' Pearl queried.

Joy smoothed over the awkward silence with, 'Come on, Pearl – it's time to get a move on.'

'I was only asking.' Pearl softened her manner. 'Look, Sylvia – if Vernon moving in with you is what you both want, I'm happy for you.'

'Quite right.' Sylvia handed Pearl's handbag to her with a grateful smile. 'None of us stick to the old rules these days; except you, Joy.'

'Ha ha!' Joy responded by flashing her wedding ring in their faces. 'You two are jealous.'

'Too true!' Pearl and Sylvia wailed.

It was only when they'd said their goodbyes and Joy

and Pearl were out on the pavement that the two friends grew serious.

'I'm worried that Vernon has rushed Sylvia into this,' Joy confessed as they headed for the seafront. 'Did you see her face last night when he made his announcement?'

'She wasn't expecting it,' Pearl confirmed. 'And he was vague about the details – will he move in lock, stock and barrel or will he stay with Sylvia only when it suits him?'

'Who knows?' Joy tried to end on an optimistic note. 'It's clear she's head over heels, though. What can we do except hope for the best?'

'They say that love conquers all.' Pearl held up her firmly crossed fingers. 'I remind myself of it every night, lying awake thinking of Bernie, or whenever someone gives me a sideways look as Errol flings me across the dance floor. I know my own heart and that's all that matters.'

They reached the bustling prom, where they must go their separate ways. The sun was bright in their eyes and noisy gulls circled low over the heads of families eating sandwiches on benches overlooking the beach.

Sylvia loves Vernon, Joy reminded herself as she made her purposeful way along the prom, past a Sally Army band playing 'Onward Christian Soldiers'. *And let's hope he loves her back.*

It was a rare treat for Mildred to stray beyond Rossi's ice-cream parlour except for weekly visits to the ante-natal clinic. The only other time had been for the Whitsuntide parade, almost a month previously.

'*Si, si*, it does you good.' Lucia had encouraged her to accompany Joy to the circus. 'My Tommy; he make tricks and you laugh. You see *elefanti*, you see *leoni*, *cavalli*.

As she'd spoken she'd mimed the action of an elephant swinging its trunk then roared like a lion before turning to Joy for a translation of *cavallo*.

'Horse,' Joy had explained.

'*Si, si* – you go to circus!'

At first Mildred had made excuses – she had nothing to wear, she had no money to pay for a ticket, she was feeling under the weather – but it had boiled down to the fact that she was afraid that people would somehow know that she was expecting and her fragile self-esteem would then crumble under unkind stares.

'No one will stare at you,' Joy had assured her. 'You're not starting to show yet and anyway, if necessary we can make you a loose-fitting dress.'

'I've never been to a circus,' Mildred had admitted with evident longing. 'They say Blackpool has the best one in the whole of England.'

'So come and judge for yourself.' Gradually Joy had overcome Mildred's objections and shown her how to unpick the darts in one of her skirts to extend the waistband.

When the day came they finished getting ready together, sitting at Joy's dressing table to powder their noses and brush their hair.

'Lipstick?' Joy offered Mildred her favourite coral-pink tube.

'May I?' Mildred's face was flushed with excitement.

'Of course you may.' As Joy watched the girl's reflection in the mirror her heart ached for what she'd already been through and what was still to come. Though her condition was rarely mentioned, now felt like an opportunity to address the subject head-on. 'Your next visit to the clinic is on Wednesday,' she reminded her. 'I'll take the morning off to come with you.'

'I can go by myself.' The response was brusque. 'I know where it is and what to do.'

'Are you sure? I really don't mind coming along.'

Mildred turned her head with a determined expression. 'Please don't take this the wrong way, but I'd rather you didn't.'

'Very well. But if you change your mind . . .'

'I won't.' After weeks of painful dithering, she felt it was time to prove that she could stand on her own two feet. 'And before you ask, I won't need to see one of those midwife ladies, if that's all right with you.'

Joy took the news in her stride. 'I won't mention it again.'

'I couldn't . . . I wouldn't . . .' Mildred faltered.

'I understand.'

'Yes, I'm young – but that doesn't mean I won't cope. I'll go to classes about how to feed and look after a baby, or else I can ask Nurse Myers at the clinic. She'll give me some leaflets.'

'And I'm sure Lucia will help.'

Joy's comment brought Mildred up short. 'Will I . . .?' The look of determination was replaced by one of bewilderment. She turned away with tears in her eyes.

'Will you what?'

'Will I still live here after . . .?'

'After the baby is born?' Joy leaned across to squeeze her hand. 'Yes, if you want to.'

'I won't have to find new lodgings?'

'We wouldn't dream of turfing you out.'

Mildred let out a long sigh of relief.

'One step at a time,' Joy reassured her. 'And while we're looking ahead, why not try and get out of the house more often? We've got the circus tonight then later this week

Tommy and I have a Viennese waltz lesson with Mrs Ellis. You could come along?'

'To watch you dance?'

'Or to join in.'

It was as if Joy had suggested climbing aboard a space ship and travelling to the moon. Mildred's eyes widened as she ran through the implications. 'Would I be able to in my condition?'

'Yes; being pregnant doesn't mean you're not allowed to dance.' Joy was amused. 'If you don't believe me, ask Nurse Myers on Wednesday.'

A dreamy smile crept across the girl's freckled face. 'I do love dancing. I used to save up to go to the Mecca every Saturday.' Painful memories brought back the frown. She stood up clumsily, knocking Joy's lipstick to the floor as she did so. 'I'm ready now.'

'Yes, let's go.' Joy picked up the lipstick and slid it into her handbag. Lions and tigers would rise up on their hind legs and jump through hoops, horses would prance and clowns would tumble. She and Mildred would take their ringside seats and settle into some well-deserved fun.

That same afternoon Lorna arrived at the Spanish Hall to meet with Cliff and Sylvia at three o'clock prompt. Scanning the long colonnades and checking the balconies, she gave an impatient shake of her head. They were late; of course they were! Young people were rarely prompt, seemingly unaware that to keep a person waiting was a very poor show. Lorna resolved to start the meeting by reminding Sylvia of basic manners.

'Here we are, Mother.' Sylvia burst through the door to one side of the proscenium arch with Cliff following close behind. 'We've been backstage, talking to the caretaker about how many chairs and tables he should set out for us when the time comes. He reminded us that the hall has a capacity of six hundred people; four at each table makes one hundred and fifty tables in all.'

Lorna pursed her lips and held back the criticism about poor timekeeping. Sylvia was in one of her excitable states, talking too quickly and smiling too broadly. 'Three hundred couples?' she queried. 'I'm afraid I have nowhere near that number of entries as yet.'

'How many do you have?' There was a hint of worry in Cliff's voice as they walked the length of the dimly lit colonnade.

'One hundred and fifteen.' Lorna kept a meticulous record of names and addresses. 'Less than half the number I require. How many do you have for the Latin section?'

'More than that.' Cliff was less certain of the exact number. 'Possibly a hundred and eighty.'

'I've exhausted my list of contacts.' Lorna emerged from the colonnade to gaze up at the unlit battlements and realistic murals of an Andalusian village nestled against mountains and backed by a deep blue sky. The hall seemed cavernous and oppressive in its unlit state, adding to her uneasy feeling that they'd bitten off more than they could chew. 'Current entries don't come close to covering our costs,' she pointed out.

Sylvia was having none of it. 'True, but we still have a month to go.'

'A little less.' Lorna wore her pedant's hat. 'Our calculations are based on attracting a bare minimum of two hundred and fifty couples for each day, just to break even.'

Cliff nodded. 'Anything above that will be pure profit.' Sylvia's mother had given voice to the worry that he'd been hiding from Sylvia, who seemed determined to ride a wave of blind optimism in the run-up to the big weekend. 'So how can we improve our chances?'

There was a long silence, interrupted by activity on the stage as the caretaker and his assistant appeared with a long ladder and began to push aside painted flats to reveal the dusty backstage area with its battery of overhead lights, ropes and pulleys.

'We have to rely on Mr King's article appearing in the *Gazette*.' Lorna stared pointedly at her daughter. 'Sooner rather than later.'

Sylvia gave an exasperated sigh. 'Mother, I've told you before that it's entirely up to Vernon and his editor.'

'It's a tricky one,' Cliff admitted. 'But I agree with you, Mrs Ellis – we could certainly do with the publicity boost that the article will bring. Leave it with me.'

'Why not Sylvia – surely she has more influence than you?' Lorna gave the characteristic tilt of her head that demanded further explanation.

'My maxim is: never mix business with pleasure.' Cliff cleared his throat awkwardly. 'Not that I always follow my own advice,' he added with a self-conscious smile.

Sylvia made a dismissive gesture while Lorna's head tilted further to the side.

'I mean that there are no personal entanglements for me as regards Vernon King, whilst there are for Sylvia, especially now that he's moved in with her.'

It was as if a bomb had exploded at their feet. Lorna gripped her handbag more tightly while Sylvia let out a low, despairing groan. Onstage a badly positioned ladder slipped then clattered to the floor. The caretaker yelled an apology then went on with his work.

Cliff's gaze darted from one to the other. 'You didn't

tell her?' he muttered at Sylvia under his breath. Damn and blast – now he'd really set the cat among the pigeons.

Her mind whirled dizzily as she recalled the endless wait for Vernon to put in an appearance the previous day. Joy and Pearl's visit had helped pass the time, but after they'd gone Sylvia's nerves had been in tatters. As the evening had progressed minute by never-ending minute, she'd hovered by the window, looking out for him until, unable to bear the sick feeling in her stomach any longer, she'd resorted to futile, everyday tasks – tidying and dusting articles that were already orderly and spotless. It had been no use; time had dragged on until at last, as dusk fell, the silence had been broken by the longed-for sound of her sweetheart's car engine in the street below. Her heart had jolted and missed a beat at the slam of the door and his footsteps on the stairs.

Vernon had burst in, dropped his suitcase on the floor and showered her with apologies – he'd been delayed in Manchester; there were loose ends to tie up, various farewells to exchange. He'd taken Alfie out for a drink by way of a thank-you for providing a roof over his head. Alfie was a good pal; one of the best. 'Say you forgive me,' Vernon had cajoled.

There had been nothing to forgive. He was here now and that was all that mattered. The sick feeling had given way to overwhelming relief. Sylvia had showed him where to put his clothes. 'I've made room on this side of the wardrobe for your shirts and suits.'

'All in good time.' Vernon had abandoned his open suitcase on the bedroom floor. He'd pressed his fingers over her mouth to forestall objections before lifting her up and carrying her to the bed, where they'd made love with warm rays from a flaming sunset streaming in through the window.

In the quiet aftermath, Vernon looked down at Sylvia and murmured, 'This beats everything – you name it, it's never a patch on us being in bed together.'

Sylvia had listened with her head resting on his bare shoulder and her eyes closed, letting her worries fade as she'd soaked up every loving word.

'Sorry again that I was late,' he'd whispered between kisses.

It hadn't mattered. *Nothing* mattered now that Vernon was here, his body warm against hers, his soft words drifting down and landing on her skin like blossom petals from a cloudless sky.

'Is this true?' Lorna demanded once the dust had settled. Cliff had made a rapid excuse and left the Spanish Hall, leaving mother and daughter to sort things out between them. 'Has Mr King moved into your flat?'

'Not officially.' Sylvia stood her ground as best she could. 'Nothing is set in stone. It simply makes sense for him to have digs closer to where he works. And please don't call him Mr King, Mother. His name is Vernon.'

'Digs?' Lorna repeated the word with disdain. 'Does that mean you're sharing lodgings with a man you scarcely know?'

Sylvia met the accusation with a defiant stare. 'It's more than that and you know it.'

'But nothing is official?' No ring, no proposal of marriage. Once again scornful disapproval blazed through Lorna's stiff query. 'And whose idea was it, pray?'

'Really, Mother, why can't you be glad for me for once?' Sylvia was on the verge of tears. 'Let me spell it out – Vernon and I are in love; it's as simple as that.'

'Love?' Lorna echoed faintly.

'Yes. Why must you repeat everything?' On the point

of making a swift exit, Sylvia made a final, exasperated attempt to make her mother understand. 'Surely you of all people know how it feels to adore someone and worship the ground they tread on? You'll do anything for them and you hang on their every word – don't you remember?'

The question flung Lorna back to her brief affair with Sylvia's father. His image appeared in her mind's eye – tall, elegant, with swept-back fair hair and remarkable blue eyes that Sylvia had inherited. Twenty-three years had passed yet still Lorna kept his portrait inside a gold locket that she wore every day. 'Yes; to my cost,' she admitted with a nod of her head.

Sylvia breathed in sharply. Her mother rarely made reference to her father's disappearance but this was surely what the phrase 'to my cost' implied.

'I was young.' Lorna's scorn faded – the time had come for total honesty. 'Two years younger than you are now – a mere girl. And yes, I worshipped your father; that's precisely the reason why I ask you to step back and consider. Not because I'm out of touch with the modern way; in fact, quite the opposite. It's because I'm desperate for you not to make the same mistake.'

At the far end of the hall, the caretaker flicked a switch that instantly flooded the stage with light. His assistant climbed the ladder to replace a bulb. 'Third from the left,' he instructed before flicking off the switch.

'Please don't misunderstand,' Lorna said softly. 'I haven't regretted for a single moment that you were the result of that affair. Everything I've done – all that I've achieved – has been for you and you alone.'

'Without anyone to help you.' Her mother's lurch into intimacy had caught Sylvia off guard. 'But you've made a success of your life.'

'Of *our* lives,' Lorna insisted. 'Oddly enough, I knew from the start what I would do, despite the naysayers who advised me not to keep you. I was certain I could offer my baby a good life, with or without their help.' Poised on the brink of glittering success as a professional dancer all those years before, Lorna had taken an early-morning walk along Blackpool's deserted beach and gazed far out to sea. There had been a moment of clarity. *I can do this. We will be happy.*

'How were you so sure?'

Lorna shrugged her slight shoulders. 'Call it stubbornness. I was considered a strong-willed child by my grandmother who brought me up after my mother died. Then I lost my father in the Great War and after that I had no one – I had to make my own way. Luckily I had a talent.'

'That you passed on to me.' Sylvia slipped her arm through Lorna's and together they walked out into the corridor, past the Renaissance Room and the clickety-click of a dozen War Office typewriters. 'I'm sorry I haven't been more grateful,' she observed.

'And I'm sorry that all through your childhood I tried to shelter you from the nastier aspects of the outside world. Perhaps that was a mistake.'

'Yes, you did.' Sylvia's laugh lightened the mood as they descended the stairs. 'Pearl and Joy always say that you spoiled me rotten.'

Down in the foyer leading out on to Coronation Street, Lorna hugged Sylvia. 'What do Pearl and Joy think about your new living arrangement?'

'The same as you; they warned me not to rush into things,' Sylvia admitted with a sigh. 'I ignored their advice.'

'Like mother, like daughter – strong willed to a fault. But what's done is done.' Lorna embraced Sylvia again. 'And if you really love this man and hope for a future together, who am I to stand in your way?'

'I do love him, Mother, and I look up to him too. Vernon's seen so much more of the world than I have. He knows about everything that interests me – dance, theatre and cinema. And don't you think he's handsome?'

Lorna took her daughter's hands and squeezed them. 'Yes – very.'

'So you'll be nice to him?'

'Yes, I promise.' It was time for them to part. Lorna leaned forward to kiss Sylvia's cheek. 'You must both come to tea next Sunday,' she said brightly. 'Tell Vernon I'll bake a Victoria sponge cake in his honour.'

Mildred's visit to the circus proved a success. Sitting beside Joy, she gasped at the high-wire acrobatics of a world-renowned Polish troupe, laughed at the outlandish antics of Tommy's Trio Rossi and marvelled at the breathtaking beauty of Emmy Truzzi's *Cavalerie de Grâce.* She joined in the applause, clapping louder than everyone as the Enchanted Cascade brought the show to a magical end.

'My favourite was the Devils of the Forest,' Mildred confessed on the leisurely stroll home. 'When the man in the white top hat stroked the panther, my heart almost jumped out of my chest.' Panthers, lions, leopards, pumas, cougars – a whole range of jungle creatures had prowled around the ring, responding to the crack of their trainer's whip. 'Where do they go after the show?'

'They live in stables under the circus ring.' Joy had seen for herself how the animals were kept underground – well fed and looked after, but without a glimpse of daylight.

'Poor things,' Mildred lamented. 'Actually, I liked the Trio Rossi better. I didn't know Tommy under his make-up until he played the trumpet and I recognized the tune he's been practising at home.'

'He's good, isn't he?' Joy was enjoying the calm dusk light, when colours faded and a faint pink glow on the horizon provided just enough light for them to find their way home. 'So you're glad you went?' she asked as they walked underneath South Pier, taking care to skirt shallow pools left by the ebbing tide.

'Yes – I loved every minute.' Mildred needn't have worried; no one had stared at her or given her funny looks – they were all too busy guffawing at the clowns or holding their breath at the high-wire risks taken by the world's leading lady equilibrists – a strange word that she'd never heard before. 'Thank you – it was marvellous.'

'You're very welcome. Let's get a move on, shall we?' The rosy glow on the horizon had vanished and before long it would be completely dark.

They hurried up the beach and took the nearest steps up to the promenade. Five minutes later they reached the ice-cream parlour and let themselves in by the side door to be met by a flurry of questions from Lucia in her dressing gown and slippers. 'My Tommy, he is the best? He fall over, he jump up, he play *musica* – you like?'

Mildred agreed that Tommy won the prize for best clown, best costume, best juggler, best trumpet player, submitting to Lucia's warm hugs with a self-conscious smile before declaring it was time to head upstairs.

'*Si, si* – you sleep, *sonno* – is *bene*.'

Joy and Lucia packed Mildred off to bed then waited in the kitchen for Tommy to arrive. They chatted pleasantly until they heard his key in the lock. He entered the house in high spirits, still energized from his performance and eager to find out if Mildred had had a good time. 'Where is she?' he enquired, running a hand through his tousled hair.

'In bed.' Joy held a finger to her lips for him to keep his voice down. 'She was tired out.'

'In that case – there's something Joy and I need to tell you, Momma.' He sat down next to Joy and opposite his mother, his expression serious.

Joy had been dreading this moment. 'Your mother's tired too – perhaps we should wait?'

'No – Momma needs to know,' he argued. 'We've been keeping it a secret for long enough.'

'What is this?' A look of concern crept over Lucia's features. 'Is bad or good?'

'Good,' Tommy insisted, drawing the estate agent's crumpled sheet from his trouser pocket and pushing it across the table for her to see. 'Joy and I plan to buy this house,' he explained calmly and simply.

'To live?' Puzzled, Lucia turned the sheet to expose its blank side as if expecting to find answers.

'Yes, to live there together.'

'No, is not possible!' His mother threw up her hands in great distress. 'You and Joy leave this house? You go to new one?'

'It's all right – King Street isn't far away.' Joy went round the table to reassure her mother-in-law.

Her words fell on deaf ears. 'You leave this house?' Lucia wailed.

Upstairs in her bedroom Mildred heard a commotion. She was half undressed, sitting in her petticoat with her legs dangling over the side of her bed. It sounded as if Lucia was upset.

'Not straight away,' Tommy reasoned. 'There's work to do on the King Street house before we move in.'

'And we don't even know yet if our offer will be accepted.' *Too soon, too sudden*; Joy had warned Tommy what the effect on his mother was likely to be but he'd steamed ahead regardless.

'*No*,' Lucia cried. '*Per favore, no!*'

'Listen to me.' Tommy's stomach churned with guilt. 'Joy's right – you can't get rid of us that easily. We'll only be round the corner.'

'But why, my Tommy?' Lucia covered her face with her hands. 'Why you leave here?'

Upstairs, Mildred crept from her room then along the landing, leaning over the banister and picking up every word that was spoken.

'Because this house is too small for four people,' he explained carefully. 'You, me, Joy and Mildred – it's too many.'

As if reacting to an electric shock, Mildred stepped back from the banister and retreated to her room. She sank on to the bed and pulled the sheets over her ears. *Too small. Too many.*

'Besides,' Tommy went on, 'now that Joy and I are married, it makes sense for us to have a place of our own.'

'But only if we're sure that you can cope without us,' Joy added. 'We promise not to leave you and Mildred in the lurch.'

'Yes; think about it, Momma – Mildred will still be here and before you know it, Hitler will be forced to surrender then this damned war will be over and Papa will be allowed home – with luck before our new house is ready to move into. So you see, it's not so bad.'

Lucia's chest heaved as she fought to control her

distress. '*Si* – no so bad, no so sad. *Bene*.' Nevertheless tears streamed down her plump face.

Mildred's body shook as she hid beneath her sheets. *Too small. Too many.* It was perfectly true: she was in the way and had no right to be here in the first place. It was only because Mrs Rossi had taken pity on her for getting herself into this awful fix. Other bosses wouldn't have been so kind. But the problem would go away if she, Mildred, wasn't here.

'*Bene*,' Tommy soothed. Lord, he felt awful. Bloody tactless fool – he should have broken it to his mother more gently.

It was left to Joy to pick up the pieces. 'Don't cry,' she pleaded with Lucia. 'Everything will look better in the morning. And Tommy, tell your mother you'll always love her, no matter what.'

'I will.' He reached for Lucia's hands, clasping them firmly and waiting for her to meet his gaze. 'I just want us all to be happy, *capisce*?'

CHAPTER TWELVE

All went ahead as Sylvia and Vernon had planned; his move to Blackpool wouldn't take place in one fell swoop and there would be times when his work would keep him away. Still, when she woke up alone after only three nights together she felt bereft.

'Where will you spend the night?' she'd asked the previous day when he'd warned her not to expect him home that evening. He'd popped into the studio with the news that he'd lined up an important interview back in Manchester.

'Oh, don't worry about me – I can always find somewhere to kip. I'll be back before you know it.'

Cliff had observed the exchange then later mentioned it to Terry. 'Sylvia was upset but tried not to show it. Vernon breezed off without a care in the world.'

'Trouble in paradise?' Terry suggested with a grimace.

'Let's hope not.' Cliff had crossed his fingers and they'd carried on cooking their evening meal of liver and fried onions with plenty of mashed potato.

At six o'clock in the morning it was already daylight and Sylvia lay in bed, drifting between sleep and wakefulness. She was reluctant to get up and yet the longer she stayed in bed the more the unwelcome thoughts plagued her. What exactly had Vernon meant by always being able to find somewhere to kip? Would he go back to his old lodgings or would Alfie already have rented his room to someone else? What was so important about the interview that meant it had to take place too late in the evening for him to drive back to Blackpool? Questions buzzed inside her head like angry bees until at last she got up, determined to plan her day. First there was a breakfast of toast and marmalade, which she would force herself to eat. Then she would make a lesson plan for a midday samba class with Bill and Shirley Jones, who had their eyes set on a Latin prize at the dance weekend. After that there was a pile of ironing to tackle or perhaps instead she could squeeze in a mid-morning excursion to see Pearl in the arcade. But then, no – Sylvia didn't want to risk not being at home when Vernon got back.

She was sitting at the table by the window, making notes for her lesson – remember to focus on the controlled bounce and rapid steps of Brazil's national dance – when Vernon put in an appearance.

'How's my girl this fine, sunny morning?' he cried, flinging his jacket over the back of the sofa and brushing aside her ponytail to kiss the nape of her neck. 'Have you missed me as much as I've missed you?'

When Sylvia stood up to embrace him she noticed that he hadn't had a chance to shave.

'What's the matter – do I look a sight?' he said with a grin before holding her at arm's length. 'You, on the other hand, are the picture of perfection.'

'I did miss you,' she confessed, stooping to pick up her notebook, which had slid to the floor.

Vernon used the moment to retrieve his jacket, delve into a pocket and produce a sheet of paper with a list of names scribbled in pencil. 'Three new couples for your dance weekend,' he announced triumphantly. 'Never say I don't do anything for you.'

Sylvia recognized two names on the list: Wilfred Perkins and Betty Stevens were among the foremost Latin dancers in the North of England. 'How did you manage this?'

'I have my contacts.' Vernon was confident that a wink and teasing look would disarm her. 'Better warn your local contenders to be on their mettle – Wilf is convinced that he and Betty are an odds-on certainty.'

'That remains to be seen.' Sylvia gave him another hug. 'Was Wilfred Perkins the person you went to interview?'

'No, it was someone else. As a matter of fact, that fell through at the last minute.'

'So it was a waste of time?'

Vernon shrugged as he strolled into the kitchen and bit into a slice of toast leftover from Sylvia's breakfast. 'It happens in my line of work. At least I didn't come home empty handed; I brought you those entries for your big day. On top of which, I bumped into Art, who suggested two more couples for your mother's competition – good old quickstep and foxtrot specialists.'

'Did you write their names down?'

He tapped his forehead then spoke with a mouthful of toast. 'They're in here. I'll add them to the list after I've had a shave.'

Sylvia relaxed as Vernon disappeared into the bathroom, wondering why she'd let herself get into such a state in the first place. But then another question wormed its way inside her head – where had Vernon been when he'd 'bumped into' Art Richardson? At a night club, perhaps. Had Vernon watched the band perform then gone for a drink with them afterwards? Come to think of it, there was stale alcohol mixed with tobacco on his breath. *Stop it!* She brought the train of thought to an abrupt halt. Vernon was here now and that was all that mattered. So Sylvia sat down at the table to transfer the new names to her list of entrants, wondering how and when they intended to pay their entry fees.

Vernon reappeared shirtless, with a towel slung over his shoulder and smelling of shaving soap. 'By the way,' he began as he hovered behind her, 'I've a bone to pick.'

'Oh?' she glanced up from her work.

'Yes – Cliff Seymour has had a go at me and I'm not happy.'

'When? What about?'

'A couple of days ago. About the damned article – he demanded to know when it'll appear in print. I told him I'd handed it over to my editor, Sam Pearson.'

Sylvia frowned as Vernon, leaning over her, rested his hands on the table to either side of her then nestled his cheek against hers.

'I'm tired of repeating the same old thing – it's the editor's decision, not mine.'

She shifted uneasily on her chair. 'But you can see why we're worried?'

'Not really.' He stood up straight then wandered across the room, hands in pockets, speaking with his back to her. 'So please ask Cliff to stop pestering me – tell him it gets my back up.'

A fresh knot of anxiety formed in Sylvia's stomach. 'I'm sorry,' she breathed. 'I'm sure he didn't realize.'

Vernon swung round to face her with a fixed smile. 'Not your fault – but don't let it happen again.'

Was he serious? Studying his expression, she was unable to tell.

'Just kidding.' Vernon burst out laughing as he came towards her and stooped over her once more. 'Honestly, my sweet; you should see your face!'

'Are you sure you don't want me to come to the clinic with you?' Joy checked with Mildred. The kitchen window was open to let in cool air after Lucia's recent burst of baking activity. Fresh loaves stood on a wire tray and a bread crock and dirty utensils were piled in the sink. 'I can easily phone Alan and tell him that I won't be in today.'

Mildred shook her head. 'I'm fine, thanks.'

It was clear she was anything but. In fact, Mildred had looked distinctly peaky these past few days; quieter than ever and keeping to her room instead of offering to help Lucia in the ice-cream parlour. It saddened Joy to find that the girl's cheerful mood following their visit to the circus had evaporated so quickly.

'What's up with Mildred?' Tommy had asked the evening after the circus trip, on his way out to work. 'I just said cheerio and she ignored me.'

Joy had promised to investigate but had come up against a brick wall. 'Knock-knock,' she'd said, while tapping on the girl's door. There had been no reply and no sound of movement so Joy had assumed that Mildred was taking a nap.

'Mildred, she is in her room. She cries,' Lucia had reported to Joy next day. 'She does not talk.'

Once more Joy had gone up to check. This time the door had been ajar and Joy had found the girl sitting on her bed with her arms folded and her face pale and serious. 'What's wrong?' she'd ventured as she'd closed the door behind her.

'Nothing.'

'You haven't had a change of heart about the baby?' Joy reasoned that this could be behind the dramatic shift in Mildred's mood.

'No.'

She'd said nothing more; just the one emphatic syllable. Joy had tried to bring her out of herself by chatting on about this and that. 'Robert Finchley's wife brought their new baby into work today for us all to see – a little girl called Rita. She has a mass of dark curly hair just like her mother.' There'd been no response so Joy had quickly changed tack. 'Did you decide to come with Tommy and me to Mrs Ellis's Viennese waltz class tomorrow night? We'd really like it if you did.'

'No, it's not for me.' A flat reply without an explanation; head hanging, eyes closed.

'Well, Lucia will be here to keep you company,' Joy had reminded her just as Tommy had arrived home. She'd dashed downstairs to greet him.

'Duh-dah; our offer on the house has been accepted!' he'd announced to Joy and Lucia with an imaginary blare of trumpets. 'How about that?'

He'd swept his wife clean off her feet then embraced his mother and done the same with her. Lucia had shrieked and pleaded to be put down. Great news indeed!

Upstairs in her room Mildred had heard excited voices, too muffled for her to understand. It didn't matter; whatever the family were celebrating was no longer any of her business. She had already made up her mind about what she would do.

So when Joy knocked on her door on the Wednesday morning and offered to go to the clinic with her it was easy to turn her down. 'I'm fine thanks.'

Joy glanced at her watch. She must leave now or run the risk of missing her train. 'If you're sure . . .?'

'Quite sure.'

'Well then; I hope it goes well. I'll see you later.'

She was gone; fresh and delicate as a daisy in her pale yellow dress and cream jacket, her long, dark hair pinned up and hidden beneath a straw hat. The young Mrs Rossi was a beautiful woman; generous to a fault and with a heart of gold. Mildred would be forever grateful.

Listening for movement below, she heard Lucia call goodbye to Joy before making her way through to the café to prepare for another busy day. Mildred knew that Tommy had already left the house. The kitchen was empty; now was her moment.

She stooped to pull her canvas duffel bag from under the bed. It was already packed with her few belongings. Mildred unbuckled the front pocket and took out a note addressed to Mrs Joy Rossi, written the night before. There was no need to read it through; she remembered it word for word.

Dear Mrs Rossi,

I am leaving because Mr Rossi is right – this house is too crowded for all of us. The last thing I want is to be in your way. Thank you for everything you've done for me. I will never forget you.

Yours truly,

Mildred Kershaw

Her hand trembled as she placed the note on the pillow. She picked up her bag and crept from the room, down the stairs and through the empty kitchen, ignoring the two slices of bread, knife, plate, cup and saucer that the older Mrs Rossi had set out for her. The kitchen was the warm, safe heart of the house; a place to which Mildred would never return.

The side door was open. Swiftly crossing the small yard, she didn't dare to look back in case her courage failed. Leaving was the right thing to do. The latch clicked as Mildred opened the gate then clicked again as she closed it behind her.

At last; a letter from Bernie had arrived! Pearl tore it open to find that it was written more than two weeks earlier, on 28 June. He was in southern Italy; that much was now certain. The regiment's aim was to help drive the enemy out of Sicily but there might be a long, hard road ahead. Bernie could say no more.

The main thing is, I'm still in the land of the living. Apart from a gippy tummy due to filthy latrines and Lord knows what else, I'm in decent nick. Anyhow, you don't want to hear me moaning on. How's life in dear old Blighty? More to the point, how are you, my Pearl? Missing me as much as I miss you, I hope.

It took her a full hour to absorb the contents. Bernie had continued his letter with a few flippant remarks about the Italians' disorganized way of fighting compared with the goose-stepping Germans in North Africa. He reckoned the Allies already had the Italian troops on the run in some areas and the shipping channels in the Med would soon be opened up, barring enemy reinforcements. Then the tone of the letter altered in an attempt to commit to paper his deeper feelings.

Dearest Pearl, it's hard to believe that one day I'll be holding you in my arms again, like we did on the night we were married – remember that? I can't wait. If I didn't carry your picture with me everywhere, I'd think that I'd made it all up. As it is, I just have to look at the photo and suddenly everything is all right again. Pearl, I don't mind admitting that I've shed a few tears, wondering how long it might be before we see each other. 'We'll meet again, don't know where, don't know when . . .' Sorry to go on like an idiot. You're probably wondering what happened to the happy-go-lucky bloke you fell for. It's still the same old me, I promise.

Pearl finished reading the letter then clutched it to her breast, which was how her father found her when he clomped downstairs demanding his breakfast, braces dangling and shirtsleeves rolled up.

'Where's your mother?' Henry grunted at Pearl.

'Here I am.' Before Pearl had a chance to reply Maria carried in four pints of milk from the front doorstep. 'Get yourself off to work,' she told her daughter briskly. 'I'll sort out your dad's porridge.'

As if floating on air, Pearl tucked Bernie's letter inside her blouse and made her way to North Pier. She kept it close to her heart throughout the day. Customers rolled into the arcade and fed their cash willy-nilly into the rows of Lucky Stars and Chip and Busts until their pockets were empty. Pearl played the latest hit records and sat at the desk gazing out at the sparkling sea and clear blue sky, oblivious to her surroundings and thinking back to the days when a carefree Bernie had spun the waltzers at the Pleasure Beach – 'Scream if you want to go faster!' – and how the girls had obliged. Or else she recalled him scaring her to death on the ghost train or deliberately crashing into her on the dodgems or jumping out from behind the distorting mirrors inside the Fun House. Memories, glorious memories! All before she and Bernie had grown up and fallen in love and the war had snatched him away.

At the end of the day she forced herself back to the present, to go and meet Errol at the North View Parade studio.

'Someone looks like the cat that got the cream.' Sylvia's greeting was accompanied by a sly nudge.

Pearl patted the letter that was still tucked inside her blouse. 'He wrote.'

'Of course he did.' Sylvia had never doubted it. 'Happy now?'

'Over the moon,' Pearl confirmed. 'And you?'

'Likewise.' There was little time to talk – Sylvia had taught her last class of the day and had promised to meet Vernon at the Galleon, which had become their favourite haunt. 'Vernon brought me three more entries for our Latin competition.' What she didn't admit was that there was still a long way to go money-wise before they broke even.

'I didn't mean that. I was asking about you and Mr Entertainment.'

'Tip-top, if you must know.' Slipping on her canvas sling-backs, Sylvia hastily stored her dancing shoes under a bench in the alcove. 'Sorry, must dash.'

Which she did, crossing paths with Errol as she left the building.

'Ready to jive?' he asked Pearl without any build-up. The summer sun had deepened his tan, set off by an open-necked white shirt and dark blue slacks.

'Yes, as soon as I find the right record.' She flipped

through the rack, only to find that Sylvia had left it ready for them on the turntable.

Errol observed her quick, light movements as she searched. 'Good news from foreign fields?' he guessed.

Pearl stood with the needle raised over the record. He said 'noos' for news and his voice lilted upwards at the end of the sentence. 'How did you know?'

'One look at your bright eyes was all it took.'

'As it happens, you're spot on.' She took out Bernie's letter and waved it triumphantly. 'It arrived this morning all the way from sunny Italy.'

'I sure am happy for you.' And in one way he was sincere. On the other hand, *Goddammit!* He quickly buried this unworthy thought and offered her his hand. 'Shall we?' Pearl lowered the needle then let him lead her into the middle of the room. They began with a few basic moves – bounces, kicks and shimmies – giving her a chance to share the dance weekend news that Sylvia had imparted.

'New entries – should I be worried?' Errol asked as he swung Pearl out.

'Yes – they include the top Latin couple in the North of England,' she explained. 'Apparently Vernon knows them personally.'

'Vernon?'

'Vernon King, the journalist at the *Gazette*. He's Sylvia's new beau.'

'Oh yeah, I know the guy you mean.' Step, kick, step again. 'Cary Grant's double.'

'That's the one.' Step and bounce, swing out then back. The music gathered speed, building to the point when they would attempt Pearl's Tiller Girl kick while Errol ducked and did his Cossack impression.

'Art Richardson's band played at our base last night.

We had the full works: trumpet, sax, drums, piano and the cutest girl singer you ever saw. Your journalist guy was there to report on the gig.'

'He's Sylvia's journalist, not mine,' Pearl corrected as she pivoted and Errol ducked. 'She let him move in with her at the weekend – love's young dream.'

'Gotcha.' Errol grunted with the effort of kicking out from a crouched position. Kick, kick, kick and spring back up then catch hold of Pearl's hand and swing her out – bounce and shimmy. There was more he could have said about the good-looking journalist and the cute girl singer, but this seemed like a time to keep his mouth shut. 'Wanna try a lift?' he suggested as the record finished and they took a quick breather. 'You run at me and jump, one leg either side of my waist. I catch you then start to spin on the spot while you lean out and arch your spine until the back of your head skims the floor – you trust me?'

'With my life.' Pearl nodded eagerly and restarted the record. 'Come on, let's give it a go.'

Joe was at a loose end. He'd closed his stall for the day then hung around in the market square to chew the fat with fellow stallholders, discussing the worsening shortages of citrus fruit and bananas, petrol and paraffin. Afterwards, since it was a pleasant evening, he fancied a stroll along the beach before heading home to King Street. Others had followed suit – he nodded a greeting at young Len Fraser who walked hand in hand along the shoreline with Valerie Ward, before spotting several old school pals engaged in a casual kick-around. A couple of deckchairs, spaced several feet apart, served as goalposts.

'Now then, Joe – come and join us.' One booted the ball high in the air and Joe caught it.

'Why not?' He spent a few minutes in goal, diving sideways or leaping high as the others fired at him. *Oof!* He caught the ball and clasped it to his stomach or reached up to bat it away with his fingertips. When the game finished he dusted himself down. 'See you later,' he called to the gang as they went their separate ways.

Deciding that a quiet night at home was on the cards, Joe headed for the prom, where he bumped into Joy as she alighted from a tram. 'Smashing evening,' he remarked.

'Lovely.' She was in a rush to get home to see how Mildred had got on at the clinic. 'Sorry, Joe – I have to dash.'

He watched her hurry off, marvelling at how much Joy crammed into her life these days. And now there was a plan to do up the house close to his on King Street, not to mention the small matter of entering Sylvia's big dance competition. *Lord knows how she does it,* he said to himself as he turned for home.

'How about that – a lift and two cartwheels!' Pearl exclaimed. She and Errol ended their practice session on a high note. They both gasped for breath and their foreheads were damp with sweat.

'Not bad.' Errol grinned.

'Not bad? It's blooming marvellous!'

'But will it be enough to win the darned thing?' He undid another button of his shirt to help him to cool down. 'Just how good are Vernon King's guys?'

'I don't know and I don't care. So long as we polish our routine and don't make any mistakes on the day, I'm pretty sure we stand a chance.'

'So how many more sessions like tonight?' Errol closed the gramophone lid.

'As many as we can fit in during the time we have

left – let's see; just over three weeks. Say three rehearsals per week; that makes nine altogether.'

'Sure thing.' He would grab with both hands every chance to spend time with Pearl. 'I'm free Monday, Wednesday and Friday evenings.'

Planning ahead, they tidied the studio then locked up and left.

'What do you plan on wearin'?' Errol asked as they sauntered down North View Parade towards the prom.

'I haven't decided – it has to be something that lets me kick high and do cartwheels; maybe a skirt with a split up the side. I want it to look modern.'

'Honey, you could wear a sack and still look a million dollars.' It seemed natural to keep on walking as they talked, even though they'd passed the bus stop where Errol would normally wait for his ride back to base. The sun was low in the sky, casting long shadows across the wide promenade. 'Luckily I don't have that problem; guys can turn up in shirts and pants and nobody gives a damn what we wear, so long as we lift our girls without dropping 'em on their heads.'

'Don't even think about dropping me.' Pearl gave him a sideways shove.

'Trust me, I won't.' Laughing, Errol dug into his pocket and produced a pack of chewing gum. 'I knew from the get-go that we'd make a good jive team – you had all the right moves, plenty of natural rhythm, plus whatever it takes to stand out from the crowd.'

'You're too kind.' Pearl's fingers touched his as she took a piece of gum. There was a burst of mint and sugar on her tongue as she popped it into her mouth. 'I'm lucky to have such a great teacher.'

'I'm the lucky one,' he insisted. They'd reached the

Tower building. Every detail of its brickwork and arched windows was drenched in sunlight, the intricate steel structure of the Tower soaring overhead. Errol gestured towards the shaded alley up the side of the building that led to the market square and Empire Street. 'I guess this is where we say goodbye?'

Pearl's mind was still on the competition. 'Your trousers – what colour will they be?'

He took a second to figure out what she meant. 'Oh; my pants.'

'Pants – trousers; it's the same thing.'

'Potato, potatoe,' Errol responded, grinning, and they both broke into laughter before linking arms and turning into the alley together. 'If you wear your dark blue trousers, I'll make a dress to match,' she decided.

'What the . . .?' Coming up from the beach after his kick-about, Joe stood dumbfounded. Were his eyes playing tricks or was that Pearl and the Yank getting too friendly by far? *Surely not. Pearl would never . . .*

But then yes. Joe waited for a gap in the traffic before crossing the road. *I saw them with my own eyes, fooling around outside the Tower entrance.* They'd been laughing their heads off then disappeared arm in arm up the alley, not dreaming that anyone was watching.

Joe was the type to mind his own business. He regarded himself as level headed and fair. But blimey, this took the damned biscuit! Pearl and the GI – after all the nasty gossip that Joe had chosen to ignore. Bernie was his best mate, for crying out loud! They'd joked their way through school together and Joe had been best man at the wedding. Now Bernie was stuck God knows where, in some rotten hellhole, while Pearl and Errol Jackson laughed and bloody well linked arms without a care in the world.

Angry, disjointed thoughts ricocheted inside Joe's skull as he followed them up the alley. He would go straight home and put pen to paper. *Dear Bernie, I hate to tell you this but there's something you ought to know . . .*

'I'm back!' Joy put down her handbag on the kitchen table then took off her hat and jacket. There was no response so she went through to the café to find her mother-in-law standing at the hatch overlooking the prom, serving ice cream to the last customers of the day.

Lucia took their money then slid the hatch closed, wiping her hands on her apron as she turned towards Joy. 'Ah, it is you,' she murmured.

'Yes; who did you think it was?' Joy's gaze flicked around the sunny room, taking in the green gingham tablecloths and the small vase of fresh flowers set out on each table, the shiny glass counter, the shelves stacked with crockery and the ice-cream refrigerator humming quietly in the background.

'I wait for Mildred,' Lucia explained. 'She doesn't come.'

'Oh dear.' Joy was disappointed but not immediately worried. 'Perhaps the clinic was busy. She might have had to wait longer than usual to be seen.' Or, more alarmingly, perhaps the nurse had discovered an unexpected hitch: a further rise in blood pressure or concern about Mildred not gaining enough weight – in which case, she'd have held her patient back until a doctor was free to examine her. 'Still, she ought to be home by now.'

'*Si, si.*' Lucia was the first to hurry upstairs to knock on the girl's door, with Joy following close behind. 'Mildred, *mia cara* – you are there?'

No answer.

Lucia turned to Joy. 'She sleeps?'

'Maybe.' Joy frowned as she ran through various scenarios. 'But surely she would have popped into the café to tell you that she was back?'

Lucia knocked again then put her ear to the door. Still silence.

Joy felt her chest tighten. This wasn't right. She recalled how definite Mildred had been first thing that morning about attending the clinic without her. 'Something's up – she hasn't been herself lately,' she muttered.

'I open the door?' Lucia asked.

'Yes.' With mounting anxiety, the two women entered the room.

All seemed normal – there were yellow roses in a vase on the bedside table and the pristine net curtain cut out the sun's glare. But then, no – not normal. 'Where are her things?' Joy wondered out loud. There were no slippers by the bed, no dressing gown hanging on the door hook; no sign that the room was inhabited.

Lucia gasped and pointed towards a note on the crisp white pillow.

Joy scooped it up and began to read with a rapidly beating heart. '"Dear Mrs Rossi, I am leaving because Mr Rossi is right – this house is too crowded for all of us."' Aghast, she handed the note to Tommy's mum, who read out Mildred's final sentence.

'"I will never forget you."' Lucia let the note drop to the floor then sat on the bed and sobbed.

Joy flung open the wardrobe door to confirm their worst fears. It was empty. Stooping to search under the bed, she saw that the girl's duffel bag was missing. 'This was no spur-of-the-moment thing,' she muttered. 'Mildred planned to do this.'

'Where does she go?' Lucia wailed. 'Who helps her now?'

Joy gave her answer. 'No one,' she whispered faintly. 'You, Tommy and I are the only friends Mildred has in the whole world.'

CHAPTER THIRTEEN

'The thing is . . . Mildred is expecting. I promised I wouldn't say a word, cross my heart and hope to die. ' Joy stood in Pearl's living room and stated the bald facts. After a day at work worrying herself sick over the girl's disappearance, she'd hurried to Empire Street to ask for advice.

'Hush – let me shut the door.' Pearl jumped up from her sewing machine, where she'd begun work on her competition skirt. 'Walls have ears,' she reminded Joy. 'Now, say it again – slowly.'

'Mildred has run away,' Joy repeated. 'Yesterday, while I was at work. She packed her bag and left a note.'

'And she's pregnant?'

'Yes. I couldn't tell you before – she swore me to secrecy.'

'Who else knows?'

'Only Tommy, Lucia and a few people at work. She has a mother who's as nasty as can be.'

'So Mildred won't have gone back home?'

Joy shook her head. 'Never in a million years. But where will she go instead? That's the question. She's all alone in the world – she has no one.' All night Joy had tossed and turned, trying to work out what to do.

Lying awake beside her, Tommy had suggested getting

in touch with Nurse Myers to find out if the girl had kept her appointment at the clinic. He'd gently reminded Joy that it had been Mildred's choice to do what she'd done. 'You're not to blame,' he'd murmured.

'But where did she get the idea that the house was too crowded?' Joy had thought back over the past few days. 'You don't suppose she overheard the three of us talking – me, you and your mother?'

'When we were explaining our reasons for buying a house?' Tommy had considered this most likely. 'But she can't have heard the part about us moving to King Street.'

'It was thoughtless of us not to include her.' Unable to forgive herself, Joy had sworn to leave no stone unturned until they discovered the desperate girl's whereabouts.

'I've come to you because your family knows everything that goes on in this town,' she explained to Pearl.

Pearl nodded. 'I'll ask Mum to keep her eyes and ears open. Customers flock to her fish and chip stall at this time of year; maybe she'll hear something. And Dad, too – he prides himself on keeping his ear to the ground.'

'Oh, thank you.' Joy took a deep breath. 'Mildred can't just have vanished into thin air.'

'I'll ask Ernie and his pals to keep a lookout too,' Pearl promised. 'And I'll mention it to my arcade regulars.'

'I know Mildred doesn't have much money.' Joy continued to paint a bleak picture. 'I doubt that she has enough to pay for a room in a boarding house or even for a train ticket out of town.'

'Poor girl – she must be at her wits' end.' Pearl couldn't imagine what it must be like to be pregnant, penniless and friendless. 'Have you told Sylvia about this?'

'Not yet.' For now Joy had done all she could. 'It's partly my fault,' she confessed as Pearl saw her to the door. 'I didn't include Mildred in my plans for the future. If I'd explained that Tommy and I were buying a house and that she could stay with Lucia for as long as she liked, this wouldn't have happened.'

'You weren't to know.' Trust Joy to take the blame. 'Honestly, you've been an angel as far as that girl is concerned. And try not to worry – we'll pull out all the stops.'

Joy hovered on the doorstep. 'It can't be that difficult, can it?'

'No; we'll find her sooner rather than later.' Pearl sent Joy off with a firm reassurance but deep down she felt less certain. She pictured the warren of narrow streets behind the market area and the miles of respectable boarding houses leading off from the prom, not to mention the huge seafront hotels, each with backyards containing large storage areas – ideal spots in which to lie low. 'Mildred's gone missing,' she informed her mother when she went through to the kitchen. 'It's all hands on deck to find her. Will you spread the word?'

'I'll do my best.' Maria raised a cautionary eyebrow. 'But I can't promise miracles. Let's face it, if the girl doesn't want to be found, Blackpool has a thousand places for her to hide.'

Mildred slipped through the crowds unnoticed on this, the end of her second day on the run. It had been easier than she'd anticipated, mingling with holidaymakers who flocked to the Golden Mile or sitting quietly in one of the wrought-iron and glass shelters overlooking the sea. She'd watched the comings and goings of cheerful families and groups of pensioners and had wandered the streets as far as Stanley Park without attracting attention. For a time on the Wednesday evening, when she'd basked in the setting sun close to the park's central fountain, in the shadow of an enormous statue of a lion and looking out over the boating lake, she'd almost let her troubles slip away amid the sweet scent of roses and the tinkling, chattering sounds of customers in the café nearby. Almost, but not quite – the queue for tea and cakes had reminded Mildred that she was hungry. Rather than spend the little money she had on food, she'd decided to wait until the park had emptied then gone from one litter bin to the next, picking out people's leftovers before a park attendant had shooed her away. Ashamed of her actions, Mildred had shoved the scraps into her duffel bag then scurried off.

Wandering back towards the town as daylight had faded, she'd gone in search of a place to sleep. By this time the crowds had thinned and she'd felt there was more chance of a solitary, aimless girl being noticed so she'd avoided the most frequented places such as cafés and pubs, lurking in side streets until the coast was clear. Finally she'd reached the seafront and watched as the fortune tellers' booths and stalls selling cheap knick-knacks were closed down. Weary to the bone, she'd risked discovery by swiftly crossing the prom when there was still a trickle of people taking late-night strolls.

Once on the deserted beach, Mildred had breathed a sigh of relief. The blackout had been in full force but as her eyes had grown accustomed to the gathering darkness she'd got her bearings. She was close to Central Pier, with the ramp leading from the lifeboat station to her left and a stack of deckchairs covered in tarpaulin to her right. Her feet had sunk in the warm, soft sand as she'd lifted a corner of the canvas. There'd been enough space to creep underneath and once she was certain that she hadn't been spotted she'd managed to squeeze between the folded deckchairs and find a place where she could lay her head. Eventually the final tram had passed and the prom had fallen silent. Mildred had drifted off to sleep to the rhythmical sound of waves lapping the shore.

Thursday had taken her out of town as far as the American base at Warton Aerodrome, past the factory where Wellington bombers were made. Mildred, who was mostly ignorant of military matters, was astonished to see huge sheds where men worked on noisy production lines that manufactured planes for the war effort. Even from a distance, the clanking of metal and the shunting of engine parts along conveyor belts had been deafening. Beyond the sheds she had spotted three runways and several vast hangars, dominated by a tall control tower. Behind that were row upon row of huts – the living quarters for American airmen stationed there.

She'd turned away from the base then drifted towards the sand dunes in search of peace and quiet, sitting for a while next to a concrete pillbox on the side sheltered from the wind. Then gnawing hunger had driven her back towards the town, through more rough dunes, using the Tower as a landmark until she'd reached the first of Blackpool's three famous piers. The tide was out and she'd stood beneath its enormous iron structure, feeling cold drops of salty water land on her upturned face.

What next? Losing heart, with the string of her duffel bag cutting into her shoulder, Mildred had approached the water's edge then gazed far out to sea. A solution had suggested itself – why not walk into the swirling, foaming water, knee deep then up to the waist, wading on until she was out of her depth? She had no idea whether or not she could swim. She'd imagined a strong wave washing her off her feet and carrying her out between the tall black legs of the pier. *How long would I float, staring up at the clear blue sky? How long before I was dragged under by a current too strong to resist?*

Shaking off the temptation to end it all, she'd forced herself to walk on along the beach, trying her best to merge with the colourful holiday crowd too busy enjoying themselves to pay her any attention. As on the previous day, she'd scavenged for scraps of food; this time from bins on the promenade, until a kind elderly woman in an old-fashioned grey dress with a high, lace-trimmed collar had noticed Mildred picking at the remains of fish and chips abandoned by their owner.

'Here.' The old lady, thin and delicate as a sparrow, had offered Mildred a sandwich from her small picnic basket. 'Help yourself – I made too many for one person.'

Sorely tempted, still Mildred had hesitated.

'Please,' the observant old lady had insisted. 'A girl in your condition must keep up her strength.'

No more had been said. Mildred had eaten her fill, shyly thanked the woman then moved on. Eventually, after the sun had set, she'd cautiously made her way to the same stack of deckchairs as the night before, only to find that on this occasion their owner had wrapped a heavy chain around his tarpaulin to secure the chairs beneath.

For the first time since she'd fled the safety and comfort of Rossi's Ice Cream Parlour, Mildred had broken down and cried. How would she ever get out of the mess she was in? How would she manage from one day to the next as the baby grew inside her? With only a vague idea of how many weeks would pass before she was ready to give birth, driven beyond any sense of shame, she wept bitter tears. Hardly caring who noticed her, she climbed the steps on to the prom then drifted on towards the Pleasure Beach where two employees, about to close up for the night, discussed their plans for the rest of the evening.

'Fancy a pint?' one asked.

'Aye, a quick one,' the other agreed. 'You go ahead; I forgot my jacket.'

As one man headed for the nearest pub, the other disappeared inside his ticket office. Still crying, Mildred seized her opportunity – she slipped through the gates and hid behind a billboard advertising the delights of the Fun House before the gatekeeper emerged. She heard the clang of the gates as he closed then locked them behind him.

Mildred crept out from behind the advertising hoarding. Alone at night in the strangely silent grounds, she was able to make out a giant Ferris wheel and a roller coaster silhouetted against a moonlit sky. She walked in a daze past the entrance to the sleek, stuccoed casino, ignoring silent dodgems to one side and waltzers to the other. Might she find shelter under the Fun House awning? No, she needed somewhere with more cover. So she wandered on until she came to the ghost train, where she discovered a row of miniature carriages stationed next to a narrow platform. Recoiling from garish paintings of ghosts and skeletons above the entrance to the tunnel, Mildred shivered. But the carriages offered protection from the wind, so this was where she chose to spend her second night without a roof.

She stepped into the one furthest from the grinning skulls then lay down on the hard wooden seat, using her duffel bag as a pillow. Though it was cramped and uncomfortable, it was the best she could do.

*

Vernon loved orderliness. His habit was to roll pairs of socks into neat balls and store them in a drawer that Sylvia had emptied for him. Insisting on doing his own ironing, his shirts were perfectly pressed before being hung in his side of the wardrobe and if she left dirty dishes by the side of the sink, he took it upon himself to wash them and put them away.

They reached the end of their first week together with scarcely a cross word. In the evenings there was laughter followed by nights of passion that amazed Sylvia and left her breathless and wanting more. He knew what pleased her and spoke tenderly as they made love, kept her close all night long.

So Saturday began with affectionate kisses before Vernon left for a meeting with his editor and Sylvia went next door to the studio to discuss with Cliff the latest developments in the build-up to their dance weekend.

'I'm still worried that we won't meet our target,' Cliff confessed. He was casually dressed in a checked shirt with fawn slacks held up by a smart brown leather belt. The outfit was finished off with a pair of brown suede brogues. When Sylvia arrived he was ready to set out for the market with Terry. 'We've handed out leaflets and put up posters in every possible place, but we need at least fifty more entries to break even, and your mother requires another seventy-five. What more can we do?'

'Take some leaflets to the market with you,' she suggested as she chose records for her first lesson. 'And we can dish some out at the Tower tonight. We're bound to scrape together more entries there.'

'Will do.' Buoyed by her optimism, Cliff took leaflets from the pile next to the gramophone.

Terry entered the studio, rivalling Cliff's dapper style

in a linen jacket and Panama hat. He greeted Sylvia with a light kiss on the cheek. 'How are you and Vernon rubbing along in the same billet? Still billing and cooing like a pair of turtle doves?'

'That's right – feel free to make fun of me.' Sylvia smiled and blushed. 'Do you really want to know how he's settled in?'

'We do,' Terry and Cliff chorused with sideways glances at one another.

'Well then, hear this – Vernon is perfect in every way.'

'Is that it?' Terry had hoped for solid titbits.

'Yes.' She was adamant. 'Now mind your own business and run along.'

It was time to prepare for her first lesson – Saturday was a busy day and soon she was up to her ears in progressive walks and whisks, kicks and flicks, spot turns and left finishes. Samba music filled the room and pupils wobbled and mixed up their right foot from their left. Still, sun streamed in through the plate-glass window and there were smiles and some minor successes. 'One – a – two!' Sylvia tapped out the rhythm. 'Left foot to the side, close with the right foot, transfer weight to the left foot. Very good, Marlene; excellent flexing of the knees.'

The difficult samba lesson was followed by the far easier jive. 'Remember to swing out then come back into hold with plenty of bounce,' she called to a large group of enthusiastic beginners ranging in age from twelve to fifty. 'There's no rule book – just improvise and enjoy yourselves.'

Taking the instructions to heart, her pupils experienced many a bump, mixed with cries of delight and triumphant yells before the lesson ended at twelve on the dot.

'Thanks, Miss Ellis – I enjoyed that and I learned a lot.'

‘Ta, miss – see you next week.’

Sylvia waited until the studio was empty before locking up. She reckoned she had time for a quick sandwich before the start of an afternoon session with locals Andrew and Margaret, who had also learned of the stiff competition they were to face in the shape of rivals from further afield. She slipped next door to the flat and was surprised to find Vernon sitting at the living-room table with his notepad open in front of him.

‘I didn’t expect you back.’ After planting a kiss on the top of his head, she went through to the kitchen. ‘Shall I make you a sandwich while I’m at it?’

‘Not for me, thanks.’ He scribbled down a few sentences. ‘Sam needs five hundred words from me by five o’clock on *For Whom the Bell Tolls* – it’s the new Gary Cooper film with Ingrid Bergman, based on a book by Hemingway.’

‘What did you make of it?’ she called through to him.

‘It’s damned good – especially Bergman.’

Sylvia came back into the room, sandwich in hand, glad of Vernon’s presence as he sat hunched over his notes, hard at work. How unbelievably lucky she was to have a sweetheart who was so talented and handsome.

‘Incidentally . . .’ Putting down his pencil, he patted his chair and invited her to perch next to him. ‘I found myself in another spot of bother this morning.’

‘In what way?’ Not suspecting that anything was amiss, she sat on the edge of the chair.

‘My editor had a go at me. It was bad enough when Cliff wittered on about my piece not appearing in the paper, but now it seems your dear mother has been on the telephone to Sam three times this week, demanding to know when he’s going to print it.’

Sylvia's stomach lurched. 'Oh dear; what exactly did she say?'

'I don't know, but whatever it was ruffled his feathers – "I'm the editor here and I'll print it when I damn well please," et cetera. He blamed me for not keeping Lorna in check until I pointed out that it was your job to do that.'

She swallowed hard to settle a rising sense of unease. 'I'm sorry – I'll have a word with her.'

'I'd appreciate that.' The sentence was dry and clipped. 'And make sure it doesn't happen again – I'm serious this time.' He got up and reached for his hat. 'I have to nip out for a while.'

'But I thought you had a deadline.' She glanced at his notebook and pencil, which he promptly picked up and shoved into his jacket pocket.

'I do, but I promised to meet Alfie and the gang at the Galleon this afternoon. I'd have invited you along but I knew you'd be busy teaching.' Setting his trilby at a jaunty angle, he kissed her quickly on the cheek. 'I'll probably drop in at the office afterwards and use one of the typewriters. Don't look so glum,' he cajoled. 'I'll see you later.'

'When? Where?' Her chest felt tight after she'd pulled away from the kiss.

'Half seven at the Tower. Put your glad rags on.' He was on his way out but he paused in the doorway. 'By the way, you won't mind if Alfie ends up back here with us?'

'How come?'

'Art's band is playing at the Hydro again this evening but they'll be finished by seven then Alfie fancies coming along to the Tower for another spin around the dance floor. I said he could kip on our sofa afterwards.'

Sylvia's face creased into a frown. 'I'm not sure that's allowed.'

'Oh, come on!' A smiling Vernon darted back into the room to embrace her. 'Alfie won't be any trouble, I promise. Anyway, I've already told him he could.'

The frown deepened as she looked at his face in close-up to learn that the smile she'd grown so used to on this occasion didn't reach his eyes. 'Mr Ibbotson might not like it.'

He kissed her forehead. 'Mr Ibbotson doesn't need to know, silly. We'll be quiet as mice on the way up. Come on, what do you say?' Without waiting for an answer, he released her and was on his way again. 'I'll take that as a yes,' he called over his shoulder as he skipped down the stairs two at a time. 'Remember, put on your best frock. And don't worry if I'm not there on the dot, go ahead without me and I'll join you as soon as I can.'

'My, you look a million dollars,' Pearl complimented Joe as she stood under the awning at the entrance to the Tower. She'd watched him approach from the direction of King Street wearing a double-breasted, pinstriped suit, with his hair neatly parted for once and slicked down with Brylcreem.

He received the compliment with a stiff smile. 'I thought I'd make the effort for once.'

'Girls will fall over themselves to partner you,' she assured him with a wink. She steered him to one side as a bus stopped to offload its passengers, who then made a beeline for the entrance.

'If you say so.' He pulled away and walked on into the foyer.

Pearl breezed after him and tapped him on the shoulder. 'Was it something I said?'

'Give it a rest, Pearl – I'm meeting someone.'

'Ooh, anyone I know?' Seeing that he wasn't in the

mood, she threw in a more serious question. 'I take it you've heard about Mildred?'

Joe nodded. 'She's gone missing.'

'Yes, no one's clapped eyes on her since Wednesday. We've got the whole town searching for her. I don't suppose you've heard anything?'

'Not a dickie bird.'

'The Rossis are desperate to have her back. We've promised to help track her down.'

'Can't help you there.' Joe spotted a couple of market pals. 'Sorry, I have to go.' And he melted into the swelling crowd without a backward glance.

Pearl turned with a shrug and resumed her place under the awning, seeking refuge from a fresh sea breeze since she was wearing only a pleated skirt teamed with a thin white blouse. Sylvia, Cliff and Terry soon joined her and took her mind off Joe's odd behaviour. They greeted each other with hugs and compliments. Pearl awarded Sylvia the best-dressed prize, saying she looked stunning in a dress with a silvery sequinned top and jade-green, frilled skirt.

'How long have you been standing here?' Sylvia darted a quick question at Pearl, followed by, 'Vernon's due any minute – have you seen him?'

Cliff puffed out his cheeks in exasperation. 'Good Lord, woman; calm down. She's been like this all day,' he explained to Pearl. 'I honestly don't know what's got into her.'

'Yes, she definitely has ants in her pants.' Terry backed him up.

'No sign of Vernon, as far as I'm aware.' Pearl hadn't seen Sylvia so on edge for a long time. 'But don't worry; if he said he'd be here, he'll keep his promise.'

'He only gave me a rough time,' Sylvia admitted. 'He had to call in at the office to write a review first.'

'So maybe it's taken longer than he thought.' Terry, who was intent on joining the queue at the bottom of the stairs, guided Cliff in that direction.

Sylvia and Pearl watched the two men walk on ahead of them. 'You go with them,' Sylvia suggested.

'No – I'm not in any rush.' In fact, Pearl had decided to wait for Errol's bus to arrive. 'Are you sure you're all right?' she checked.

'I'm fine. Why shouldn't I be?' Sylvia fidgeted with the contents of her handbag. 'Dash it – I forgot my lipstick.'

'You don't look fine.' Pearl suspected that a rash on Sylvia's neck and the fretful rummaging in her bag were signs that something was wrong. 'Come on – out with it.'

Snapping the clasp of her handbag shut with a sharp click, Sylvia tossed her head impatiently. 'Oh really, Pearl; why do you always stick your nose into other people's business? I've had a busy day and I've come here to enjoy myself, not to be given the third degree.'

'That's rich, coming from you.' Pearl watched her friend stalk off, sequins glinting under the bright lights, blonde ponytail swinging. *Jeepers, creepers – sorry I asked!* The evening had got off to a bad start – fingers crossed it would get better.

She was rescued from the doldrums by the surprise appearance of Joy in one of her lovely ballroom outfits – the cream one with an embroidered bodice and knee-length, flowing skirt. 'I thought you weren't coming,' she began.

'I changed my mind.' Originally Joy had planned to stay in to keep Lucia company. Tommy was working and Joy was still eaten up with worry over Mildred, having spent every spare moment searching for her. She'd checked obvious places first – yards behind the big hotels, café buildings at the ends of the piers, even the changing cubicles at the open-air baths, and had gone as far as Stanley Park, thinking that Mildred might have taken refuge in one of the many shelters there. All for nothing – it seemed as if the girl truly had vanished into thin air.

Tonight it had been Lucia who had shooed Joy out of the house with, 'Go – dance with friends – be happy!' She had refused to take no for an answer, helping to choose Joy's dress and sending her off with repeated *ciao*s and a cheerful wave. 'Or rather, Tommy's mother changed my mind for me,' she added with a smile. 'She insisted it would do me good.'

'She's right.' There was still no sign of the GI bus and an increasingly chilly Pearl had grown tired of waiting. 'Shall we go in?' Linking arms, they tagged on to the end of the queue.

Half an hour later, with tickets in hand, they entered the ballroom in time to see the dramatic raising of the crimson curtain and the appearance on stage of a five-piece band, given a big build-up by an MC in a white dinner jacket and black dickie bow. 'Ladies and gentlemen, please welcome the one and only Jack Noble Dance Band, straight from the Astoria Ballroom in London's West End!'

'You don't say!' Pearl dragged Joy from their table under the balcony. Jack Noble was a well-known band leader who rarely travelled this far north. He played swing music, led by a saxophone and two trombones, with a jazz pianist and a drummer to complete the line-up. 'Sylvia, what are you waiting for?' she cried as she and Joy rushed by.

'Care to dance?' Joe stepped in to offer Sylvia his hand.

She'd kept her eyes peeled for Vernon for long enough and there was still no sign of him. 'Yes, why not?'

Soon they were on the floor and jiving away like there was no tomorrow. The music was fast, the mood buoyant.

'Watch your step, Sylvia.' On the part of the floor closest to the stage Eddie side-stepped to avoid her and Joe, who had almost crashed into him and Mavis.

'Sorry; I wasn't looking where I was going.' She righted herself then carried on dancing – off into a space beneath a huge loudspeaker where the insistent beat of 'Boogie Woogie Bugle Boy' almost deafened her and Joe and pushed them into evermore extravagant moves.

'I wonder where the man of the moment has got to,' Mavis commented with a wry grin as Sylvia shimmied and kicked. Every time Eddie encountered his old flame she noticed a cloud on their generally sunny horizon – he would frown and give an awkward cough and for a few minutes he would remain serious, seeming to shut her out in a way Mavis couldn't put her finger on. True to form, he ignored her remark and suggested they sit out the rest of the dance.

Meanwhile, a couple of uniformed Royal Navy lads, already well oiled after downing several pints at the Queen's Arms, squeezed between Pearl and Joy. 'You don't mind if we join you?' One grinned broadly as he seized Pearl's hands, pulled her clumsily towards him then swung her out.

'A pair of bobby-dazzlers like you need two strong chaps to swing you around the dance floor.' The second man leered at Joy as he leaned forward and shook his shoulders, clicking his fingers in time to the music.

'Do you mind?' Pearl was having none of it. She broke

away then dragged Joy free before heading towards the bar, where Terry and Cliff offered to buy them a lemonade apiece. 'Bloomin' cheek!' she exclaimed.

Terry laughed. 'Those two not your cup of tea?' he guessed.

'They reeked of booze.' Pearl's face was flushed and animated.

'And they couldn't dance for toffee,' Joy added.

For the next few minutes, they were happy to stay by the bar, listening to the band move on from the boogie-woogie number to Benny Goodman's 'Jungle Blues' then on to a smooth Glenn Miller tune that allowed couples to go into ballroom hold.

'This was always one of my favourite bands.' Cliff sang the band leader's praises to Pearl. 'I knew Jack back in the day.'

'He knew everyone "back in the day".' Terry gave Joy a playful nudge as the GI contingent put in a late appearance and Pearl shot off to join them. 'That's the last we'll see of her for the rest of the night,' he predicted.

Sure enough, Pearl spent the next few dances running through complicated jive moves with Errol. The floor was too crowded to allow cartwheels and leapfrogs, but they rehearsed a lift or two, drawing admiring glances from other dancers, who stepped back to allow them more space in the middle of the floor. Errol lifted Pearl with ease, slinging her over his shoulder as he turned on the spot then lowering her, without missing a beat.

'Show-offs,' Joe grumbled to Sylvia after they'd retreated to the bar area. 'Pearl ought to know better.'

'Don't be so quick to judge.' The knot of anxiety in Sylvia's stomach had tightened. Where on earth had Vernon got to? 'I thought the same until I learned what

Pearl's going through on the quiet.' The sentence was hardly out of her mouth before she spotted him. He'd come in through a door used by staff at the side of the stage and he wasn't alone. With him were Alfie Matthews and Rosie Johnson.

'Blimey; that's what you call making an entrance.' Joe's gaze followed Sylvia's, landing on the woman's tight black dress, hour-glass figure and cascade of blonde curls.

Sylvia watched as Vernon collared the MC, who listened then nodded before stepping up on to the stage and having a word in Jack Noble's ear. Meanwhile, the glamour girl soaked up countless admiring glances, head to one side, smiling. As soon as Vernon spotted Sylvia at the bar, he beckoned her across and greeted her with a quick kiss on the cheek.

'You already know Alfie; he'll be coming back to our place later on,' he reminded her. 'And of course you remember Rosie, the singer in Art's band.' The hurried introduction was interrupted by the MC, who whisked the newcomer on to the stage. She raised her tight skirt almost to thigh level in order to negotiate the stairs. 'Watch and learn.' Vernon winked at Sylvia.

'I thought you said she wasn't your type.' Sylvia immediately regretted her peevish reminder and was relieved when Vernon ignored it.

He casually offered Alfie a cigarette. 'Did I also mention her voice? Pin back your ears and listen to this.'

Removing a microphone from its stand, Rosie tapped it to make sure it was live. Her actions were smooth and unhurried as she took centre stage, waiting for the band to complete the introductory bars to 'Swing Low, Sweet Chariot', a recently recorded Bing Crosby number. When she opened her mouth, the voice that emerged was sweet and mellow, smooth as honey. Throwing back her head and swaying her shoulders as she pressed her lips to the microphone, the sight and the sound were mesmerizing. Many couples on the floor broke out of hold and simply listened.

'"Swing low, sweet chariot, coming for to carry me home."' Transfixed by the pure sound, Sylvia paid little attention to lyrics about bands of angels and Jesus washing away sins. She experienced a peculiar sensation of fading into invisibility beside the vision of loveliness onstage.

Vernon stared at Rosie through a cloud of blue cigarette smoke. He ignored something that Alfie said to him and when the song had ended he joined in with the wave of applause and a call for more that echoed around the ballroom. 'See?' he said, sidling up to Sylvia and sliding an arm around her waist. 'How lucky are you to have a singer like her on board? With Rosie Johnson to draw in the crowds, your weekend will be a sure-fire hit.'

CHAPTER FOURTEEN

Walking along the prom late on Saturday night, Mildred heard strains of music coming from the Tower Ballroom. She felt a sharp pang of envy as she imagined girls dancing away their cares under bright lights in swirling skirts and sparkly shoes, with glimpses of petticoat and the heady scent of sweet perfume in the air. A cold mist had blown in off the sea and created a darkness so thick that she was scarcely able to find her way down on to the beach to investigate the stack of deckchairs where she'd spent Wednesday night. But no; the security-conscious owner had padlocked his property once more.

So Mildred wandered on, ghost-like, towards South Pier until she came to the open-air baths, a mere stone's throw from Rossi's Ice Cream Parlour. Drawn to the curved white facade, she slowly made her way towards its grand entrance then crept between tall columns into dark shadows, only to find that others had sought shelter here before her.

'No vacancies.' A hoarse male voice barked out a sarcastic warning, accompanied by a clink of bottles and the strong smell of tobacco smoke and alcohol.

Startled, Mildred retreated on to the broad pavement.

'Only kidding.' It was a cackle this time, followed by a thick, phlegmy cough.

'Take no notice.' A second voice, seemingly belonging to a younger man, invited her to join them. 'Can you spare a fag, love?'

Mildred shivered. 'Sorry, I don't smoke.' As her eyes grew accustomed to the gloom, she made out half a dozen huddled forms close to the turnstiles allowing entry into the baths.

The second man quickly lost interest while a third got to his feet and lurched towards Mildred. He was wearing a tattered army greatcoat that hung loose over an emaciated frame. 'What's a nice girl like you—' Without bothering to finish his sentence, he made a clumsy lunge in her direction.

She gasped then ran, fleeing all the way to South Pier until she was sure she wasn't being followed. Out of breath and terrified, she slumped against a tall brick pillar. What should she do now? Was nowhere safe? Alert to every sound, she picked up the ripple of water and realized that she must have reached the entrance to a paddling pool that she'd been able to see from the Rossis' café. It was a place where children sailed toy boats and where there was a stone shelter on one side, hopefully unoccupied. Sure enough, it was deserted – an ideal place for Mildred to spend her fourth night on the run.

Sylvia left the flat while Vernon was still fast asleep. Creeping out of the bedroom, she held her breath as she edged past Alfie, who lay sprawled on the sofa under an eiderdown that Vernon had provided.

Once out of the house, she took a few seconds to gather herself and tie a silk headscarf under her chin. The air was damp and she had a long walk to King Alfred Street ahead of her. She was annoyed with herself. Why had she agreed to let Vernon's friend stay overnight? Surely he could have shared the taxi to Lytham that Rosie had ordered at the end of the evening?

'We're playing at the Clifftop Hotel tomorrow,' Rosie had announced as the group – Rosie, Vernon, Alfie and Sylvia – had parted company outside the ballroom. Her guest spot with the Jack Noble Band had gone down a storm and people kept coming up to congratulate her. 'Art has booked a room for me there as part of the deal, so see you later, alligators!' With a cheery wiggle of her fingertips, she'd stepped into the taxi and sailed away.

When Sylvia had pulled Vernon to one side to ask why Alfie hadn't gone with her, Vernon had shrugged it off with, 'Rosie makes things up. Who knows where she's heading in that taxi, but you can bet it's not the Clifftop.'

Alfie had come back to Sylvia's flat as arranged and the two men had carried on drinking into the small hours. So much for them promising to tiptoe around the place to avoid alerting Mr Ibbotson. They'd been too drunk to do any such thing and the elderly tobacconist had sent his lad to knock on her door and ask for them to keep the noise down.

Pushing this incident firmly to one side, Sylvia stepped out along North View Parade, her attention fixed on the awkward visit she was about to pay to her mother. Keen to avoid confrontation, she planned her strategy carefully. She would arrive unannounced and cheerfully accept the tea and toast that would inevitably be forced on her. Together they would study the latest lists of entries for their dance weekend, which would hopefully include more competitors from further afield. This would provide a natural lead-in to what Sylvia really wanted to discuss.

She found her mother in the flat above the dance studio, already fully made up and coiffed and apparently irritated by her daughter's unexpected visit. The room was immaculate as usual – every cushion plumped up, every ornament and dance trophy perfectly positioned. Sylvia tried to ignore several copies of the *Gazette* on the coffee table but Lorna noticed her eyes flick towards them then away again.

'Quite,' she said in a frosty tone.

'Quite what?' Sylvia retorted.

'There's been no article about our competition, as you very well know.'

'No, not yet.' Damn; there was a danger of them plunging straight in after all. 'Shall I put the kettle on?'

'We can have tea later – don't try to change the subject.' Lorna picked up one of the newspapers. 'Earlier this week I took the trouble to go through the latest editions with a fine-tooth comb before making a telephone call and demanding to speak to Mr Pearson, the editor. The woman who answered was less than helpful.'

'I can imagine,' Sylvia said under her breath, imagining receptionist Angela's frosty response.

'On the first occasion she insisted that Mr Pearson was busy and that I must try again later, which I did. This time she told me that he was out of the office but that I might leave a message if I so wished. Well, you know me, dear – I informed her that her response was unsatisfactory, as was the fact that we were still waiting for Vernon King's article to appear. Apparently, my message was not passed on so I was obliged to make a third telephone call—'

'Mother, stop,' Sylvia pleaded as she sank on to the sofa. 'I know all of this and it's the reason that I'm here. Vernon asked me to come.'

Lorna breathed in sharply before crossing the room to stare out of the window. 'I see.'

'He said I should point out that no amount of pestering will make Sam Pearson print the article before he sees fit.'

'Pestering?' The word brought a frown to Lorna's face. 'As I see it, my request to speak with the editor was perfectly reasonable. I simply wished to convince Mr Pearson that three weeks before the event is the perfect time to generate maximum interest. Besides, it might be that Vernon's article had been overlooked; in which case, a gentle reminder would not go amiss.'

Again Sylvia begged her mother to stop talking. 'You don't need to justify making the calls,' she said faintly. 'I happen to agree.'

'You do?' Lorna turned her head sharply in her daughter's direction. 'But Vernon doesn't?'

'He assures me that it's more complicated.'

'In what way?'

'He says it depends on what else is happening in the entertainment world and whether or not there's room for our article. We're at the height of the summer season so there's plenty going on – tea dances, beauty pageants, open-air concerts in Stanley Park, et cetera.'

Lorna sat down next to Sylvia. 'But surely Vernon has some influence over what's given priority?'

'He says not,' Sylvia said limply. 'You saw for yourself how difficult it is to get through to Sam Pearson.'

'Oh dear; I seem to have put my foot in it.' Once the realization had sunk in, Lorna sounded apologetic. 'I hope it didn't lead to an argument.'

'Between me and Vernon? No, not at all.' The brittle reply led to a short silence that Sylvia ended with, 'We have to take his word for it that the article will appear in the next few days.'

'Forgive me.' Lorna patted Sylvia's hand. 'It's hard not to fret, knowing what a difference it will make. As it is, I lie awake at night worrying what will happen if our competition turns out to be a failure. I have no idea how I would pay off the debt.'

'And I'm sorry, too. I'm the one who came to you with the grand scheme – Spanish Hall, a live band, thousands of leaflets, big posters everywhere – who convinced you to take the risk in the first place.'

'And it may yet pay off.' Lorna emerged from under her grey cloud, determined to look on the bright side. 'I'll make some further telephone calls – this time to colleagues at the Imperial Society, encouraging them to spread the word. We can also place advertisements in *Dancing Times* and other specialist magazines. After all, why rely on one solitary article in the *Blackpool Gazette*?'

'That's right.' Sylvia sounded unconvinced.

'Then chin up, dear.' Giving her daughter's hand a second light pat, Lorna went off to the kitchen to make tea. When she returned with the tray she saw that Sylvia was staring blankly into space. 'You look tired,' she remarked as she poured from the pot. 'I hope you're not overdoing it.'

Sylvia's eyelids flickered shut. 'I'm all right.' She sighed. 'I stayed up late last night with Vernon and a pal of his from Art Richardson's band.'

'And you liked Vernon's friend?'

'Well enough. His name's Alfie Matthews. He's quite quiet – unlike the band's singer, Rosie Johnson, who I also bumped into last night.'

'Ah!' Lorna sipped her tea.

'Yes; "Ah!"' Sylvia smiled faintly. 'She had all the men chasing after her, and who can blame them?'

'I see.'

'You'll find out for yourself soon enough, though even Art Richardson warned me that she's not reliable. She may not turn up for rehearsal or even for the event itself.'

'I hope you're not comparing yourself with her,' Lorna said softly, though she knew that this was exactly what her daughter was doing. 'In my experience, girl singers love to hog the limelight but seldom have the discipline to succeed in other areas. Take our world of competition dance, for instance – the hours of training, the attention to detail, the endless repetition needed to reach perfection – which you, my dear, have always had, ever since you were little.'

'Thank you for that.' Sylvia gave her mother's hand a grateful squeeze.

Lorna returned it with added emphasis. 'I wish you realized how talented you are,' she murmured, 'and how proud I am of you.'

Sylvia's eyes opened wide in astonishment. Such praise from her mother was rare.

'I mean it – even though you abandoned the waltz and the quickstep in favour of all that vulgar swinging out, bouncing and gyrating.' Lorna's humorous challenge made Sylvia smile. 'There – that's better.'

'The thing is, Mother, Vernon was keen to sing Rosie's praises to me. I found that hard to swallow.'

'Naturally.' Lorna considered what advice to offer. 'But try not to show that you're jealous and please don't dwell on it – men are often drawn to showy women like this Rosie person, but it's seldom more than skin deep.'

'I'll try.' Sylvia accepted her mother's suggestion with a sigh of relief.

'Now, what do you say to taking a trot down memory lane with me?'

'What do you mean?' Sylvia watched her mother stand up and smooth her skirt in a businesslike way then check her appearance in the mirror over the mantelpiece.

'Why not join me in the studio? Tommy and Joy have booked a lesson, along with several other entrants in our competition; all Viennese waltz specialists.'

'Yes, why not?' It had been a long time since Sylvia had assisted her mother. 'I haven't had a chance to chat with Joy recently – we've both been too busy.'

'There'll be no time for chatting,' Lorna warned as she led the way downstairs. 'This morning is all about heel leads, forward changes and reverse turns, with eyes firmly on the top prize.'

'I didn't know that you and Mavis would be here,' Sylvia informed Eddie after the waltz lesson was over and Eddie's partner had dashed away on an urgent errand for her mother.

'If you'd known would you have stayed away?'

'Of course not,' she said sharply.

'So how did Mavis and I do?' he prompted. 'Did you spot any glaring mistakes?'

'Only one or two mistimed rise-and-falls towards the end of your routine – otherwise top marks.' How strange it was to act as if there had never been anything between herself and Eddie; Sylvia wasn't used to it, whereas he seemed to have closed the door on their past and be perfectly at ease. 'You're still not quite on a par with Tommy and Joy, though,' she teased.

'Steady on!' he protested as he stooped to tie his laces. 'I'm sorry I asked.' They were in the alcove next to the piano where pupils stored their outdoor clothes. Lorna stood by the studio door talking to two competition entrants who Sylvia didn't know. Joy and Tommy had left at the same time as Mavis, intent on visiting the house on King Street that they were in the process of buying. 'Do I detect a certain bias?'

'Certainly not.' Sylvia defended her opinion with a toss of her head. 'Tommy swings into the first beat of each bar with more gusto than you and Mavis's head position requires a slight adjustment.'

Eddie nodded. 'More gusto,' he repeated with a wry smile. 'The story of my life, eh?'

'If you say so.' Wondering why the twinge of regret that she experienced in Eddie's presence felt sharper than usual, she was about to turn away.

'This is your jacket, isn't it?' Ever the gentleman, he held it ready for her to slip on. 'By the way, what did you make of Rosie Johnson's performance last night?'

Sylvia slid her arms into the sleeves of her jacket without immediately giving an answer. That woman's name was on everyone's lips!

'She's quite something, isn't she?' Eddie added.

Sylvia gave a quick shrug. 'Everyone seemed to think so. I didn't know you were there.'

'Yes you did – you and Joe almost upskittled Mavis and me during the jive.'

'Ah yes; come to think of it.' Picking up her handbag, she hurried off, scarcely pausing to say goodbye to her mother.

Eddie watched her go. He hadn't had time to make his point about Rosie Johnson's flighty reputation – the real reason for mentioning her name – and perhaps this was just as well. After all, Sylvia was an adult and must fend for herself, even though it had pained him to see how Vernon King had fawned over the singer and ignored Sylvia.

'Goodbye, Edward dear.' Lorna saw that he was the last to leave the studio. 'And thank you.'

'For what?'

'For being a perfect gentleman,' she said softly and sincerely. 'I only wish there were more like you in this harsh and uncertain world.'

'There's an awful lot to do.' Joy stood in the front room of what was to be their house on King Street. The wallpaper was peeling and there was a heap of soot in the hearth from the unswept chimney. The rooms were still lit by gas and there was no hot water supply, since the previous owner had been elderly and without the means to modernize. Everywhere smelt damp.

'Nothing that we can't learn to do ourselves.' Tommy tried not to show that his shiny optimism had been dented on this their first real look around. 'I'll borrow a manual about electrics from the library; how hard can it be?'

'And I'll pick up a paintbrush and give everywhere a lick of whitewash. We'll learn as we go along.' It wasn't in either of their natures to be defeated before they'd even begun. Still, Joy was daunted by the scale of the task. She rested her head on Tommy's shoulder. 'Perhaps Joe will muck in.'

'Yes and I'll ask around at the circus to see if there are any volunteers there.'

'Just don't mention it to Ted and Leo,' she said with a smile. 'Those two would be squirting water everywhere, crashing into things and tripping over their own big feet.'

Tommy laughed. 'I meant one of the lighting men. They could help me to wire the place.'

'I know you did.' She hugged him hard. 'Wherever will

we find the time?' she wondered. Increasingly this was the one thing she felt desperately short of – time to continue the search for Mildred, time to see friends, time to pursue her passion for ballroom dancing.

Tommy hugged her back. 'I've been thinking.'

'Please don't,' she teased.

'I could ask my boss Jerry Martin if I can alter my shifts at work – do matinee and evening performances on Sunday through to Thursday; ten shifts per week, leaving me free to do up the house on Fridays and Saturdays.'

'And what if I could rearrange my working hours, too?' There was a faint possibility that Joy could cut back to four days a week in the office and put Alan in charge for the fifth day. 'I'd have to discuss it with George and promise to catch up on paperwork at home if I fell behind.'

Tommy tightened his embrace. 'That might work.' His heart brimmed over with tenderness for the girl he'd married. 'We'll *make* it work,' he vowed. 'When we set our minds on something there's no stopping us.'

They wandered arm in arm into the kitchen with its old-fashioned cooking range then Tommy led her upstairs to what would be their bedroom, at present empty of furniture, with more soot in the grate, more peeling paper and the gaslight fitting hanging loose on the wall. 'Picture it once it's done up,' he whispered.

She closed her eyes to visualize pretty floral wallpaper, soft, warm rugs, a double bed where she would lie with Tommy and feel certain that she was the luckiest woman in the world.

Pearl had set her mind on finding out what was wrong with Joe.

'What do you mean, he was off with you?' Maria

was busy making Sunday breakfast for Henry, the only member of the household to have bacon and eggs while the rest had to make do with toast and dripping.

Pearl's feet still ached from jiving with Errol the night before. 'I think I've pulled a muscle in my leg,' she complained as Elsie scraped the last of the butter from the dish and Wilf protested.

'I said, what do you mean, Joe was off?' Maria refused to be fobbed off.

'He ignored me all night, which is not like him. I'll call at his house on my way to the arcade to find out why.'

'Perhaps he was just in a bad mood.'

'Joe's never in a bad mood.' Pearl reached for her jacket. 'He was perfectly fine with everyone else. I noticed him dancing with Sylvia before Vernon arrived.'

Maria turned two rashers of bacon in the frying pan. 'Shout up to your father on the way out,' she called after Pearl. 'Tell him his breakfast's ready.'

Pearl left the house clutching a half-eaten piece of toast. Empire Street was quiet at this time on a Sunday morning, which was how she liked it. The doors of the Black Horse were closed and many of the blinds in neighbouring houses were still down. As usual, she kept her eyes fixed on the Tower and didn't cross the road until she was safely past the entrance to Mason's Yard – a habit she'd developed ever since the awful incident that she didn't like to talk about. Once on the market square, she slowed her pace and thought out what she would say when Joe answered her knock. She had ten minutes at the most to sort things out.

'Yes?' He took an age to come to the door with his hair ruffled from sleep and his collarless shirt unbuttoned. When he saw Pearl he took an involuntary step back.

'What have I done wrong?' Straight to the point, demanding an answer.

'What time is it?' he muttered.

'Time you were up. I want to know why you gave me the cold shoulder last night – come on; be honest.'

'Give me a break, Pearl.' Joe stood his ground as she barged past. 'It's too early in the morning to be having this conversation.'

She went ahead into the living room, which Joe kept in good order – his books and magazines carefully arranged on a shelf next to his football programmes, hearth neatly swept, the sofa of his modern three-piece suite carefully covered with a blanket to keep it clean. 'I mean it, Joe; I don't like it when we argue.'

'We're not arguing,' he muttered.

'Yes, we are. I want to know what I've done to put your back up.'

He stayed by the door, hands thrust deep into his pockets, eyeing Pearl with open hostility. 'You know what you've done.'

'I don't have the faintest idea,' she protested. 'Tell me.'

She was asking for it so Joe went in all guns blazing. 'You and your Yank, that's what!'

Not this again! 'For heaven's sake, Joe – how often do I have to explain to people? Errol is not *my* Yank, he's just my dance partner. Anyway, what was I meant to do: hide myself away behind closed doors, waiting for news of my husband's next home leave and writing letters to him, waiting and writing and all the time in agony over where Bernie was and what he was having to face?'

'I'm not saying that. But honestly, Pearl, do you and the Yank have to jive together every chance you get? Why not dance with someone else once in a while?'

'Because we've entered Sylvia's competition so we have to rehearse. I'll say it again – Errol is my dance partner; nothing else.'

'It didn't look like that to me.' Joe spat out the words. 'Not when I saw you two laughing and cosying up.'

She smarted under the sting of his rebuke. 'When? Where?'

'Outside the Tower on Wednesday night. You didn't see me but I saw you.'

'And why shouldn't Errol and I laugh and have a joke together? He's my friend, the same as you are.' A pleading note crept into Pearl's voice.

Joe refused to listen. 'The whole town is talking. I hear my customers bad-mouthing you behind your back, sniggering over how much time you two spend together. Bernie is my best pal, remember – all that nasty gossip leaves a bad taste. And then when I saw you with my own eyes—' He broke off abruptly with a gesture of disgust.

'Then what?' Pearl demanded. Her face was burning, her heart racing.

'When I saw you together on Wednesday it was the final straw.' Joe delivered the knockout punch. 'That was it; I wrote Bernie a letter.'

Pearl felt a chasm open up beneath her feet. She tumbled through darkness, clutching thin air and still falling.

'I told him there was something off about the way you've been carrying on behind his back, said he deserved to know.'

'How could you?' she breathed. Still falling, still clutching at nothingness.

'I did it because Bernie is out there, sodding well risking his life for his country, that's why. And you're married to him and should know better.'

'Oh!' She sank on to the sofa and covered her face with her hands.

'Get up.' Joe roughly seized her arm and pulled her to her feet. 'What was I supposed to do – carry on as if nothing was the matter? He's my pal, I tell you.'

Pearl swayed then pulled free. 'You're wrong – nothing's happened between Errol and me,' she wailed.

Joe put his hands over his ears to shut out her excuses.

'Why didn't you tackle me about it to my face before you wrote to Bernie?' She prised his hands from his head. 'There's more to this than you know; much more.'

'Go on; I'm listening,' he grunted.

'The truth is that I was attacked late at night by three GIs and it was Errol who saved me.' Sobs broke from her as she experienced yet again the stomach-churning sensation that accompanied every attempt to explain. 'Sylvia got the wrong idea too but once I gave her the facts, she understood.'

'Attacked?' Joe repeated.

'Outside Mason's Yard. It was dark, no one else was around. Two stood guard while the third pushed me down on the ground. He was too strong – I couldn't fight him off. You can guess what would have happened if Errol hadn't come along.'

'Good Lord!' Joe sat her down on the sofa. 'So why keep this to yourself?'

Pearl dug deep for the truth. 'Because I didn't want anyone to pity me – I'm Pearl Scott, the life and soul of the party, the girl who makes jokes and loves to dance and always speaks what's on her mind, not some pathetic ninny you have to feel sorry for.' She slumped exhausted against the back of Joe's sofa. 'There – now you know why Errol is the best friend a girl could have.'

'Does Bernie know this?'

She nodded. 'I told him during his last home leave.'

'Damn, damn, damn!' Joe paced around the room. 'If only you'd let me in on it.' He'd written the letter, kept it short and to the point.

Dear Bernie, There's something you ought to know. Brace yourself. Pearl's been carrying on behind your back with a GI sergeant from the Warton base. They make no effort to hide their affair; as a matter of fact they've entered a big dance competition together. Sorry to be the bearer of bad news, chum. It's up to you what you do next. All the best from your pal, Joe.

He'd posted it first thing Thursday morning. God knew how long it would take to reach him.

Still Pearl drifted down through darkness, falling less quickly but nonetheless unable to stop herself. She prayed to God that Joe's letter would be held up by the censors or get stuck in the postal system – anything to give her some breathing space, because once Bernie had received Joe's letter there was no way back up into daylight and never would be, ever again.

CHAPTER FIFTEEN

'Don't worry – I was just leaving.' Alfie winked at Sylvia as she entered her flat after her visit to her mother's. He picked up his jacket from the back of the sofa and slung it over his shoulder. 'I have to see a man about a dog.'

Hearing voices as she'd come up the stairs, her heart had sunk. She'd recognized the visitor's light, lilting tone and was sure that Rosie's name had been mentioned followed by Vernon's throaty laugh. But when she'd opened the door they'd suddenly gone quiet and acted as if they were busy: Vernon with some papers on the table by the window and Alfie with collecting his belongings.

'Don't believe a word,' Vernon quipped. 'He can't stand dogs, can you, Alfie boy?'

His friend didn't linger. 'Later,' he called over his shoulder as he closed the door behind him.

'And how's the girl of my dreams?' Vernon embraced Sylvia and landed light kisses on her cheeks and neck. 'You smell nice; what perfume is that?'

'It's not perfume, it's soap. Have you arranged to see Alfie later on?'

'What makes you think that?' More kisses, a tighter embrace.

'He said as much on his way out.' She disentangled herself. 'I was wondering, that's all.'

'No firm arrangement.' Vernon shrugged and went back to his papers. 'I mentioned I might drop in at the Clifftop this afternoon if I have time. They're playing there this evening, remember? Art sent a message via Alfie asking if I'd be up to writing a short review for tomorrow's *Gazette*. It's work again, so I doubt you'd be interested.'

'But maybe I would,' she argued. 'A pleasant tea dance on a sunny Sunday evening – I can think of worse things.'

Vernon shook his head. 'The fact is, I'll be holed up in a corner jotting down notes about the play-list, and so on, while you, my gorgeous girl, would be fending off hordes of chaps wanting to waltz you round the dance floor. I'd have to be made of stone to sit by and watch that happen.'

Still she pushed to be included. 'Surely I could sit quietly in the corner with you and watch the band?'

'Drop it, will you? I don't even know if I'll bother going.' He shuffled the papers into a neat pile. 'Where've you been, anyway?'

'To see my mother, as you asked. You were still asleep – I didn't want to wake you.'

'Long visit,' he muttered under his breath.

'We had the chat about your article then I stayed on to help her with a waltz class.'

'Hmmm. How did the "chat" go?'

'You can be sure that Mother won't telephone your editor again. But the fact remains, we're struggling to attract entries.' Keeping her answer brief, Sylvia went through to the bedroom where she began to change out of her blouse and trousers into her pink cotton dress.

Vernon leaned against the doorpost to watch her undress. 'I take it Lorna still thinks that I'm responsible?'

'She did at first,' she conceded, 'until I put her straight.'

'That's all right then.' He crept up behind her and nuzzled the back of her neck.

'Mother's worried, that's all.' Sylvia held on to the dress as Vernon turned her round then held her close.

'What's the hurry?' The dress fell to the floor as he backed her towards the bed, stroking her neck with the side of his thumb then letting his hand slide down over her breasts. 'You do something to me every time,' he whispered in her ear. 'I swear I can't help myself.'

She loved that low whisper of his and the touch of his lips. Lacking the will to resist, she sank on to the bed and gave herself up to him, arching her back to let him unfasten her bra, feeling the straps slip from her shoulders then the warm weight of him on top of her, pressing her down, kissing her all over until she swooned.

When it was over she lay for a long time, eyes closed, breathing in the smoke of Vernon's cigarette, feeling desired and safe. 'Mother gave me a piece of advice about Rosie Johnson,' she confided out of the blue, doing the very thing that Lorna had warned her against.

'Oh?' Vernon's lips popped softly as he practised making smoke rings. 'Do go on.'

'It seems silly looking back, but it did bother me at the time.'

'What did?' he asked lazily.

I told Mother that you seemed to have changed your mind about Rosie – at first you'd said she wasn't your type.'

'Did I?'

'Yes, but last night at the Tower you arrived with her and Alfie, and I have to admit that I felt left out.'

'Yes, that's very silly.' Vernon sat up then swung his legs

over the side of the bed. 'Anyway, you're wrong – I never said Rosie wasn't my type.'

'Yes, you did. I remember the conversation word for word. You said she was brassy.'

'No, it would be a stupid thing for me to say – one look at her and you realize that Rosie is every man's type.' Stubbing out his cigarette, he lay back down next to Sylvia and rested his arm across her chest. 'Sometimes I haven't the faintest clue what goes on inside that pretty little head. You come out with this guff about Rosie without any evidence to back it up.'

His arm felt heavy across her body and the smell of nicotine lingered on his fingers. 'But I can't have made it up.'

'Yes, that's exactly what you did.' Vernon spoke as if it was a trivial point that nonetheless needed clearing up. 'It's happened before – a few times.'

'When?' Sylvia did her best to ignore the alarm bells that had begun to jangle.

'Just small things like putting my clothes into drawers without telling me then forgetting you'd done it or insisting that we'd arranged to meet when we hadn't . . . Don't worry about it; I know you've got a lot on your mind.'

Sylvia slid sideways to free herself then drew her knees to her chest and pulled the sheet around her. 'I'm sorry,' she breathed.

'I said not to worry.' Vernon reached for his trousers. 'It's only a teeny-weeny problem. This happens when couples decide to move in together; you get to see each other warts and all.'

She hugged her knees to stop herself from shaking.

'I know you don't want to admit to warts,' he acknowledged with his trademark smile. 'You, my love, want the never-ending fantasy: the glass slipper, the ball gown, the glass carriage. But let's face it, that's not how it works.'

'I know,' she whispered. 'I've said I'm sorry.'

Stooping to kiss the top of her head, he spoke more briskly as he pulled on his shirt. 'Now I really do have to see a man about a dog, or rather, several dogs at the circus.'

A miserable, numb feeling had crept over her. 'More work?' she murmured.

He nodded. 'No rest for the wicked, eh? Everyone except Alfie has a soft spot for canine caperers. The poster outside the Tower Circus advertises them as "Fifteen Marvellous Maltese Dogs". Sam needs a bright and breezy three hundred words on their act by this time tomorrow.'

There was one small chink of light for Pearl at the end of a very dark tunnel – no; make that two. First was the hope that Joe's letter had been held up in the post; second was for her to set the record straight by dashing off one of her own to Bernie then pray that by some miracle he would receive it before Joe's.

> *Dear, darling Bernie,* she began during a short break from the arcade. *I'm writing in a hurry to tell you not to take any notice of an upsetting letter that Joe has written. Maybe you've got it already, but if not it's about me entering Sylvia's dance competition with Errol Jackson. A lot of people, including Joe, have got the wrong impression, but you and I both know how Errol helped me last winter and why we stay firm friends because of that. Believe me, there's nothing more to it – cross my heart.*

Pearl's hand shook as she scrawled the stiff-sounding, shallow words. If only she could explain to Bernie face to face and let him see for himself how desperate she was, instead of having to hide away in her bedroom to write it down in a way that didn't come close to expressing her deeper feelings.

Errol and I have never overstepped the mark – you can trust me on that. I love you and no one else. Please remember our precious times together and the promises we've made. Know that every morning I wake up thinking only of you and every night when I go to sleep you fill my dreams. There'll never be anyone else – Your ever-loving wife, Pearl.

There; it was done. Blotting the ink dry before sliding the letter into an envelope, she felt hot tears trickle down her cheeks. There was no knowing how long it would take to reach its destination, if ever. She knew she would be in agony until she received Bernie's reply.

'Pearl, what are you doing up there?' Henry sounded irritated as he called from the hallway.

'Nothing.' The letter needed a stamp. Today was Sunday so the post office was closed.

'Then shift yourself,' her father ordered. 'You've left Ernie in charge at North Pier for long enough.'

'Coming.' Roughly wiping away her tears, she appeared at the head of the stairs. 'Anyway, shouldn't you be minding your own arcade?'

'Wilf's holding the fort for me.' Henry was hungry – he'd popped home for a quick sandwich and had been surprised to find his daughter there too. 'What's up?' he asked as she squeezed by him in the narrow corridor. 'You've got a face like a wet weekend.'

'Thanks a lot, Dad.' She brushed away the insult. 'Wilf's only twelve, for goodness' sake. You can't leave a boy his age in charge of all that cash.'

'Says who?' Henry glanced in the hall mirror then ran a hand through his thick, greying hair. *Not in bad nick, considering,* he thought in passing. 'I was working at the Pleasure Beach full time when I was Wilf's age, fixing up dodgem cars when they broke down.'

'I might as well talk to a brick wall,' was Pearl's parting shot.

Her route to North Pier took her across the market square then along the bustling prom. The stalls selling ice cream and souvenirs were doing a roaring trade and there were long queues at the entrance to the Pleasure Beach and outside many of the fortune tellers' tiny booths. The beach itself was crammed with day trippers who had set up striped windbreaks and settled into deckchairs while their sunburned, sparrow-legged offspring built sandcastles or pestered for sixpences to pay for donkey rides. Still preoccupied with the dark threat hanging over her, Pearl ignored the everyday smells and sights as she reached the turnstiles at the entrance to the pier.

'Howdy, Miss Pearl.' A familiar voice greeted her as she searched her purse for the required penny. Errol broke free from a group of friends to offer her the coin. He was out of uniform, dressed in a short-sleeved pale blue shirt that brought out his tan, which in turn emphasized the striking blue-grey colour of his eyes.

'Thanks.' Pearl frowned as she accepted the coin.

'"Hello, Sergeant Jackson, how are you?"' he mimicked, head to one side, eyeing her quizzically.

'Sorry.' She drew breath then managed a faint smile. A decision that would change everything flashed into her mind. 'Actually, I'm glad I ran into you.'

'Yeah?' He stepped to one side, gently drawing Pearl with him. The questioning gaze intensified.

'There's something I need to talk to you about.' She hated with all her heart what she was about to say, but events had forced her into this corner – the town gossips had won. 'I've had a change of heart. I can't enter the jive competition with you after all,' she blurted out.

Errol slowly absorbed the information. 'Jeez!' he breathed.

'I know – it's rotten. After all our hard work—'

'I get it,' he interrupted. He did; instinctively he totally got it. Leaning against the side of a newspaper stall, he waited for her to continue.

'I know I'm letting you down,' she acknowledged.

'Forget it; not your fault.'

'It is – partly. I didn't pay enough attention to how it – us dancing together – looked from the outside. And now that's backfired on me in a big way.' Errol's face was shaded by a canvas awning so she found it hard to judge his reaction.

'Still not down to you,' he assured her. 'The small-minded guys out there – they're the ones who got it wrong.' *All wrong, damn it. And after the care I took not to step out of line.* Sure, he'd been tempted and would've dived straight in if Pearl had been willing, but she wasn't and Errol had respected that. Her friendship was what mattered above all else. Whenever he'd felt homesick he'd always known he could chat with her about his life in Georgia, how his parents hadn't got along but he'd stuck around for the sake of his kid sister then enlisted in the army as a way of getting as far away from his argumentative, temperamental folks as possible. He'd met Pearl soon after he'd arrived in Blackpool and looked out for her with a protective urge that came naturally to him. And he and Pearl had made the best jive team around. 'You don't have to do this,' he said in his quiet, low drawl. 'Why not ignore the rumours and carry on in the same old way?'

'I've done my best to ignore it.' A strong gust of wind blew the hat from her head. He stooped to retrieve it. As he handed it back she could see his face more clearly and the look of hurt in those dazzling, blue-grey eyes. 'But it didn't work out. I'm so sorry, Errol.'

'Sure.' He felt the need to establish exactly where this left him. 'Is it OK for me to say hi when I see you – in the arcade or at the ballroom?'

Pearl nodded. 'Hi is fine but we won't be able to dance.'

So no more lightning-quick kicks and hops, no more sweet swinging out and coming back into hold. 'Will it be OK to buy you a drink?'

'Better not.' She cast around for a way to soften the blow. 'There are plenty of other girls out there; my friend Doris would kill to enter the competition with you. Or what about Ruby? She loves to jive.'

'I guess.' Errol shook his head. *Talk about kicking a guy when he's down.* 'You don't have to worry about me, though. I'll be just fine.'

'I'd better go.' Pearl glanced along the length of the pier to the cluster of buildings at the far end.

'So, you know where I am.' It was hard as hell to let go of Pearl, his English firecracker, his livewire, the girl of his dreams. 'I'll always be there . . .'

To catch me when I fall. No need to complete the sentence; she understood his meaning.

And they parted. The iron turnstile squeaked as she pushed through, the wind tugged at her skirt and she glimpsed waves swirling and foaming between gaps in the wooden boards. The sky overhead was pure blue.

*

'About time!' Ernie let Pearl know that he was fed up. She'd promised she'd be gone for an hour and it had been twice that. 'It's been flippin' mayhem in here. A bunch of Yanks were hoggin' the best machines – the Spitfires and the Lucky Stars. A couple of old geezers weren't happy about it – I had to ask the Yanks to move on. Then I spotted a kid from my school – Dennis the Menace we call 'im – crawlin' under the old Chip and Bust in the far corner with a dirty great screwdriver. He was tryin' to unscrew the back and rob the jackpot but I kicked him up the backside and threw him out. And that's not all. After I got rid of Dennis, guess who turned up. No, you won't guess—'

'Stop,' Pearl pleaded. 'I'm here now, so you're off the hook. And thanks for holding the fort.' She'd promised Ernie two shillings for his trouble, which she duly handed over with: 'Don't spend it all at once.'

Ever the joker, he proceeded to bite the coins to check that they were genuine. 'See ya later alligator!' he grinned as he shot off along the pier.

Severely downcast after her conversation with Errol, Pearl took up position by the entrance, next to a colourful billboard inviting customers into Great Scott's North Shore Amusement Arcade with the catchphrase, 'You too could strike lucky!' Ernie's choice of gramophone record came to a scratchy end so she lifted the needle and was about to set one of her own on the turntable when she picked up the sound of a scuffle taking place beyond the Seaview Café at the very end of the pier.

'Everyone stand back!' a man's voice cried above a hum of consternation.

A woman gave a short, high-pitched squeal and there was a clamour of other voices shouting out warnings – 'Take it easy. Steady, steady – easy does it.'

Café customers scraped back their chairs and rushed to see what had caused the commotion. Soon a crowd had gathered, all craning their heads to see what was going on.

'Move back, everyone,' the original voice warned. 'Easy, easy there.'

'Shouldn't we call the police?' someone asked. 'Or the lifeguard – just in case?'

'Good idea,' was the response.

Curiosity drew Pearl towards the action. She crept round the side of the crowd to join two regular anglers who had abandoned their rods to join the melee. 'What's going on?' she asked.

The older of the fishermen, his bald head the colour of polished copper, jabbed a thumb towards a figure at the centre of events who had climbed on to the railing and now sat with legs dangling over the edge, gazing down at the water. 'Seems like she wants to jump; don't ask me why.'

It was a girl or a woman, then. Being short, Pearl could only catch glimpses over other people's shoulders. She made out a slight girl with mousy hair. Her back was turned to the crowd and she was hunched forward, looking as if she would at any moment launch herself into the sea. A shock of recognition ran through Pearl – something to do with the slope of the girl's shoulders that gave her a frightened, hunted look. 'Sorry – excuse me,' Pearl said as she pushed her way forward. 'Excuse me – I think I know who this is.'

Several nights of sleeping rough had taught Mildred many things, not least the kindness of strangers. First there had been the old lady who had shared her sandwiches and then a boy and his father who had come early in the morning to sail their toy yacht in the paddling pool. She'd been asleep on a stone ledge in the shelter when the little boy's excited cries had wakened her. The father had spotted her and, taking pity on her, had pressed a few coins into her hand with, 'Buy yourself some breakfast, love.'

Of course there had been bad times, too; the drunken tramps outside the outdoor pool for a start and another occasion late at night when three louts had emerged from a pub and surrounded her. They'd made vile suggestions but luckily been too drunk to act on them. Her heart had been in her mouth as she'd escaped on to the deserted beach.

Mildred now understood a phrase she'd once overheard – 'hiding in plain sight'. It meant mingling with the crowd and not doing anything to attract attention; something she'd been good at all her life. The sunny days had drifted by and now she knew most of the quiet back streets between the town centre and the Hydro to the north and the Lido swimming pool to the south. She'd watched from the sidelines as families had queued for the Fun House and had listened to the shrieks of delight that issued from within. Tommy and Joy had mentioned that the building contained a steep, four-lane slide, a moving staircase and a huge barrel that rotated. Joy had promised to take her there one day. Now that would never happen – Mildred had flown that nest once and for all.

Late on Saturday afternoon she'd passed through the turnstile on to North Pier. A cheeky lad in a Boy Scout's uniform had seen her hovering by the entrance and suggested that two littl'uns could squeeze through together. 'No one's looking,' he'd said with a mischievous wink. Mildred had taken up the offer, thinking that the pier could provide the ideal spot for an overnight stay once the crowds had departed. There was bound to be a shelter with a bench or else a doorway to sleep in. In the morning she might use the last of her money to buy hot tea from the café.

And so it turned out. The sun went down and holidaymakers returned to their boarding houses. The café owner shut up shop. Mildred made sure to stay well hidden as Joy's friend Pearl turfed out the last of her customers from Great Scott's Amusement Arcade. This only left anglers fishing off the end of the pier, attaching bait to their hooks and casting out to sea with an expert flick of the wrist. The sight of the men leaning motionless against the ornate iron railing, waiting for a bite, left her feeling unexpectedly calm. No fish were caught, though seagulls soared overhead in expectation. Dusk gathered and the anglers packed away their tackle and left.

Mildred slept in a shelter facing out to sea. She woke to a cool dawn, only aware of the sound of waves breaking on the shore then receding – breaking and receding until the end of time. Then awareness of her situation rose to the surface. The foremost was hunger – a strong, gnawing sensation in her stomach. Running her hand over her belly, she thought she felt her baby give a small kick. But was it too early? Was it simply hunger? She had no idea. Sitting up straight, she gripped the edge of the bench as slow footsteps approached.

'My *Sunday Express* says we've got Mussolini well and truly on the run in Sicily.'

'Aye, and the Russkis have surrounded Kursk, according to the wireless.' Two early-bird anglers discussed Allied progress in Europe.

'Not before time,' the first grumbled. 'Now all we need is for the Yanks to finish off the Japs in the Far East like they promised.'

Mildred slipped around the side of her shelter, hoping to avoid notice – only to encounter a third fisherman already busy with rod and line. He saw her but didn't react. Retreating into the shelter, she decided there was no harm in sitting it out until the pier grew busy and she could slip away.

'I've a lad in the Royal Engineers – he's been taken prisoner out in Burma. They've got him building a bloody railway.' The latest arrival had chosen to set up not ten yards away. 'His mother's worried sick.'

'Can't say I blame her.'

Before long other anglers arrived. Some noticed Mildred and nodded a greeting. None seemed curious about her reason for being there. They were all middle aged or older, dressed in faded jumpers or threadbare jackets, most with cloth caps pulled well down over their faces. Eventually, as the sun gathered strength, one would leave his rod in his neighbour's charge then head off to the Seaview Café.

'Here you are, love.' A small man with a bushy ginger moustache opened his vacuum flask then poured Mildred a mug of tea. 'Get that down you.'

Another offered her two digestive biscuits. He was the chatty type and told her about his daughter who had married a Belgian before the war and gone off to live in Antwerp, wherever that was.

Soon the end of the pier came alive with day trippers fresh off coaches and families ordering breakfast at the Seaview. Warmed by the sun, Mildred changed her mind about moving on – why not stay here for the day and watch the world go by? The morning passed. Stallholders stood in their doorways, arms folded, enjoying a good gossip. Off-duty soldiers crowded into Pearl's arcade and mothers scolded children for climbing on benches then leaning too far over the railing. Midday came and went and the afternoon drifted on in a sunny haze. Venturing away from her shelter and taking care not to be observed by the boy taking money at the entrance to Pearl's arcade, Mildred stopped outside a newspaper stall to read the day's headlines then strolled on a little way to look in the window of a souvenir stall selling little wooden boxes decorated with sea shells. It was then that it happened.

She turned back the way she'd come. The sun was hot on her bare shoulders and arms. The light was so bright that it dazzled. For a second she thought she was mistaken – it couldn't be the same man! But she recognized the skinny frame and the dark, swept-back hair. He had the same broad, lopsided smile and was wearing the identical blue jacket that he'd worn to the dance on the worst night of her life. It was Frank.

Blind panic had Mildred in its grip. She pushed past café tables and stumbled on. If she didn't look back then it would prove not to be real after all. Reaching the shelter at the end of the pier, she fought for breath, collapsing on to the bench, her stomach heaving, still desperate not to draw attention, to be anywhere except here. *Please, please, let it not be true!*

Her heart was pounding so fast and hard she thought she would die. It was out of control, hammering as if trying to break out of her chest. Try as she might to take a deep breath, her ribs were locked and air was squeezed from her lungs. *Breathe, breathe. I can't do it! Try! I can't!*

The nearest angler – the one with the ginger moustache who'd given her tea from his flask – saw that she'd collapsed forward with her head between her knees. He hurried towards her to help her to sit up. 'What's wrong, love?'

As if reacting to an electric shock, Mildred sprang to her feet, her eyes wide with terror. *I can't breathe! I can't bear it!* She fixed her gaze on the railing at the end of the pier and the glittering sea beyond. She ran towards the barrier and climbed on to it. *Please make it stop!*

'Move back, everyone. Easy, easy there.'

Someone ran to alert the police and the lifeguard as Pearl rushed from the arcade and began to push her way through the crowd. A bald angler with a tanned, weather-beaten face stood in her way and warned her that a young girl intended to jump off the railing into the sea. Struggling to make sense of the spectacle, Pearl finally made out who it was.

'Sorry – excuse me. Excuse me – I think I know who this is.'

'She's serious.' Another angler blocked Pearl's way. 'She'll jump if anyone goes near.'

'Mildred.' Pearl pushed past him to reach the front of the crowd then stopped and uttered the name in a low, urgent voice.

Deafened by the thud of her own heartbeat, Mildred failed to hear. The water below was deep and blue. The smallest shift forward would send her plummeting. She would hit the cold, cold water then vanish below the surface and not struggle. Down she would sink, further and further beneath the waves, until she reached the sandy bottom. Her fearful, frantic heart would stop. The horror would end.

CHAPTER SIXTEEN

Pearl risked taking a small step forward. 'Mildred – it's me.'

The terrified girl gazed down at the water where oblivion beckoned.

'Joy has been looking everywhere for you. We all have.'

Joy – the sound of the familiar name caused Mildred to turn her head towards Pearl then swiftly look away again. Everything was a blur – the staring faces, the bright pink, blue and yellow of women's dresses and the white dome of the café roof against a clear sky.

'Joy is desperate for you to come home. So is Tommy. So is Lucia.' Pearl ventured towards the rail one cautious step at a time. The crowd held their breath.

Mildred grasped the rail more tightly. Her heart still threatened to burst through her ribcage and the vision of Frank at the door of the arcade refused to fade. His sharp features and jaunty smile were imprinted on her memory.

'I promise we won't let anyone harm you,' Pearl said in a calm, clear voice, suppressing a gasp as Mildred leaned forward as if preparing to jump.

Was this the only way? To make a dizzying, cold end and never to see that man's face again, hear his voice, feel his hands on her and remember the terrible, shameful things he did?

'Please let us help you,' Pearl whispered.

Turning again, Mildred made out the figure of Joy's friend – the small one with dark hair who smiled all the time. Why was she here?

Pearl spotted the flash of recognition. 'That's right; it's me – Pearl.' She reached out a hand, palm upwards. 'Let me take you home.'

Pearl had said the word 'home'. Mildred dragged air into her lungs.

'Good girl.' Pearl inched forward. 'I'm so glad I've found you – Joy will be thrilled.' She sensed that the crowd of worried onlookers was being quietly shepherded out of sight. 'Please take my hand,' she urged.

Safety was within reach. Twisting her torso, Mildred made a great effort to swing her legs over the railing towards Pearl. Then she hesitated. Where had all the people gone? Might Frank be hiding among them, ready to pounce? The iron band around her chest tightened again. The world tilted on its axis – the sky was beneath her feet, the sea rose up to swallow her.

'What is it?' Pearl spotted the wide-eyed look of terror. She ran forward in time to catch the swooning girl and hold her tight. 'It's all right,' she murmured. 'I've got you – you're safe now, I swear.'

'All I can tell you is that after Mildred came round she refused point-blank to wait in the arcade until you arrived,' Pearl told Joy when she called in at Rossi's Ice Cream Parlour early the following morning. The two women sat in the empty café with the blinds still down and tables unset, reflecting on the previous day's events.

'And you've no idea why?' Joy had already made an emergency appointment at the maternity clinic. The last twelve hours had been a blur. News of Mildred's re-appearance had reached her and Tommy while they were working on the King Street house, by which time Mildred was safely home. They'd rushed to join Lucia and spent most of the night settling the girl back into her room and making sure that she was warm and comfortable.

'It's a total mystery,' Pearl replied. 'Mildred wouldn't set foot inside the arcade and she refused to utter a single word of explanation. In the end, I decided the best thing was to bundle her into a taxi and bring her here.'

'She still hasn't spoken.' Joy's relief was tempered by bewilderment.

'Not to anyone?'

'No and it's not for want of trying. Lucia, Tommy and I – we've all done our best. But Mildred gets into a state whenever we press too hard.'

'Perhaps she's suffering from shock.' Pearl was no expert but she'd heard of such things; when a serviceman had witnessed terrible sights in the heat of battle, for instance, then lost the power of speech. 'You have to wonder what drove her to consider jumping off the end of the pier.'

'Nurse Myers might provide us with answers.' Joy went on to admit to the guilt that had plagued her during the last few days. 'I've said it before and I'll say it again – I wish with all my heart that Tommy and I had included her in our plans from the beginning.'

'Don't feel bad; you had a lot going on.'

'We would never have let Mildred down – I hope she knows that now.'

'I'm sure she does. And if it turns out to be a type of shell shock that stops her from speaking, let's hope Dr Evans can prescribe a medicine to calm her nerves.'

'One that doesn't harm the baby,' Joy reminded her. 'I

didn't have time yesterday to thank you properly for what you did – without your quick thinking, Lord knows what would have happened.'

'I'm glad I was on the spot.' It was high time for Pearl to go and open her arcade. 'Good luck at the clinic,' she said as she made preparations to leave. 'By the way, I should mention that Errol and I have pulled out of Sylvia's competition.'

The news jolted Joy out of her preoccupation with Mildred. 'Whatever for?'

Pearl was already out of the door, glancing along the prom as a tram approached. 'Just because.' And off she dashed, bright and quick as a kingfisher in her blue dress, heels clicking along the pavement, head held high and showing no sign of the turmoil in her head and heart.

'The baby is doing fine.' Nurse Myers, brisk and professional as ever, completed her examination behind a set of green canvas screens while Joy hovered near by, reassured by the clinical surroundings and by the quiet bustle of nurses in their blue uniforms and white caps going about their business. Surely Mildred would understand that the crisis was over and she would be well looked after between now and the birth of her baby. 'The heartbeat is strong and the pregnancy seems to be progressing normally. You can get dressed now.'

Joy relaxed a little as she waited for the nurse to emerge.

'Could we have a quiet word?' Frowning, Nurse Myers took Joy to one side. 'The baby is certainly fine but Mildred's blood pressure is high and she's lost more weight – she needs to put it back on as quickly as possible.'

'I understand. My mother-in-law will make sure she eats properly from now on.'

There was an awkward pause. 'Frankly, it's not her physical condition that concerns me so much as her mental state. She seems extremely tense and her lack of response is worrying.'

Joy quickly brought the nurse up to speed with recent events. 'There was a huge misunderstanding that made her run away. We don't know where Mildred's been or why she did what she did.'

'She almost jumped to her death?' the nurse asked for confirmation.

'Yes; and she hasn't spoken a word since we got her back.'

'I see.' Nurse Myers looked at a small silver watch that was pinned to the bib of her starched white apron. 'Let me go and see if Dr Evans is free.'

Minutes ticked by and Joy decided to join Mildred behind the screens. She found her half dressed, sitting on the edge of the bed and staring into space. Joy sat down next to her. 'We're waiting for the doctor – he won't be long.'

Mildred's pale face showed no reaction. Her lank hair was pushed behind her ears and her shoulders slumped forward. All she knew was that words signalled danger. Silence equalled safety.

Soon a young doctor entered the cubicle with a stethoscope tucked into the pocket of his white coat. He was tall with an angular face, high forehead and a hairline that was already receding. 'Hello, Mildred. I'm Dr Evans – we haven't met before. Nurse would like me to have a few words with you. Is that all right?'

No response.

He lowered himself to his patient's level by sitting in a chair at the side of the bed. 'I hear that your baby is developing normally. That's good news, isn't it?' There was a long pause. 'Is there anything you'd like to ask me? No? Well, we won't force the issue.'

Do not speak and unleash the terror within. Mildred turned her expressionless face towards him. All her energy had drained away and every movement was an effort.

'We're very glad you came back to clinic; you've done the right thing for you and baby. Our job is to look after you both so we would like to check your blood pressure and weigh you twice a week for a while. Nod if you understand.'

Mildred communicated by an almost imperceptible downward movement of her head.

'That's champion. No one at the clinic will pester you with questions that you don't wish to answer but if ever you feel ready to talk we're here to listen. For now the best course of action is for you to go home with Mrs Rossi and get plenty of fresh air and rest.'

Mildred closed her eyes to shut out the kind doctor's face and the green screens that trapped her. She could take in no more. 'Home' was the one word she clung to.

'Nurse Myers will help you to get dressed.' Dr Evans departed with a word of advice for Joy. 'Fresh air, rest and absolutely no stress,' he insisted.

Joy followed him. 'Can't you give her some medicine to calm her nerves?'

The doctor shook his head. 'Let's wait and see. I hope it won't be necessary.'

'Will she get better?' was Joy's next anxious question.

'Perhaps. But don't expect miracles – progress is likely to be slow.' The soft manner he'd used with his patient became firmer as he delivered the unvarnished truth. 'This is the result of severe shock. Mildred isn't choosing not to talk; she simply can't – it's a rare condition called selective mutism. So you must try to be as normal as possible around her and avoid undue excitement. Bring her back here on Wednesday if you can.'

Joy promised she would do her best and left the clinic with a heavy heart, ordering a taxi to take her and Mildred home. Tommy was there to greet them. Fresh air and rest, Joy told him. Patience and tender loving care. Soon Lucia came in from the café and took charge. Mildred was shivering despite the midday heat, so Lucia brought a cardigan from her room. She must eat, so Tommy's mother warmed the hotpot she'd prepared earlier in the day. Anyone could see that the poor girl was exhausted, so it was up to bed with her and when she woke there would be a sunny seat in a corner of the café where she could sit quietly and watch the world go by.

Tommy waited to see that all was under control before he left for his matinee performance. 'What the doctor ordered applies to you too,' he told Joy, who had insisted on going into work for the remainder of the day. 'You need to rest.'

'Not today,' she answered with a serious expression. 'I promised Alan that we'd go through the latest sales figures.'

'For any special reason?'

Joy was ready to leave the house, handbag over her arm containing a file of papers that she'd prepared, wearing white gloves and a straw hat that perched at an angle over her dark hair. 'To get ready for George's visit later this week.'

'George is travelling down from Glasgow?' Tommy was intrigued. 'Is this to do with rearranging your office hours?'

'Yes.' Joy crossed her fingers. 'Nothing is settled but I'm working on a proposal that I hope he'll accept.'

With two weeks to go before their big dance weekend, Sylvia, Cliff and Lorna had arranged to meet again at the Spanish Hall. They gathered under the colonnade that ran the length of the vast room, staring out glumly at what seemed like acres of polished dance floor and at the painted battlemented balconies which in the cold, clear light of day had a cheap and tawdry aspect.

'I'm afraid we've bitten off a good deal more than we can chew.' Cliff voiced what the other two surely felt. None of their efforts so far had brought in the required number of contestants; not widespread leafleting, nor posters placed in prominent positions in the town's libraries, theatres, WI centres, ARP posts or anywhere else that could be persuaded to accept them. Likewise, Lorna's adverts in the national dancing magazines had produced only a trickle of new entries.

'This is supposed to be our big break,' Sylvia reminded them. 'Our chance to shine in the world of competitive ballroom dancing.'

'Yes, dear – we're well aware.' Lorna, who had been caught in a sharp shower of rain without an umbrella, let her irritation show. She turned to Cliff. 'I suppose it's too late to call the whole thing off?'

He nodded. 'I looked into it. Even if we were to refund the couples who have paid in advance, we'd still have to stump up for the hire of the hall, and Art Richardson would be well within his rights to demand payment too.'

'You've considered calling it off without telling me?' Sylvia was outraged.

'I was being practical. Unless we can achieve the magic

three hundred entries each, we might as well be pouring our money down the drain.'

Their gloomy mood matched the weather outside. While Lorna distracted herself by removing her hat and shaking off the raindrops, Cliff justified going behind Sylvia's back. 'In my experience, it's best to be prepared for the worst.'

Major disappointments had dogged him for much of his adult life: events beyond his control such as the Nazis coming to power in Germany, which had forced him to quit a successful cabaret spot in Berlin, followed by mixing with the wrong, high-society set in London – a combination of poor judgement and bad luck that had sent him scurrying back to Blackpool with his tail between his legs.

'Well, I for one am not going to give in without a fight.' Sylvia marched on to the floor, gazed up at the vaulted ceiling and spread her arms wide. 'With the lights on and live music playing, this place will be magical. I don't care if I have to tramp around the whole of Lancashire on foot, recruiting more couples – Bury, Burnley, Manchester – whatever it takes.'

'Bravo – that's the spirit.' Arriving unannounced, Vernon strolled on to the stage, clapping his hands and making a hollow sound that echoed around the hall. He wore a light mackintosh and had a folded newspaper tucked under his arm. 'Greetings, people; I come with glad tidings.' Descending the stairs at the side of the stage, he waved the paper at Sylvia. 'Hot off the press: my long-awaited article has appeared in today's edition.' As Cliff and Lorna hurried to join them in the middle of the dance floor, Vernon opened the copy of the *Gazette*. 'See for yourselves.'

Major New Dance Competition Welcomes Final Entries. The

bold headline was set out in thick black print. There was one photograph – not of Lorna, Sylvia or Cliff, or of couples dancing in their studios, but a picture of Art Richardson's band. Underneath was a subheading: *Famous Swing Band Brings in the Crowds.*

'Not quite what I was hoping for,' Lorna said under her breath.

Cliff was more positive – Vernon's preview took up half of the entertainments page, above smaller reviews on an end-of-pier variety show, a dog act at the circus and various cinema showings. 'Very good,' he commented. 'Hopefully this will do the trick.'

Sylvia couldn't take her eyes off the photograph. Rosie was at the centre, flanked by Art, Alfie and other members of the band. She was wearing a strapless, fitted gown, with her halo of blonde hair falling softly around her face. 'Why this one?' she asked Vernon. 'Wouldn't it have been more to the point to show our couples dancing in the studio?'

'Not my choice.' He brushed aside her question. 'The picture editor must have decided that the band is the biggest draw. Anyway, aren't you pleased with what I've written?'

They read on. Lorna's studio was mentioned near the top of the piece, where she was described as a 'sometime ballroom queen'. Vernon had included a little of Cliff's background: namely his lowly beginnings in Blackpool and his international reputation as a cabaret dancer and MC.

'I avoided mentioning Berlin,' Vernon told him. 'I didn't think that would go down too well with our readers.'

Sylvia took the paper from him and read to the end. 'I'm not in here,' she said with a sense of crushing disappointment.

'Yes you are,' he argued.

'Where?'

'Here.' He took the paper back and read out loud. '"The Latin section of this exciting dance weekend is led by Cliff Seymour and his associate." I had to be careful to avoid accusations of favouritism,' he explained. 'Some of our readers will be aware that you and I are sweethearts.'

Lorna gave Sylvia's hand a sympathetic squeeze. 'Never mind, dear. The main thing is that the article has appeared at last.'

'And at the best possible time to generate maximum interest,' Vernon assured them. 'Didn't I say that Sam Pearson is an old hand at judging these things? All that worrying your pretty head for nothing, eh?' He brushed the underside of Sylvia's chin with his forefinger.

'Please thank your editor for giving us so much space.' Cliff stepped forward to shake Vernon's hand.

'Will do. Now it's over to you to make your event a runaway success.'

'Thank you, Vernon; rest assured we will.' Lorna's expression was pinched, her tone formal despite them being on first-name terms. 'We'll stand by, ready to receive calls.'

'Yes, yes.' Cliff grew businesslike. 'We must be sure to write down names and addresses plus the category – ballroom or Latin – so we can forward the relevant forms.'

Vernon and Sylvia walked with them to the door. 'With luck Sam will ask me to write a follow-up article – a review.' Vernon held out a carrot that he was sure they would grasp. 'That'll be solid proof that your hard work has paid off. Who knows? It may even open the door to making this an annual event.' One last shake of the hand sent them off in different directions.

Sylvia was subdued after she and Vernon left the Winter Gardens and drove home. His chipper mood grated on her as he talked again of his ambitions and of how the best way to achieve them was to concentrate on music reviews rather than spreading himself too thin over theatre, cinema and dancing. Swing bands were all the rage; if he used his contacts and became known for his journalistic expertise in that area it was bound to come to the notice of editors in Fleet Street. And by the way, she did see the reason for keeping her name out of it, didn't she?

Another heavy shower began as they parked close to the studio on North View Parade. Sylvia too had come out without an umbrella and the rain quickly soaked through her thin cotton dress.

'It's called a conflict of interest.' Vernon's explanation was condescending. 'That's when someone in business is set to benefit from a close personal connection that isn't revealed.' When she raised her eyebrows at him he quickly apologized. 'I'm sorry – of course you know that, which is why you're not angry with me.' He used the key he'd had cut to unlock the door to the flat then led the way upstairs.

'I don't care about that but I don't like the picture they chose.' It didn't make sense to Sylvia to highlight the band rather than the competition itself.

'Yes, it's a pity.' As they entered the living room, Vernon gave her a consolatory peck on the cheek then drew her towards the sofa. 'Never mind; it can't be helped. Looking on the bright side, Sam did print the article in its entirety – with hardly any cuts and rewrites. I thought it read well.'

'Very well,' she acknowledged. An inner voice warned her to leave it at that. 'We'll know within the next couple of days what effect it's had and whether or not we'll meet our target.'

'I'd bet my bottom dollar you will.' The confident phrase was accompanied by an invitation for her to sit on his lap. 'There, that's nice and cosy. We should make more time for this instead of dashing about, trying to prove ourselves – you with your dance studio, me with my reviews.'

Sylvia rested against him. 'I don't mind working hard – I'm used to it.'

'But secretly wouldn't you rather be at home with me, playing the little housewife?'

She pulled away and gave his face a smart tap with the back of her hand.

'Kidding!' He gave a gesture of surrender. 'I'd never ask you to stop dancing. But let's face it, most women give up their careers at some point in their lives.'

'I ought to get changed.' Sylvia escaped his clutches and stood up. 'This dress is wet through.'

He went with her into the bedroom then straight across to the wardrobe where he took out several dresses. 'Which of these will you wear to the Tower tomorrow night?'

'I haven't thought about it.' She stood still while he held her jade-green, sequinned number against her to judge its effect. 'It ought to be long, though – tomorrow's competition is the Viennese waltz.'

'Is it? That's a shame – I like this one on you. It shows off those beautiful long legs. To heck with the waltz competition – couldn't you wear it just to please me?'

'I could if you ask nicely.'

'Plee-ease!' Running his fingers through her damp hair, he kissed her softly on the lips. 'Is that nice enough?' he murmured. 'No? Then how about this?' Before she had time to resist he swept her up and carried her to the bed, showering her with kisses as he gathered her to him.

'Not now,' she protested. 'I have to teach a tango class at three.'

Vernon put his finger to her lips. 'Shh! We've got fifteen whole minutes before then – plenty of time.'

'No,' she repeated, though she felt her resistance weaken.

He sensed it too. 'See?' he whispered. 'You want to, too. Like this and like this.' More kisses on her shoulder and neck, him pressing against her, waiting until she responded before rolling on top of her so there was no escape.

And so she gave in once more and loved him and let him do what he wanted until it was over and he lay naked on his back smoking the customary cigarette. He watched lazily as she quickly washed and dressed in freshly pressed trousers and a clean blouse.

'I have to pop out for a while,' he informed her.

Sylvia brushed her hair then twisted it on top of her head.

'Did you hear me?' He went to the wardrobe as she finished getting ready. 'What have you done with my pale blue shirt?'

'I haven't touched it.' She was already late; glancing out of the window, she saw her first pupils arrive at the studio. She counted on Cliff being there to let them in.

'It was here earlier today.' Vernon searched with growing impatience. 'I ironed it then hung it up in its proper place. You must've moved it.'

'I swear I didn't.' She hated it when this happened, especially when she was short of time. Vernon's face darkened in an instant and he clenched his teeth, his movements grew jerky and impatient.

'You must have.' He slid hangers noisily along the rail.

'I know exactly where I put it. Why can't I trust you to leave my things alone? It's as if you move them on purpose, just to annoy me. Pale – blue – shirt!' With each word he shoved her dresses to one side.

'Vernon, please!' The dresses slid from their hangers and spilled out of the wardrobe on to the floor. She watched him kick them to one side.

'Here it is – at the opposite end of the wardrobe from where I left it.' He pulled the shirt clear then advanced towards her. 'Look – it's creased to hell; I'll have to iron it again because of you.'

It was pointless to argue. 'I have to go,' she murmured, edging towards the door.

'I'm sick to death of telling you not to move my stuff – it drives me round the bloody bend.'

She left with Vernon's angry voice following her down the stairs. It was time to pull herself together and teach her tango class. When she went back to the flat he would probably be gone. She would spend the evening alone, not knowing when he'd be back. Tomorrow night she would style her hair and do her make-up then put on the sequinned jade-green dress.

CHAPTER SEVENTEEN

If anyone was capable of nursing Mildred back to health it was Lucia. Tommy's mother was born to care. She cooked delicious meals made from the plainest of ingredients and sat down with the girl each evening to mend and darn, clean and polish whatever came to hand. Then there were the small touches, the one-off acts of kindness – like making sure that the flowers in Mildred's room were refreshed or simply humming the tune to '*O Mio Babbino Caro*' as they sat together in the kitchen while Lucia knitted a matinee jacket for the baby.

'My Tommy and his Joy – they buy house, very old, very dirty,' she said with a sigh as she broke off from the tune. 'But they are *contento* and I also. You must see house. I take you.'

On another occasion she showed Mildred a framed photo of Tommy's father in his youth, with thick, wavy hair like Tommy junior, the same broad shoulders and lively smile. 'See, he is handsome man. My heart is sad without him.'

On the Wednesday of that week Lucia casually invited the girl to come shopping with her, as if it was the most natural thing in the world. 'I buy food at market – tomatoes and peas. You like? Then we see *il dottore* – the doctor.'

Mildred simply nodded then went upstairs to fetch her hat.

Joy was amazed that Mildred had agreed to leave the house. 'Your mother worked her magic,' she informed Tommy later that day. 'She took Mildred to the clinic for a check-up and Nurse Myers reports that all is well, thank heavens.'

'Still not speaking, though?'

'Not as yet.' Joy pictured a block of ice melting in the warmth of the sun, slowly, drip by drip. 'But soon, I hope.'

Friday came round; the day when Joy must meet with her cousin George. 'Wish me luck,' she called to Lucia and Mildred as she set out to catch her train.

'*Buona fortuna!*' Lucia rushed out on to the pavement to wave her off. 'Joy is good girl,' she murmured to Mildred when she returned. '*Una buona moglie* for my Tommy, *si*?'

Mildred nodded and almost smiled. *Buona* meant good. *Buona, buona.*

Much was riding on the outcome of the meeting and Joy knew she must keep a clear head if she wished to win the argument. She was aware that the main stumbling block would be a condition written into their grandfather's will. To cut a long story short, she and George were named as joint inheritors of Hebden Knitwear, but only if both were based in the Glasgow factory. George had already made a major concession by agreeing to reopen a distribution warehouse in Manchester, which allowed Joy to work from there. It had turned out well so far, but she was afraid that her new plan might be a step too far.

'Good morning, Mrs Rossi.' Alan greeted her at the gate with an easy smile. 'Mr Hebden travelled down on the overnight sleeper. He's waiting for you in your office.'

Joy braced herself. 'Thank you, Alan.'

He walked with her across the yard past vans bearing the Hebden Knitwear logo parked close to the wide warehouse doors. There was already a busy, bustling atmosphere as two men stacked cardboard boxes into the back of one of the vans while its driver studied delivery details for the day. 'I've arranged for Dora to bring tea and biscuits,' Alan informed her.

'A good idea – thank you.'

He felt her hesitate as she entered the office building. 'Mr Hebden invited me to join the meeting if that's all right with you.'

'It's more than all right,' she said with a sigh of relief.

So they went upstairs to find George at Joy's desk sifting through papers that Alan had already provided. He stood up to shake her hand. 'Always good to see you, Joy.'

He ran through the pleasantries in his usual brisk and straightforward way, saying he was glad that married life suited her. He was interested to hear that she and Tommy had bought a house. A slight, trim figure with dark hair and refined features, the family resemblance was clear – though George's manner was more authoritative than Joy's, with a hint of impatience suggested by quick movements and a piercing glance. He'd spent the previous night on the train, scarcely sleeping and all the time wondering what could be so urgent that his young cousin and business partner had requested a face-to-face meeting.

'Now let's get down to business,' he began once they were all seated around the desk. 'I've been running through the latest sets of figures. Sales are holding up well, despite the problems we've been experiencing on the manufacturing side. The supply of raw materials is the main issue there. Nothing will come through from Italy in the foreseeable future but we can now source the wool more locally. In terms of nationwide distribution of the finished product, we do have to deal with petrol rationing. How much of a problem is that for you, Joy?'

'It's not too bad,' she assured him. Settling into familiar surroundings – her typewriter and telephone in front of her, shelves stacked with files behind her and a view of the warehouse roof across the yard – her nerves settled and she was able to explain to her cousin how she'd switched to sending out many orders by rail in order to cut back reliance on petrol.

'Very good.' Still unsure where the meeting was headed, George drew another sheet of paper to the top of the pile. 'How about staffing expenses, the cost of heating and lighting, and so on? Could we make economies there?'

Alan stepped in with the relevant facts and figures: the distribution arm of the business employed twelve full-time warehouse workers, five drivers, one caretaker and one cook who ran the canteen single handed at present. 'We're stripped back to the bone as far as staffing is concerned,' he assured his boss.

'All members of staff are up to scratch?' George enquired.

'Yes; the new caretaker, Robert Finchley, is excellent,' Alan confirmed.

George gave a brief nod then moved on without comment. 'Now to the main business: your proposal, Joy.'

This was it; the moment they'd been building towards. She must sound cool, calm and collected – above all confident that her plan was practical and cost effective. 'We're agreed that Hebden Knitwear has performed as well as can be expected since I joined the company.'

'True,' George acknowledged with his Scottish burr.

'We're holding our own, in spite of this damned war.' Tension built as he waited for Joy to continue.

'True,' Alan echoed.

'I enjoy the work a great deal and with Alan's help I've learned a lot in a short space of time.'

A knock on the door startled George. It signalled the arrival of a stout, solemn woman bearing a tea tray, which she carried in without fuss before backing out of the room.

'Thank you, Dora.' Joy breathed in deeply as she came to the main point. 'At present I work in the office for five full days a week.'

'As agreed,' George said quickly, his face inscrutable.

'However, I believe that I could work as efficiently from home for one of those five days.'

Alan shifted uncomfortably in his seat while George tapped the desk with the end of his pencil. So they'd reached the heart of the matter – and it was not what either had expected.

'Hear me out,' Joy continued. 'Each Friday I would leave Alan in charge of running the warehouse while I caught up with paperwork at home – preparing and sending out invoices, answering customer queries, calculating wages, and so on. In the event of any difficulty here on site, Alan and I would solve it over the telephone.'

George raised a warning finger. 'All well and good, but would that comply with the terms of our grandfather's will?'

'It would,' Joy insisted. 'I've looked again at certain codicils and, contrary to what we believed, nowhere does it state that all hours must be worked in one place.'

Alan sat forward, alert to the ding-dong exchange between his two bosses. It seemed that Mrs Rossi would give as good as she got.

'Take you, for instance, George – roughly what percentage of your time do you spend out of the factory, travelling to meet suppliers and drumming up new custom in department stores across the country?'

A pertinent point, well made. 'Thirty to forty per cent, perhaps,' he admitted.

'So how does that differ from me choosing to do my paperwork from home in future? I wouldn't be idle. In fact, I might even be putting in more hours per week if necessary.'

'How so?'

'By working during the time it takes me to travel back and forth on the train.'

Still tapping his pencil on the desk, George glanced in Alan's direction. 'You know the distribution side of the business inside out. What's your opinion?'

'It might work,' the manager conceded. *Clever girl – sharp as a tack.*

'I'd *make* it work.' Joy grew more determined. 'Monday to Thursday based here then Friday working from home. We could begin with a three-month trial then reconsider if necessary.'

George checked again with Alan, who nodded. 'It's rather caught me off guard,' he confessed to Joy, his expression softening. 'To be frank, I travelled down from Glasgow half-expecting to learn that you and Tommy – er – planned to start a family.'

'Oh no.' She felt her face colour up. 'Not yet.'

'In which case, I feared I might have lost you altogether.' George rested his elbows on the desk and made a tent shape with his long fingers. 'Alan, any further thoughts?'

'I'd be happy enough with the new arrangement.' He smiled at Joy as he delivered his verdict.

'Sure?'

'Aye. I trust Mrs Rossi to do what she thinks best.' The experienced manager had been impressed by how quickly Joy had learned the ropes and how well she managed those who worked under her; quite a feat in one so young.

'Very good.' George continued to consider all the angles. 'That's all for now, Alan – thank you.'

He made an unobtrusive exit, leaving the two cousins facing each other across the desk.

'I will have to look closely at Grandfather's will before going ahead,' George warned.

'Of course.' Joy's preparations had been thorough. She swiftly pulled her copy of the document from a file on her desk, turned the pages then pointed to several underlined passages. 'You see here – the small print stipulates full-time work but not location.'

'Hmm – interesting.' George read the relevant sections then paused to review the situation. He thought back twenty years to when his father had done the dirty on Joy's father and cut his younger brother out of the family business by making false accusations and by concealing documents that only came to light after George's father had died. Deprived of their inheritance, Joy's family had gone through much hardship in the twenties and thirties while George's had prospered. 'I've done my best to make amends,' he reminded her at last.

'Yes and you turned my life around. I can never thank you enough.' She'd always recognized that honour had been the driving force behind George's decision to track her down and offer her a fair share of the business.

'And I can never apologize enough for my father's actions,' he continued.

Joy waited with bated breath.

'I'm very fond of you, Joy.'

She braced herself for what might follow. 'But?'

'But – nothing,' George declared. 'I'm fond of you and I trust you. Let's begin the experiment as soon as we can – four days in the office and one day at home. We'll review it after twelve weeks.'

'But?' she prompted a second time. There was definitely one lurking in there somewhere.

'But the new way of working relies on something you haven't considered.' His mouth twitched.

'Does it?' Joy felt sure she'd dotted all her i's and crossed her t's.

'Yes – it depends on your having a telephone at home.' George's serious expression relaxed into a smile as he presented Joy with a logistical flaw. 'You know, the new-fangled contraption sitting here on your desk?'

'Of course!' She shot up from her seat and paced the room. How had she overlooked something as simple as this?

They both quickly collapsed into laughter – part relief, part embarrassment – then came together in a hug. The small technical hitch could be easily solved so the cousins went out for a leisurely lunch then Joy saw George to his train, mission accomplished, before hurrying home.

'Tommy, Lucia, Mildred; we need to buy a telephone!' she announced the second she was through the door. 'Tommy, where are you? Is anyone at home?'

Lucia was the first to put in an appearance. '*Un telefono? Perché?*'

Mildred followed Lucia into the kitchen while Tommy could be heard clattering downstairs. 'What's this about a telephone?' he demanded as he burst into the room.

'We'll need one for me to do my job!' Joy skipped

around the room, inviting them all to celebrate. 'Put the flags out – George has agreed that I can work from home!'

The next morning Tommy rose early to marshal the troops. 'Joy, here's a mop and bucket and a scrubbing brush for you. And Mildred, one broom and one dustpan and brush for you. Momma, you'll have to hold the fort here while we three get to work on King Street. I've roped Joe into lending a hand once he's finished in the market.'

'*Si, si – vai!*' Lucia shooed them out on to the street armed with their cleaning materials.

'We'll begin upstairs then work our way down.' Tommy's high spirits were infectious as he marched the girls along back streets, metal buckets swinging. 'This might not be the most glamorous job – Lord knows what we'll find lurking up unswept chimneys and behind rotting skirting boards.'

'We're ready for anything, aren't we, Mildred?' Joy said.

Mildred gave a determined nod.

'Off we go then – just like the seven dwarfs!' Marching single file along the narrow pavement, Tommy took the lead, singing the well-known Disney tune as he went.

'Have you seen the *Snow White* film?' Joy asked Mildred. 'They work awfully hard digging, but don't worry – in your condition you're allowed to take plenty of rests.'

'Joy is Doc, the clever one, and I'm Happy, which speaks for itself,' Tommy decided. 'Mildred, you're Bashful.'

'The names of three of the seven dwarfs,' Joy explained.

With Mr and Mrs Rossi by her side, Mildred made her second daring outing of the week. By looking straight ahead and putting one foot in front of the other, she managed to control her anxiety and reach Joy and Tommy's new house without incident.

'Heigh-ho, heigh-ho!' Tommy hummed as he turned the key in the lock.

And then began a morning of mopping and sweeping, of taking down ripped blinds, nailing broken pelmets, fixing sash windows and screwing loose door knobs firmly into place. In the afternoon Joe showed up with a couple of market pals to help Tommy cut off the gas supply before dismantling old light fittings.

'Let's leave the boys to it,' Joy suggested to Mildred. 'We can walk back along the seafront if you like.'

Mildred signalled her agreement by helping Joy to stow away their cleaning materials in a cupboard under the stairs.

To reach the promenade the two girls crossed the market square then made their way down the side of the Tower building, emerging close to Central Pier at a busy time of day. Music from the Pleasure Beach mingled with the rattle of passing trams. Joy and Mildred were forced to thread their way through crowds of carefree holidaymakers, past the large temporary water tank until a lorry loaded with sandbags blocked their way. A man in shirtsleeves shouted a warning from the back of the wagon – 'Watch your backs, girls!' – before a heavy sandbag landed with a thud right at their feet.

Mildred shrank back with a look of confusion.

'It's all right,' Joy assured her as she began to work her way past the obstacle. 'It's safe to go this way – follow me.'

But the thud of a sandbag had shattered the girl's fragile confidence. Smiling mothers in sundresses; fathers with red, bad-tempered faces; children running hither and thither across her path – it was all too much.

'This way,' Joy repeated.

Mildred put her hands to her ears in a futile attempt to

block out the noise then, without warning, she darted in blind terror across the prom, dodging between cars and buses without a thought for her safety.

'Mildred, wait!' Joy set off in pursuit, managing to catch a glimpse of the girl's pale green dress as she reached the far pavement then disappeared up the alley beside the Tower. Car horns blared and drivers shouted as Joy followed in her wake before losing sight of her in the market square. Which way now? Another flash of pale green provided the answer – the frightened girl was heading back the way they'd come.

Mildred fled from the funfair screams, the music, the car horns, the shouting, but most of all from the faces in the crowd. Every single one could be Frank. He was here in Blackpool, around every corner, in every dark shadow – his pale face, his sharp features, the dark sweep of hair across his forehead, the glinting brass buttons on his blue blazer. Not knowing which way to turn, she sank to her knees and sobbed.

Joy found her on the corner of King Street, surrounded by a knot of concerned onlookers.

'What's up with 'er?' one asked as Joy crouched down beside Mildred and put an arm around her shoulder. 'Why won't she speak?'

'Looked like she's seen a ghost,' another muttered.

Joy motioned for them to stand clear with her free arm. 'Can you stand up?' she asked Mildred as the door to number 24 opened and Tommy and Joe came out on to the street. 'That's right; try. Help is on its way.'

'Poor lass,' a woman murmured. 'It looks to me like she's in the family way.'

With Joy's help Mildred struggled to her feet. She shielded her face with her hand as Joy led her to safety.

'Slowly does it,' Joy urged. 'We're almost there – let me help you. Now up three steps and through the door.'

Tommy and Joe brought up the rear and the door clicked shut behind them. 'Take her into the front living room,' Tommy suggested. 'We'll be in the kitchen if you need us.'

Joy guided Mildred towards an old, threadbare armchair and sat her down. 'I'll stay here with you,' she whispered. 'Take as long as you like.'

Mildred drew her legs to her chest then rocked forward and back, forward and back, breaking her long, locked-in silence with, 'Oh – oh – oh!' and again, 'Oh!'

'There, there,' Joy murmured.

'Don't let him . . .' Mildred's wall of silence crumbled and words tumbled from her mouth. 'Please don't let him . . . please.'

'Hush – no one is going to hurt you,' Joy promised.

'Mrs Rossi, I saw him.'

'Saw who? When?'

'Frank.' The name was heaved from deep within. 'North Pier, Pearl's arcade. I did see him.' She'd opened her mouth and spoken the dreaded words and the world hadn't come to an end. Joy was still there beside her.

'This Frank – he won't hurt you again. Do you hear me?' Joy waited for Mildred to raise her head and look her in the eye.

'Yes.' The wave of terror had broken over her head and was slowly ebbing. Through tears and sobs, Mildred spoke again. 'Thank you, Mrs Rossi. Thank you.'

Many days had passed and there was still no reply from Bernie. Reason told Pearl that it was too early to expect one, even if her airmail letter had got past the censors and arrived in Italy without delay. Time after time she'd thought of writing again in case the first one had got lost, and every morning she'd waited on the doorstep for the postman's delivery. 'Sorry, love – none for you' and, 'Sorry, Pearl – still no go,' and finally a curt, 'Nothing.' It had been one dull disappointment after another.

'For heaven's sake, stop moping around the house.' Maria told her off when she arrived home from work. 'Why not do what you normally do on a Saturday? Go out dancing with the girls.'

'Not tonight – I'm not in the mood.'

'You will be once you get there. Go on – up those stairs with you and get changed.'

'Aye aye, captain.' Following the line of least resistance, Pearl did as she was told and arrived at the Tower earlier than usual.

'Someone's an eager beaver,' Brenda, the girl from the ticket office, remarked as Pearl swung through the glass doors into the foyer.

She was in two minds whether to stay or go – she really didn't care either way. Unless someone she knew turned up shortly, she would probably drift off and have an early night. But then Joy and Tommy arrived and dragged Pearl inside. While Tommy went on ahead to buy tickets, Joy declared that there'd been a major breakthrough with Mildred – the runaway had broken her silence at last.

'The reason why she wanted to end it all was because she'd just seen her rapist coming out of your arcade.'

The news snapped Pearl out of her low mood. 'Out of my arcade? What time was this?'

'Late on Sunday afternoon.'

'I'd left Ernie in charge. Is Mildred sure it was the same man, not someone who looked similar?'

'The same, without doubt.' Joy explained how she and Tommy had managed to get Mildred home from King Street in a taxi. 'At first she didn't make much sense but Lucia soon settled her down and got more of the story out of her. Mildred had been sleeping rough. She'd spent most of last weekend on North Pier with nowhere to go, hoping that no one would notice her. She got the shock of her life when she spotted her attacker.'

'I'm not surprised.' Pearl drew a deep breath then exhaled through pursed lips. 'Give me a description so I can quiz Ernie.'

'He had a slight build, not tall. Picture Frank Sinatra – he joked with Mildred that his nickname was Frank because they looked so alike.'

'That's something, I suppose.' As more people arrived, Pearl and Joy found a quiet spot to one side of the foyer.

'Dr Evans warned us not to put pressure on Mildred. She's making progress but any small thing could cause a relapse. You should have seen the poor girl sobbing her heart out this afternoon – it was like a dam bursting.'

'I'll take my lead from you,' Pearl promised as she spotted Tommy waving from the balcony. 'He's bought your tickets – you'd better go,' she told Joy. 'If Ernie remembers anything important, I'll let you know.'

Joy ran up the stairs and Pearl watched from her quiet corner as more people crowded into the foyer and formed a queue on the stairs. She spotted the usual suspects – the tall figures of Eddie and Mavis in their elegant attire, a few ARP first-aiders and wardens, young Len Fraser and Valerie Ward, whose sweet romance was still going strong, and then inevitably, a posse of GIs swaggered in, talking in loud American accents and flashing smiles in the direction of unaccompanied girls.

Errol was among them. Hoping to avoid notice, Pearl slipped into the Ladies, where she intended to wait until the coast was clear. She pushed through the cloakroom door and entered a room lined with cubicles down both sides.

'Bad luck, Pearl – all occupied.' Ida was there with Thora, busy with lipstick and rouge at the mirror above the sinks. Ida was in shiny green satin, Thora in slinky crimson.

'It's all right – no hurry.'

Ida pressed her lips together then pouted. 'Pearl, what's this latest rumour we heard about you and Errol?'

'I've no idea, Ida – what have you heard?'

Thora, meanwhile, patted her fair curls then turned to face Pearl with an unconvincing smile. 'That you two have broken up – such a shame.'

Pearl bristled. 'We can't have broken up because we were never together – fact.'

'Ha ha; you could've fooled us.' Ida put away her lipstick. 'And Thora and I aren't the only ones who thought so. But anyway, is it right that you and Errol have pulled out of Sylvia's competition?'

'Yes, that part is true.' Pearl longed to hear a toilet flush followed by the slide of a bolt that would mean she could escape into a cubicle.

'Do tell!' It was Thora this time, shamelessly squeezing every drop of enjoyment out of Pearl's embarrassment.

Pearl had never much liked Thora and Ida and now she knew why. 'There's nothing to tell.'

'Ooh-hoo; touchy!' Ida's turn to twist the knife. 'Come off it – Errol Jackson was smitten from the start. He couldn't take his eyes off you – still can't.'

Enough was enough. Pearl turned around and departed without another word. There were muffled giggles as the door swung shut and Pearl set off across the foyer. Girls like Thora and Ida wouldn't get the better of her; who gave a fig if one of them pounced on Errol and they danced all night under the open roof? Pearl queued for her ticket before entering the magnificent ballroom. She looked up at the twinkling stars – let the music begin!

Vernon had done it again – floated off after lunch without telling Sylvia when he'd be back.

'No need to wait for me,' he'd called on his way out. 'I'll see you at the Tower if not before.'

Sylvia had convinced herself that this was fine; she understood that Vernon was permanently at his editor's beck and call, sent out to interview a fading music hall star or an up-and-coming circus performer. Before he left he'd mentioned that a famous film star was staying at the Norbreck – it would be his job to find out if the whiff of scandal surrounding her private life had any substance.

Fine! Sylvia had had a busy afternoon ahead of her. Teaching would keep her mind off yesterday's argument over Vernon's shirt, which had left her trembling from head to foot. *You moved it without telling me. I did not. You did – you know you did.* She had gone over and over the incident in her mind. Had she in fact committed the offence without realizing? It could happen sometimes – when she was so busy or preoccupied that she became absent-minded. Perhaps Vernon had been in the right all along. But if so, why be so angry over such a small thing? He'd thrust the shirt in her face and yelled that it was creased when it really hadn't been and it had been her dresses that would need ironing after he'd dragged them from their hangers.

She'd taught her tango lesson and returned to the empty flat. She'd picked up the dresses, still on the floor where Vernon had left them, and hung them back on their hangers, taking great care not to touch his shirts. She'd waited up for him and when he returned just before midnight he'd been his charming self, telling her about his night out with other journalists from the *Gazette*. He wasn't keen on the sports reporter (who banged on and on about football) but had found more in common with Hugo Wilkinson (who covered town council affairs and who could drink all the rest under the table). A good night, all in all.

They'd gone to bed and straight to sleep. Or rather, Vernon had. Sylvia had stayed awake, taking shallow breaths and hardly daring to move. In the morning she'd got up first and made breakfast for them both. He'd come to the table half dressed and in need of a shave – still achingly handsome. He'd called her sweetheart and love, told her that he would work from home all morning and made a sad face when he'd learned that she would be in the studio. 'Don't be too long – I'll miss you,' he'd murmured softly and held her in a long embrace before she'd departed.

Perhaps she'd made too much of the previous day's argument. Since she was a child Lorna had criticized Sylvia for taking small setbacks too much to heart. Couples had rows over trivial things – it was normal. So when she'd come home for lunch to learn that Vernon had been asked to interview the aforesaid famous film star she'd been excited on his behalf.

'Who is she?' she'd asked as he'd checked that he had his notebook and pencil.

'Nancy Marlowe.'

Sylvia had confessed that the name meant nothing to her.

'Really? She's only the biggest starlet to emerge from Ealing Studios in the last couple of years.' Vernon had smiled indulgently at her ignorance. 'With luck I can get her to dish the dirt on other stars and come away with a scoop.' So don't wait for him, he'd insisted – he'd see her at the Tower. 'Wear your green dress,' had been his parting shot.

Which was the reason Sylvia was alone when she followed Pearl into the ballroom, to find the evening already underway.

'Don't ask,' a grim-faced Sylvia muttered as she sat at Pearl's table.

'It's like that, is it?' Pearl picked up on her friend's tense mood. She looked stunning in her sparkly dress but something was obviously amiss.

'Vernon's working.' Sylvia immediately broke her resolution not to mention him.

'Of course he is.'

They sat in silence as organ notes swelled and filled the ballroom, rising through the open roof into the starlit sky.

'Lovely evening,' Pearl remarked listlessly as a foxtrot ended and a jive began. And yes; she saw that Thora had beaten Ida to it and was having a whale of a time being swung around the floor by Errol. 'Do you want to dance?' she asked Sylvia.

'No, I'd rather sit this one out, thanks.'

Joy and Tommy beckoned them on to the floor as they passed by but Sylvia and Pearl shook their heads. Sylvia spotted Mavis and Eddie heading for the bar. Pearl waved at Sandra and Eileen. Swing out, triple step on the spot, low kick, retract and swing back in – the lively ARP pair had the moves off pat. Back at the bar, Eddie and Mavis seemed to be having a difference of opinion – he shook his head at something she'd said then Mavis walked off in a huff. Ruby was jiving with a GI who lifted her clean off the floor then swung her over his hip before bringing her round to face him again, rocking forward then back then on again. 'I'm a killer-diller, yes, I am! Wham, Be-Bop-Boom-Bam!'

'"I can do it, you can too!"' Sylvia mouthed the lyrics with a couldn't-care-less shrug. Where on earth had Vernon got to?

'Here he comes.' Pearl had read Sylvia's thoughts. She pointed to the main entrance, where Vernon stood next to a slim, dark-haired woman in a strapless silver dress with a fitted, fish-tail skirt. 'Is that who I think it is?' She gasped at the dazzling vision.

Sylvia followed the direction of Pearl's finger. Vernon had placed his hand under his companion's elbow and had started to guide her towards the table where she and Pearl sat. Her stomach churned as they drew near.

'Is that Nancy Marlowe?' Pearl could scarcely believe her eyes. 'You know; the actress who starred in *Snows of St Moritz* and *Lovers' Leap*. What on earth is she doing here?'

Others were wondering the same thing. Jaws dropped and dancers made room for Vernon and his glamorous companion to pass. Could it possibly be? Surely not! It's her – I swear on my life!

Sylvia's body went rigid. Her face was pale and blank when Vernon spoke.

'Sorry we're late,' he apologized as he pulled out a chair for the raven-haired woman with the scintillating lipstick smile. 'Time flies when you're having fun. I'm sure no introductions are necessary,' he added with a complacent smile.

'Hello, I'm Nancy.' Giving him a nudge with her elbow, the actress extended a gracious hand towards Pearl and Sylvia. 'He's a card, isn't he? He's had me in stitches all afternoon.'

'He's a card all right.' Pearl spoke through gritted teeth. 'I'm Pearl Greene, by the way. And this is . . .'

'Sylvia,' Vernon completed her sentence. 'She teaches ballroom dancing.'

'Pleased to meet you.' Seemingly oblivious to the frosty atmosphere, Nancy basked in the sunshine of a thousand admiring glances. 'Isn't this place an absolute wonder? Look up; you can see the stars!'

'There's one star here that outshines all the rest.' Vernon sat beside her with his elbow on the table and his back turned to Sylvia.

Pearl slipped her hand under the table and grasped her friend's fingers so hard that Sylvia winced.

'You silly so-and-so!' Nancy's laugh was light and tinkling. Her diamanté earrings and necklace sparkled. She leaned forward to confide in Sylvia. 'Mr Silver Tongue here promised me that I'd have more fun if we came to the Tower than if we stayed at my stuffy hotel so we gave my manager the slip and here we are.'

'Ready to dance the night away.' Vernon seized the moment. As the jive finished and Reggie Dixon segued seamlessly into a quickstep he leaped to his feet and offered Nancy his hand. 'I'm sure you two girls don't mind,' he said to Pearl and Sylvia as he whisked her away.

'Please don't say a word.' Sylvia had been holding her breath. As she let it out she felt herself begin to tremble. Tears welled up and threatened to spill.

'I could kill him,' Pearl muttered.

'No, don't make a fuss – I'm fine.' Sylvia picked up her

handbag then scraped back her chair.

'Where are you going?'

'To the ladies' cloakroom. I tell you, I'm fine.'

'I'll come with you.'

'No, stay where you are.' Sylvia was afraid that if she accepted Pearl's offer her thin crust of self-possession would crumble. 'I won't be long.'

She walked away, eyes straight ahead – out on to the first-floor balcony, past the ticket office then down the wide stairs into the brightly lit foyer, scarcely breathing, feeling more and more dizzy and oblivious to her surroundings.

'Sylvia?'

Her hand was on the cloakroom door when a voice called her name. She turned too quickly, her knees buckled and she sank senseless to the floor.

CHAPTER EIGHTEEN

There'd been a tiff and Mavis had stormed off to the Ladies. Eddie had waited at the bar but she hadn't returned.

A row over nothing – she'd jumped down his throat for not listening to a word she'd said; an increasingly common occurrence, apparently. 'You're always thinking of something or someone else.' He'd apologized. No good; Mavis had tossed her head and walked away, leaving him high and dry.

Eddie had downed his drink then decided to go and find her. There would be more humble pie – he was sorry and yes, it was true he had a lot on his mind and was sometimes distracted. He would try to do better in future. Once he'd smoothed things over, they would return to the dance floor.

He was halfway down the stairs when he saw Sylvia making her way towards the cloakroom ahead of him. She seemed unsteady so he called her name. She turned and fainted so he ran to her aid.

She lay face down. Her hair had come loose and fallen over her face. 'Sylvia?' Eddie stroked back strands of hair, unsure whether or not to move her. Her skin was cold but there were beads of sweat on her forehead. He pressed his fingers against her wrist to check her pulse then straightened her skirt to cover her legs.

Meanwhile, the cloakroom door swung open and Mavis emerged, to be greeted by a picture of Eddie crouching over Sylvia, who seemed dead to the world. Mavis gasped and shrank back.

Eddie relied on his first-aid training – once he'd checked Sylvia's pulse, he turned her on to her back then raised her legs. 'Fetch cushions, a pile of coats – something to raise her feet off the floor,' he called out to whoever was close by.

A quick-thinking doorman rushed to his aid. Taking off their jackets, they rolled them up and placed them under Sylvia's legs.

'Has she had one too many?' the hard-bitten doorman asked.

'No – it seems she fainted. She'll come round soon, I hope.'

And sure enough, Sylvia's eyes flickered open. Through blurred vision she saw the outlines of two men bending over her and made a panicky attempt to sit up.

Eddie slid an arm under her back to raise her. She was light as a feather. 'Easy does it; take your time.' He kept his arm there as a support, cradling her while she came to. 'She needs a drink,' he told a woman standing by the cloakroom door, only to discover that it was Mavis. 'There you are! Fetch Sylvia some water, please.'

Mavis reacted as if someone had flicked a switch. She sprang into action – obviously there were taps in the cloakroom but how would she carry the water back?

'Where am I?' Sylvia's head swam. There were bright lights high above her and the sound of organ music. She thought she recognized Eddie's voice.

'You're at the Tower,' he murmured. 'You passed out, that's all.'

In the cloakroom Mavis discovered a used glass on a window sill. It contained dregs of sweet martini which she rinsed out. By the time she'd filled it with cold water and rushed back out into the foyer, there were others on the scene.

Back in the ballroom, Pearl had been uneasy. Sylvia had looked dreadful; she ought not to have let her go to the Ladies by herself. So she'd grabbed hold of Joy mid-quickstep and gabbled an explanation – Nancy Marlowe and bloody Vernon were dancing together – Sylvia was in a right state. The two girls had dashed down the stairs to discover Eddie administering first aid.

Eddie took the glass from Mavis then offered it to Sylvia. 'Drink it slowly,' he told her. 'A few sips at a time. How do you feel now? Stand back, everyone – give her space to breathe.'

While Joy offered Eddie one of the rolled-up jackets to place around Sylvia's shoulders, Pearl pulled Mavis to one side and demanded an explanation.

'You'd better ask Eddie. I wasn't here when it happened.' Seeing that Sylvia was recovering, Mavis backed away. She wished to be anywhere but here.

'Eddie?' Sylvia clung to his hand.

'Yes, it's me. Take a few more sips. Tell me when you feel ready to stand.'

She recognized his voice, soft and kind. There were people all around and Vernon pushing his way through to the front.

'Stand back, everyone. I'll take it from here.' Vernon thrust Eddie to one side. News had travelled fast from foyer to ballroom – Sylvia Ellis had fallen down in a dead faint. Eddie Winter was giving her first aid. Vernon had been obliged to make speedy arrangements for his film star to leave the building by a back door. 'There's an emergency – I have to go,' he'd told one of the MCs. 'Miss Marlowe will require a taxi to take her back to the Norbreck.' But it turned out that Nancy had come out without her purse. Vernon had paid for her fare. Apologies for spoiling her evening and he hoped she wouldn't hold it against him. But now, after this short delay, he was down in the foyer and back in control. 'What happened, sweetheart? Are you all right? Let's get you home.'

Eddie kept a reluctant distance as Vernon put his arm around Sylvia's waist then raised her to her feet.

'I'm sorry,' she mumbled. 'I'm sorry.'

'Hush now.' Still supporting her, Vernon led her towards the exit.

Pearl discovered Sylvia's handbag at the foot of the stairs and hurried after them, out on to the promenade. 'This belongs to Sylvia.' She handed the bag to Vernon. 'How will you get her home?'

'I parked my car just around the corner.'

'I'm so sorry.' Sylvia turned her face away from Pearl.

'Are you sure she can manage?' Pearl was reluctant to let them go.

'Quite sure.' He kept on walking. When Sylvia stumbled, he lifted her up and carried her around the corner, out of sight.

Mavis refused to go back into the ballroom with Eddie.

'What's the point?' she asked as he walked her home to Duke Street. 'The evening is already ruined.'

'But Lorna's competition is only two weeks away. We need to put the finishing touches to our waltz routine.'

'Is that all you ever think about – our blasted waltz

moves?' Mavis was furious. Striding ahead, her skirt flared out as she whirled around and walked backwards, gesticulating wildly. 'Perfecting our frames, swaying into the first beat of the bar, forward change right to left then left to right, blah-blah.'

'Watch out!' The warning came too late as Mavis collided with a litter bin.

She recovered her balance then walked beside him. 'I mean it, Eddie – I'm sick to death of the Viennese waltz. Why can't we let our hair down once in a while?'

'I thought we'd agreed . . .?' He let his sentence drift, thinking back to the time when he'd been without a dance partner and Lorna had picked out Mavis for him – a diamond in the rough but with bags of potential. True, they'd made an unlikely couple but he felt it had worked out well.

'We did agree, but that was then. Now I'm green with envy every time I watch Pearl dance the jive.'

'Not any more,' he reminded her.

'That's beside the point. Think of any other Latin couple: Bill and Shirley, Andrew and Margaret. They don't have to stick to a set pattern; they're free to improvise. And their music is so modern.'

'But we chose Standard ballroom from the start.' He began to suspect that there was more to this than she was letting on.

'You and Lorna chose – I didn't.'

'Point taken, but why didn't this come up before now?'

'It did but you didn't notice.'

'Did it? When?'

'Ages ago – whenever the band played swing or boogie-woogie and I wanted to stay on the floor; that's when you carted me off to the bar for a drink.'

'I suppose you're right. I'm sorry for being such a

stuffed shirt.' They'd walked as far as North Pier, where they must turn off on to Duke Street. 'I've always had my heart set on ballroom; it's in my blood.'

Mavis knew that Eddie didn't get the point. She tugged at his sleeve to stop him from crossing the road. 'Let's face it, you've had your heart set on something else too.'

About to step off the pavement, he came to a sudden halt. Good Lord, she meant Sylvia!

'Yes; finally!' As the truth dawned, Mavis turned and walked slowly down some steps on to the beach, where she stooped to take off her shoes. 'I suppose I've always known.'

'Mavis, wait.' Eddie followed her. The full moon cast enough light for them to see the silhouette of the pier standing out against a starlit sky. 'I swore to make a clean break from the past – you and I are the future.'

Shaking her head, she walked on towards the shoreline. 'When I saw you with Sylvia tonight, I knew in a flash that it's simply not true.'

'You don't understand. I was worried about her, that's all.'

He'd cradled Sylvia in his arms like a lover; that was the moment when Mavis had admitted defeat. 'Be honest, Eddie. She's the only girl for you and always will be.'

He wanted to protest but the words stuck in his throat and in the end he couldn't deny it. They stood side by side, watching the dark waves swell and break.

'It's all right. Deep down I've always known.' Plucky Mavis managed to strike a more cheerful note. 'We've had fun, though. And you've taught me a lot – not just about fleckerls and quarter turns. You're a blooming walking encyclopaedia, you are. I've learned the whole history of the Tower – how many feet high it is, the number of nuts and bolts that went into building it.'

Eddie forced a smile. 'Never mind the nuts and bolts; I've learned something much more important from you – namely, how to seize the moment and live life to the full.'

'That's all right then.' So it was settled between them with regrets but without too much hurt. 'It's a pity, though.'

'What is?' The horizon stretched on for ever, wave after restless wave.

'We could've won that waltz competition hands down and made headlines in the *Gazette*.'

'Two trumpet players, two saxophonists, one pianist . . .' As a reminder for Pearl, Sylvia counted off on her fingers the members of Art Richardson's band. 'Oh, and one double bass player and one drummer.' Excitement was building. Now there was just over a week until the event at the Spanish Hall and Sylvia, Cliff and Lorna had almost met their entry targets.

'Don't forget the singer,' Pearl added with a knowing look. She'd been relieved to see Sylvia walking along the pier, seemingly back to her old self after Saturday's fainting fit. When she reached the arcade, dressed in her favourite white capri pants and a pale blue top, the sea breeze had ruffled her fair hair and brought colour to her cheeks.

'How could I possibly forget Rosie?' Sylvia had the grace to shrug off Pearl's pointed remark with a smile and a laugh. 'Or Nancy Marlowe, for that matter.' The two glamour pusses had made a lasting impact.

'I'm not busy in here – let's step outside.' Pearl summoned Ernie, who'd been given the task of collecting money from the Chip and Busts and Lucky Stars. She asked him to man the desk for a short while.

'How long?' He dumped the bag of coins by the side

of the till. Pearl's 'short while' could stretch to hours and hours, going by recent experience.

'A few minutes. And try not to sulk.'

Once out in the fresh air, the two girls strolled past the Seaview Café towards the end of the pier, where they leaned against the railing and gazed out to sea. 'Vernon's article did the trick,' Sylvia told Pearl. 'Entries are coming in thick and fast. Now it looks as though we might even have to turn people away.'

Pearl left a comfortable pause before asking, 'How are you, anyway?'

'Excited, nervous . . .'

'No; I mean how are you and Vernon getting along?'

'Like a house on fire,' Sylvia rushed to reply. 'Honestly, he's made such a fuss of me these last few days. He's made my breakfast and generally tidied up around me. Last night he came home early and drove me to Stanley Park for an evening stroll.'

'That's good to hear. And you took it easy after last Saturday, I hope?'

'What do you think? No, I was back in the studio on Sunday, putting the finishing touches to Andrew and Margaret's routine. I'm convinced they stand a very good chance of lifting the Latin trophy now that you and Errol have pulled out.'

'Typical – there's no stopping you, is there?' Pearl glanced over her shoulder to see new customers forming a short queue outside the arcade. They were the usual mixture of day trippers and off-duty servicemen. She turned away quickly, preferring not to know whether Errol was among them. 'Joy and I were worried about you.'

'No need.' Sylvia brushed aside her concern. 'How about you? Any letter yet?'

Pearl shook her head. 'I'm worried sick, if you must know.' Nothing; not a word from Bernie. Silence, never-ending, nerve-jangling silence.

'I'm sorry that you and Errol won't be competing.'

'In the end we agreed that it was the right thing to do.' She glanced round again in time to see that yes, her ex-dancing partner was there. She watched him pay his money then stoop to enter through the low door of the arcade.

'Still, it's a pity to miss out. Couldn't you find a replacement?'

'Let's not talk about it.' The permanent knot in Pearl's stomach tightened. 'The whole thing has been such a mess.'

It was time for them to say goodbye – Sylvia had arranged to meet Lorna while Pearl must relieve Ernie. 'Chin up,' Sylvia said as she hurried off.

Determined to act normally, Pearl took charge of the till while her brother went back to collecting coins from the machines. Players were silent as they focused their attention on winning. At the drop of a coin, a silver ball bearing would appear. The player would pull a lever to propel the ball around a metal maze then watch it drop, be redirected then drop again and again until the ball rolled out of sight. No jackpot this time around.

Stepping back from his machine, Errol sauntered up the aisle towards the till. 'Howdy, Miss Pearl – how you doin'?' Just friendly and casual as agreed.

'I'm fine, thanks.' The lie tripped from her tongue but she knew that he knew that she was far from fine.

He assumed that she still hadn't received the longed-for letter. 'And Miss Sylvia?'

'She's fine too. She was here just now.'

'Yeah, I saw her. Not long to go now, huh?'

'Till her dance weekend? Nine days.' The conversation threatened to peter out. In the background there was a rattle of coins landing in a metal dish. One of the Playball machines had paid out. Pearl forced a smile for Errol's benefit. 'Sylvia has high hopes it'll be a roaring success – even without us.'

Ouch! He made way for new customers to enter. 'Yeah, I guess. Hey, it turns out your friend Thora is quite a gal.'

Pearl prepared herself for what was to follow. 'Don't tell me – you and Thora have entered the jive competition.'

Errol shook his head. 'No, Miss Pearl – Miss Thora sure as hell wanted to but I told her no way. She made eyes at me, sayin', please, please! I told her thanks but no thanks.'

Pearl bit her lip. It wasn't good to gloat.

'Quite a gal,' he repeated with a low laugh. 'How about you? Did you find a new partner?'

'No and I haven't looked.' End of story. 'I'll be there on the night but only to offer Sylvia moral support.'

'So, see you around.' Members of Errol's group had spent their small change and were drifting away from the machines, out on to the pier. He followed them. They gathered by the café, exchanging cigarettes and flirting with a bunch of local girls.

Back in the arcade, Ernie approached the till with another bag of coins. 'Can I go now?' he asked Pearl.

'Soon.' Here was an opportunity to quiz her brother to see if he remembered any more about what happened on the day Mildred had threatened to jump. 'First I need you to get your thinking cap on about a week last Sunday.'

'Oh heck.' Ernie grumbled and growled and would have scarpered if she hadn't cornered him.

'Run through what you told me before,' she insisted.

'The arcade was busy. There was a bunch of GIs. Who else?'

'Leave off.' He squirmed out of Pearl's grasp. 'Dennis was here – I booted him out. That was it.'

'Ernie, this is important. We must have had other customers you haven't mentioned.'

He narrowed his eyes. 'Why do you want to know?'

'Because Mildred swears there was a man in the arcade that day who did something awful to her a little while ago. He committed a serious crime.'

'Blimey!' Pearl's whispered account had piqued Ernie's interest – he'd recently read a Sherlock Holmes mystery and had fancied life as a detective ever since. 'Does that make me a witness?'

'Maybe. Think back to what happened – you kicked Dennis out, then what?'

His face took on a look of pained concentration. 'I was goin' to tell you this bit but you cut me dead. After I got rid of Dennis this woman comes in with a load of blokes. I didn't know her from Adam but a geezer playin' on the What's My Line by the door rushes up and asks for her autograph. It turns out her name's Rosie Johnson and she sings with—'

'Art Richardson's band.'

'How did you know that?' Ernie was amazed at his sister's grasp of the facts.

'Never mind – I just did. Did you get the names of the men she was with?'

Ernie screwed up his features. 'There was a short, fat bloke called Harold and one they called George.'

'What did he look like?'

'Dunno, I didn't notice.'

'Concentrate. Was there a man called Frank?'

'Not that I know of. The lanky, bald one was ordering the others around – he was the boss.' Ernie felt the pressure; major criminal investigation or not, he longed to be let off the hook.

Pearl realized she'd gleaned all she could for the time being. 'Good lad – you've been a big help.'

'Can I go now?'

Pearl nodded and he galloped off, leaving her to mull over what she'd learned. She might be on to something; Art Richardson's band performed in ballrooms across the north-west so it was perfectly possible that they'd played at the Manchester Mecca on the fateful night. Pearl decided to lose no time in sharing the information with Joy. Together they would follow up this new lead. Until then she resisted the urge to run before she could walk.

Joy gave Alan her new telephone number then took the train home with mixed feelings, trying to convince herself that she'd done the right thing. 'Get in touch if there's a problem,' she'd insisted before leaving. 'The call will go through to Lucia's ice-cream parlour and either she or Mildred will come and fetch me.'

The first day of working from home was fast approaching. George would be in the Glasgow office, ready to step in if necessary, which shouldn't happen because Joy had carefully scheduled every delivery and chased up every outstanding invoice before she left. At least, she hoped she had. She sat in the train gazing out at summer fields; the wheat was turning from green to gold and brown Hereford cows were dotted across sunny hillsides. The train swayed around wide bends and rattled over gleaming steel tracks as fields gave way to houses and Joy caught her first glimpse of the sea.

With her head still full of work matters, she alighted in North Station then headed straight home, where she found Lucia bustling around her café and Mildred putting her feet up in her room.

'I went to the clinic all by myself,' Mildred announced with a touch of pride. She sat on her bed propped up by pillows, with her short hair freshly washed, dressed in a loose blouse that covered her expanding baby bump.

'And?' Joy perched on the side of the bed.

'Nurse Myers was pleased with me.' Mildred had slipped into the waiting room, careful to avoid eye contact with the other pregnant ladies. When her name had been called, she'd kept her head down and hurried behind the green screens, got undressed then lain on the bed. Nurse Myers had pressed a cold metal trumpet against her belly and listened. 'The baby's heartbeat is strong,' she'd told her. 'You're both doing very well.'

'She said I was a good girl,' Mildred told Joy shyly.

'So you are.' Joy smiled and patted her hand. 'And you caught the tram home?'

'No, it's a nice day so I walked.' With her head held high and a blossoming sensation that she had as much right as anyone else to enjoy the sunshine.

'And why not? Fresh air does you good.' Joy absorbed the pretty orderliness of the room – the crisp white pillows, blue counterpane and a framed print of roses on the chimney breast. Perhaps it was time to suggest another outing. 'How do you feel about coming out for tea on Friday?'

Mildred clasped her hands tightly together. 'Who with?' Going to the baby clinic was one thing; sitting in a tea shop like an ordinary, everyday girl was quite another.

'With me.'

'Where to?'

'To my friend Sylvia's. It'll be just the three of us.'

So not to a café where people might stare. 'I don't know. I'm not sure . . .' Untwisting her fingers, Mildred rested her hands across her stomach.

'No need to decide straight away.' Joy stood up and smoothed down the bedspread. 'Think about it and tell me later.'

CHAPTER NINETEEN

'Did you two know about this?' Lorna arrived at the North View Parade studio unusually flustered and armed with a copy of that morning's *Gazette*. She flung it down on top of the gramophone player and pointed to a feature on the entertainments page.

Sylvia and Cliff read the headline: *Dance Weekend in Disarray*. Beneath it was a publicity shot of Rosie Johnson and a subheading: *Sick Singer Backs Out*.

Stunned by the news, Sylvia was at first unable to speak.

'We had no idea.' Cliff read on. 'It says here Rosie's got diphtheria; it started with a high temperature and sore throat earlier this week. She'll be out of action for at least a fortnight.'

Lorna turned to Sylvia with an accusatory glare. 'Didn't Vernon warn you?'

'No, he didn't say a word.' Sylvia was still trying to take in the news. Diphtheria was serious but it was an illness that could now be treated. Today was Friday, which meant there was just over a week to go before the start of their competition.

'But he wrote the article.' Lorna pointed to the reporter's name. 'Why didn't he mention it?'

Cliff stepped in between mother and daughter. 'That's

hardly the point, if I may say so. The fact is there's no way that Rosie will recover in time to sing for us if this report is true.'

'*If* it's true?' Lorna turned her gaze to Cliff.

'Yes – instances of Rosie Johnson being unwell appear in the news from time to time. The word on the grapevine is that "unwell" is a polite way of saying that she's too sozzled to stand up straight and has to be sent away to a health resort in the countryside to dry out.'

Lorna took a sharp intake of breath. 'And Art Richardson continues to employ her?'

'Yes – if she manages to stay sober she's a marvellous singer.' Not wanting to go into further detail, Cliff bit his tongue.

Sylvia got over her initial shock. 'Art must have a reserve singer in mind. Surely this isn't a complete disaster?'

'Vernon is exaggerating when he says we're in disarray,' Cliff conceded. 'He knows what makes a good headline.'

'And I suppose there's no such thing as bad publicity.' Sylvia did her best to look on the bright side. 'Vernon's article may turn out to be a good thing after all.'

Lorna refused to be placated. 'But we have all the entries we need now. What if this article puts couples off and they decide not to compete after all?'

'It's a little messy,' Cliff agreed, pacing the floor and frowning. 'Perhaps Vernon could call Art and find out the name of Rosie's stand-in – what do you think, Sylvia?'

Lorna was all for this idea. 'Yes; then he could write another short article that would give us a last-minute boost.'

Sylvia's chest tightened. 'I could suggest it,' she murmured reluctantly.

It was agreed – Sylvia would speak with Vernon and

meanwhile Lorna and Cliff would finalize arrangements at the Spanish Hall, checking that the billboards advertising their weekend were in place outside the entrance to the Winter Gardens. There was even talk of a wireless interview for the BBC as part of a current affairs programme describing how the fun-loving British were determined to keep on carrying on in dance halls all around the country.

'All will be well,' Cliff assured Lorna as they left the studio together. 'With or without Rosie Johnson, Art's band is a big draw. Entries have come flooding in from far and wide, excitement is mounting and nothing I can think of will stop us now.'

Vernon came up behind Sylvia, put his arms around her waist, swayed her from side to side and crooned the chorus of 'You Are My Sunshine' into her ear. He'd called in at the studio and caught her unawares as she put away records after her morning's teaching. 'You are, you know – you make me happy every time I see you.'

She turned to face him with a tentative smile. 'Hello; have you had a busy morning?'

'Not too bad.' Releasing her, he loosened his tie and undid his top button. 'I have to go out again this afternoon, though. I was thinking we might fit in the flicks later this evening.'

Lorna had left her copy of the *Gazette* next to the record player. Sylvia watched Vernon's eyes skim over his report.

'Or would you rather skip the cinema and get an early night?' He sidled up to her and nuzzled her cheek.

'I'm not sure. I'll see how I feel.'

'A nice early night,' he repeated as he stroked her cheek with his thumb. 'What do you say?'

Sylvia took a deliberate step back then reached for the newspaper. 'Why didn't you tell me about Rosie?'

'Sorry – must've slipped my mind.' Shrugging, he reached for a cigarette.

'When did you find out she was ill?'

'A couple of days ago – Alfie happened to mention it. When news got out, Sam thought it was worth a few hundred words in today's paper. Why? What's the problem?'

'You said we're in disarray.'

'Yeah – sorry,' he acknowledged through a cloud of smoke. 'That was the sub-editor's doing – you know how it is. Anyway, no need to get hot under the collar about a silly headline, is there?'

His arms encircled her and again she stepped away so she could see him clearly. 'Cliff and Mother want to know if Art has found a stand-in.'

'I can check with Alfie if you like.' Vernon picked a shred of tobacco from the tip of his tongue with his thumb and forefinger. 'Can you please stop going on about it and tell me what we're having for lunch?' As he strode towards the door, his image was reflected in floor-to-ceiling mirrors on three sides of the studio. 'Are you coming?' he called over his shoulder.

Sylvia had learned to recognize the cool, dismissive tone, so she was on tenterhooks as she followed him to the flat.

'What is there to eat?' He went into the kitchen and rummaged in cupboards, scattering cigarette ash over the floor.

'There's a fresh loaf in the bread bin.'

'Anything else?' He slammed one cupboard door then opened another.

'We've used up all the eggs and cheese.'

'I give up.' Another door slammed then he pushed past her into the living room. 'I'll get something while I'm out. This stupid fuss about Rosie – it's not really coming from Lorna and Cliff, is it?' Still ultra-casual, said with a slight sneer.

Sylvia felt a constriction in her throat that made it hard to swallow. It was better to say as little as possible and let Vernon get whatever it was out of his system.

'Admit it – you never liked her. You're probably happy that she's dropped out; it means less competition.'

'That's not fair,' Sylvia breathed.

'Isn't it?' He came close, to within inches of her face. 'Swear to me you're not jealous.'

'Stop it, please.' He was looking down at her, taking advantage of his height, frightening her with the ferocity of his gaze.

Vernon laughed suddenly and raised both hands in surrender then he turned to the mirror to fasten his shirt button and straighten his tie. 'Anyway, I can't blame you or any other girl who has to compete with Rosie. But don't worry; you can't get rid of me that easily – you, Sylvia Ellis, are still officially my sweetheart.'

The phrase brought hot, shameful tears to her eyes. It somehow made her sound like a trophy or a medal. It made her feel small.

'I'll be back later,' he promised on his way out. 'And remember, leave your evening free for that early night.'

Joy was glad that she'd been able to coax Mildred out of the house, despite a grey sky that threatened rain.

'We'll take umbrellas,' she promised Lucia. Tommy was at King Street with a member of the circus lighting crew, starting to install wiring throughout the house.

'*Si, si – ombrelli!*' Lucia waved them off with a broad smile '*Pioverà* – soon it rains.'

The past few days had run smoothly at work so there was a spring in Joy's step as she and Mildred walked along the prom. 'So far the day has gone without a hitch, thank goodness. I've had just one phone call from Alan about a rush order for V-neck jumpers from a department store on Oxford Street. That's in London,' she explained to her naive companion. 'So that was good news and me being here in Blackpool didn't cause a delay since I could organize delivery over the phone. Next week I'll order a small, portable typewriter. Then it will be like having two offices – one in Manchester and one in Blackpool.'

Mildred didn't take in much of what she was being told but Mrs Rossi sounded happy. Meanwhile, a light rain started to fall and with their umbrellas up they could stroll along unrecognized, past a long row of souvenir stalls on one side and the wide open sea on the other.

'There aren't many people around,' Joy remarked as they reached Central Pier. 'Everyone's inside, keeping dry. Are you happy to carry on walking, or should we catch a tram?'

'Walk,' Mildred decided. She liked the salty tang of the sea in her nostrils and was in no hurry to arrive at Sylvia's flat. But when they'd walked as far as North Pier she was feeling tired. 'Is it far?' she asked.

'No, we turn up the next street,' Joy promised. 'Five more minutes and we'll be there.'

The shower eased so they closed their umbrellas and shook off the raindrops. On North View Parade they passed a row of boarding houses with 'No Vacancy' signs outside each one then a butcher's shop with two men in straw boaters and striped aprons serving behind a shiny, glass-fronted counter. They passed some more houses and finally reached a bright sign above a plate-glass window which read 'Live Your Dream' in big, shiny letters.

'This is it,' Joy announced. 'Or rather, the one next door.'

Mildred followed her into a dark shop entrance with an intriguing sweet smell. Inside the shop she caught a glimpse of a boy using brass scales to weigh out a small heap of loose tobacco.

'Up these stairs.' Once more Joy led the way, knocking on the door at the top then waiting for Sylvia to appear.

'There you are.' Sylvia looked pleased to see them as she opened the door. She was lovely and slim in her pale blue blouse and tapered, three-quarter-length trousers, with her hair up in a ponytail that swung as she turned. 'Come in. Tea's ready.'

Mildred had managed the outing well so far but now her nerves would be put to the test. Would she be able to drink her tea without spilling it? Would she have to make small talk with someone she hardly knew?

'Come in,' Sylvia said again. She sat them down on her sofa and made them feel at home. 'Here – give me your umbrellas. I'll put them in the sink in case they drip. Joy, have you heard the latest? Art Richardson's singer has had to drop out.'

'What; no singer for your dance weekend?' Joy picked up the note of anxiety beneath Sylvia's breathless chatter. 'What happened to Rosie Johnson?'

'She's poorly. But Cliff says not to worry – it shouldn't affect us too badly.'

'Yes, I suppose the band can manage without her,' Joy agreed.

The talk veered off in a direction that Mildred didn't follow so instead she took in her surroundings. So this was what it was like to make your own way in the world as a single girl. You had a flat with pretty things in it, such as the daintily embroidered linen covers for when you rested your head back against the sofa and ornaments of beautiful dancing ladies on the mantelpiece and a lamp in the corner that was modern and sleek. You earned your own money by teaching dancing and running a competition and you paid your own rent – it was wonderful.

'Here's your tea.' Sylvia handed Mildred a cup and saucer. 'I'm afraid there's no sugar. You look very well, by the way; positively blooming.'

'Thank you.' Mildred smiled and balanced the precarious cup and saucer on her knee.

Joy and Sylvia chatted on. Joy told Sylvia that she felt she'd made the right decision to work from home for one day a week. 'It should give me more time to help Tommy with the house.'

'And even an hour or two to practise your Viennese waltz?' Sylvia teased. 'Mother will be thrilled.'

Mildred risked raising the cup to her lips. So far so good. Mrs Rossi's friend was very nice and Mildred felt under no pressure to join in the conversation. She fixed her gaze on the silver dancing girls and dreamed of a future that could have been hers. 'I love to dance,' she volunteered during a short silence.

'You do?' Silvia was immediately all ears.

'Yes – to swing music. I listened to it all the time on the wireless. I saved up and went to our local dance halls every Saturday.'

'Then you must come to me for lessons.' Sylvia saw panic in the sudden red flush on Mildred's neck. 'Having a baby needn't stop you from dancing,' she said quickly. 'My mother did it so why shouldn't you?'

'When you're ready,' Joy added calmly. 'And perhaps not the more strenuous stuff – not straight away.'

'Of course, whenever you like. The door's always open.'

'I felt the same as you, Mildred,' Joy confided. 'I thought dancing wasn't for the likes of me. I was very shy and I didn't earn much money as a cleaner at the Tower. It was thanks to Sylvia and her mother that I dipped my toe in the water.'

'And she's never looked back,' Sylvia added brightly. 'She and Tommy are in the running to win the Viennese waltz section next Saturday.'

'I wouldn't go that far,' Joy said with a blush. When Mildred excused herself to go to the toilet she thanked Sylvia for drawing the girl out of herself. 'With a bit of luck, this time next year we'll see her out on the dance floor while Lucia stays at home and babysits.'

Mildred was gone longer than expected and meanwhile Sylvia and Joy heard footsteps on the stairs accompanied by men's voices.

'Vernon,' Sylvia said quietly. She stood up and swiftly carried the tray into the kitchen then reappeared with an anxious expression.

'And?' Joy enquired.

'Probably Alfie.'

Sure enough, the door opened and the two men entered. They were in mid-conversation – Alfie was telling Vernon a tale about a girl he'd just met; a good-looker but with not much between the ears.

Vernon said something about not looking a gift horse in the mouth then he noticed Joy. 'Sorry, I didn't realize we had a visitor,' he said with a breezy smile. 'Sylvia never mentioned it.'

Joy stood up awkwardly. She could never quite relax

with Sylvia's beau. The reason was hard to pin down; he was always charming but it was as if he was enjoying a private joke at her expense. Perhaps it was the half-smile that played constantly on his lips. 'Hello, Vernon – how are you?'

'I'm tip-top thanks, Joy.' He sauntered through to the kitchen and noticed three used teacups on the tray. 'Cuppa?' he called through to Alfie, who had taken Mildred's place on the sofa.

'Go on then,' Alfie agreed, unbuttoning his jacket and making himself at home.

Joy heard Mildred returning down the corridor. 'We'd better be off,' she told Sylvia as she hastily gathered their things.

Mildred had grown anxious when she heard male voices in the living room but since there was no other way out of the flat, she breathed in deeply and opened the door.

He was sitting on Sylvia's sofa in the same dark blue jacket with shiny metal buttons as before, with his brown hair combed across his forehead. He was grinning. His legs were spread wide, one arm resting along the back of the sofa. *Frank.*

Joy saw all colour drain from Mildred's terrified face. Her eyes were wide and dark, her mouth open. Alfie stopped smiling.

Frank. Here, right in front of her, staring at her from under hooded lids.

Something was dreadfully wrong. Joy rushed towards Mildred, who looked as if she might faint. Sylvia hurried into the kitchen to fetch Vernon.

Frank was staring at Mildred as if trying to place her, slowly coming to an unpleasant realization.

The same thin face and blue eyes. 'Frank.' Mildred said his name out loud.

Alfie gave an uneasy laugh. 'What's up with her?' he asked Joy.

'Frank,' Mildred repeated.

Joy took her hand. 'Are you sure?' she whispered.

Mildred nodded. Her legs felt weak and she sagged against Joy.

'Is she right in the head?' Alfie sprang up, then backed away towards the window. Yes, it had taken a little while but he remembered clearly now – Manchester Mecca, way back in the spring. He'd have to weasel his way out of this one double quick. 'She doesn't look it.'

In the kitchen Sylvia launched into a hurried explanation. 'Joy's pregnant friend Mildred is here. She's feeling faint – she needs water.'

Peering over her shoulder into the living room, Vernon saw what was going on then immediately used his foot to slam the kitchen door shut. 'Let Joy sort it out,' he muttered. When Sylvia reached for a glass then turned on the tap, he grasped her wrist. 'I said, let Joy deal with it.'

Noting the slam of the door, Alfie realized he was without back-up. 'Why does she keep calling me Frank?' He turned to Joy for an answer. 'Tell her my name's Alfie Matthews; at your service!'

Mildred shuddered at the sound of his voice. 'I saw him at the arcade. I knew it was him.'

Joy supported her weight. 'It's all right – I believe you.'

It took every shred of Alfie's willpower to maintain his flippant tone. 'You're as daft as her. Watch my lips – I've never clapped eyes on the girl until right here, right now.'

'It's him.' Mildred took a step towards him. 'It's you.'

'Alfie – Alfie Matthews,' he repeated slowly, as if to a child. *Spell it out – treat her like a simpleton.* 'Tell her,' he barked at Joy.

'No. You match the description she gave me. She's four months pregnant. You're the father.'

He gave the same dry, nervous laugh as before. *Bloody hell; a kid in the picture. Could it get any worse?* 'Prove it,' he said through gritted teeth.

'Oh, we will,' Joy assured him. 'We'll go to the police and tell them what you did – the exact details of where and when. There were hundreds of people at that dance hall in Manchester – dozens of witnesses who must have seen you leave with Mildred, a doorman who can pick you out in an identity parade.'

'And me.' Mildred surprised herself. 'I can do that.' In the clear light of day she saw that he was a weedy chap, a sneaky liar; not the monster of her imagination. She had a glimpse of how she might stand up to her attacker and make him pay.

'Sod you!' He made a fist then lashed out at thin air. 'It's still my word against yours, whatever sob story you give to the police.'

'You're admitting you were there, that it was you who did this?' Joy challenged.

Alfie swiped the air for a second time. 'I'm admitting nothing of the sort. And even if they could prove it was me, I'd say she led me on. She's a little tart who hangs out in all the dance halls, scrounging drinks off blokes in return for favours – you know the type. Who do you think they'd believe?'

'Us,' Joy replied calmly. 'Me, Tommy, Lucia, Sylvia and Pearl – we'll all back up Mildred's version of events. You'll be caught out in your first big lie – letting on to her that your name was Frank when really you're Alfie Matthews, the drummer in Art Richardson's band.'

'And I didn't want to do what you made me do.' Mildred's voice grew stronger as Joy guided her towards the door. She paused on the landing at the top of the stairs. 'I said no and tried to fight you off. It didn't make any difference – you did it anyway.'

CHAPTER TWENTY

'I tell you, they're on to me.' Immediately after Joy and Mildred had made their exit, Alfie barged into Sylvia's kitchen in a state of panic. 'What am I meant to do? Think of something, for Christ's sake!'

Vernon dragged him back into the living room. 'Stay there,' he ordered Sylvia, slamming the door behind him. 'Keep your voice down,' he warned Alfie as he shoved him down on to the sofa. 'Go ahead – explain.'

'The girl who was here just now . . .' Alfie gesticulated wildly.

'Calm down.' Vernon lit a cigarette then handed it to him. It was important to play for time so he could plan his tactics. 'Which one?'

'The one from the Mecca in Manchester, early April; don't pretend you don't remember. She only went and recognized me.'

'Jesus Christ!' Vernon paced the room. Of course the penny had dropped with him the moment the girl had stepped into the room – it was the reason he'd stayed hidden. 'I hope you denied it?'

'Yes, I bloody denied it – I'm not stupid.' Alfie took a deep drag on the cigarette. 'The other one – the tall one – she threatened to go to the coppers. So what do I do now?'

In the kitchen Sylvia heard their muffled voices. Her heart was in her mouth as she put her ear to the door and listened.

'You hold your nerve,' Vernon insisted. 'And you plan an alibi that doesn't involve me.'

'Such as?'

'Such as being in another place with some other floozy or playing with the band when this is meant to have happened – anything to prove you weren't there.'

'The kid's up the duff.'

Vernon gave the nearby table leg a sharp kick. 'I warned you, Alfie – time after time, I told you to be careful and you took no bloody notice.'

Sylvia heard snatches of their conversation – 'hold your nerve', 'plan an alibi', 'some other floozy'. The heartless words made her feel sick.

'Listen to me,' Vernon continued. 'You carry on as normal. Chances are the girl won't really go to the cops, and even if she does, it'll be your word against hers.'

'And you'll back me up?' Alfie grasped at the only straw within reach.

Vernon gave his response in a measured tone, emphasizing every word. 'How can I when I wasn't even there? You hear me?'

Sylvia heard Alfie groan then fall silent.

'If she does involve the police it'll be your word against hers,' Vernon repeated. 'That's if they even bother to follow it up. They have their hands full arresting burglars, coupon cheats and black market men – I doubt they'll take any interest in a pregnant girl's sob story.'

'You're right.' Stubbing out his cigarette and getting to his feet, Alfie appeared calmer. 'No one will believe her. Carry on as normal – that's the thing. We're playing at the Liverpool Rialto tomorrow.'

'And keep your mouth shut,' Vernon warned him. 'Not a word about this to anyone – understand?'

Their voices grew more muffled as Vernon escorted Alfie out of the flat and down the stairs. Sylvia struggled to make sense of what she'd heard – though no name had been mentioned, Mildred was obviously the girl they were talking about, which meant that Alfie was under suspicion and had come to Vernon for help. She was still putting the pieces of the puzzle together when Vernon stormed back into the flat and she ventured into the living room.

'The stupid fool keeps his brains in his trousers.' He opened his packet of cigarettes, then finding it empty, crushed it and flung it on to the floor. 'What a bloody mess. But it serves me right for not keeping my distance – it's well known that Alfie Matthews can't keep his hands to himself.'

'Vernon, please . . .' She put a hand on his arm.

'Sorry.' His frown disappeared in an instant, replaced by a superficial smile. 'It's nothing – ignore me.'

'Is it true – is Alfie the man who attacked Mildred?'

He pulled his arm away. 'I don't want to talk about it. And anyway, I have another bone to pick.'

'With me?'

He went through to the bedroom in search of a fresh packet of cigarettes. 'Yes, you. Why didn't you tell me you were expecting visitors this afternoon?'

Sylvia framed a careful reply. 'I wasn't sure they would come.'

'Why not?'

'Mildred doesn't like to leave the house. She could easily have changed her mind.'

'Still, you might have thought to warn me. If you had,

I'd have taken Alfie for a pint and saved us all a hell of a lot of trouble. Anyway, have you seen my ciggies?' Opening the wardrobe door, he felt inside various pockets.

'There they are.' She pointed to the small cabinet by the bed.

Vernon made a tutting noise as he unwrapped the cellophane, flipped open the lid and slid a cigarette from the pack. 'There you go again; moving stuff around without telling me.'

She watched the small flame of his lighter illuminate his even features. Its flickering light was reflected in his eyes.

He glanced at her before sitting on the edge of the bed. 'Why so jumpy? You know I was joking, don't you?'

'I wish you wouldn't,' she murmured.

'Wouldn't what – try to lighten the mood? You'd rather I went around with a scowl, worrying about this and that small problem like you do, never having any fun? Come here, come and sit with me.' He patted the counterpane invitingly.

'I don't have time.' She backed into the living room, praying that he wouldn't follow.

Vernon approached from behind then put his arms around her waist, resting his chin on her shoulder. 'There's always time for a quick cuddle, isn't there? Come on, you know I can't resist you.'

She twisted out of his grasp then turned to face him. 'Why did Alfie think you could give him an alibi?'

His lips stretched into the characteristic thin smile. 'Search me.'

'There must have been a reason.' She steeled herself for the blast of anger that would surely follow.

'No reason.'

Two short, sharp words. She held her breath – here it came: the wrecking ball behind the smile.

'I said I didn't want to talk about it. And while we're at it, I'd prefer to go about my business without being cross-examined at every end and turn. "Where are you going and who with?" "How long will you be?" It's getting boring, sweetheart.' Vernon thrust his face close to Sylvia's. 'The problem is you're so bloody unsure of yourself; never thinking you're good enough, always needing me to prop you up. I've tried; honest to goodness I have. How often have I flattered you, explained how your hair looks best up in a ponytail, what clothes you look good in. I've done all I can to boost your confidence. And does it work? Does it heck!'

A hollow laugh was accompanied by a contemptuous wave of the hand designed to crush her completely. But for once she felt a spark of defiance. 'To boost *my* confidence?' she echoed. '"Wear your green dress to show off your legs." That's to make you look good, not me – my choice doesn't come into it.'

'If you say so.' Vernon turned away as if brushing a stray thread from his coat sleeve, as if she didn't exist. 'I was only trying to help.'

The spark was extinguished, leaving Sylvia in darkness. She watched him take a comb from his back pocket and flick it through his hair, ignoring her presence as he prepared to leave. Straighten tie, button up jacket, reach for hat. Gone.

'Don't wait up.' He dropped in his usual parting phrase as he left.

True to their word, Mildred and Joy had gone straight to the nearest police station. A world-weary sergeant behind the desk had written down details without showing the slightest reaction – Mildred's name, age, address, followed by details of her attacker, followed by date and nature of alleged offence.

'That's what Mildred had the most trouble with,' Joy reported to Sylvia and Pearl when they met as arranged at the entrance to the Tower the next evening. 'Imagine having to describe exactly what Alfie had done – all the sordid details.'

'Brave girl.' Sylvia would far rather have stayed at home this evening, having spent the previous one on tenterhooks, wondering where Vernon was and again the whole of today as he'd prowled around the flat with a scowl on his face and without any of the usual attempts to kiss and make up. He'd sat at the table and scribbled a few notes for his next review, chain-smoked his way through a packet of cigarettes then gone off again without saying a word. When Pearl had dropped by unexpectedly on her way home from the arcade, she'd been the one who'd insisted that Sylvia should put on her glad rags and come to the Tower.

'Good for Mildred.' Pearl was keen to learn all she could from Joy. 'I couldn't believe it when Sylvia told me how she stood up to Alfie even when he lied through his teeth. Thanks to you, Joy, I'm sure.'

'Mildred was shaking like a leaf when she confronted him but she wouldn't back down,' Joy recalled. 'Even when we got to the police station she kept her nerve as the sergeant took her through it step by step. It was a torment for her but she managed it in the end.'

'Now what?' Pearl asked.

'The sergeant will check Mildred's condition with the maternity clinic. Proof that she's pregnant will help to corroborate her version of events.'

'And what about Alfie? Have they arrested him?'

Joy shook her head. 'Not so far as we know. We didn't have an address for him but the sergeant knows that he plays in Art Richardson's band. He shouldn't be hard to track down.'

'Maybe by this time tomorrow, then.' Pearl drew Sylvia and Joy to one side as a sudden influx of dancers surged through the glass doors – lovey-dovey couples strolled arm in arm; shop girls dressed to kill skipped by, determined to impress a gang of young funfair workers who strutted towards the stairs leading up to the ballroom. 'I say, Sylvia – if they make an arrest before your competition, how will Art Richardson get by without a singer *and* a drummer?'

'I've no idea.' She'd been so preoccupied that this obvious hitch hadn't even occurred to her. 'If the worst happens and we end up with no band, Cliff or my mother might know someone who can step in.'

Pearl and Joy held up their crossed fingers. 'Shall we go in?' Pearl suggested.

So they entered the foyer, greeting friends as they went. Joy spoke to Mavis and her cleaning pals, just ahead of them in the queue. She said she was sorry that Mavis and Eddie had decided to withdraw from next week's competition and was backed up by Sylvia.

'Quite right.' Ruby, who stood near by, added her opinion. 'Their Viennese waltz was second to none.'

'Such a shame – after working so hard – it's Eddie Winter's loss, not hers.' Various voices chipped in.

Pearl gave Sylvia's hand a sympathetic squeeze. 'Take no notice,' she murmured.

Meanwhile, the foyer grew more crowded. Joy was collared by Doris, who remarked she hadn't seen her at

Lorna Ellis's classes lately and demanded to know if she and Tommy were still set to compete next week. All being well, Joy told them, but she didn't hold out much hope of winning a prize.

The buzz of excited voices increased as the ballroom doors were opened. Soon the stage spotlights would be switched on and the music would start. Several RAF men at the head of the queue paid for their tickets and entered ahead of their arch rivals, the GIs. The two groups would compete for the pick of the bunch among the girls already at the bar.

'There's Errol.' Sylvia pointed him out to Pearl as he entered the ballroom and they moved closer to the ticket booths. 'Will you dance with him if he asks you?'

Pearl shook her head. 'I'll leave him in Ruby's capable hands,' she said with a sigh. The queue edged forward until finally their tickets were bought. They entered the ballroom to strains of organ music played tonight by a stand-in for Reggie Dixon, who was currently entertaining the troops in Egypt. A murmur of disappointment soon gave way to excited chatter as couples launched into a jaunty quickstep.

'Shall we?' Joy asked Pearl, while a quieter-than-usual Sylvia went to claim a table under the balcony.

'Why not?' Better to join the action than sit and brood. Letting Joy lead, Pearl was swept into a promenade chassé followed by a pivot turn – keep it light, leave the world behind, be happy.

Sylvia found a vacant table close to the loudspeakers at the side of the stage. As she sat down, the swelling notes, bright lights and swirling movement on the dance floor brought on another spell of dizziness so she refused several offers to dance. She would sit this one out, thank you.

'Are you sure?'

Sylvia glanced up to find that the latest offer had come from Eddie. He stood tall and serious, immaculate in a dark, double-breasted suit, his wavy hair newly trimmed.

'Yes, I'm sure,' she murmured.

'Can I buy you a drink – your usual?'

She nodded then watched him work his way around the edge of the dance floor towards the bar. What was wrong with her? Why was she so exhausted?

Eddie returned as the quickstep ended and a swing number began. He sat beside her and watched her sip at her martini. 'Joy and Pearl seem to be having a good time,' he remarked conversationally. Then after a long silence, 'Are you ready for next weekend?'

'More or less.' Sylvia sighed.

'Oh dear, that doesn't sound good.'

'The truth is, I'm not sure we'll have a band,' she confessed. 'Art Richardson's singer is ill and now a question mark hangs over his drummer.' She'd given away more than she'd intended. 'Please don't say anything.'

'I won't.' Eddie had the sense not to press her.

Without warning Sylvia lowered her head and began to sob uncontrollably, her chest heaving as she struggled to draw breath.

'Oh dear – come with me.' Eddie helped her to stand up. 'It's all right; no one will notice.' There was an unattended exit close by so he ushered her from the ballroom, along a dimly lit corridor leading backstage. 'What is it?' he urged. Muffled strains of a Glenn Miller number reached them as he found a quiet alcove where they could sit.

'Please don't . . . I can't bear it.' Sylvia teetered on the edge of a dark, dreadful realization that she'd been desperately holding off since yesterday.

'You can tell me,' he urged. 'I promise it won't go any further.'

'Oh, Eddie, it's too awful – I'm such a fool.' The sobs continued to rise from deep within.

He lifted her hands away from her face and spoke calmly. 'You're not a fool – far from it. The pressure of organizing the competition, the problem with the band – is it too much?'

'No – yes; that's part of it.' She couldn't bear even to look at him. 'Rosie Johnson has diphtheria.'

'And the drummer?'

'Alfie Matthews,' she cried. Speaking his name tipped her over the edge of denial and sent her plummeting towards the truth. 'I think – in fact, I *know* – that he attacked Mildred Kershaw.'

'Damn.' One quiet word escaped through gritted teeth as Eddie held her hands in his.

'They met by accident yesterday at my flat and Mildred identified him. I believe her – I'm convinced she's telling the truth. Worse still – Vernon knew,' she confessed. And now the words came in a rush, scarcely coherent. 'I heard him ordering Alfie to hold his nerve . . . act normally, he said . . . create an alibi for the police. I'm scared, Eddie.'

He put his arms around her and held her close. 'Hush, there's no need to be frightened.'

'Vernon says he loves me but . . .'

'But what?'

'I can't explain. I don't know where I stand with him; not really.' She pulled away. 'I shouldn't be telling you this – you of all people.'

'Why not? I'm your friend and that will never alter.'

'Vernon can be lovely sometimes . . .' She faltered then fell silent, drowning in utter misery.

'But sometimes not?'

Sylvia nodded. 'He gets angry with me over little things I don't remember doing then he makes a joke of it. I know I shouldn't take it to heart but I can't help it. And now it's clear he's covering up for the man who raped a fifteen-year-old girl.'

In the name of God! Eddie fought to control his reaction as she sobbed anew. 'Are you absolutely sure?'

'Deep down, yes – I'm certain.'

'But he'll deny it?'

She nodded. 'I heard Alfie pleading with Vernon to back him up. Vernon said how could he do that when he wasn't even there? His voice was cold as steel.'

Eddie understood in a flash that Vernon King was prepared to ditch Alfie in the dirt in a callous attempt to save himself.

Sylvia had shared the facts and was exhausted. 'Joy, Pearl and I knew that a second man looked on but did nothing to help. That man was Vernon – his job was to act as a lookout while Alfie went ahead and did his worst.'

It was close to ten o'clock when Bernie stepped off the train. He swung his kitbag over his shoulder as he left North Station then tramped in his serge battledress through Blackpool's dark streets. It was Saturday, so he headed straight for the Tower ballroom, where he expected to find Pearl dancing with the Yank that Joe had written to him about.

After recovering from the initial shock of receiving his friend's letter, Bernie had stewed over its contents for days. The 'something he ought to know' and 'a GI sergeant from the Warton base' were phrases that he'd replayed in his head a hundred times, swinging between rage and disbelief – 'I'll wring her bloody neck!' to 'Never; not Pearl – not in a million years!' – and everything in between. Maybe he should write to her, demanding an explanation? But then, what if Joe had got it wrong? After all, Pearl had made no secret of the fact that she enjoyed dancing with GI Errol Jackson and perhaps that was all there was to it. Then again, what if their friendship had gone further than it should have in his absence? Joe had sounded pretty certain that something was up.

To and fro Bernie went, waiting and waiting for a letter from Pearl that would set his mind at rest. It never came; the one note from Joe was all he received. He lost sleep, stopped eating, went around like a bear with a sore head. Eventually he'd been in such a poor state that he'd passed out from heat exhaustion while on parade. He'd been hauled in front of his sergeant major, who'd demanded to know what the hell was going on. This had led to Bernie being seen by the doc who had scanned his medical records and diagnosed delayed shell shock after his close call in North Africa. The result: tablets to help Bernie's nerves plus ten days' leave.

Now here he was, a stranger in his home town. The sun sank below the horizon as Bernie reached the prom and kept on walking towards his destination, looking straight ahead with only one thing on his mind. He'd told no one he was coming, not even Joe.

Had anyone seen Sylvia? Joy and Pearl were worried. They'd danced the first two dances of the night together before Joe and another market trader had stepped between them and whisked them into a jitterbug followed by a nice, simple waltz – no treading on toes or bumping into people. The girls had been carried along by the music, losing themselves in the thrills and spills of the crowded dance floor. It was only towards the interval that Joy had reminded Pearl that they'd left Sylvia in the lurch. They searched for her without success. On asking around, Ruby recalled that yes, Sylvia had definitely bagged an empty table. And later Ida had noticed that – surprise, surprise – Eddie Winter had sat down next to her.

'Maybe she was tired and Eddie took her home.' To Pearl this was an encouraging sign.

'But surely she would've said goodbye before she left.' Joy carried on searching. Had anyone seen Sylvia, by any chance?

Before long a second, more alarming possibility occurred to Pearl. 'You don't think Vernon showed up and found her having a heart-to-heart with Eddie?' she asked Joy. 'That wouldn't have gone down well, would it?'

'Let's hope not.' The interval came and the dance floor emptied.

'I hear you're looking for Sylvia.' Mavis approached them, glass in hand, looking the height of fashion in a white V-neck blouse and pleated skirt. 'I happened to notice her crying her eyes out earlier on. But don't worry – Eddie was there to mop up the tears. They snuck away through a side door.'

So Joy and Pearl relaxed a little. Before they knew it, the curtain lifted and the music began again as the MC invited everyone back on to the floor. The girls' faces lit up at the sound of Ken 'Snakehips' Johnson's 'Tuxedo Junction' being played at a terrific lick. They knew that only the best, most agile dancers could keep up with this one. Kick and click, kick and click, spin and swing in, swing out and repeat. Shake those shoulders, snake those hips. Joy and Pearl threw themselves into a jive. Bold Mavis raced ahead of Ruby to grab Errol as her partner. Errol caught Pearl's attention as she and Joy whirled past. They exchanged looks that said, *There but for fortune*. But both knew it wasn't to be.

They danced on towards midnight.

The evening ended in a slow waltz and a gentle shower of confetti as Bernie waited in the alley down the side of the Tower building. He'd planned to march straight into the ballroom and catch Pearl and Errol off guard, but when he got there he'd had second thoughts. Why set tongues wagging by creating a scene? Whose business was it except his and Pearl's? No; far better to wait outside and confront her as she left.

He stood under a clear, starlit sky, quietly smoking a cigarette, keeping to the shadows as happy, footsore dancers spilled out on to the prom.

On the first floor of the building Pearl and Joy queued to collect their jackets from the cloakroom. They were joined by Tommy, who had been performing at the circus. Joe happened to tag on to the merry gang as they descended the stairs. All agreed it had been a good night.

'Did you miss me?' Tommy teased Joy as he linked arms with her.

'Not the least little bit,' was the light-hearted reply.

Errol and his GIs were a few steps behind. He heard them laughing then caught sight of Pearl preparing to split off from the others.

'Joy and I will walk you home,' Tommy offered.

'No need – it's not far,' Pearl insisted, stubborn as ever.

Errol saw Pearl set off by herself up the alley at the side of the building. 'You go ahead,' he told his buddies. 'I'll catch you later.' He'd decided to follow Pearl at a discreet distance to make sure she made it home OK.

After the bright lights of the ballroom, Pearl's eyes took a while to adjust to the darkness of the deserted alley. Never mind; every step of the way was so familiar that she could have found her way home blindfolded, but then she gasped as a figure suddenly stepped out in front of her.

Errol was some thirty paces behind. He saw a tall guy in uniform emerge from the shadows, saw Pearl stop dead in her tracks.

'Bernie?' No, it couldn't be. She was mistaken. She recoiled then set off at a run towards the cobbled market square.

It happened quickly in semi-darkness, in the shadow of the Tower – Bernie overtook Pearl and blocked her way, Errol sprinted after them, Pearl dropped to her knees in shock, Errol stooped to help her up.

'Take your hands off her!' Bernie shoved Errol out of the way. Anger exploded inside his head like a grenade – everything Joe had said was true.

Pearl staggered sideways. It was Bernie's voice, Bernie's face – teeth bared like an animal. 'Stop – you don't understand!'

Errol reeled backwards then quickly recovered. He ran at Bernie and landed an uppercut with the sickening crunch of knuckles against jawbone. Pearl gasped as Bernie withstood the blow then socked Errol full in the face. 'For God's sake, Bernie!' She used all her strength to drag him back, allowing Errol to land a body blow.

It was only when Pearl spoke her husband's name that Errol realized what he'd done. *Good God Almighty!* He backed off, rubbing his knuckles, breathing heavily.

Bernie wrenched free of Pearl and challenged Errol, arms spread wide. 'Can't take it, huh? Come on, why don't you?'

Errol shook his head.

'No? Not so slow to move in on my wife behind my back, though,' Bernie taunted, blood trickling from the corner of his mouth.

Pearl darted between them as Bernie advanced. 'It's not true.' She forced him to take a step back.

'So what's he doing here, sneaking up the alley after you?' Bernie jerked his thumb in Errol's direction. 'Caught red handed, I'd say.'

'It's not how it looks,' Pearl pleaded. He was here in the flesh; her Bernie but not her Bernie, wild eyed and acting like a savage. 'I wrote you a letter – I swear we haven't done anything wrong.'

'I never got any letter.' Bernie advanced again.

'Listen, buddy . . .' Errol attempted to calm things. He ducked a second blow aimed at his jaw then, staying low, tackled Bernie to the ground. They landed with limbs entangled then wrestled furiously. Pearl's screams carried as far as the prom.

'Fight!' A raucous voice rang out.

'Where?' a second voice yelled.

'Over there. Between a Yank and one of our lads, by the looks of it.'

Four or five youths were eager to join the fray but Joe beat them to it. He headed them off, yelling at them to bugger off back the way they'd come. Thank heavens he'd realized in the nick of time that it was Bernie rolling on the ground with Errol Jackson, and Pearl screaming blue murder for them to stop.

'Joe, tell him the truth,' Pearl begged as he sprinted to join them. 'He won't listen to me.'

Bernie gained the advantage. He sat astride Errol, fist raised. Joe grabbed his wrist just in time. 'Easy,' he muttered as he dragged him off. 'No need to go breaking his bloody jaw.'

Bernie struggled and swore as Pearl stood frozen to the spot and Errol hauled himself upright, ready to fight again if necessary.

'Easy, easy.' Joe restrained Bernie by pressing both palms against his chest. 'Beat it if you know what's good for you,' he told Errol.

'Do as he says,' Pearl implored.

'You sure?' Errol picked up his forage cap from the gutter and slapped it against his thigh. His nose hurt like hell but he was prepared to finish what he'd started.

'Yes – go!'

'OK, Miss Pearl, I'm outta here.' Squaring his shoulders and straightening his jacket, he strode back towards the prom.

'All right, pal?' Joe kept hold of Bernie to make sure that he didn't follow.

'No, I'm not all right.' Bernie couldn't even bring himself to look at Pearl. Fragments from the explosion of rage still ricocheted inside his skull. 'Turns out you were right – I can't trust her as far as I can throw her.'

Pearl let out a despairing groan.

'Why did I even bother coming back? And no, don't try to talk your way out of it,' he yelled at her. 'I saw what I saw.'

'You're coming with me to my house.' Joe took control

as Pearl started to weep. 'Pearl, you head on home. You both need to calm down. In the morning we can talk.'

Go home, calm down. The dark world was spinning. Pearl watched Joe lead Bernie across the square towards King Street. Her beloved husband was walking away. Their love was shattered into a thousand pieces and would never be whole again.

CHAPTER TWENTY-ONE

For a few moments after she woke Sylvia wondered where she was. She came round slowly, recognizing the flowered curtains of her childhood bedroom then the framed ballroom dance certificates that she'd been awarded hanging above the small fireplace.

Eddie had refused point-blank to let her go back to North View Parade. 'It's not safe,' he'd insisted. 'At this stage of the game there's no telling what Alfie will do if and when the police catch up with him. What if he goes running to Vernon for help? What then?' He'd insisted on taking her to King Alfred Street then outlined the situation to Lorna, who had reacted calmly and promised to take care of Sylvia. 'I'll check in on you tomorrow morning,' Eddie had promised before he left. 'Expect me around midday – there's something I have to do first.'

Lorna had put Sylvia to bed without fuss. One look at her daughter's pale, tragic face had told her all she needed to know. 'The explanations can wait until morning,' she'd murmured as she'd stroked stray hairs back from Sylvia's forehead. As Sylvia had drifted off into uneasy sleep, Lorna had stayed at her bedside, sitting through the night and only leaving the room at eight o'clock to prepare a breakfast tray.

She brought it in as Sylvia woke. 'You look rested,' she said with a relieved smile. 'Your face has more colour.'

Sylvia sipped tea from one of her mother's dainty china cups. 'What time is it?' Looking at her watch, she put the cup to one side then thrust back the bedclothes. 'Why did you let me sleep in? I have a lesson to teach.'

Lorna objected but Sylvia was adamant – she couldn't possibly let her pupils down; it was Andrew and Margaret's last session before the competition and they still needed to finesse their jive routine.

Lorna did her best to talk her out of it. Sylvia's safety was more important than any dance contest. It made no difference; Sylvia was determined to go to her studio.

'May I borrow a blouse and a pair of slacks?' she asked when she emerged from the bathroom. Her face was scrubbed clean and her hair brushed loose around her shoulders. Obviously the dress that she'd worn to the Tower wasn't suitable daywear.

Lorna reluctantly obliged. 'Won't you at least wait until Eddie comes back?'

'I'm sorry, Mother, I don't have time.'

'And what if . . .?' Lorna hesitated before finishing her sentence. 'What if you run into Vernon?'

Sylvia flinched at the sound of his name. 'I won't go to the flat,' she promised. 'And Cliff and Terry will be on hand if there's any sign of trouble.'

So Lorna was forced to let her go. She watched from her first-floor window as Sylvia set off down the street, proud of her daughter for refusing to be cowed but fearful too.

It was a transformed Mildred who came down for breakfast. She'd thrown off her shackles by the simple act of standing up to her attacker, and from now on she wouldn't hide – no, she would be bold and hold her head high.

Frank wasn't Frank, he was Alfie Matthews and Mildred had seen fear in his eyes. He was small and mean and powerless and he would not win.

'Here she is.' Tommy greeted her with a broad smile and made room for her at the breakfast table. Lucia presented her with bacon and eggs, 'For the *bambino*', while Joy made a list of King Street jobs for the day – strip wallpaper, emulsion the ceiling, paint skirting boards.

'Would you like to help?' she asked Mildred.

'Yes please.' The answer came in a heartbeat. A new girl with freckles and a smile that lit up her face. A girl with a baby on the way who she would love and cherish.

Lucia provided some work clothes – her own wrap-around apron that swamped Mildred and a headscarf to tie turban-style around her head.

'I look a sight,' she giggled as she looked in the mirror. 'But I don't care.'

'That's the spirit.' Joy had already phoned the police station for an update on Alfie Matthews. No arrest as yet but officers were following up several leads. The sergeant promised to contact Mildred as soon as they'd located him.

King Street beckoned on a bright Blackpool morning. It was still early as Tommy, Joy and Mildred left Rossi's Ice Cream Parlour and walked along the prom – no hurry, enjoy the sunshine, breathe in the sea air and listen to waves lapping against the shore, to the screeching of gulls and the braying of Clive Rowse's plodding donkeys as he led them down to the beach.

When they arrived at King Street Joy gave Mildred a job that she hoped wouldn't prove too strenuous – some gentle wallpaper stripping in the main bedroom. 'Don't climb any ladders,' she warned. 'If something is out of reach, leave it for me and Tommy.'

First Mildred had to wet the walls with a large paste brush then leave the water to soak in so that the paper would scrape off more easily. It turned out that some patches were more stubborn than others but she worked away at the task while voices drifted through from the bedroom next door.

'How about dividing this room into two?' Tommy proposed what had been in his mind from the start. 'One half can be the bathroom with plumbing for a sink, bath and toilet. The other half can stay as a bedroom.'

Joy took her time to picture how this might work. 'It would make a very small bedroom.'

'Yes,' he acknowledged. 'One very small bedroom for one very small person?' There was a rise at the end of the sentence accompanied by a questioning look as he put his arms around her. 'I don't mean straight away,' he added quickly.

Joy laughed and hugged him, laughed again and kissed him. 'I do love you, Tommy Rossi,' she declared. 'I love you with all my heart.'

'I notice your bed's not been slept in.' Maria went downstairs in her dressing gown to find Pearl sitting at the kitchen table. She'd popped her head around the door to check on Elsie, who was still fast asleep, but of Pearl there'd been no sign. 'Good Lord, girl; you look like death warmed up.'

'Bernie's back,' Pearl told her in a faint voice. She was still wearing her dance outfit and the make-up she'd applied so carefully the night before was smudged and streaked.

‘Back where?’ Maria asked sharply as she filled the kettle then set it on the hob.

‘He’s here in Blackpool.’

‘So where is he now?’

‘At Joe’s.’ Pearl was in a daze, hardly aware of her surroundings. ‘There was a fight.’

‘Over what?’ It was clear to Maria that certain birds had come home to roost. ‘No, don’t tell me – Bernie found out about you and the GI. He came home to sort you out.’

‘I don’t need sorting out.’ Angry tears welled at the implications behind her mother’s words. ‘Errol and I don’t dance together any more. We’re hardly even on speaking terms.’

‘I see.’ Maria stood by the cooker, waiting for the kettle to boil. ‘But your husband has got the wrong end of the stick.’

Pearl nodded. ‘Please don’t say I told you so. Bernie started a fight with Errol; fists flew then they wrestled on the ground. Joe managed to stop them.’

‘Good for him.’

‘Yes, but it’s thanks to Joe that this has happened in the first place.’ Pearl sighed loudly. ‘He wrote to Bernie saying I was carrying on with Errol behind his back.’

‘No point blaming Joe,’ Maria said curtly. After warming the pot, spooning in the leaves and adding boiling water, she gave the tea a quick stir.

Tears ran freely down Pearl’s cheeks. ‘I wrote to say I was sorry there was a misunderstanding but Bernie didn’t get my letter.’

Maria handed her a handkerchief. ‘Blow your nose. If I were in your shoes I’d be round to King Street quick as a flash, saying sorry to his face.’

Pearl dabbed her cheeks. ‘Oh Mum, I’ve gone and ruined everything. You should’ve seen Bernie last night – he was so mad at me. What if I go round there and he slams the door in my face?'

'Go upstairs and get changed.' Maria dished out the orders sergeant-major fashion. 'Wash your face, brush your hair.'

Taking a deep breath, Pearl stood up. 'Please will you come to King Street with me?'

'No.' She propelled her daughter towards the door. 'You got yourself into this pickle, now it's up to you to get yourself out.'

Andrew and Margaret's dance routine was well-nigh perfect. 'Keep up this standard and you'll do me proud,' Sylvia insisted. 'If you win a prize you might even think about turning professional. But remember, timing and synchronization will be key.'

The exhausted couple got ready to leave the studio. There was mention of the strong opposition that they would no doubt face, followed by a parting comment from Andrew that left Sylvia feeling uneasy.

'Fingers crossed that Art Richardson finds a stand-in for Rosie Johnson; otherwise the whole event could fall flat on its face.'

'Don't worry about that,' she called after him with false cheeriness. 'You two just concentrate on your routine and leave the music side of things to me and Cliff.' She heaved a sigh as the door swung closed after them.

It was soon opened again by Cliff who, as it happened, had come to update her on the Rosie situation. 'Art's found a singer called Connie Simpson,' he reported.

'Is she any good?' Sylvia wished she'd had breakfast at her mother's – she was feeling distinctly light-headed through lack of food.

'Yes – more of a homely, Vera Lynn type; nowhere near

as showy and glamorous as Rosie. But she'll definitely do a good job.'

'Excellent; that's one less thing to worry about.' Sylvia concentrated on rearranging records in the rack.

Cliff closed the lid of the gramophone and watched her closely. 'Yes, the build-up should go smoothly now that the mysterious case of the missing singer is solved. Are you by any chance free tomorrow evening to come to the Spanish Hall with me?'

'What for?'

'To finalize Sunday's playlist with Art and the band?'

'Of course.' Smiling briefly, she continued to sort through the records.

'Is everything all right?' Of course it wasn't – Cliff could tell by the way Sylvia avoided looking at him.

'Tip-top,' she fibbed.

'Well then . . .' He hesitated.

'Cliff, I'm perfectly fine. Now, if you don't mind, I have to prepare a lesson for Bill and Shirley.'

'In that case, I'll leave you to it. I'll be upstairs in the flat if you need me.'

Left to herself, Sylvia sank weakly on to a chair. The parched, dizzy feeling was getting worse. Perhaps it would be a good idea to follow Cliff upstairs and ask him for a cup of tea and something to eat. She was putting this thought into action when the door swung open again.

'Hello, sweetheart.' Vernon breezed into the studio with a broad smile and his usual swagger. His hair looked windswept and there was plenty of colour in his cheeks. 'How about coming for a drive on this sunny Sunday?'

Sylvia's stomach turned. The grin sent her into a tail-spin; had recent events completely slipped his mind?

'Let's head south.' He swung the car key in front of

her face to tempt her. 'We can find a nice little café in Lytham, have tea for two and two for tea, just me for you and you for me—'

'Vernon, I can't.' She stepped back.

'Can't you see how happy we would be?' he crooned before seizing her around the waist then waltzing her across the floor.

Sylvia struggled to free herself. 'I really can't. Not after Friday.'

He tightened his hold. 'What about Friday? Oh, you mean Alfie and the girl. What an idiot, losing his head like that. If he'd kept his mouth shut he could've saved himself a lot of bother. As it is . . .' He turned and steered her down the length of the room.

'Stop – please!' He was pressing against her, her head was spinning and their reflection in the full-length mirror was blurred.

Laughing, Vernon swept her off her feet and into his arms. He carried her towards the alcove where he sat her in his lap and started to cover her face with light kisses. 'I'm sorry we had a little tiff,' he murmured. 'Let me make up for it by taking you for that drive.'

No; she wouldn't let him draw her back in – not this time. She pulled away with all her might. 'Where were you last night?' she demanded fiercely. 'No more lies – just tell me the truth.'

Vernon leaned against the wall, genuinely amused. 'Oh, so the cat has claws! I was working – I have to earn a crust.' He sprang up from the bench and took firm hold of her arm. 'And where were *you*, I'd like to know? A man comes home at midnight expecting to find his other half keeping the bed warm. She can't just swan off without a by your leave.'

'I was at my mother's.'

'All night?' His grip tightened and his expression grew cold.

'Yes – all night. Stop – you're hurting me.'

'One last chance, princess – do you intend to come on that drive with me or not? No? All right then; go to hell.' He shoved Sylvia backwards so hard that she overbalanced and sent the record rack flying. He stooped to pull her back to her feet and that was how Alfie found them – Sylvia on the floor with gramophone records scattered around and Vernon crouching over her, about to do God knew what.

Alfie sprinted across the studio with surprising speed. 'For Pete's sake, man – leave the girl alone!' He swore loudly as he pulled him away and Sylvia struggled to her feet. 'We're in enough trouble as it is.'

'What the . . .?' Alfie was no match for Vernon, who easily shrugged him off. 'How the hell did you track me down?'

'I tried the flat. No one was there so I came here to ask Sylvia if she knew where you were.' Alfie backed away, wary now that he recognized Vernon's dangerous mood. Light the blue touch paper then stand well clear. 'Sorry if I interrupted something.'

'Shut your mouth!' Vernon advanced towards Alfie. 'Let me spell it out one last time: you're to stay the hell away from me from now on – understand?'

Sylvia put a hand over her mouth to stifle a scream. Terror had her in its grip.

'I said, do you understand?' Vernon's eyes bulged as he prodded Alfie in the chest and forced him back towards the door.

Alfie stumbled but recovered. 'Vernon, you can't turn your back on me – I'm your pal.'

With one final shove, Vernon sent Alfie reeling backwards through the door and crashing on to the pavement. 'I swear to God you're no pal of mine – now sod off!'

Len Fraser burst through Ibbotson's shop door into the street. He'd heard a racket – some sort of row going on in Sylvia's dance studio. Cliff and Terry, too – they ran down their stairs to the sound of raised voices and the sight of Vernon King manhandling Alfie Matthews. What in God's name? And that wasn't all – the gathering crowd spotted two police patrol cars speeding up the street, squealing to a halt and disgorging four boys in blue plus a plain-clothes passenger.

Vernon retreated into the studio but before he could trap Sylvia inside, she slipped past him, out on to the street where she collapsed trembling and gasping on the pavement.

Two officers swooped on Alfie and handcuffed him. He was arrested on suspicion of committing a serious sexual offence against a fifteen-year-old girl outside Manchester Mecca on Saturday the third of April 1943. One read him his rights while Alfie kicked and punched, yelling at the top of his voice, 'What about him?' In a final, desperate flare of vengeful anger he pointed the finger at Vernon lurking in the doorway to the dance studio under the bright red and yellow 'Live Your Dream' sign.

'What about him?' the arresting officer echoed.

'If I go down, I'll take that bastard with me.' Spit flew from Alfie's mouth and sweat trickled down his forehead. 'Vernon King is his name. He was with me that night at the Mecca, keeping a lookout. We took it in turns; the week before it was him who got the girl and the week after it would've been him again.'

*

Eddie stepped from the first police car to help Sylvia to her feet. 'Vernon has been arrested,' he told her gently. 'He can't harm you any more.'

She struggled to take in what he said.

Cliff and Terry shielded Sylvia and Eddie from the inquisitive crowd. 'Take her up to our flat,' they told him. 'We'll make sure you're not disturbed.'

'I told you last night that there was something I needed to do,' Eddie reminded Sylvia once he'd got her upstairs and settled her on the sofa. Noises from the street faded as onlookers slowly dispersed. 'I went to the police station to report your suspicions about Vernon.'

'And they believed you?'

Eddie nodded. 'It turns out he and Alfie had been in trouble with the police for something similar before he came to Blackpool. Nothing was ever proved but his previous editor sacked him because of it. I gave the police his address. They brought me here in one of their cars.'

'All those lies . . .' she whispered. Lie after lie after lie. She'd witnessed Vernon's attempt to flee but he'd only got a few yards up the street. One officer had rugby tackled him, another had pinned him to the ground, while a third had clapped handcuffs on him. They'd led him away in sullen silence, hands behind his back, head hanging. No more 'Don't wait ups' – Vernon was gone, once and for all. He would never come back.

The inevitable calm came after the storm, during which Eddie stayed with Sylvia. He accompanied her to the police station, where a detective inspector interviewed her about the circumstances leading to Vernon's arrest, then Eddie took her back to her flat.

'Can I come in?' he ventured as they stood hesitantly in Ibbotson's doorway.

Weary to the bone after the day's traumatic events, she nodded then led the way upstairs. 'But don't fuss over me,' she warned. 'I'll be perfectly fine.'

Fine on the surface but not fine underneath – Sylvia's lifelong habit brought a wry smile to Eddie's lips. 'I'm here,' he murmured as they entered the living room. 'And always will be, if you'll allow me?'

She sank on to the sofa and absorbed his simple words.

He sat next to her and waited.

Resting her head on his shoulder, Sylvia knew at last that this was where she belonged; here with the man whose heart had always been true. 'Yes,' she murmured at last. 'Hold me tight, Eddie. Don't let me go.'

CHAPTER TWENTY-TWO

Maria collared Ernie as he crept under the counter to scrounge a bag of chips from her busy stall. 'I need you to go to the arcade,' she informed him.

'Do I have to?' he whined. 'I'm meant to be playing footie with my pals.'

'Yes, do as you're told.' There'd been no sign of Pearl since Maria had packed her off to King Street and it was now late in the afternoon. Had she and Bernie patched things up or not? 'Check that your sister is all right. Help her to shut up shop if need be.'

Still grumbling, Ernie trotted off along the prom, batting away a gull that showed too close an interest in his chips. 'Clear off!' The rubber soles of his worn pumps slapped against the pavement and a lively breeze lifted his mousy-coloured hair clear of his face as he approached North Pier.

Sitting at her till, Pearl was going through the motions. Pennies were slotted into Spitfires and Little Mickeys, ball bearings whizzed around Playballs, jackpots were won or lost. She was there in body but her mind was elsewhere.

Following her mother's orders early that morning, she'd rushed from Empire Street to knock on Joe's door but received no answer. With her heart in her mouth she'd walked swiftly round the block then knocked again, peering anxiously through the letter box and calling Bernie's name. Still no one had come to the door.

'You're wasting your time, love.' A well-meaning neighbour had leant through his open window and informed her that the house was empty. 'I saw them go out half an hour ago – Joe and his army pal.'

'Have you any idea where they went?' Pearl had pleaded.

'Sorry, I haven't the foggiest.'

She'd wondered frantically what to do next. What if Joe had been unable to calm Bernie down after the fracas of the night before? In which case, Bernie might be stepping on to a train right that minute, steaming out of her life for ever. The thought had entered her head like an arrow then lodged there. It had sent her all the way to North Station in a blind panic. She'd arrived at the main concourse breathless and full of fear and had been stopped at a barrier by an officious station employee – she couldn't pass without a platform ticket and yes, he'd seen plenty of soldiers boarding trains that morning but what of it? Pearl had dashed up and down the concourse, studied lists of departures, even searched in the station café in a last, desperate hope that she would discover Bernie and Joe there. In the end she'd admitted defeat and made her way to the arcade in the faint, fast-receding hope that Bernie would know where to find her if and when he was ready to talk.

Every second of every minute of every hour had been agony.

'Mum says are you all right?' Ernie burst through the door as she was contemplating closing up. Trade had been slower than usual, thanks to bright blue skies that had tempted people on to the beach and kept them there all day.

Pearl jerked back into the present. Two RAF men – her only customers – sauntered down the aisle towards the door, telling each other better luck next time. 'Yes, I'm all right,' she told Ernie wearily.

'She says do you need me to help you close up?'

Pearl nodded. 'You can bring in the sandwich board then pull down the blind.' She opened the till and scooped handfuls of sixpences into a canvas bag, promising herself that she would cash up properly later. 'I need a breath of air,' she told Ernie as she stepped outside.

She'd given up all hope when Bernie emerged from the café. He'd kept out of sight for a full hour, biting his nails and wondering what to do.

'Just talk to her.' If Joe had said it once he'd said it a dozen times as he and Bernie had walked along the beach early that morning, trying to shake off some of Bernie's fury. 'For goodness' sake, listen to what Pearl has to say.'

It had gone in one ear and out the other. Bernie hadn't been able to rid himself of the image of Errol Jackson sneaking up the alley after his wife, hoping that no one would notice them. In the end Joe had given up trying to persuade him and returned to King Street.

Bernie had walked on alone as far as the golf course at Fleetwood then turned back the way he'd come. He had two choices – go to Joe's to pick up his kitbag then catch a train, get the hell out of town and cut off all contact with Pearl. Or he could find her and tell her to her face – she'd made him a laughing stock and he would never forgive her; their marriage was on the rocks, end of story.

He trudged through the sand dunes, hot as hell in his uniform, swinging between the two options, lurching towards the second one as he'd passed through the turnstile and slowly made his way along North Pier. But then he'd dragged his feet as he approached the arcade; as on the previous night, perhaps this was neither the time nor the place to have it out with Pearl? So at the very last moment he'd slipped into the Seaview Café to gather his thoughts.

Now there she was – a small, slight, dark-haired figure in a pale blue summer dress – and his heart almost broke in two. Her face was pale and drawn, without its usual sparkle. She closed her eyes and tilted her head back to absorb the sun's rays as Bernie made his way out of the café.

Their eyes met and they stared at each other without moving for what felt like an age, trapped under the weight of uncertainty.

A group of day trippers came between them – mothers with beach towels and picnic paraphernalia, fathers carrying rolled-up windbreaks, barefoot kids with buckets and spades.

Bernie took one step towards Pearl, who immediately darted inside the arcade.

'Here's the key,' she told Ernie. 'I want you to lock up.' Then, quick as a flash, she was back outside and running towards Bernie with words tumbling from her lips. 'Where have you been? You weren't at Joe's. I went to the station to look for you. I've been worried sick.' He stood with feet wide apart, hands by his side, more gaunt than she remembered – tall and upright thanks to his army training but now unmistakably her Bernie.

'I needed time to think,' he said quietly. His voice was deeper and slower than before. His eyes searched hers for answers. 'We have to talk.'

They set off along the pier, waves washing far below, with the sun behind them and the row of seafront hotels ahead.

'I'm sorry.' Simple words from Pearl broke a long, agonized silence.

Bernie glanced at her face then stared straight ahead again. His jaw ached with the effort of holding back a torrent of harsh words. 'What for?'

'For not listening to advice.'

'Whose?'

'My mother's, Sylvia and Joy's. Everyone warned me how it would look but I went my own sweet way.'

'Doing what?' Bernie drew her towards a bench overlooking the beach, knowing that they'd reached the heart of the matter.

'Having a good time at the Tower, dancing with Errol, entering the jive competition with him.'

The golden sands stretched as far as the eye could see, fringed by white waves. 'Anything else?'

'Nothing; I swear.'

Bernie stared at his bitten fingernails. 'So Joe got it wrong?'

'Yes.' Her voice was so faint that Bernie could scarcely hear.

Could he believe her? 'You and Errol must've spent hours practising your dance.'

She nodded. 'In the studio, mostly with others there too.'

'Sometimes alone?'

Another nod as a wave of misery crashed over her.

'And you swear . . .?'

'Nothing happened – on my life!' Words were weak – would they ever be enough? 'I never thought of Errol in that way. It's you that I love.'

'I know what your dancing means to you,' Bernie conceded. 'I'm not saying you should've stopped.' Still the picture of Pearl and Errol jiving the night away refused to fade. He stood up abruptly and set off for the turnstiles.

She ran to keep up. 'It's because of dancing that I was able to carry on without you – learning the steps, being carried away by the music. Please don't blame me for that.'

'I don't.' The turnstile squeaked as he pushed through ahead of her.

'I hardly knew how to get through the day, not knowing where you were and dreading another telegram.'

Listen to her – that's what Joe had said. *Really listen*. Bernie waited for her to join him on the prom.

'Look what the war has done to us – not just to you and me but to thousands of couples up and down the land. It's torn us apart. And we women are left at home while you men go off to fight. We're not supposed to show how scared we are – no, we're meant to keep calm and carry on. And I realize that even telling you this is a poor show because you men have it far worse.'

Bernie walked on, deep in thought. 'It's not that bad,' he muttered. 'Most of the time we're dying of bloody boredom, awaiting orders or being yelled at by our sergeant major on parade – "Attention! Forward march; left, right, left right; at ease!"' Best not to dwell on the rare days when his regiment saw action; the ack-ack-ack of machine guns, the relentless trundle of tanks, the sight of an unexploded grenade landing ten feet to your left, the mangled bodies of comrades caught up in a tangle of barbed wire.

'Fibber.' Pearl always knew when he wasn't telling the truth.

He gave a faint smile then almost absent-mindedly took her hand. 'Fair enough.'

They walked past the lifeboat station next to Central Pier before crossing the wide road and heading for the Pleasure Beach. The perfect circle of the Ferris wheel rotated slowly against a cloudless blue sky. Riders on the Big Dipper screamed and laughter from the Fun House drew Bernie and Pearl back to their old haunt.

'How bad is it out there in Italy?' she asked. 'Truly.'

'Better than Egypt. Our boys have bombed Rome to bits, Sicily is ours, the navy has opened up sea lanes in the Med, Mussolini is *kaput* – finished.'

Pearl gripped his hand more tightly but said nothing. It was an unbelievable relief just to walk in the sunshine with Bernie's hand holding hers, to hear his voice regain energy, for him to sound more like his old self.

'I'm sorry too.' He stopped next to the dodgem ride to watch the small cars whizz by, sparks flying overhead, drivers crashing head-on then veering off in the opposite direction – more sparks, more crashes, more glee.

'Why are you sorry?'

'For not trusting you.' A string of carriages on the most famous roller coaster in the world plunged from a great height, down and then up again, soaring skyward, and now it was the turn of riders on the Side Winder planes to dive-bomb, to hold on to their hats and scream.

'But now you do?' Everything hinged on Bernie's reply.

He led her towards the Whip, where he'd worked as a youngster. *Scream if you want to go faster!* The colour, the lights, the thrill of it, the centrifugal force as the waltzers whizzed round. 'Remember this?'

'Of course I remember.' Crystal clear; Bernie spinning the carriages, leaning over to grin at her as she clung to the steel safety bar. The dizzy thrill of the very moment when they had fallen in love. Still she waited for his answer as the roundabout slowed to a halt.

'I do trust you.' He murmured into her ear then waited for the nearest car to stop spinning. 'Shall we?' he asked.

'Why not?' Pearl stepped in first while Bernie held it steady then jumped in beside her. A new tune blared out from the loudspeaker and the ride began again, slow at first but steadily gaining speed. Her skirt billowed and her head was thrown back against the cushioned support.

Scream if you want to go faster into an unknown future. Hold each other tight. Never let go.

CHAPTER TWENTY-THREE

So much to do and so little time to do it in. With less than a week to go before the main event, Sylvia rallied quickly. Vernon was the past, Eddie was the future. So was her work with Cliff in the dance studio; a step into a brighter future beckoned and her mood was buoyed by the familiar thrill of doing what she knew she was good at: teaching Latin dance and organizing the final details for the competition.

'Nervous?' Cliff asked as he and Sylvia joined Lorna at the entrance to the Spanish Hall on the Saturday morning. The days had flown by and they stood on the brink of a life-changing event.

'Yes,' Sylvia and her mother admitted.

And with good reason. Would all contestants arrive on time? Had Art Richardson managed to find a replacement drummer? Had the caretaker arranged the correct number of tables and chairs?

Cliff held up his firmly crossed fingers before pushing open the doors and entering the empty dance hall. 'Let's do it!' His cry echoed along the deserted colonnades and up to the vaulted rafters. 'Come along, ladies; the moment has arrived.'

*

Tommy felt Joy's hands tremble as they stood in hold. They were surrounded by dozens of fellow competitors, all dazzlingly beautiful in a rainbow display of lace, chiffon, silk and satin, and standing nervously under rows of glittering chandeliers, listening to the introductory bars of their Viennese waltz.

Joy pressed her lips together and held her breath. Only by looking directly into Tommy's eyes could she hope to ward off the jitters she'd been experiencing since the moment she'd stepped on to the floor.

'What's wrong?' he whispered as he tightened his hold.

Everything! The fear of making a mistake through lack of practice – of missing a beat or leading with the wrong foot – was turning her legs to jelly.

'Relax,' he murmured. 'Pretend there's no one watching; it's just the two of us dancing under the moon and stars.'

For a brief second Joy closed her eyes and listened to the swell of the music. She remembered how much she adored the build-up to this moment, when Tommy would sweep her across the floor and they would glide and spin, dip and turn in perfect harmony.

'And one, two, three . . .' They were off; Tommy led with his right foot, Joy followed with her left. She was in seventh heaven.

'How about that – third prize!' Joy and Tommy returned triumphant to their table to loud applause. They proudly showed their rosettes to Lucia and Mildred, who clapped loudest of all.

Lorna was at the microphone announcing the final results. Second prize for the Viennese waltz went to Joan and Archie Newbold from Morecambe and overall winners were, as expected, Lionel Mason and Beryl Sharpe.

Pearl and Bernie had joined Cliff, Sylvia and Eddie on the balcony of the Spanish Hall in time to see Joy and Tommy compete. They'd crossed their fingers as Art's band had played the introduction to 'Red Sails in the Sunset' and kept them crossed as Connie Simpson had begun to croon the words, 'Oh, carry my loved one home safely to me.' They'd watched the judges eliminate couples by a tap on the shoulder until only three remained. From their high vantage point they'd admired the poised performance of their favourites as Joy and Tommy had kept strictly to tempo and swept across diagonals, leaning into each turn then swaying into the centre and rising high on the balls of their feet. Joy's elegance had been clear for all to see. Her cream dress with its embroidered bodice and flowing skirt was understated perfection, while Tommy in white tie and black tails had led his partner into chassés and pivot turns without putting a foot wrong.

'Not bad considering they didn't have much time to rehearse.' Eddie passed judgement on their friends' achievement. The dance hall was jam-packed, the atmosphere magical, thanks to its glittering chandeliers and exotic Andalusian flavour. 'Shall we join them?'

So down they went as Tommy and Joy basked in Lucia's praise – '*Bello! Stupendo!*' – and smiled at Mildred's excited congratulations. 'You were marvellous – by far the best of the bunch!' How wonderful to have seen the Rossis win their rosettes, to have styled her hair and put on her best frock and had the courage to step out with her friends to share in their success.

'And now, ladies and gentlemen, all that remains is

for me to thank Art Richardson and his band.' Onstage Lorna drew her Saturday event to a gracious conclusion. The band leader took his bow to a round of enthusiastic applause. 'And a special thank-you to our competitors for making the first day of our ballroom dance weekend a sparkling success. We hope to see you all next year,' she concluded as they began to disperse.

The stage lights dimmed and the curtain came down. Joy and Tommy's small, happy gang moved off to continue their celebrations elsewhere, leaving Cliff to shake Lorna's hand enthusiastically. 'Very well done; it couldn't have gone better,' he assured her.

Relief flooded her fine features. 'Thank you, Cliff.'

'Taxi for Mr Winter,' a driver called from the entrance, his voice echoing across the almost empty hall. One by one the chandeliers dimmed, leaving only the red Exit lights glowing.

'That's us.' Eddie had thought ahead, as usual. 'First stop King Alfred Street, second stop North View Parade.' He departed with Lorna on one arm and Sylvia on the other, with Cliff close behind.

Bernie and Pearl were in no hurry to follow. 'Lorna Ellis put on a jolly good show,' he acknowledged. 'There'll be no holding her back from now on.'

'Welcome to the big time,' Pearl agreed. 'Let's hope that tomorrow goes as well as today, for Sylvia and Cliff's sake. It starts with the samba and ends with the jive.'

'About that.' Bernie hesitated before taking the plunge. 'Would Sylvia be willing to accept a late entry or has that ship sailed?'

'Why do you want to know?' A glance at his face in the dimly lit hall failed to enlighten her. 'Come on, Bernie; what are you on about?'

'This,' he said, taking her by the hand then swinging her out and pulling her in again. He shimmied his shoulders then bounced-and-kicked – one, two, three, four.

Pearl's eyes lit up. 'You want us to . . .?'

'Enter the jive competition together.' Kick, swivel and bounce, kick, swivel and bounce. 'Yes – why not?'

Sunday night and the Spanish Hall was bursting at the seams. Cliff was at the microphone and Sylvia was in charge of checking competitors' details prior to the start of the jive section, the final dance of the evening. 'Good luck,' she murmured to hot favourites Wilf Perkins and Betty Stevens as she handed them their numbers.

'Ready?' Bernie asked Pearl. He was in uniform, she dazzled in her blue sequinned skirt.

'As I'll ever be.' Excitement oozed out of every pore as Art Richardson announced the jive section's opening number – Count Basie's 'One O'Clock Jump'. The pianist's hands flew over the keys, soon joined by saxophones and a double bass in a fast-paced introduction.

All day long, for eight hours straight, Pearl and Bernie had rehearsed in the North View Parade studio, swivelling their feet, flapping their elbows and pecking with their heads, loosening up before they'd progressed to high kicks and leapfrogs. 'It's all coming back to me.' Bernie's natural rhythm hadn't deserted him and by late afternoon they'd perfected what they felt was a decent routine.

They'd gone back to Joe's house on King Street where they'd lived for the past week and where they'd fallen easily into a routine of working all day in the arcade then walking home along the beach each evening, perhaps stopping for a drink in the Queen's Arms or strolling through the Pleasure Beach for old times' sake, convincing themselves that this was how it would be when the war ended. They'd made the most of every moment, as the clock had ticked relentlessly towards the end of Bernie's home leave.

Now, under the bright lights of the ballroom floor, they were surrounded by well-wishers. Joe was there to give his pal an encouraging slap on the shoulder. Eddie, Joy and Tommy propelled them out of the shadows into the spotlight and at the very last moment Errol appeared out of nowhere, smart and handsome as ever in his GI uniform.

'Don't let me down, Miss Pearl,' he said in his familiar drawl. 'Go win that prize.'

'We'll try,' she promised, while Bernie shook his hand to show there were no hard feelings.

And then they were out on the floor with fifty other couples, throwing themselves into the dance – underarm turn and side step out, bounce and kick, side step in again, loose and free.

Sylvia joined Joy on the sidelines to watch the judges eliminate couples one by one. She frowned as Bill and Shirley received the dreaded tap on the shoulder and told them better luck next time. Joy couldn't take her eyes off Pearl and Bernie. Their high kicks were spectacular, their synchronization faultless.

All was movement and flow, colour and sparkle. Five couples remained.

Bernie swung Pearl to arm's length then let her go. The tempo quickened as she ran towards him then flung herself into his arms. He raised her on to his shoulders and spun her around. Their rhythm was unbroken as he lowered her to the floor. They were in hold, rocking in perfect harmony.

A judge tapped the shoulder of the couple next to them. Only four remained. Maybe, just maybe, the prize would be theirs.

It wasn't to be. Pearl and Bernie failed to knock favourites Wilf and Betty from the top spot. They had to settle for second.

'Runners-up!' Sylvia and Joy fought their way through the crowd to congratulate them.

'Well done, you!' Joy hugged Pearl, while Tommy dragged Bernie off to the bar.

'If you'd thrown in an extra cartwheel or two you could've beaten them.' Ever the perfectionist, Sylvia's opinion was drowned out by Art's closing number: a rendition of 'We'll Meet Again' by popular demand.

'Ignore her – you were marvellous.' Joy linked arms with both girls then guided them across the floor. '*We* were marvellous!'

'Yes, we were,' Sylvia heartily agreed. The weekend had gone without a hitch and requests were pouring in for a repeat performance next year.

'Happy with second place?' Joy checked with Pearl as the three girls paused at the edge of the dance floor to take in some final magical moments – Connie Simpson at the microphone, Art Richardson conducting his band, the crimson curtain slowly descending.

'I'm over the moon.' Pearl waved at Bernie, who was motioning for her to join him – *Come quick; every moment of my home leave is precious!* She gently squeezed her friends' hands then slipped away.

'How about you?' Sylvia asked Joy. 'Was third place good enough?'

'You know me – I'm happy as long as my nearest and

dearest are happy.' Tommy stood at the bar, holding up a drink for her to claim.

Off she went, leaving Sylvia to join Eddie at the table that they'd shared all evening. She sat next to him as the stage lights dimmed.

'There you are,' he said with a smile.

'Yes, here I am.'

He leaned over and kissed her; his Sylvia, his golden girl.

Have you read other books by Jenny Holmes?
Find out more about her novels, available
now in print and ebook.

The Ballroom Girls

Book 1 in *The Ballroom Girls* series

It's time to take their first steps on to the dancefloor!

Blackpool, summer 1942

Sylvia, the daughter of one of Blackpool's pre-eminent ballroom dancing teachers, has been coached to win prizes all her life. But when she secretly takes lessons in the popular new Latin dances, will mother and daughter end up at odds?

Pearl sells fish and chips at the Pleasure Beach by day, but on a Saturday night she partners her best friend Bernie at the Tower Ballroom. As their dancing improves, might friendship turn to something more?

Joy lost her family in the Blitz and feels alone in the world. But when dashing Tommy invites her to dance, could this be her chance to find the life and love she's always dreamed of?

It may be wartime, but can the magic of the ballroom help our girls dance their cares away?

Available now

The Air Raid Girls

Book 1 in *The Air Raid Girls* series

May, 1941

Connie's life has taken an unexpected turn since her husband died – she's living at home and working in the family bakery – but night shifts as an ARP Warden give her a firm sense of purpose.

Her younger sister **Lizzie** is eager to play her part too, perhaps as an ambulance driver. Her fiancé refuses to support her decision . . . but does he really know what's best for her?

Twenty-year-old **Pamela** has led a sheltered life, but when her family's home is destroyed in a raid she must learn to stand on her own two feet – helped by new friends.

As bombs fall and fires rage, the young women face the destruction of everything they've ever known. Can their fighting spirit prevail?

Available now

The Spitfire Girls

Book 1 in *The Spitfire Girls* series

'Anything to Anywhere!'

That's the motto of the Air Transport Auxiliary, the brave team of female pilots who fly fighter planes between bases at the height of the Second World War.

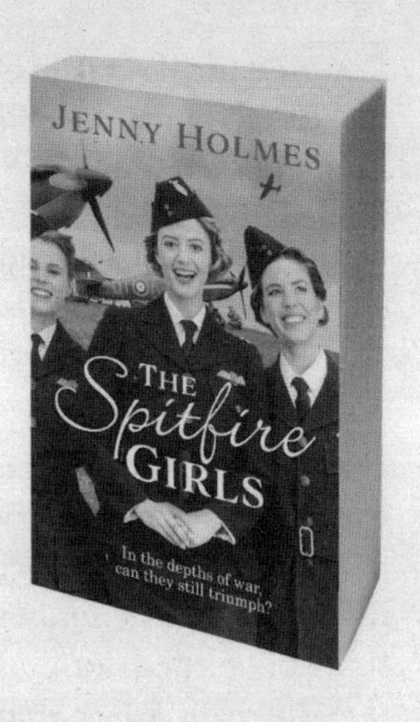

Mary is a driver for the ATA and although she yearns to fly a Spitfire, she fears her humble background will hold her back. After all, glamorous **Angela** is set to be the next 'Atta Girl' on recruitment posters. **Bobbie** learned to fly in her father's private plane and **Jean** was taught the Queen's English at grammar school before joining the squad. Dedicated and resilient, the three girls rule the skies: weathering storms and dodging enemy fire. Mary can only dream of joining them – until she gets the push she needs to overcome her self-doubt.

Thrown together, the girls form a tight bond as they face the perils of their job. But they soon find that affairs of the heart can be just as dangerous as attacks from the skies.

With all the fear and uncertainty ahead – can their friendship see them through the tests of war?

Available now

The Land Girls at Christmas

Book 1 in *The Land Girls* series

'Calling All Women!'

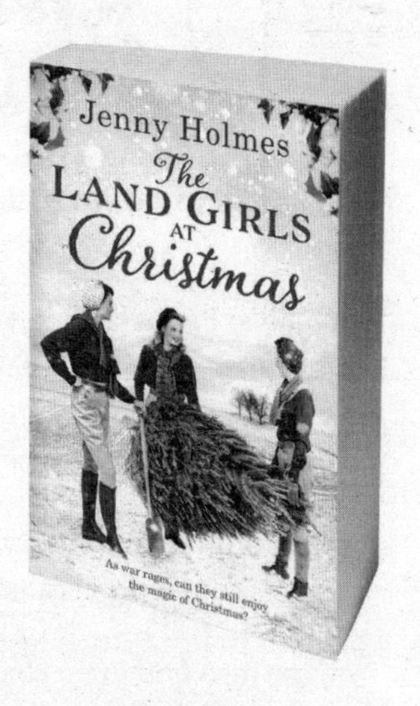

It's 1941 and as the Second World War rages on, girls from all over the country are signing up to the Women's Land Army. Renowned for their camaraderie and spirit, it is these brave women who step in to take on the gruelling farm work from the men conscripted into the armed forces.

When Yorkshire mill girl **Una** joins the cause, she wonders how she'll adapt to country life. Luckily she's quickly befriended by more experienced Land Girls **Brenda** and **Grace**. But as Christmas draws ever near, the girls' resolve is tested as scandals and secrets are revealed, lovers risk being torn apart, and even patriotic loyalties are called into question . . .

With only a week to go until the festivities, can the strain of wartime still allow for the magic of Christmas?

Available now